THE GOOD TWIN

DIANE SAXON

Boldwood

First published in Great Britain in 2023 by Boldwood Books Ltd.

Copyright © Diane Saxon, 2023

Cover Design by Head Design

Cover Photography: Shutterstock

A CIP catalogue record for this book is available from the British Library.

Paperback ISBN 978-1-83518-052-5

Large Print ISBN 978-1-83518-048-8

Hardback ISBN 978-1-83518-047-1

Ebook ISBN 978-1-83518-045-7

Kindle ISBN 978-1-83518-046-4

Audio CD ISBN 978-1-83518-053-2

MP3 CD ISBN 978-1-83518-050-1

Digital audio download ISBN 978-1-83518-044-0

Boldwood Books Ltd
23 Bowerdean Street
London SW6 3TN
www.boldwoodbooks.com

To all the furbabies that bring such joy to my life. I've stolen their names often to feature in my books.

This one is for Skye, my beautiful Dalmatian, who inspired my DS Jenna Morgan series and is wholly responsible for my desire to kill...

Also, for Cleo, who appears as herself.

1

With a long drag of the last cigarette in the packet, I blow a puff of smoke into the late autumn air until it plumes in a halo of white to hover around my head. My long black hair, shiny, dyed and straightened to perfection, swings in a heavy curtain just past my shoulder blades.

I run my fingers through it, sectioning it so one luscious thick lock falls over my shoulder and lies perfectly across one breast. I take my time admiring it. After all, it was no easy job to get it done.

Dad had an absolute tantrum when he saw it. *What the hell have you done? Your hair was perfectly all right before, why would you do that? Why would you want to change it?*

I take another, longer pull of my cigarette and hold the smoke in my lungs until they burn.

Of course, he doesn't understand. Mum would have, but Mum is no longer here. I turn my mind from that train of thought. I don't want to go there. Today is supposed to be a good day. A hopeful day. Which is why I dyed my hair.

I love the colour, it's so much nicer than dull-as-dishwater brown.

More than that, it gives me a certain individuality. Right now, I feel the need for that uniqueness.

The deep raven is even better in sunlight.

There is no sunlight today, though. Typically, it's the dullest day we've had all week. I'm hardly going to get the chance to show off my shiny hair. Still, it's better than it was.

LJ had said he liked black hair. It was going to be a surprise for him.

With a delicate move, I pincer my thumb and forefinger to pluck the minute speck of tobacco from the tip of my tongue. There's not really anything there, but I once saw some film actress do it in an old film. Retro. It's cool.

My freshly stuck-on nails feel unfamiliar, numb, as though I've lost all feeling in the tips of my fingers. I won't be able to paint with them this long, but perhaps I can clip them when I get home. Once the glue has set to cement. Otherwise, they will simply ping off, leaving me with dried-on glue on my own bitten-down nails.

I hold them out in front of my face to admire my long, slender fingers, elongated with those square-tipped, fluorescent pink mani-cured nails. With a burst of defiance, I'd stuck a matt black one on the ring finger of each hand.

I've slid delicate silver rings onto each finger, with one on both thumbs too. They're all different. Sweet.

They look good.

I look good.

I glance at the time and give a little shiver of anticipation. He should be here by now. He will be. Any minute. I'm sure of it.

I've really gone to a great deal of effort, and I hope it's appreciated.

A thin shudder washes over me as the damp from the miserly drizzle seeps deep into my bones through the thin jacket I shrugged on as I headed for the door.

I sneaked out before Dad arrived home and stopped me.

It's not like it's a problem. I just didn't want to stay home, that's all.

My little sister, Jade, has afterschool club anyway, so there would only have been me there, rattling around in a house which always feels empty these days. I know I could clean the bathrooms or vacuum, but I'm sick of that too.

Provided I'm back by the time Dad gets home from work, and I bet he's working late, he'll never even know.

I don't want him to know.

He wouldn't understand. Overprotective since Mum died. Almost eight months ago now.

My breath hitches on a sob and the quick sting of tears rushes in before I can block them. Pain lances my heart as I try desperately not to allow it to cripple me.

Dammit, I don't want to smudge my carefully applied black eyeliner. It would look like a shitstorm.

If Dad had seen me with this much make-up, he'd have a hissy fit.

He always has a damned hissy fit these days. The slightest thing sets him off. It's not like I'm not old enough. He's treating me like he does Jade and she's six years younger.

He'd not been amused when I dyed my own hair black, and there'd hardly been a mark on the bathroom sink, and only a couple of splashes up the white tiles. He'd gone a little crazy. He's been a little crazy since Mum died.

Haven't we all?

'Be back by 10 p.m., Summer.' 'Don't be late, Summer.' 'You really shouldn't wear make-up to school, Summer. In fact...' 'Watch who you talk to on social media, Summer.' 'Dammit, Summer, do you have to splurge your whole life out on Facebook and Instagram? Nobody wants to see that. It's just too much.' 'You leave yourself so open...'

Well, school's over and I'm no longer a child.

I grip the cigarette between my lips, inhale deep, and pull the zipper up on my jacket. I squint as smoke burns my eyes and tears sting, which is almost welcome. I thought I was all cried out.

If LJ doesn't turn up, I won't be cried out. It'll break my bloody heart.

As I raise my head, smoke streams from my nostrils and I watch while it whips away on the cooling air. There's another thing Dad would hit the roof about. Me, smoking. I never did until recently. As far as I know, Skye doesn't. Then again, who knows what effect university life has had on her? I know she drinks a lot and parties now. Good for her. I mean, we all like a drink and it's not like we're underage. But that's the sum total of my knowledge of her uni life. Maybe she doesn't want us to know how much fun she's having. Not while we're at home. Miserable.

I scissor my fingers around the cigarette and take it from my lips so I can grind my teeth against the rolling anger deep in the pit of my stomach that surges up every time I think of her. Leaving me.

It's not my fault my identical twin sister, Skye, decided to go against Dad's advice to take a year out before starting uni. He'd thought with Mum dying, it would be better if we didn't go to university. We wouldn't be able to make the best of it, with our loss. We'd flounder. If we just stayed at home and deferred our acceptances.

I did as he suggested.

Skye did not.

Who could blame her for wanting to get out of here? For wanting her freedom?

Me. That's who.

Most girls our age embrace the opportunity to take a year out. I did. I thought it would help us heal if we stuck together as a family. Ride this year out.

Turns out that wasn't such a great decision.

Not the same decision Skye made either. She wasn't stupid. The reason Dad suggested a year out was not so we could travel the world, taking in the sights and learning how to live independently. It was so we could stay at home. Huddled together in a safe cotton wool haven. Stifling. Smothering. A fact I'd not taken long to realise.

Skye had said no. No to the year out. She decided to go direct to university. A fresh start.

Skye had made the right choice. There was no doubt. I don't blame her. The only blame I lay at her door is that she's left me. Alone to cope with all of this.

I raise my face to a cloud-laden sky which is being swallowed by the encroaching night, just as regret threatens to swallow me.

I wish I'd been brave. I should have gone, too.

Away from Dad's choking overprotectiveness, which has only become worse since Skye left. God knows, I love him, I really do, but most days I wind up wanting to kill him. And him, me.

Much as I love him, we're driving each other insane and that's another reason. If I'd known this would happen, I would quite happily have gone. Left. But how was I to know he'd become a flaming nightmare? Too possessive. Too concerned. Anxious to know every single thing I do, every place I go.

I put it down to the fact that he's lost that tie, not only with Mum dying, but with Skye, too. She cut the umbilical cord and flew the nest. We barely hear from her.

He can hardly keep tabs on her while she's at university, which means he tightens the reins on me instead. Suffocating me with his constant concern. Anxiety.

A hard chill invades my bones and I hunch my shoulders up to my neck to ward it off, clenching my teeth against the rattle of them as an icy finger of wind manages to sneak its way under my collar.

'Fuck this.' A guilty thrill runs through me at saying the word out loud. I never used to drop the F-bomb, keeping it inside my head, but lately it feels good to say it.

I flick the cigarette butt. It pirouettes, sending out sparks before it hits the floor where I grind it beneath my heel into the tarmacked footpath with grim satisfaction.

I glance both ways along the street. Puff out a breath.

I cross my arms over my chest.

Great. Just bloody great!

I've been stood up.

Disappointment grabs at me, but I allow the little stab of anger to take over.

LJ's had quite long enough. If he isn't going to show, that's his loss, but he could have at least let me know. It's only polite. And we are a family with good manners.

I check the phone for any messages.

A million of them on the 'School leavers of 2016' bloody WhatsApp chat. All of it varying shades of shit.

They're all such kids. When will they fucking grow up? You'd think they were twelve-year-olds, not closer to nineteen. All drama and hysteria, as though their petty lives have been destroyed because someone's boyfriend dumped them, or their mum wouldn't allow them to borrow the car. Boo-bloody-hoo.

They are lucky they have their mums.

Unlike me and my sisters.

I miss my mum every single moment of every single day. I can't breathe without thinking of her. It's so unfair.

My mum was the most vital, energetic person I know. She's gone.

All the group can do is moan about their mums. I never did that when mine was alive. I wish I had her now.

I think I have more to whine about than any of them. But I've distanced myself from them. Can't involve myself in their shit any longer.

I swipe my finger across the screen, my false nail scraping over the glass.

I scroll down, and then up again.

Nothing from LJ. The swine. Has something happened to delay him? Has he had to work late?

I sigh as I take a look at our family chat. Skye hardly comments on our thread at all.

She makes me bloody mad. Too busy to send her little sister a few messages a day, never mind me, her twin. There's a twinge of sadness that insists on making itself felt beneath the bubbling annoyance.

I wish she'd keep in touch more. No matter how angry I was... am... with her, I miss her like crazy.

She's due home next week for a quick break, but I doubt she'll bother. She hasn't confirmed it. It seems she's found her niche, her little clique, settling in to all the partying and fun with no mention of any actual work she's supposed to be there for.

I know I'm angry with her, but I still feel anxious for her too. Mum would want her to work. To make sure she's keeping up with things. She wouldn't want her to party away her time at university. Embrace it, by all means. That's what Mum would advise her. Us.

Both our lives have been sculpted towards success in our separate fields. Both Mum and Dad had gone to university. It had been their ambition for us to go too.

When I have the opportunity to next year, I'm going to make sure I always keep in contact with Dad, and more specifically with our younger sister, Jade.

After all, we all lost our mum. All three of us. But Jade was probably the one most affected. Eleven when it happened, now twelve, she needs that motherly figure. Skye could have helped share that burden. Instead, she buggered off and left us to it.

It's not her fault. I'm just being a total bitch. I'm jealous as hell and wish to God I'd made the decision to go with her. But a few months ago, when Mum died, I wasn't ready to leave home, Dad, Jade.

It was during those precious few months that we needed to make a decision I wasn't ready to take. So, I deferred until next year.

If it was now, my answer would be different. I'd go in a heartbeat.

Of the two of us, I'm the worrier. Mum used to say I carried the world for both of us on my shoulders, whereas Skye gained all the confidence.

We may look identical in every way, but we're not. Skye is the left-brain thinker. Terrific at mathematics and problem solving. I am a right-brain thinker. Artistic, visual.

Mum and Dad both knew that. Nurtured our talents and made us feel like individuals.

I tug on my bottom lip with my teeth, probably chewing the dark wine lipstick off as I dig my hands deep into the pockets of Skye's favourite jacket with only a small prod of guilt. What can she expect? If she left it behind, it's obviously no longer her favourite.

She hasn't mentioned it. And nor have I mentioned the fact that I've taken to wearing it.

I dip my head so I can tuck my face into the collar of her jacket and take comfort from Skye's familiar smell while tears I'd been so determined to ignore trickle down my cheeks. I breathe in deep, then huff out.

It wasn't just Jade and Skye and Dad. It was everything. Every bloody thing seems to have gone wrong since the moment Mum died. Little things.

I squint at the empty street.

I might as well go. If LJ turns up now, I'm going to look like a hooker in any case with my tear-smudged make-up and bright red nose. I've probably got lipstick stuck to my teeth. He'd hardly be impressed, and first impressions count.

Right?

Six weeks we've been chatting online and this was supposed to be the first time we meet. Only he's stood me up. I've never been stood up before. Not that I've ever gone out with anyone apart from a couple of the spotty-faced boys at school.

I haven't got the wrong place. This is definitely it. He said it was the cut-through from his work on his way home. Otherwise, I wouldn't be standing here like a loser.

Loser. That's me.

Fucking typical.

I've been so excited and now I feel foolish.

Can anything else really go wrong with my life? It simply can't get any worse. I like to think so, anyway.

With a defeated sigh, I push away from where I've been leaning against the brick wall under a narrow overhang that had provided minimal protection from the drizzle. I peer up and down the deserted road before I head off along Watling Street towards Wellington town centre.

The dark car that cruises alongside me is long, with blacked-out windows, and earns itself a momentary disinterested glance as I quicken my step. This is one of the reasons my dad has become overprotective. I'm not being conceited when I say Skye and I attract attention, because we do. Unwanted attention. More often than not when we are together because of our identical twin status. Often lewd suggestions accompany graphic hand signs from drivers leaning out from open windows of vehicles with music playing too loud.

This sleek car has none of those elements. Any feeling of

discomfort fizzles away as I'm more concerned with the sudden closing in of weather to draw the night down faster than I anticipate.

I need to get home in case Dad gets there before me. I've been out longer than I thought. Hanging around for LJ like some sucker.

Just over an hour. I should have cut and run by now. But hope had kept me hanging on.

Disappointment etches itself into my soul. I can't believe after all this time LJ has let me down.

It was only supposed to be a brief meet-up, maybe a quick coffee at one of the steamed-up cafés which are all now shut in any case. Just to see if we like each other in person.

I certainly like his profile pictures. He's just a couple of months older than me, with a beautiful shock of dirty-blond hair swept up in what's meant to look like an effortless peak that falls to one side. The other side of his head is shaved in that sexy textured crop hairstyle only the most confident of boys are wearing.

My heart gives a little squeeze as I allow my mind to wander and I slow down, hoping he'll lope along the road all apologies and wide smile.

LJ isn't a boy. Not like the ones I went to sixth form with. His face has the thick stubble of a mature, masculine man, contoured beautifully around a square chin.

He's gorgeous.

But he's not here. Disappointment claws at me.

I thought from our online chats that I was as important to him as he had become to me. Evidently not.

I sigh.

Right. That's it! I'm off. No more bloody loitering like he's about to appear in front of me. He's had his chance. I'm done.

If I continue to the end of the road, I can nip into Morrisons, pick up a loaf of bread, some milk and those bloody awful cheap biscuits Dad likes. A 'healthy' biscuit, Dad declares. Full of oats which dry the spit in your mouth until it sticks in your throat like lumpy glue. The more you chew, the stickier it becomes.

Still, Dad enjoys them. A little too much, if you ask me. His waistline has definitely thickened in the last few months without Mum to control his poor eating habits.

I shouldn't buy him biscuits, but he'll be pitifully pleased that I've thought to pick him up a treat, and it will deflect any annoyance that I'm late home and don't have dinner on. On the off-chance he's home before me.

I look at my watch. Time has flown, it's creeping up to almost 6.15 p.m., which means by the time I go into Morrisons, grab those things and race home, Dad could well be there before me, making dinner.

Dinner. My stomach rebels at the thought.

Dad's shit at cooking. He could burn soup. If it wasn't for me whipping up a quick pasta dish or scrambled eggs on toast, we'd live permanently on take-outs. I don't mind an occasional one, but four nights a week is too much. Too unhealthy. And I really do prefer healthy food – I don't include oat biscuits in that preference, though. Admittedly, the fact we don't have chocolate biscuits in the house has helped me to keep my own weight down.

Jade, I've noticed, has plumped up a little after the initial drastic weight loss when Mum died. She'd needed to gain weight, but if I'm honest, she needs to be careful she doesn't slide too much the other way, if you get my drift.

I touch a hand to my own stomach, which up until recently has been concave and is now just tipping over into the convex. I can hardly speak. I don't need to put on any weight either. The bitches, male and female, so-called old school pals were all too quick to pick up on anything like that. Which is another good reason I have little to do with them. I'm more of a 'lurker' on the chat groups and I can't be arsed to go out with them.

There's so much talk about being kind to each other, acceptance, tolerance, understanding. It was all a pile of shit the teachers doled out at school and the kids ignore as they stab you in the back and happily ruin any kind of image you have at the drop of a hat.

Since leaving sixth form, instead of becoming kinder, there was a core group who'd honed their skills and escalated their bitch status.

One slight head tilt from Kellie Balding, accompanied by the lift of a perfectly micro-bladed eyebrow, and her little clique couldn't resist. They didn't need to say anything, their looks spoke volumes. Lips pumped with filler pouted in that judgemental way. Eyes filled with spiteful humour.

Skye and I were the lucky ones. We had each other. They rarely targeted us. We rarely gave them the opportunity. Only Skye was no longer here, and I was on my own. An easy target. I've always been an easy target.

They didn't give me any more leeway because Mum had died. No one seemed to care about that any more. They'd ceased to care about a month after she'd gone, once the funeral was over. We were supposed to have got over it. Pulled ourselves together. No one mentioned it. Or asked how I felt. Mum dead, Dad a bit useless, Skye self-centred and Jade really needy.

The summer holidays dragged. It brought distance, even from my closest friends, as I argued with my twin. Each of us determined we were right. Nobody wanted to take sides.

Turns out I don't have many friends. Being a twin seems to have brought that, because Skye has always been my best friend and no one else has ever been that close. No one came between us. Once Mum died, our so-called friends drifted even further.

None of it mattered to them. It wasn't their lives. Not their catastrophe.

How could they understand? According to Facebook, which is the sum total of my contact with ex-school pals apart from WhatsApp, a whole host of them are at university, got jobs, the ones with a little more money have taken a year out to travel the world.

Which is how I came to find an online friend. One who understood. Who was there whatever the time. Day or night.

Sweet LJ, who was happy for me to rattle away about what a shit life I have. Messages poured from me, sometimes positive, but more often than not whiny or bitchy. I couldn't help myself. It was so easy to chat with him online. He never seemed to mind, however much I divulged to him.

He's a secret even my twin doesn't know about. I even told him that and he agreed. He's my secret. She couldn't know, because somehow, she would ruin that. Just because she wasn't here for me didn't mean I couldn't have someone else to fill that yawning chasm of emptiness.

I need someone other than Skye. I need LJ.

Only he isn't here now. When he'd promised to be, and all my growing excitement for this day shrivels and dies like a dried leaf that crumbles into powder and wafts away on the wind.

Disappointment and bitterness take its place.

Just another person who thinks nothing of letting me down. For weeks we've been trying to arrange a meet-up. A time when LJ could take a little while off at the end of the day from his new job as an apprentice engineer – I think my dad would like him. Intelligent, empathetic. That's LJ.

Just older than me, he lost his sister some years ago. She must have been older than him. He spoke about it once, but I've found it hard to coax much detail out of him after that. He said it was too painful. That she'd taken her own life.

Perhaps he'd be more comfortable talking about it face to face.

My heart squeezes every time I think about it. How painful it must be to think of someone you love, not loving you enough to stick around. So many people call it the easy way out. It can't be easy. Knowing you're leaving behind people who love you and whom you love back. Even on a bad day.

Mum didn't leave deliberately. Her death had been swift, painless they said, and instant. Although I have my doubts as to how painless it is to have a blood clot explode in your brain. An embolism they called it.

She'd complained of a headache that morning before Skye and I went to school, Dad went to work, dropping Jade off on his way. It was Jade's last year at the junior school.

We'd pretty much ignored Mum. She'd complained of a headache for a few days. We'd not even given her a second thought. Who does? Mums aren't there to complain, they're there to complain to. That was another secret I'd shared with LJ. A sneaky guilt that we'd ignored Mum when we could have saved her, if only we'd listened. None of us had.

By the time we arrived home at the end of the school day, Jade was already there, upstairs, where Mum had collapsed on the bathroom floor. The paramedics were hovering over Mum, their faces pulled into masks of sympathy.

According to the coroner's report, she'd been dead for several hours before Jade came across her.

That's life, hey? That's what the thoughtless tell me. The inconsiderate, the superior, the ones who still have their own mothers alive and kicking.

My lips twist with cynical bitterness.

I've given up on LJ arriving and quite frankly, unless he has an excuse and a grovelling apology, I'll have nothing further to do with him, the thoughtless prat.

I consider blocking him on Facebook, but I'll give him the opportunity to explain first. Maybe. If I ever hear from him again. Maybe he thinks it's a game.

I'll give him a chance, though.

I tuck the phone into my pocket and squint into the dusky light as I look right and then left, ready to dash across the deserted street to the far side that will take me from the quiet row of mainly empty old houses, where most people are probably still at work.

A gust of wind whips up and hurtles wet leaves and twigs in a whorl towards me in an advance warning of the weather front setting in.

I duck my head and stride towards a more commercial area, lit by huge orange sodium lights from the supermarket car park, their warmth pulling me in their direction.

I frown, thinking it would have been far more logical to have arranged to meet LJ somewhere like Morrisons, but I'd agreed to his suggestion without thought. I trust him. After all, we've got to know each other.

The same black car lingers further along at the kerbside, now on the same side of the road as me, engine gently idling, headlights off. Probably waiting for someone to knock off work and walk through that same passageway.

I hesitate for a split second, not really bothered by the presence of the vehicle. Just a fleeting sense of unease at the quietness. The street is more often than not deserted. It's not the most salubrious part of town and the black BMW is probably not the normal class of car that cruises along here.

I shrug off the feeling. All the more reason not to be worried.

I step out onto the tarmacked road.

The car's engine revs. Headlights blaze and instead of creeping towards me, it shoots forward, a quick kangaroo hop, then a roar.

My heart crashes against my ribcage as I raise my arms in an automatic defence, but the car jolts to a halt right in front of me, the bumper barely kissing the side of my knee.

Fury courses through me at the sheer stupidity of the person behind the wheel. Who the hell do they think they are? Vin Diesel? Without thought, I smack one open hand on the bonnet of the car and the other on my chest, gasping for breath as I glare at the person behind the windscreen. What an arsehole.

The car door flies open and someone steps out, a mere shadow as my vision is filled with tears of fright and the bright, glaring beam from the headlights which spark out in all directions.

'You moron.' The tears I've staved off for the past few weeks prick the back of my eyes for the second time this evening and a senseless terrified rage takes over, my voice breaking on every word. 'You absolute fucking…'

I barely see the silhouetted person as they stride around the open car door, fast and furious, before a fist ploughs into my face. My head snaps back and the burning shock of that punch throbs through my entire system as I try desperately to draw in a breath through a nose instantly filled with thick fluid. Blood, mucus.

I raise a shaking hand to my face, no longer the aggressor but the victim, and shock holds me in its thrall so I can't move, can't run, can't scream.

When the second punch comes, my knees crumple beneath me. I stagger back a pace before I sag to the ground in front of wide car tyres, where wet leaves have circled around to bunch up in the gutter.

A laboured sob breaks from me, my voice cracking as I cover my face with both hands and roll my head downward into my knees. Into a tight ball. A protective ball.

'Don't. Please don't.' I hate to beg, but there is nothing I wouldn't do to make this pain stop. The words bubble through the gush of blood coating my fingers, which drips into the lap of my jeans.

Cold, oily mud soaks through the material at my knees and I quake as another gust of wind rushes through, snatching cruelly at my life.

Why me? What have I done to deserve this?

I raise my head to appeal to my assailant, and a surge of blood fills my mouth so whatever words spill out are accompanied by crimson bubbles spilling down my chin to run down the jacket I took from my twin. Stole from her wardrobe. She's never going to forgive me for getting it so bloodied.

That's if she ever sees it again. Ever sees me again.

Skye.

'*Summer!*' Her panicked voice screams inside my head. She'll know. We always know. My pain will be her pain.

I look up and the glaring lights fill my vision. The shadow towers over me and before I can plead for mercy, the sole of a boot stamps into my face. My head snaps back.

Skye. Help me.

A heavy cloak pulls over me and I'm not sure if that is something physical my attacker has done, or whether my mind has shut down to protect me from further damage.

Darkness rises up to engulf me until there is nothing.

Not even sound.

2

SATURDAY, 20 MAY 2023, 11.30 A.M.

Two hours before the wedding

Skye nudged her dad's fumbling fingers aside and took hold of the two ends of his bow tie. 'Why didn't you buy a ready-tied one?'

'I already had this one in the drawer.'

Her own fingers fumbled. 'What?' She gave the ends a quick yank and jerked her dad's head towards her, so their noses almost touched. 'You're not using an old bow tie, Dad? You can't. It's your wedding day.'

An unperturbed smile lingered on his lips. 'It's only been used once. But something old, something new...'

She blinked up into his eyes. 'Please don't tell me this is from when you married Mum.'

He held still, then a smile spread over his face as his eyes twinkled with amusement. 'All right. I won't then.'

A snort of disbelieving laughter burst from her, and she stepped back.

Skye dropped one end of the tie and, ignoring yet another pleading message lighting up the screen from her recent ex, hit the play button on the phone she'd balanced on the edge of the bedstead.

Determined not to let Jordon ruin the day for any of them, she studied the YouTube video and deftly tied the bow tie around her dad's pristine, stiff white collar. At least that was brand new. The suit was hired, so technically his something borrowed.

'There.' She stepped back to admire her workmanship and tilted her head. 'A little crooked, I think.' She grimaced. An understatement as the bow settled in a twenty-to-two position.

Skye reached out and tugged the bow tie undone. Retying it, she smiled. 'That's better.'

She patted her dad's chest and left her hand there, just above his frantically beating heart. 'Nervous?'

He placed a clammy hand on her cool one and gave it a squeeze. 'Terrified.'

'You know you're doing the right thing?'

'I know.' He lifted her hand from his chest and placed a kiss in her palm, his voice thickened. 'You're so much like your mum. You know I will always love her. No matter what.'

'I know that, Dad. But she's been gone over seven years now. You can't be expected to live your life alone.'

'You tell that to Jade.'

'Jade might understand when she grows up a bit.'

'She's nineteen.'

Skye shook her head. 'It doesn't mean to say she's mature.' Less forgiving than her dad, she stepped back and dropped her hand from his.

Sadness oozed from him, but Skye ignored it. If her little madam of a sister didn't turn up today, she'd never forgive her. They'd both lost their mum. They'd both lost their sister. It might be seven years ago, but it still hurt her as much as anyone else. After all, how could you get over that?

All three of them dealt with it in entirely different ways. Skye chose to tuck it away. For now.

Just as she'd decided to lock away her fury at her ex too. She'd switched off the notification sound on her phone, but it didn't stop the messages from streaming over the screen. She could turn it off, but what if Jade needed her? She could block him, but...

Determined not to dwell on it today of all days, her dad's wedding day, Skye snatched up both glasses of Prosecco she'd brought into his bedroom and, forcing a smile, handed one to her dad. 'Here. Cheers!'

He looked at the glass, a rueful smile quirked his lips. 'I'd have preferred a whisky.'

He clinked his glass to hers and took a long pull of the drink, wrinkling his nose with distaste as he swallowed it like was lemonade. She guessed not everyone was a fan of Prosecco.

Skye squeezed his arm. 'Take it easy, Dad. We don't want you drunk before you take your vows.'

He smiled back, placed his glass down, picked up his jacket, and shrugged into it. As he turned, he studied himself in the full-length mirror. 'Not bad, for an old geezer.'

Skye laughed. 'Old? You're only fifty-two. It's taken you long enough.'

She picked up the buttonhole that had been laid on the dressing table, positioned it on his jacket lapel then threaded through a pearl-headed pin to secure it in place. She smoothed the material with her hand and grinned at him.

At five feet ten inches, she still had to look up at him, but once she had her heels on, she'd be about eye-level with the six feet one he claimed to be.

'Martha's going to be swept off her feet, you handsome devil.'

Her dad's rare laughter filled the room.

'Aha, we're ready, I see.'

Skye whirled in the direction of the door where Jacob, her dad's best man, loitered.

A little younger than her dad, a tall, slender man, sandy hair shot through with streaks of grey, pale grey eyes twinkling with warmth.

She sent him a cheeky grin and spread her arms wide before she pirouetted to show off the ripped jeans and baggy grey T-shirt she currently wore. 'What do you think, Jacob?'

Jacob pushed away from the doorframe and stepped into her dad's bedroom. He was dressed impeccably in a suit to match her dad's. 'I think it's great to see what an effort you've made.'

Skye swiped up her drink and made for the door, giving him a shoulder bump on the way. 'Cheeky beggar. It won't take me more than ten minutes to slip into my bridesmaid's dress.'

The one she'd had the honour of picking herself as Martha had claimed to have no idea about young women's fashion, despite the fact she was only in her late forties and always looked impeccable. Classic maybe, rather than modern.

Skye had gone for a cerulean sleeveless empire-line full-length dress to complement her chestnut hair and make the blue in her eyes zing.

Her eye colour was the reason her parents had named her Skye. According to her dad, when they were born, her twin's eyes and hers had been such an intense blue that they changed their names from the jewel names, Topaz and Jade, the moment he remarked they were like a summer sky.

Summer and Skye.

Only now, it was just Skye.

Her chest gave a light squeeze at the painful reminder always hovering on the edge of her conscience, which was as much as she could allow today. This was a happy day. A good day. The best thing that had happened to them as a family for the past seven years.

She wasn't about to dwell on history. On bad things.

She took a small sip of Prosecco and held it in her mouth while she stared at the closed door at the end of the hallway. She could have got changed at her own place, just a twenty-minute drive away, but she wanted some special time with her dad before the wedding. Just the two of them.

A quiver of anticipation trickled through her like the bubbles down her throat.

She was ready for this. This was what they all needed. To move on. To live again. Here was their chance. Martha was a breath of fresh air.

Skye took a long breath in. There was plenty of time. As she'd told Jacob, she only needed to pull on her dress and slip into her heels, and she was ready. She'd applied her make-up before checking on her dad. A fortuitous moment that turned out to be, as he'd needed her help.

The touch of foundation she'd applied dimmed the smattering of bright freckles scattered over the bridge of her nose, spilling onto her cheeks, to give the illusion of the smooth alabaster skin she would rather have had. The light dusting of bronzer warmed her pale skin, together with a soft dusky blue on her eyelids blending into the oyster she'd brushed up to high, arched eyebrows she'd defined with a subtle swipe of brown powder.

Skye suspected Martha had allowed her the freedom of colour choice for the dresses to get her on side. The truth was, it wasn't needed. She'd been on Martha's side from the moment she'd met her. The woman had brought a new lease of life to Skye's dad. A life that had dulled after the death of her mum, and extinguished after the disappearance of Summer, her twin sister.

Skye pushed open the door to what was now the guest bedroom. She no longer had a room of her own since Martha moved in and made changes. Changes that had been desperately needed.

It didn't matter. Skye had a place of her own. Always had since she'd left university with a first-class honours degree in mathematics and finance. She could have chosen to stay in Lincoln. She could have moved to London. She'd wanted to be closer to her dad and little sister at the time. Not so close it brought back constant memories.

The commute by train from Wellington to Birmingham where she worked was hellish, but she didn't want to live in the city. She wasn't a city girl, but for the field of meteorology she'd selected, she had no other choice but to commute.

She stared at her old room.

After the wedding, her dad and Martha were talking about selling both houses. Martha claimed she didn't need to live with ghosts, because despite changing things around, they still haunted Skye's dad.

Skye didn't necessarily agree those ghosts would be left behind once they moved. Summer's disappearance had left a gaping wound that would forever ooze, the torture of not knowing what had become of her twin. But she understood Martha's viewpoint.

It appeared both Martha's son, Luke, three years younger than Skye, and Skye's younger sister, Jade, had differing opinions on that philosophy.

Which was one of the reasons Jade had elected not to attend the wedding at the last minute, despite helping to choose the bridesmaids' outfits only the two of them would wear. Whatever it was that had prompted Jade's outburst two days earlier had sent her running for cover. Or, more precisely, back to university.

Skye suspected it had something to do with Martha sending Summer's old clothes and toys to the charity shop despite the fact that they probably wouldn't accept the balding, one-eyed Care Bear she'd dug from the bottom of Summer's wardrobe. That, more than anything, appeared to have upset Jade. She was the one guilty of removing that Care Bear's eye when she was a baby. It had been a standing joke, one Martha could not have been expected to understand.

Then there had been the boxing up of all the girls' precious belongings from school reports through to dressing-up clothes and photographs that their dad had found too hard to face.

The insult had stung. Not so much Skye, as Jade.

So, Jade had gone.

Reluctant to tell Martha that she may be one bridesmaid down, Skye and her dad had kept the outburst between them. Or at least that's what Skye had believed, but there was something in Martha's intelligent gaze that made Skye wonder just how much she knew. The secrets she and her dad had kept in the past were now shared as he took Martha into their circle.

It was good for him. She was good for him.

Shame Jade and Luke thought otherwise. Skye didn't know what Luke's problem was, but Jade was twitchy that Martha was a money-grabbing gold-digger, and all she wanted was to get married, get the will changed and steal their inheritance.

It was laughable.

Personally, Skye thought it was an insult to their dad. He was handsome, in good nick for his age and a lovely, if slightly sad, personality. There was no reason he shouldn't be attractive to the opposite sex. He needed this. He needed Martha. She brought a warmth and a vitality to him Skye had no memory of.

Skye wasn't entirely sure what Luke's issue was with her dad. She didn't know him well enough, but considering his age, he acted like a spoilt teenager around them. Petulant and gruff. He dug his hands deep into his pockets and rounded his shoulders as he cast them wary looks from under a long, floppy blond fringe.

Maybe his anger and distrust were because his girlfriend had broken up with him. Or maybe his girlfriend had broken up with him because of his attitude. Whichever order the break-up came in, Skye had no desire to be in his company any longer than she needed to be.

She had her own break-up to deal with.

Jordon, her ex-boyfriend, who'd been invited to the wedding until Skye had caught him sexting a woman on the other side of the world. Oklahoma or Alabama. One of those states that had a rousing song with the name in the title.

Eight months they'd been seeing each other. She'd actually fancied herself in love with him for a while. They'd even been talking about moving in together.

When she discovered his deception, she also realised he wasn't really the man for her. She wasn't that bothered by their split.

He was. He'd turned up on her doorstep a little worse for wear and begged her forgiveness on more than one occasion.

She forgave him.

She simply didn't want him back. Any affection she'd held for him had been wiped out in one little indiscretion. An indiscretion which, had she loved him, she might have been able to forgive. But she didn't love him. She never had.

Skye had started to believe she was incapable of love. True love. She loved her dad, and she loved her younger sister. That being said, she often felt a strong inclination to murder Jade.

Apart from those two, there was no one in her life she'd allow under her skin. Even Aunty Judith, her mum's sister, was kept at arms' length. Just in case Skye became too fond, too close. Because then the inevitable happened and they would disappear, one way or another, and they'd be gone from her life, leaving her to straggle back the loose ends of her very ragged life once more.

Despite promising herself not to look, Skye sank down onto the

bed and checked the messages from Jordon. The man she'd
thought she would marry one day.

She closed her eyes against the pain.

Jesus, he'd sent reams of them. She scrolled through, not both-
ering to read them all in detail, but she got the general gist.

Skye, losing you is the worst thing that has ever happened
to me...

Well, he should have thought of that before turning to another
woman for comfort.

Please don't leave me.

She hadn't. He'd technically left her. He may not have had a
physical relationship with the other woman, but somehow this was
worse. It was a desertion of her mentally and emotionally.

I can't stop thinking about you and how we could so easily fix
this.

No. No, we can't, she thought, because Skye didn't want to fix
something that was broken so badly. She wasn't sure she cared
enough about Jordon to fix it. Right now, she was still angry, but a
thin layer of 'I don't give a shit' coated her feelings. She didn't care.
All she felt was intense relief that she'd not committed to him. Not
after she'd read the text he accidentally sent to her instead of the
woman on the other side of the world. A text confessing how awful
Skye was, how she made his life intolerable, and he couldn't wait to
leave her. According to his text, he'd booked a flight from London
Heathrow to OKC with a stop-over at JFK in three weeks' time. She
was never quite sure how he'd expected to explain that journey to

her. She'd looked it up. The flight alone could take him anything between twelve and seventeen hours.

Skye had no way of checking the truth of his texts, but she had no reason to doubt it either. The man was a lying shit. She swallowed any fragment of emotion.

Skye had imagined this would be her dream. What her dad was doing. A wedding day. A ring on her finger.

Relief and fury still battled together. Relief that she'd found out in time, before she'd committed herself heart and soul to Jordon. Fury that he thought he could so easily make it better. There was no better.

The final message in the string garnered the first response from her.

I'll be there for you at the wedding. We can talk.

What?

No!

Skye surged to her feet. White noise filled her head.

How could he even think that he might still be welcome at her dad's wedding? There was nothing about their situation that made any of it all right.

He couldn't mean it. Was he just trying to get a response from her?

She sank back down onto the bed again, wildly tapping at the phone.

Do NOT even think about turning up at my dad's wedding. Not even by the longest stretch of imagination could you think you would be welcome. You are NOT. STAY AWAY!

Sky hit send and snatched up her drink, taking a large gulp and instantly regretting it as the bubbles fizzed up the back of her nose while she watched the cursor flashing madly as Jordon typed an answer.

No need to shout. I have no intention of coming. I just wanted you to stop ignoring me.

Skye placed her empty glass back on the dresser and covered her face with her hands, relief flooding through her. Her phone burred to signal another incoming message.

I love you. I miss you. Please can we talk?

FFS. What do you not understand about I don't ever want to see you again? Stay away from me. No. Not today, not tomorrow, not when I have space to think. NEVER... LEAVE. ME. ALONE!

She slapped the phone face down on the bed and jumped to her feet again. She poured herself another glass of bubbly and this time sipped it slowly.

If she'd had an inkling of affection still left for Jordon, he'd wiped it out. Did he really imagine he would still be invited to the wedding?

Skye scrolled back in her mind through the brief conversations they'd had after she'd caught him out. She'd never actually said he was uninvited, but really? How thick-skinned was he?

He was supposed to have sat next to her on the top table.

Sadly, now she had been partnered with Luke for the walk down the church aisle followed by having to endure being seated next to him for the entire duration of the wedding breakfast.

As if it wasn't bad enough that she'd broken up with her

boyfriend and Luke had broken up with his girlfriend, now it looked like they were being paired.

Why Martha and her dad couldn't have got married in a registry office was also beyond Skye. Personally, she'd have rather been barefoot on a faraway shore with the sea lapping at her toes.

Each to their own. Only now it meant she was stuck next to misery guts for the whole of the meal without even her sister around as a distraction. Jade should have been on the other side of Luke, in which case at least Skye could have leaned over him to chat to her, rude or not.

Maybe if Jade turned up, Skye could jiggle the places around, so she sat next to Jacob instead.

Skye dug into the holdall she'd placed on the new sofa-bed that had replaced her double bed. The bright whites and yellows of the bedding had filled the room before and despite her agreement about making changes, she couldn't stifle the quiet shunt of melancholy. Instead of the bright splash of light, the room had been dimmed with ochres and rusts. Certainly not Skye's taste. But it was no longer her home. She no longer had a say.

Thank God Martha had allowed her the choice of her own bridesmaid's dress, otherwise they could have had a disaster on their hands. She wasn't averse to colours, but she really hadn't cared for the Barbie pink Martha had suggested.

She laid out the underwear she'd bought especially for the occasion. Not her normal pretty floral bra and knickers layered with lace and flowers, but smooth, big knickers and matching bra in flesh colour. Not that she knew anyone with flesh the colour of her underwear. If she did, they'd already be classified as dead.

It was practical. The shape of the bra perfectly lifted her breasts and the halter neck sneaked neatly under the halter strap of the dress.

Skye stripped and laid her clothes on the sofa-bed ready to roll up and stash in her holdall. She whipped off her bra and edged her knickers down her thighs, letting them drop to the floor at her feet.

The familiar 'crack' sound of her bedroom door opening had her slapping her arm across her breasts and instantly dipping into a crouch. Heart hammering, she twisted her head in the direction of the intruder.

Pale green eyes glittered at her as a wide smile spread across the interloper's face.

'Well, there's a sight you don't see every day.'

3

THURSDAY, 6 OCTOBER 2016, 11.55 P.M.

With his face cupped in hands that refused to stop shaking, LJ groaned. A low groan. A powerful groan. A mixture of elation and horror.

He'd done it.

Against all odds, he'd actually pulled off the impossible.

It hadn't been difficult to entice her in. The good twin.

Little miss goody two-shoes.

She'd been all too malleable. So willing to pour her heart out.

Poor little abandoned Summer. With no one to love and no one who loved her.

He'd reeled her in so easily. Because she'd been willing to be seduced.

That part had been easy.

The problem had arisen when he realised the moment she saw him, she'd bolt. He'd thought to wait it out. Let the disappointment of being stood up wither her. He'd misjudged that part of the plan. Her withering had been momentary, then she'd rallied.

The first bit had gone beautifully smoothly.

He wasn't anything like the profile he'd stolen of a boy, only months older than Summer. Her ideal man, so to speak.

LJ had got that information by trolling her. Or stalking her, if that was a better term.

He'd followed her around Facebook, joined the groups she joined, made friends with those whom she friended before he even approached her, offering to be her friend. Just to build that profile. It didn't take much. A few months. In fact, it was dead easy. It hardly took a bright mind. It certainly took a cunning one. But he could do crafty. He was proud of his deviousness. It had held him in good stead for years and now everything was pulling together.

Initially, it hadn't been her intention to look for romance. Summer had wanted a friend. Someone not close enough so they'd gossip with real-life friends. She wanted to be able to offload. So, he'd trawled her posts and messages and made himself as close a lookalike as possible to Ansel Elgort, who she seemed to swoon over every time his name was brought up in conversation. No one noticed when he swapped out his profile picture for a blond. Nobody was interested in his life. They were all too concerned with their own.

He'd not made himself too easily available.

She'd come to him. He'd given little hints about how hard his parents were on him. Going to university was never on his programme. She was lucky to even be able to consider it. He'd had to work from the age of fifteen. Now his parents were talking about the best time for leaving home.

The sob story wasn't enough to make her back off, just sufficient to give her empathy so when he returned it, it was genuine. Or as genuine as an imposter could be.

He lowered his hands and dropped them to the kitchen table.

He clenched his jaw, determined to override that weakness that had them still trembling.

Panic had been the problem. He knew he'd panicked. If he had the chance to do it all again, he'd do it differently. Finesse that end bit. The bit he'd totally fucked up. He'd gone in too blasé, too confident, sure that he knew what he was doing. He didn't. He made a complete balls-up of the whole thing.

He rubbed his grazed knuckles. For a start, he should have worn leather gloves. Also, he probably wouldn't have chosen to injure her in that way. Now, he was going to have to wait until she was at best healed, at least lucid.

Hissing out as he dabbed anaesthetic onto his knuckles, LJ let his mind wander free. Who needed lucid? Who needed healed?

The chair scraped back, almost upending as he came to his feet.

Healing was something he needed to do.

Before he could train her, he needed to break her.

From that he would take such pleasure.

She could pay for the sins of her father.

4

THURSDAY, 6 OCTOBER 2016, 11.55 P.M.

Sound is the first thing I'm aware of. At least, the lack of it.

Pain spears my face with an excruciating pulse that radiates through my entire head so the power to think eludes me.

Barely able to breathe, I raise a hand up to touch a fat, swollen nose that doesn't even feel like my own. A painful wince comes out as I graze shaking fingers across crusted-on blood and mucus which blocks my nostrils, sending a spike of panic through me.

I open my mouth and drink in stale air as I try to blink away the darkness that presses down on me. Scary, and dense.

Fear tightens my throat. Where the hell am I?

I struggle to sit up, reaching out with tentative hands to feel along the length of what may be some kind of camping bed. A cold metal frame supporting a thin mattress.

Enveloped in shadows, with only a chink of light in a thin oblong line I presume is the outline of a door. A door I pray to be able to escape through, but I can't move. Terror has rooted me to the spot in case my attacker returns. Opens it. Comes through.

Scared enough to not even risk putting my stockinged feet on the floor, I tuck them up onto the mattress to sit cross-legged. After all, I have no idea what I would be putting my feet onto. My toes curl up tight as painful cramp takes hold of them.

Where are my shoes? Why take my shoes?

Confusion slushes through a mind full of blank holes.

If you take my shoes, I can't kick. I can't run.

I raise my fingers to my nose again to carry out a tentative exploration. With the tip of my fingernail, I gently scrape away the thick scab that plugs my nostrils until a thin inlet of air seeps through one side and then the next.

I blink.

It's pitch black and even though my eyes should have become accustomed to the dark in the last few minutes while I've been sitting here, it's too dense. Too frickin' scary. I'm petrified.

Panic is a bird's wing fluttering in the cavity of my chest where my heart used to be.

What am I doing here? Why me? What have I done to deserve this?

Pain throbs through my back, making breathing so painful, I try to control it, calm it down. I reach around, hitch up my T-shirt and touch my hot, tender skin on my back, mid-ribcage. I gasp as my searching fingers touch the solid, burning lump where he'd administered that vicious kick. It's on fire. I flinch but continue to investigate with icy fingers over scalding flesh.

It's not just that part of me that hurts. Every bit of me screams in agony. Every single muscle and bone hurts with a raw ache that threatens to consume my whole thought process.

As a whimper escapes my lips, I press them closed.

Was that a shadow flickering past the crack of light, or merely the light flickering outside the room?

Terrified, I lower myself back down onto the mattress and curl into a foetal position. I squeeze my eyes shut and force my breath to slow down as I strain to listen for any slight movement from outside the door.

A quiet shuffle. A soft breath.

I force myself to relax. Swallow my next inhale and freeze until my chest burns with the effort of holding my breath.

There it is again.

A sound. An inhale. Not me. I'm still not breathing.

Someone else.

There isn't anyone outside the door.

Because they're here. Inside the room. With me.

5

SATURDAY, 20 MAY 2023, MIDDAY

An hour and a half before the wedding

Skye gasped, tempted to tell her younger sister to fuck off as Jade stood with the door wide open for anyone looking along the hallway to see Skye stark frickin' naked. If she did, though, Jade would probably flounce along that hallway, thunder down the stairs and slam out the front door, just like she had a couple of nights ago, this time leaving the entire household to stare at the naked Skye.

Instead, she mustered up a tight smile. 'Come in. Shut the door.'

'I thought it was only the bride that was supposed to lose weight before the wedding.' Jade swept a critical gaze over Skye, her lips twisting with vague disapproval as she clicked the door shut behind her.

Skye glanced down at herself. She hadn't lost weight. She'd always been on the slim side. If anything, she felt a little wobble around her midriff. Not quite as wobbly as her younger sister. She suspected it was only a bit of green-eyed monster, as Jade's dress was two sizes larger than her own.

She skimmed a quick eye over her sister but said nothing about her wild hair and her make-up free face. Her younger sister had impeccable skin, but the tone was pale and washed out, with purple bruising under the eyes as though she'd had too many nights on the town and nowhere near enough sleep. Skye could have made the assumption that Jade was upset, but really wasn't so sure. Most likely petulant because she'd not got her own way.

Skye chose to ignore it. 'Are you getting dressed?'

Jade reached for Skye's half-filled glass of Prosecco and took a swift gulp. 'More to the point, are you?'

Skye snatched up her bra and knickers and swiftly pulled them on before anyone else barged into the room. As young girls they'd not had locks on the inside of their rooms. Never felt the need. But this was no longer their house, and the feeling that anyone could walk in made Skye's movements fast and slightly panicked.

Jade skimmed a critical eye over her. 'Nice. Gorgeous.'

'Thanks.'

Skye dipped her head to take in her appearance. Big girls' knickers and a simple, seamless T-shirt bra. Not her normal attire, admittedly, but she wouldn't be stripping off for anyone but herself this evening, and the smooth lines of the underwear would only serve to complement her dress.

She eyed her sister. 'Get dressed. Hurry up.'

Jade handed her sister's glass back to her with a crooked grin. 'How long have I got?'

Skye glanced at the screen on her phone. 'Fifteen minutes. Twenty, tops.' She reached for the open bottle and a second glass she'd placed on the bedside table in the hope that Jade would turn up. As she topped hers, then filled the second one, she smiled. 'What made you change your mind?'

Jade's eyes were flinty as Skye turned and held out her glass, instantly regretting asking the question. 'I didn't want to upset Dad.'

Skye stayed quiet but raised one brow as she waited.

Jade slumped down on the padded stool in front of the dressing table mirror and scraped her hair back from her face, twisting it with fast fingers and a skill Skye would never have into a sleek, elegant coiffure.

She leaned in close to the mirror to inspect her features, the reflection of her eyes catching Skye as she took a sip of the Prosecco Skye handed to her.

'I figured if I made my feelings too obvious, I would cut off my nose to spite my face.' She placed the glass down and picked up a bottle of Skye's cleanser. Smoothing it on with her fingers, she gave Skye a rueful smile. 'I don't want to lose Dad. We've all lost so much already. I thought if we all look after each other, nothing bad can happen again. I don't like Martha, but then again, she's not my choice, she's Dad's. I'd rather have him close where I can keep a sharp eye on her.'

Skye turned her back to Jade to hide the bubbling frustration. She slid the silk dress from its hanger. Instead of tugging it over her head, she stepped into it and drew it up over her legs, giving a gentle wriggle to get it past her hips, and pushed her arms through the armholes. As she shrugged into it, she turned back around.

'I honestly don't think he's in any peril from her.'

As Jade opened her mouth to reply, Skye continued, barely giving her sister chance to draw breath. 'But the last thing we need is to distance ourselves on the off-chance something happens.'

'We need to protect him.'

'Indeed.' Skye couldn't disagree more, but she was keeping her mouth shut. If she could keep the peace until her dad and Martha Brindley were married, then she was sure things would settle down with Jade back at university for the next couple of years.

Jade dropped the dual cotton wool pads that she'd used to wipe off the cleanser onto the dresser, and then doused another in a generous amount of toner, swiping the pad upwards over high cheekbones, a narrow forehead and down the length of her straight nose.

Her features were so different from Skye's. It made her wonder sometimes how come they were sisters. They definitely were. Jade was more like their dad in features and personality, which possibly accounted for the fact that they clashed more. Both Skye and Summer had been so like their mum. Identical twins themselves, when Skye looked at old photographs of her mum, she could have been either one of them.

'Is this the only foundation you have?' Jade wiggled the small bottle of foundation, two shades lighter than she used, at Skye.

'Well, yes. Didn't you bring your own make-up?'

The only reply from Jade was a loud tut as she tipped a little foundation onto the fleshy heel of her thumb, then took a brush and dipped it into the bronzer Skye had left on the dresser. With a liberal douse, she swirled the two together and then applied it to her smooth skin.

'Dammit, how do you manage to do that? If that was me, it would never work.'

Jade gave a casual shrug as she took a sip of her drink before picking up another brush and a palette of eyeshadow. A quick swoosh of colour over her lids and her eyes instantly darkened to almost emerald, while Skye's pale blue ones seemed to fade into insignificance beside her.

Ironically, their parents had planned to name their youngest daughter Amber because that's what colour her eyes appeared to be when she was first born. Not a bright blue like the twins had but a reflection of their dad's eyes. So they thought. Instead, within days, they'd deepened to a vibrant sea green. Their dad said that was the moment he knew she was going to be contrary.

Skye glided her feet into the mile-high heels she'd chosen while Jade finished perfecting her make-up. Nothing designer, she didn't need designer shoes. Who needed comfort either? They simply needed to look spectacular. And preferably not rub. She had blister plasters in her dainty matching clutch bag just in case.

Jade's shoes were more conservative. If she could have got away with wearing white trainers, she probably would, but they'd managed to persuade her to wear heels at least. Nothing as spectacular as Skye's, but the compromise seemed to satisfy everyone. Again, another contradiction. Make-up and hair done to perfection, but a preference for slouchy clothes and comfortable shoes.

Skye considered it again. Her university years had been like that too. She'd worn more black. With good reason. Losing her mum had been devastating. Losing her twin had been like losing a part of her.

As Jade slid her feet into her shoes, Skye felt a stab of regret that she hadn't bought the same ones. At least Jade wasn't going to have pinched feet by the end of the long day. Nor would Skye if she took her shoes off after the wedding ceremony. She could always dance barefoot.

With a quick tilt of the glass, Jade drank the remains of her Prosecco and came to her feet. Unlike her sister, she threw the dress over her head and let it slide down, taking the risk of getting make-up all over the neckline.

Typically, the dress slithered down her body, smoothing over her curves, and settled to perfection.

They both turned to look in the full-length mirror. Skye couldn't help but agree with Jade. She had lost weight. In fact, she looked pretty good.

Her heart gave a squeeze. 'Mum would be proud of us.'

Jade snorted. 'She'd have flayed us for coming to Dad's wedding if she was alive.'

A bubble of laughter came out to be cut off with unexpected suddenness.

Skye's voice thickened. 'He wouldn't be getting married if she was alive.'

They looped their arms around each other. Their eyes met in the mirror and Jade's sadness layered over Skye. How different it would be if only Summer was there on the other side of Jade.

Bookends, their mum used to call them.

A rose between two thorns, their dad always joked.

A shit sandwich, Summer and Skye had laughed.

Whatever the case, Skye felt the absence of her twin more strongly than ever.

6

SATURDAY, 8 OCTOBER 2016, 2.35 P.M.

Pain screams through me as I quietly sob into my hands, hoping he won't hear. Won't return.

I'm not sure I can bear it if he returns. When he returns. Because it is inevitable.

I'm curled on my side on the thin, dusty mattress facing the wall. Hopelessness presses down on me and I tuck my legs in tighter. To ward off the cold. To ward off the fiend.

I hurt so much. In places I've never hurt before. My face throbs, a fierce heat pulsing in my cheek so I could actually see it swollen in my vision before he went, turning out the light, leaving me in suffocating darkness.

There's a horrible warm stickiness between my thighs.

I know what he's done to me. He's raped me. More than that. I've been completely violated. I'm not stupid or naïve.

Except... I'm both of those things.

I've allowed myself to be catfished. Drawn in by someone who didn't even exist. Not the person I'd believed he was, in any case. Isn't that exactly what catfishing is?

It's not like I was on a dating app. I don't think I'd ever use one of those. They're too dangerous, so Dad tells us. Be careful, girls, I know we don't have your mum around now to give her advice, but please be careful who you speak with online. Don't talk to strangers.

And here I thought I was clever. Clever enough to have checked up on LJ. I thought I had, anyway. I'd cruised his Facebook page, and there he was with his springer spaniel puppy, and a photo from a few years earlier of his arm slung around his sister who refused to have a Facebook account because it was only for the oldies.

Everything about him had appeared genuine. He was friends with my friends. Wasn't he? Only I'd never asked any of them about him, because I hadn't wanted to share him. It had been our secret. I'd not even told Skye because we were barely talking, and he was mine. My secret.

Secrets.

We'd had more than one secret.

I told him everything. He knows everything.

My body contracts and a dull throb low down in my belly, like a period pain, starts up. Tears leak from the edge of my eyes to trickle down my cheeks. I can't help the groan that slips out. From the pain. From the... It's not embarrassment. Something deeper, much more visceral.

I fought him. With every ounce of my being, I fought him. Until I could fight no more. Until my false nails peeled back, leaving my own bloodied and ripped, some of them embedding themselves in his clothes, his flesh. I don't think they caused any damage. He barely acknowledged as his hot breath puffed out over me and he pinned me until my muscles gave out, gave in. Until my legs stopped kicking, my teeth stopped gnashing. My body betrayed me.

He continued long after I stopped fighting.

I'm left alone with my thoughts and my mind turns to how I

managed to get myself into this situation. I realise that's what we do. We victims. We blame ourselves for being tricked. For being raped.

I curl my body into a tighter C.

Oh, God. I'm mortified.

When I recall the things I've divulged to a monster. Things he can use against me.

Not only have I told him everything, revealed things to him that no one else knew so he sympathised about Mum, but I'd broken confidences. He'd encouraged me to whine on about Dad, my sisters, my life. The whole shebang, like I had the worst life ever.

He'd been there for me.

Or so I thought.

But my life isn't bad. Or at least it wasn't until now. Yes, I've lost Mum and we're all devastated, things hadn't been good. I'd fallen out with my twin for the first time in my life and we were barely talking, but now it's far worse.

Now I have nothing. Nobody. Because now, I belong to him. He made that abundantly clear as he forced himself on me. In me.

My flesh crawls as I recall words he'd groaned into my ear as he'd done that horrible thing to me. Impassioned. Crude. Declarations of love he couldn't possibly have.

Love. He doesn't know the meaning of the word.

I raise my head as a thought occurs to me.

I wonder if he will let me go now. Now he's done what he wanted to do, taken what he wanted from me. My virginity. My pride.

I stare down at my broken, battered body. My dignity in tatters.

Shame and disgust swamp me.

A soft whimper slips from my lips as I cringe remembering how, online, he'd coaxed details of my so-called love life from me. Or lack of love life. The fact that I'm still a virgin. I was a virgin. That's no longer true. But I'd told him I'm holding back until I meet that someone special in my life. Unlike loads of the girls who I was with at sixth form.

I'd waved that small nugget of information like it was a white flag of surrender. A small tease. To let him know just how special I thought he was.

Only I'm no longer a virgin and that someone special, who I'd believed was LJ, is not him.

There's no resemblance to the photograph. His hair isn't thick and lush with that modern haircut. The face nothing like LJ's photograph.

In the dull light from the single bulb suspended from the ceiling, I saw his shadowed face. His eyes deep pits filled with a manic expression of lust, of anger. His flushed skin has a leathery dimpled texture, not the smooth, beautiful complexion on the pictures of the young man he'd impersonated. A young man who probably had no idea his details had been stolen. Cloned. His whole identity, past and present, had been on Facebook for all the world to see. Only they hadn't seen, because LJ probably used all the privacy settings to keep others out of his make-believe life.

The only reality is he used his own name. I think. LJ. He said, 'Call me LJ,' his voice guttural and low.

LJ. I'd asked him once what the letters stood for. He told me all his friends called him LJ. When I'd persisted, he confessed it stood for Lying Joker. On another occasion he said it was Loser Jackass. I'd laughed. He was funny. Only he wasn't funny.

LJ was a monster.

Bile rises in the back of my throat and with a suddenness that takes me unaware, I'm heaving, throwing up over the side of the bed what little contents were in my stomach. My muscles contract, hard and painful. Between my legs hurts so much I don't even know what I should be crying about the most.

Tears leak from stinging eyes to track down my painful, swollen face.

This time, I don't try to hold back the sobs. 'Dad. Daddy.'

There's no answer in the dark. My dad isn't here. He can't rescue me.

Will LJ let me go?

'Can I go home now, please? LJ, please can I go home? My dad will be waiting for me. He needs me. He really needs me.'

My voice breaks on my sobs.

Oh, God. How long am I expected to endure this?

'LJ?' Desperate, I beg. 'Can I go home now, please? Pleeease.'

In the dark, there is nothing but silence.

7

An hour before the wedding

'Girls.'

Their dad's voice rumbled from along the hallway and Skye opened the bedroom door. She caught the brief flicker of relief on his face as Jade appeared next to her, the same height despite shorter heels. They were all tall in their family. Their mum had teetered at an elegant five foot nine, and Jade was an inch taller than Skye.

'Coming,' they chimed in unison.

The girls followed as he made his way downstairs and out the front door, where Jacob leaned his backside against the cream Morgan, the chrome gleaming in the sunshine.

'Jeez, isn't that overkill? It must have cost a fortune.'

Skye cast her sister a dark look as she stepped level with her. 'Shh. It's Jacob's. It's his wedding present to them.'

'What, the frickin' car?'

'No, you idiot, the *loan* of the car for the day. They normally cost hundreds.'

'That's what I thought. What a bleeding waste of money.'

Their dad turned at the car and looked back at them, a wide grin on his face that wiped any argument from both the girls' minds.

The loud peal of the landline ringing made the smile drop from his face to be replaced with a crease of concern. 'Skye, would you get that?'

'Dad, just leave it.' Jade took hold of Skye's arm to stop her going back inside the house.

At least Skye knew it wouldn't be Jordon. She'd not heard from him since her insistence he leave her alone. It appeared he was going to. At least for now. Until he had a drink. Then, his messages would start again. Pleading. Pathetic. After another couple of drinks, they would morph into recriminations, accusations. If only she'd paid him more attention, he would never have even looked at another woman, never mind joined a dating app and ended up sexting God knows how many other women. She'd only seen messages from one woman. But she'd seen the app on his phone.

The phone jangled again, jogging her out of her reverie.

'Leave it,' Jade repeated.

Her dad was no pushover, nor was Jade about to dictate to him, even if he was trying his best to keep the peace. 'Just get the phone, Skye. It might be one of your grandparents. There could be something wrong.'

Skye doubted it, but to make him happy she would answer it. Her job was to keep everyone calm, if not sane, and if that meant answering the phone to make sure her grandparents had no issues getting to the venue, then so be it. After all, at the age of seventy-six her grandad had been left frail since his diagnosis and treatment for prostate cancer. Her grandma was still a sprightly seventy-four-year-old who approached life like a freight train.

'For God's sake.'

Skye ignored her younger sister's muttered words and turned back into the hallway and reached for the house phone. Jade was still grumbling as she stomped through behind her.

'So, we're all happy to be late for a cold caller.'

No, they were late because she was late. One quick answer of the phone would hardly delay them interminably.

'If Dad thinks it's Grandma or Grandpa, then let me appease him by answering.' Skye shrugged.

'It won't be. I don't know why he keeps that bloody landline. It's not like anyone even uses it.'

Apart from Grandma and Grandpa... Skye sighed. She couldn't see what all the fuss was about. She could have answered the phone by now.

'Jade, chill out. How bad can it be? If it's a cold caller, I'll hang up.'

Skye reached for the phone and turned to look out of the open doorway as she did. 'Hello?' Her lips curved in a smile as she watched the sun beat down on Jacob and her dad, making their morning suits glow a silver grey. Handsome, both of them, with the backdrop of that beautiful car. Their business partnership of years had morphed into a solid, quiet friendship.

Her heart warmed.

'Hello?' She spoke into the silence, then waited a beat. Her grandpa didn't always respond immediately, being a little hard of hearing. Although often she would hear his soft, raspy breathing rattling down the phone before he'd draw it in and then speak.

This call was silent.

Jade stepped closer. 'I told you it would be a frickin' cold caller. Hang up, for God's sake.'

'Hello?' Nothing. Skye pulled the phone from her ear, intent on hanging up, and then froze at the sound of the voice on the end of the line.

'Skye?' It was a young voice. A hesitant one.

Skye pressed the receiver against her ear to hear the woman better. 'Yes?'

'Is that Skye?' The voice carried a whispered hoarseness, together with the faint trace of an accent.

'Speaking. Yes.'

She squinted out the door as her sister stared at her. Jacob and her dad stopped talking with each other and turned, enquiring expressions on their faces. She shrugged.

'Can I help you?' Her voice carried a note of irritation.

'I promised Summer.' The young voice was weak and distant.

Skye's mouth went dry, her irritation evaporating. 'Summer...' she managed to croak. Her twin's name was barely spoken of these days. It hurt too much. Summer had disappeared like a puff of steam blown away on the wind. Never heard of again. No contact. No trace.

No closure.

The pain of it lanced through her, swift and unexpected.

'Yes. I promised Summer I would phone if I managed to escape.'

Escape?

Skye's chest squeezed as she sent a beseeching look to her dad, her gaze trying to communicate the sudden desperation. She wanted him here. She needed him by her side as her knees weakened.

A dark cloud swept over the sun and plunged the brilliant day into night.

With numb lips, she repeated her lost twin's name. 'Summer?'

'Yes.' The whisper was urgent now, a frenzied hiss. 'Listen. She said to tell you she's safe.'

'Safe?'

Her dad squeezed past Jade, a gentle hand on his youngest daughter's shoulder.

'Yes, but she's not. He's crazy. He'll kill her. Like he did the others. One day, he'll kill her, too.'

'Who is this?' Skye's voice should have been a sharp snap of impatience, instead it was weak with hope, hovering on the edge of disbelief.

They'd had crank phone calls in the beginning, but this woman's tone held an element of sincerity.

'What is it, Skye?' Her dad reached for the phone, his face wreathed with concern, but Skye stopped him with a raised hand as she stepped deeper into the hallway.

'Where is she? Where's my sister?'

As though the girl on the end of the phone hadn't even heard her, her words rushed down the line. 'She said she wanted you to know she never left you. Not of her own free will.'

'Skye.' Jacob moved closer, like her dad, his eyes were filled with concern. 'Is everything all right?'

'Skye?' Jade pushed past the two men and reached her side.

There was a sharp intake of breath on the end of the line. 'I must go.' Her voice faded and Skye pressed the phone close to her ear, barely catching the woman's words, so she couldn't be sure she heard them correctly.

White noise filled Skye's head and she swayed. 'Hello? Hello?'

But the line was dead.

8

SUNDAY, 10 FEBRUARY 2019

I keep my head lowered, eyes fixed on the table as I nibble the side of my thumb while LJ eats. My nails are short and bitten down, so I've started on the skin.

'Stop fidgeting!'

I jerk my head up and meet LJ's irritated gaze. Before I can break eye contact, he reaches over, grabs a hank of my hair and wrenches at it so I sprawl full length across the table in front of him. 'I said stop your fucking fidgeting or you can go back to your room.'

I drop my gaze and stare instead at his mouth, scared to meet the manic light in his eyes.

'I don't know why you have to be so fucking ungrateful. I let you up here, don't I? And all you can do is fucking...'

'I'm sorry.' I whisper the words, desperate not to push him further, but it seems I may be too late. It doesn't take much to push him too far. Nothing, in fact. I let out a whimper as he yanks harder and brings me nose to nose with him until I think my neck might snap. My hand is only a smidgen away from his steaming mug of coffee. I curl my fingers into a fist because I know what happened last time I knocked his mug over, and I'm not willing to go through that pain again.

'You've only yourself to blame, you know. No one else annoys me like you do.'

'I know. I'm sorry.'

'If you know, then why do it?' He flings me away from him, disgust lacing his voice as he untangles threads of hair from his fingers and drops them on the floor. It's no longer the thick luscious black locks I arrived with, but mousy brown and thinner than it used to be. With no access to scissors so I can cut it, the ends have split and I imagine it looks ragged, despite LJ giving me a small plastic brush which fills my hair with static when I use it.

'I'm sorry, LJ.' I stay still, fully aware that it might not yet be over. My chest burns as I hold my breath, frightened to let it out in case it annoys him.

'Here I was thinking I'd been generous letting you up here. And what thanks do I get?'

'I'm sorry, LJ. I forgot. I'm stupid.'

'You are stupid. Fucking stupid. I can't bear the sight of you.' He sniffs. 'Or the smell. What the hell have you been doing to yourself? You stink.'

He gives my shoulder a shove, so I fall back into my chair. As it rocks backwards, I snatch at the side of the table to stop from tipping over. I've learnt that lesson the hard way, too. You do, when your head gets smashed against the floor and all he does is walk away without a backward glance.

'You need a shower.'

I nod, desperate not to show how delighted I am to be able to shower again. I can't remember the last time. It's been weeks. So long I've lost count. I keep an overall tally of the days. From the day I realised I was there long term, I started scratching. I backtracked to the best of my ability. A mark for every day I exist. I call it an existence, because it's not living. No one could class this as anything but survival.

That's all I do. Survive. Endure.

To serve him.

I stopped smelling my own dried-on sweat a while back. I can smell his, though. All over my unwashed body. My clothes stick to my skin in the heat of the day. And when I'm locked in the cool, dank cellar that seems to be part rock, they stick again in an icy sheet at night because it never heats up in there. Never gets warm no matter how hot it may be outside. I can only dream of the heat of the sun soaking through to warm my icy bones.

I don't complain. I don't dare. Not now. Not since I learnt what happens. Sometimes it will be for no reason. Just because LJ is in a foul mood. Because the day hasn't gone his way. Because the people he's been with don't agree with him, and he's not big enough in the real world to stand up for himself. So, he comes back here to show just how strong, how powerful he is. Sometimes it's just because he feels like it.

But I keep silent, just in case.

I don't want to be confined in the dark again. Week after week he slides food on a tray through the door once a day until my bones poke from my skin and daylight blinds me when he lets me out again.

LJ hasn't done that for a while, and I'm so unbelievably grateful to be allowed to stand at the open door into the high-walled court-yard. The sun touching my face instead of me being curled up in the pitch black.

Like Dad used to say, laughingly, 'Be a mushroom, they keep you in the dark and feed you bullshit.'

It was bullshit.

Only this wasn't anything to laugh about.

And the mushrooms continued to grow. Just as I grow. I'm not flourishing, but something inside me is. I can feel it. A peculiar flutter, a comforting warmth.

I resist touching my stomach in his presence.

If I do, he will know.

What will he do when he finds out? Will he be angry? Or overjoyed? I have no idea.

For now, I'll keep it my secret.

'Here!'

I jump at the gunshot sound of his voice as he holds something out in the palm of his hand.

A bar of soap. There's never anything in the small, damp bathroom with its mouldy tiles. Nothing to show anyone lives in the house. Not that LJ lives here. He only visits and I've never known him use the shower. Not that I know everything because once he locks me in my cell, I never see or hear anything. The occasional bump or scrape. That's it. Because down there in that hell-hole of a dungeon, when the lights go out, my mind shuts down.

I exercise caution as I take the soap from his hand, just in case he decides to snatch it away from me. 'Thank you, LJ.' I bob my head. 'Thank you so much.' I can never be gracious enough, never show too much gratitude. At any given moment, that appreciation can be smashed into the floor.

LJ nods over at the kitchen sink and the small towel on the draining board next to it. 'Don't be too long. And clean the shower when you've finished.'

I turn to go, and he raises a hand. I flinch and see the satisfaction on his face as though he expected it. Wanted it. But the strike doesn't come. In fact, he pauses, one finger in the air, as though he's just thought of something, but I know better. I know everything is planned, contrived, schemed.

'I've been thinking.'

I swallow, my mouth suddenly dry. What this time? What foul-ness must I endure?

'I think it's time you started earning your keep.'

I'd rather he didn't keep me. I'd rather go home. I've stopped begging to be allowed home. I no longer crave my previous life. They wouldn't want me now anyhow. Damaged as I am. That's what LJ tells me. Every time I see him. I'm no longer the person I used to be. I'm a ghost. A dirty creature that lurks in the shadows.

He jabs a sharp finger into my ribs, and I jump, almost dropping the bar of soap. 'Are you listening?'

I nod. 'Yes, LJ.'

'What did I say?'

I can't for the life of me pull through the words he'd been speaking as my mind drifted. My neck gives a sharp spasm and my head nods. 'Earn my keep. You want me to earn my keep.'

He sighs, but the light in his eyes is still mellow. 'You can start cleaning the house from now on.'

My heart gives a little stutter. He's never allowed me to do anything. Ever. Not until recently when he's allowed me to come upstairs and stare out of the open doorway, breathe in the fresh air.

Perhaps he's softening.

What does it mean? Will he be spending more time here? This is a turn-up for the books. I'm not sure I understand. Not sure I want to. What is this shift in our arrangement? Is the fact that he's allowing me to clean a reward… or a punishment? I'm not sure. What I do know is that I feel like I'm on a knife's edge. A pivotal moment.

I can barely breathe for fear of the consequences if I make the wrong move, blink at the wrong time. He likes to do that. Keep me unbalanced.

He circles his hand in the air. 'Go, have your shower, and wash your hair properly. That's a shampoo bar.'

I hadn't heard of such a thing. Normally I can't get any lather or the soap to clean my hair properly and he's never provided shampoo before, let alone conditioner. Which is why my hair is frizzy. Not that I care. There are more things to be concerned about than my looks. They are nothing. I am nothing. Or so LJ reminds me.

Now, though, I have an opportunity. A break.

I head for the stairs and sprint up like I'm being chased, before he changes his mind. Because that's what LJ does. Forever plays games.

I jump in the shower while the water is still running cold. It takes so long to heat up that LJ moans if I take too long. My body trembles with the icy water sluicing over my head, but I take no notice and scrub, scrub, scrub.

Desperate to be clean, I lather the bar of shampoo soap against my head and the first pleasure I have felt since I arrived trembles through my body. I smile. I actually smile.

The glorious scent of green apples fills my senses. I tip my head back, allowing the water to thrash down on my face, rinsing the thick suds away, swilling the dirt down the drain.

I froth up again and the clean squeak of hair against my fingers sends shudders of pleasure across my naked flesh as the water almost boils until my skin is a healthy glowing pink. The warmth of it starts to defrost the frozen bones inside of me.

I wash under my armpits where the hair has grown in thick tufts because I'm not allowed a razor of any kind. There's nothing sharp anywhere in this house as far as I know.

For some time, I've been allowed a spoon to eat. No fork. No knife.

After the frenetic washing, I simply stand for a moment and the world seems to still. There's just me, water raining down on my head, and the first flutter of life from the baby inside me.

* * *

I rest my head on Mummy's tummy as Skye and I lie either side of her on our parents' bed. Daddy is propped up on his side behind Skye, arm crooked on his pillow to prop up his head. A mad grin is on his face, his eyes filled with a joyous sparkle.

My face close to Skye's over the swell, we look into each other's faces and smile, wriggling to get closer.

'Shh.' Mummy touches our hair and we both go so still. The smile drops from Skye's face as she feels it, the same as I do. Her eyes widen with wonder.

A flutter. A butterfly trapped in a gilded cage.

I spread my fingers wide to catch the slightest movement and draw in a soft breath.

'Special.' Skye grins at me.

I glance at Mummy's face. 'A baby. Our baby.' Because I know Mummy is having this little baby especially for us. For Skye and me. Because we asked for a baby. That has to be the reason. Shelley Greenfield's mummy had a baby and we wanted one too.

Mummy's face softens. 'Another little girl. How lucky are we that our family is going to get bigger? This baby will complete us. We're the luckiest family alive.'

Excitement buzzes through me so my skin almost vibrates. But I keep it inside. Deep inside because Mummy wants me to be good. To be quiet.

She reaches to take one of our hands in each of hers. She moves them gently over a stomach I only now realise has started to get so round, so big, stretched taut like a balloon. How come Skye and I hadn't noticed until now? Mummy's legs and arms are just the same. It's her belly that has become rounded.

My breath stops in my throat and my eyes widen as I stare across the swell of Mummy's tummy at my twin. Had she felt it?

More than just a flutter, but a movement. A slide of a small foot against the palm of my hand.

Skye's eyes reflect my own awe.

We're going to have a baby. Mummy, Daddy, Skye and me.

We're going to have a baby.

Joy fills my heart as I lay my head back down, the soft swell of Mummy's tummy a warm cushion for my head.

Gentle, rapid heartbeats fill my ears and I close my eyes. A smile curves my mouth as I slip off the edge of wakefulness and drop into the soft comfort of a dream.

9

SATURDAY, 20 MAY 2023, 12.45 P.M.

Forty-five minutes before the wedding

Skye's hands still shook as she raised the small tumbler to her lips and drank down half the contents before stopping as the burn of whisky hit her stomach. It sent a backlash up her throat to singe the insides of her nose and she wouldn't have been surprised if flames had licked from her nostrils.

'It was a hoax, Skye. It had to be a hoax.' Her sister hammered the heel of her hand a little too enthusiastically between Skye's shoulder blades. Her face was probably a blotchy mess, she imagined, as breath wheezed into her burning lungs.

'Who the hell would think that could come anywhere near funny?' Jacob crouched down in front of Skye where she'd melted onto the bottom step of the stairs, his face tense as he cupped her cheek in his hand. 'Are you okay?'

'I said a hoax, not a joke.' Oblivious of Skye's neat coiffure that she'd paid more for than she could afford, Jade gave her head a rough scrub. 'Come on. It was a cruel, horrible thing to do. Some twisted mind thought they could upset you. Us.'

Jacob nodded. 'There are some sick people out there, Skye, but this wasn't real. Jade's right. I don't know why they would choose now to do this, but there's no truth in it. There can't be. Not after all this time.'

Skye leaned back and stared over Jacob's head at her dad. Chalk white, his skin slicked with sweat. If she'd had the strength, she'd run to him, fling herself in his arms. She had nothing. She was drained. 'It felt real to me. You didn't hear her. She sounded desperate.'

'Why would she hang up?' Jade held the phone in her hand and Skye couldn't for the life of her remember her sister taking it from her numb fingers. 'I tried to redial, but they withheld the number.'

'Crazy,' her dad whispered.

'No...' Maybe. The voice had sounded panic stricken. Frantic at the end. 'Perhaps we should call the police. They could trace the number, even if it is withheld. See if someone needs help.'

'They won't get help if I get my hands on them.' Jacob shuffled around, plonking himself down on the step beside her, squeezing in between Skye and the wall.

He wrapped a beefy arm around her, and she flopped her head onto his shoulder, the soft scent of soap and freshly applied deodorant a comfort. 'You're okay. We're here.'

'Thanks, Jacob.' She sighed as she glanced up at her dad. 'Do you think we should call the police, Dad?'

Her dad sighed, pushed away from the wall and paced back to the front door.

With his back to them, his wide shoulders blocked out the daylight and cast a darker shadow through the hall.

His voice, when it came, was raw. 'It's a cruel, twisted prank from some sick individual who obviously doesn't want this wedding to happen.'

Skye wasn't sure if her sister caught the quick flash of irritation he sent in Jade's direction, but Skye's stomach pitched. The last thing they needed was another family argument ending up with Jade storming out. Jade might have her issues about the wedding, but she was over them, and she would never consider doing something so cruel. So wicked. This wouldn't merely hurt Martha, but their dad. She couldn't even conceive her sister would have had anything to do with it.

'It wasn't a prank, Dad.' There'd been genuine fear in the woman's voice.

He raised his hand and swept his hair back across his head. A sure sign he was rattled. 'I can't think of any reason why someone would come forward now, today of all days, to claim knowledge of your sister's whereabouts.'

He turned. His features tortured. 'We've not heard a single thing since the day Summer disappeared seven years ago. Nothing. No trace. So why now? What would make anyone—' his nose wrinkled in disgust '—choose today, of all days, to suddenly declare their knowledge of your sister and not even verify her whereabouts?'

He leaned in, distress carving deep lines into his face. 'They're sick. Do you hear me? The police did everything they possibly could. Our first three years of searching bore nothing but dead ends and sick people who wanted their five minutes of fame for their apparent sightings, their names in newspapers, their faces on social media. None of it was true.'

He stamped his hand against the air. 'No one saw her.'

He took in a long breath through his nose. 'Summer *wanted* to disappear. She *chose* to go. To desert us. She never wanted us to find her, or she would have contacted us before now. Before *today*.'

'Dad...'

Before Skye could raise doubts she'd had since the very start, doubts she'd mentioned every time her twin's name was brought up, he continued. 'The police investigated. There was absolutely no evidence of her being taken, nothing to indicate a struggle. No trace of anything untoward. She just left. Left us. She cracked. Walked out that door one day and never came back. I don't believe for one second—' he slashed his hand towards the phone '—that caller was genuine.'

His voice broke and he shook his head, tears forming in his eyes. 'I refuse to believe it. Not now.'

His mouth compressed in a straight line. He paused. His voice when it came was calmer. Quieter. 'It's not real. It's not true.'

Skye wanted to argue. Say what she thought she'd heard. Doubt scratched at the surface. Was it her imagination? Her heart trying to convince her head of something she'd always believed. That her twin would never have left them.

Did she want it to be true? What if it was?

Worse. What if it wasn't?

She stared up at her dad, anger vibrating through him. He was convinced it was a crank call. She felt the weight of the decision on her shoulders. A decision that could once again destroy their lives if she took that step to call off the wedding.

'You're right.' She sucked in a shaky breath. 'You're right.' She thought of his bride at the church. Lovely Martha, who deserved none of this.

She touched a finger underneath her eye and one fat tear dripped over it. Her last tear today. She'd make sure of that.

Skye stared around at the faces of the people she loved. 'Sorry. I'm sorry. It shook me.' She knew it shook them all too, but there was something more for her. They never heard the voice. Felt the conviction.

She swallowed. 'It must have been a crank call.'

Relief flooded the faces of those who watched her so intently.

Jade leaned down, eyes sparkling with her own tears, and crooked her arm through Skye's, yanking her to her feet. 'Well, fuck this for a game of soldiers. No one is going to stop my dad from marrying.'

She kept her arm looped through Skye's and glared around the small hallway to take in the two men. 'No one.'

The muscles in her jaw flexed and the challenge in her eye indicated that she'd not missed that look from her dad earlier. But nor was she about to rise to the bait. The time had passed and his emotions were too raw to deal with.

There was no way Jade would have had any part in a stunt like that. No matter what she thought of her future step-mum.

Jacob struggled to his feet from a step that had been too low for him and gave a small incline of his head, his serious eyes meeting Skye's. 'What do you want to do, Skye? You're the one who took the call, heard the woman. It's your call. We can take this seriously and phone the police now—' he glanced at his watch '—or we get on with the wedding while we give it some thought. Perhaps inform the police in the morning. It depends on how urgent you feel it is. How real.'

It was real to her, but she could see the desperation in their faces. The desperate desire for her to confirm to them that everything was all right.

She drew in a jerky breath and nodded. 'Let's get on with this. It was some bloody crank caller caught me off guard.'

She wasn't convinced.

The call had shaken her, but there was no way she was prepared to de-rail her dad's wedding. They'd had crank calls before. In the beginning. There were some sick people out there. The police had investigated every single one of those leads in the beginning. As time went on, they'd become less frequent. Then they'd stopped. Until now.

Today of all days.

Skye dabbed shaking fingers under wet eyes and hoped to God

her make-up hadn't run down her face. As it was, she could only pray the strain showing would be misinterpreted for stress of the day. No one would know except the four of them.

With nimble fingers, Jade entwined Skye's hair back into a semblance of order and then patted a tissue under her eyes. Concern rippled through her sister's tear-filled expression, but she gave a sharp nod to show she was done.

Jade turned on her heel and held out her arm for Jacob to escort her to the car. 'Let's get on with this. Don't let the bastards get you down.'

Instead of her dad kicking off about Jade's foul language, he rolled his eyes and offered his older daughter his arm.

As Skye linked arms with him, she offered up a shaky smile.

'I'm sorry I made you take that call.' Her dad patted her hand, and she noticed his fingers weren't quite steady. 'There are some really sick people out there, and I suspect it's more to do with me and the fact that I'm remarrying. Your mum's family really don't think I should.'

'It's seven years, Dad. It's nothing to do with them. It's not their life. You deserve happiness.'

He pulled the door closed behind them. 'I'd like to think I do, but they've never forgiven me for Summer disappearing after your mum died. They think I should have taken better care of her. They think it's my fault she ran away. Your grandma says I was too over-bearing, held on too tight.'

She couldn't deny he had been. His fear for them had surged when their mum died, which was one of the reasons Skye had made her decision to go to university. Summer had clung on.

Had it all become too much for her?

Guilt always cast a fine veil over Skye's opinion of her sister's disappearance. Her dad blamed himself and, to a degree, so did she. Then again, she blamed herself too for wallowing in anger that Summer hadn't gone with her to university.

Skye had believed her life would be filled with fun and laughter. The reality of university had been quite different. She'd spent most of her time alone in her dorm, unwilling to join the others, unwilling to admit to her family she'd made a mistake as she'd wallowed in her loneliness. Riddled with guilt that she'd left her twin behind and unable to admit to it. Pride on both sides had destroyed their relationship.

The big question was, had all of that driven Summer away?

Skye still could not fully believe it. Summer wasn't made that way. She was always the one to come round. To give in.

Skye squeezed her dad's hand as they stopped beside the car. 'It was never your fault. Summer made that decision all by herself. No one forced her out the door.' She hoped to God no one had, but she would never be able to shake the impression that Summer didn't just take off.

Her dad swung the rear car door open for Skye to get in. With Jacob and Jade in the front seats, Skye waited for her dad to walk around the other side and slide in beside her.

Jacob peered over his shoulder at them. 'Are we ready for this?' There was a false note of cheer in his voice, but no one acknowledged it.

'Let's go.' Her dad linked his fingers with Skye's as the car glided from the kerb. He gave her hand a light squeeze. 'Put it behind you, now. It was just a vile prank.'

Skye turned her head to stare at the street lined with trees thick with blossom. A new season, a new start.

So why was it she couldn't shake off the uncomfortable sensation she had?

What if it wasn't a hoax?

What if those whispered words she barely heard at the end weren't her imagination?

She heard them now, like an echo. The woman's voice a soft breath.

'She chalked something for you.'

10

SUNDAY, 14 APRIL 2019

Doubled over, I'm retching until it feels as though my stomach and lungs are about to burst out of my throat. Agony pulses through my body, every square inch of skin on fire as I heave and heave again.

He can hear me. I know he can hear me.

Tears are streaming down my face, but I know it doesn't matter what I do, he won't come. He won't help.

I could die down here, but he'll never come to my rescue. The best he's done is push a huge plastic bucket across the stone floor at me with his foot. The rattle and clang of him shutting and bolting the door as he left is the only sound I've heard for the past several hours.

At least I think it was hours. I passed out at one point. Ages ago. It could be hours. Or even days, for all I know.

Pain spikes every muscle, every nerve ending from the continuous spasms. The icy, damp cellar floor where I collapsed doesn't help. The cold has seeped through and taken hold of any part of my body that isn't ablaze. I can't even imagine which one is best. Fire or ice.

I shudder again. Retch. This time only bile comes out. Thin and

reedy with nothing left in my stomach to purge. Because I can'
even remember the last time I had food. Or water. Did I drink tha
bottle of water? The one turned on its side with the lid off. Or did
kick it over as the contractions gripped my body?

As the shudders subside for a moment, I roll over onto my back-
side. Desperate to get to the small bed, off the floor, I shuffle back-
wards until the cold metal frame touches my back.

A quiet sob escapes my parched lips as I take a moment just to
gather my strength before heaving myself up onto the thin mattress,
away from the chill. I need to get warm. Whatever I've got is
sweeping through my body so little ripples of it swim through my
veins until my teeth chatter so hard I think they may break into
small shards.

LJ hates sickness. I've only been ill once before and he locked
me in my dungeon then, too. Only this time it's far more serious.
Maybe he knew because he left the dull ceiling light on, whereas
normally when he locks up, he plunges me into darkness.

I thought he'd been happy with me lately. I've scrubbed the
house from top to bottom. It's immaculate now. Not a cobweb in
sight, not a bit of mould in the shower. It's been a kind of outlet for
me too. Something to do, to occupy me, and it means I get to be
upstairs for far longer every day, bathe my face in sunshine that has
gone from soft and mellow to fierce over the past couple of days.

I thought he'd started to trust me.

He's even permitted me to shower every few days. I've managed
to scrub my face while scrubbing toilets. Not in the same water, of
course, but by the time the taps have run hot in the bathroom, I've
already cleaned everywhere, and I can swish water over my face
and under my armpits every day.

When the shampoo bar became a sliver, he replaced it. That's
got to be a good sign. Right?

He's also given me a warm quilt to go on my bed because even in the height of summer, it's still cold down here in the dungeon. I've never quite figured out what the set-up is, but the cellar where I live appears to be made of stone. A dense, smooth rock which arches over the top of me. Almost like a cave. But the curving stairwell is brickwork.

My teeth clench together. If only I could get under the cover, I'd warm up. I might survive.

I've never felt so unwell in all my life.

I've eaten some crap LJ's provided while I've been incarcerated, but I've never become sick off any of it.

My cellar is filthy, without running water, but since LJ's let me upstairs more often, I've managed to clean down here too. He never made any objection when I brought the broom down and swept all the dust and cobwebs from the corners of the low arched ceiling. I even managed to bring a cloth with me to wipe down the bedframe, which had dust encrusted in all the nooks and crannies.

He said nothing when I put my bedcovers in the washing machine. Although I hesitated to step into the walled courtyard to hang them over the line. Not until he said I could. I know the consequences of not asking.

The day I was allowed into the lounge was the day I knew I would never leave this place.

He'd brought me somewhere no one would ever find me. Somewhere I could never escape from.

A bank of windows dominated the enormous open plan room, all the way across one side opposite the door. It made me wonder if the house teetered off a cliff edge as the bird's-eye view was that of a rolling landscape, thick with lush vegetation.

A deep valley stretched as far as the eye could see, with high rolling hills either side appearing to reach for the sky. The house was positioned directly above the middle of a fissure, with hundreds of huge ancient trees rising up from the valley floor heavenward, reminding me of the film I'd watched years ago called *Lord of the Rings*. Even in the deepest of winter, the evergreens still rolled in velvet viridescent carpets. My artist's eye weeps for the chance to daub paint on canvas and forever capture that scene.

On the horizon, a dot of something red floats in the sky. Too large to be a balloon. But maybe a hot air balloon. Some sort of dirigible in any case. I see it often, far in the distance. A sharp reminder that, should I escape, there is nowhere I can go. Nowhere to run to. Nowhere in that vast forest to find help. I am alone.

Stranded.

Captive.

In a wilderness I have never experienced before.

I close my eyes and picture that view now as another cramp squeezes at my womb. The view itself is my escape to another world.

There's no obvious reason to have become so ill unless LJ has brought a bug back with him and I've caught it off him. Something dangerous to me, simply because I've been so isolated. Something dangerous to my unborn child.

I know I took biology lessons in school, but quite honestly, I know so very little about pregnancy. It never occurred to me, with my little secret, that anything bad could happen.

Weak as a kitten, I hitch myself up onto the side of the bed, using my elbows to brace myself.

Liquid gushes warm and sticky from between my thighs as I raise myself up.

In the shadowy light, I stare down at myself, horror gripping my insides with as much force as the contractions that have me bearing down.

A dark patch spreads across my crotch and down the legs of my cheap, thin, pale grey tracksuit bottoms, blossoming out into a pool of bright crimson.

My fingers shake as I reach down, edging them under the elasticated waist of the tracksuit bottoms as another pain, far more visceral, creases me in two. 'Oh, God.'

'LJ.' I croak out his name. The only one who can help me. For the first time, I need him.

I raise myself up off the mattress onto one elbow while my fingers investigate. Little sobs break from my lips as terror tears through me. I push the clothes from my lower body and let them drop to the floor with a soft flump. I pull my hand slowly from between my thighs and stare at the bloodied, fragile foetus I hold on the tips of my fingers.

A sob breaks from me, my pain forgotten in that instant.

I don't know how long I cradle my baby in the palm of my hands before I become aware of sound, of movement.

The scream lodges in my throat at the metallic rattle of locks being thrown back on the door. A scream of anger. Of fury. All held back.

A shaft of light slices across the stone-walled cellar.

I duck my head so he can't see the devastation on my face. A devastation that would bring him nothing but amusement. Satisfaction. I'm sure of it.

A moment ago, I believed I needed him. Now, I know better.

The clatter of another bucket, this time metal as it hits the floor, making me jerk my head upright. All attention on him.

'Clean yourself up, you filthy bitch.'

I stare up at him, his dark figure filling the doorway to block out the light from behind him.

'How did you know?' The question spills from my lips as I continue to hold that tiny, defenceless little form in my hands, almost offering it to him.

He gave a derisive snort. 'I know all there is to know about you, Summer. I know your body better than you do. I always will.

There's no escaping me and there's no fooling me either. Clean yourself up and never think you can do that to me again. Don't ever try to hide anything from me. The repercussions if you try will be far worse than your little mind could ever comprehend.'

He places two bottles of water and a plate covered in tinfoil on the floor and backs away. As though what I have may be contagious. But we all know there is nothing contagious about being pregnant. Nor is it contagious to miscarry.

As the door slams, I recall the herbal tea LJ had slid over the table to me the previous morning. The first time he'd ever offered tea.

I realise it won't be the last.

*　*　*

Gasping for breath, Skye flung herself upright in the double bed she shared with Alec, her boyfriend.

Black haired, blue eyed, from Ireland, Alec had charmed his way into her life and her bed three months previously.

She'd found him amusing, uplifting.

Skye no longer sought solace and understanding from friends. Because nobody understood. How could they? Her pals at university didn't want to be with someone who cried into their beer every Wednesday night at students' night on campus. They wanted life and laughter. Something she could have had if not for the fact that half of her was missing.

So, she stopped talking about her twin. It had been long enough for everyone else. A lifetime for her. And yet it still felt like yesterday when Summer disappeared.

There was nothing could convince Skye that her sister simply left. Nothing and nobody.

She'd spent weeks, months, years trying to convince anyone and everyone who would listen. Until they simply stopped listening.

Her stomach cramped and sweat broke out across her forehead.

She swung her legs over the side of the bed, curled down and wrapped her arms around her stomach, letting out a groan.

Had she got food poisoning? They'd been for a Chinese earlier in the evening.

Her stomach cramped and she knew. Knew it couldn't be food poisoning. This was something far worse.

'Summer.' She gasped as another pain speared into her abdomen.

Not her stomach, but lower. Much lower.

Alec stirred, a quiet mumble of protest as she shifted again. She wasn't sure if she could make the toilet in time.

She flung back the quilt and surged to her feet just as warm liquid gushed from between her thighs to run down her legs.

Skye staggered into the bathroom and yanked on the bright white light.

Blood streamed down her legs and puddled around her feet while she panted as another contraction took hold. She sank onto the white bathroom mat as tears streamed down her cheeks.

She gasped for air.

Never in her life had she suffered such a fierce period. One where she could barely move. Where a hand tightened on her womb and squeezed it in a cruel fist.

Huddled on the bathroom floor, Skye reached up and managed to flick her dressing gown from the hook on the back of the door. The loose hook flicked off and clattered across the tiles, spinning for a moment before it came to rest. The dressing gown flipped down on top of her.

She stared up at the hole the broken hook had created on the back of the door. The landlord would lose his shit over that.

She didn't care.

Her muscles clamped down once again and she moaned. 'Sum mer, oh my God. Summer. What's going on? What's happened?'

Her twin's presence hovered over the top of her and she reached out. Felt nothing.

Skye pushed up to a sitting position and tugged the dressing gown around herself. Tears spilled from her eyes and sobs came fast and uncontrolled as a small plug of mucus slipped from between her thighs.

She stilled, staring at the small jelly-like blob and then closed her eyes as everything fell into place. Her period was six days over-due, and she'd just miscarried. She stared at the bloodied clot in horror.

She'd not even known she was pregnant.

11

SATURDAY, 20 MAY 2023, 1.21 P.M.

Nine minutes before the wedding

Luke stood on the top stone step under the arched entrance to the church.

Anger permeated the thin façade of his elegant groomsman's suit while he glared at the car as it drew to a stop.

Jacob leapt out and dashed around the front of the car to help, first Jade from the front seat, and then Skye and their dad from the rear seats.

'Jeez, what's up with Dr Jekyll?' Jade murmured in Skye's ear as they walked behind Jacob and their dad up the short path through the cemetery towards Luke.

'He's probably anxious. We are very late.'

'We're not. We've still got a few minutes. It hasn't started yet.'

Typical of her younger sister to assume that because a wedding starts at 1.30 p.m. you don't have to be there until that time. They should have been there thirty to forty-five minutes earlier.

Skye took a calming breath. There was no good pointing it out. 'It's hardly likely to without the groom. Is it?'

'Well, we're here now. Everything will be fine, if he stops glaring at us. He's got a face like a smacked arse.'

'Shh, Jade. Watch your mouth. This is a place of worship.'

Jade opened her mouth, undoubtedly to give them the wisdom of her opinion on religion, when their dad glanced over his shoulder, and with a look and one quiet word silenced them. 'Girls.'

Skye elbowed her sister, casting her a dark frown.

'He started it,' Jade hissed under her breath, nodding at Luke whose grim face had taken on the look of a nine-year-old child.

'Shush!' Skye gritted her teeth and looped her arm through Jade's. She loved her sister to bits, but once in while Jade needed to be reined in.

She raised her chin and gave a wide smile, hoping the strain didn't show. She could see it on her dad's face as he glanced back at them.

Jacob never looked behind as they came to a stop.

The vicar stepped out of the church porch, concern encroaching on calm features. 'Is everything all right? I thought we understood that the groom should be here thirty minutes before the bride. It's cutting it very fine. The congregation are getting quite unsettled.'

Jacob stepped forward with a small cough. 'Just a little car trouble. My fault.' He raised his hand and tugged at the slightly crooked bow tie, his ears flushing a dull pink.

Skye felt sorry for him shouldering the blame; he hadn't needed to, but the alternative would have been a very long, convoluted explanation she was sure the vicar wouldn't be expecting. She thought it better not to contradict Jacob at this point who probably surmised this was the easiest explanation.

Luke's jaw looked tense enough to snap. 'Mum's in the car. Waiting around the corner.'

Skye's dad glanced at his watch, his own face flushing. 'I'm sorry...'

'No matter. She's a little early.' The vicar gave them a reproachful look. 'It's usually the bride's privilege to be late.' He waved them through, his voice lifting to a cheery note. 'You're here now. Don't start your married life with recriminations.'

He stared directly at Luke. 'Give your mum the go-ahead, young man.' He raised his arms, so his cassock opened into angel wings. 'Let the ceremony begin.' He smiled, exposing square, yellowed teeth that leaned on each other like falling headstones.

Jacob, the vicar, and Skye's dad disappeared down the aisle to the front of the church as Luke slipped the phone back into his pocket after muttering something into it.

Luke stared first at Jade and then Skye, his gaze direct and assessing.

They'd barely had anything to do with each other. An occasional meal out with their respective parents. Skye found him abrasive.

Skye considered his attitude might come from the fact that he'd been dumped by his most recent girlfriend, according to his mum, putting the table plans a little awry in the process. Maybe his girlfriend had dumped him because of his abrasiveness.

She looked him up and down. Perhaps he was just a prick.

'What?' Jade wasn't quite as subtle. She shot a hip forward, placing her hand on it in direct challenge.

'What are you doing here?' he shot back.

Confused, Skye frowned as Jade glared at him. 'We have every right to be here. Our *dad* is marrying your *mum*, for better or *worse*.'

Skye darted a panicked glance through the arched doorway at the small congregation, all seated awaiting the arrival of the bride. She didn't need these two having a figurative punch-up. Her nerves were frayed enough.

'I meant, why aren't you with your dad?'

Before Jade could slant him a scathing answer, Skye stepped between them. 'Because we're the bridesmaids. If you'd paid attention, you'd know. You're walking your mum down the aisle...'

'I'm aware of that,' he snapped. His grandad had died before they had met Martha, but his grandmother was presumably seated at the front of the congregation.

'Well, we're the *bridesmaids*,' she emphasised. 'We tend to your mum. And anyway, shouldn't you be with her?'

'I got out of the car to see what the hell the delay was.' His face flushed. Evidently his temper, or anxiety, had got the better of him.

'Nice. Desert your mum.' Jade slid in and earned herself a sharp look from Skye.

'Right! Here she is.' Skye raised her chin and plastered on a wide smile as the chauffeur pulled the car up to the kerb and stepped from the driver's seat.

'Come on.' She hitched the bottom of her dress up and strode out with the others scrambling behind to catch up.

They reached the end of the church pathway just as Martha alighted from the car.

A small flicker of concern filled her eyes. 'Is everything okay?'

Skye stretched the smile even further as she reached for Martha's arm. 'Fine. Car trouble. That's all.'

Relief washed over Martha's delicate features.

The complete antithesis of Skye's mum, who had been tall and slender with long blonde highlighted hair.

Tiny pearls were woven through short, dark curls, which had been teased into an upward style to suit Martha's sweetheart face. In small heels, she barely reached Skye's shoulder.

'You look stunning.' This time Skye's smile was genuine, even though she couldn't shake the uneasiness from earlier.

Martha smiled back and did a coy mock curtsy.

Rather than a traditional wedding dress, Martha had chosen pure elegance in a silver slip dress with a long-line jacket and kitten-heel pumps.

She reached into the car and took two small posies of pale pink roses from a box on the back seat.

Handing them to each of her bridesmaids, she placed a gentle kiss on their cheeks. 'Thank you for letting me into your family.'

As she stepped back, Skye thought she detected a hint of tears before Martha turned to slide her own bouquet of cascading pink roses and gypsophila from the car.

With the bouquet in one hand, she straightened her shoulders and held the other hand out to take her son's arm. The smile as she stepped forward was confident, yet serene.

Skye and Jade fell in behind as they walked along the pathway to the church.

Control slipped back into place as Skye deliberately pushed aside all thought of anything but the wedding.

For now.

12

SATURDAY, 20 MAY 2023, 9.45 P.M.

Eight and a quarter hours after the wedding

The pounding in Skye's head was nothing to do with the loud music, or the constant flow of Prosecco she'd consumed as she sat alone at the bridal table while everyone else cavorted on the dance floor.

Martha threw back her head and laughed at something Skye's dad said to her before he twirled her around the dance floor like a twenty-something. While Skye herself felt like an old hag. Her body throbbed, a deep bone-weary ache she wasn't sure she could stave off for much longer.

Was she coming down with something? A cold? The flu? Or was it the result of the earlier phone call she turned over and over in her mind? Never quite settling and robbing her of the ability to truly join in and enjoy herself. Stealing her energy.

She picked up her phone and stared at the time. Only 9.45 p.m. She rubbed her temple, closing her eyes against the bright flashing lights.

The loud music deprived her of the ability to think.

How much longer did she have to stay? Would anyone notice if she snuck out and took off back home? She needed space. Time to sit and think.

She glanced at the messages on her phone. Messages that had started up again about two hours earlier. Obviously once Jordon had got a skinful and decided to run a pity party all of his own. Well, she had no pity for him.

Can I come over tonight?

No!

That was the mistake she'd made. She's answered him and now he knew she had, he was bombarding her with messages.

Let me come to the reception. We can talk it out.

No!

Come on, Skye. Let me see you. I miss you. I miss Cleo.

She knew he didn't. Cleo wasn't fussed about him in the least.

Fuck off!

Give me a chance.

How the hell did she get rid of him? She touched her fingers to the screen and tapped out a message.

Maybe tomorrow.

Is that because you've hooked up with one of the groomsmen?
That's what bridesmaids like you do isn't it? Sleep with the best
man. You don't want me there tonight because you've managed
to snag some poor bastard.

Jeez, that turned on a coin. He was obviously pissed.

Don't bother coming tomorrow, Jordon. Just fuck off right now. I
never want to see you again, you stupid bastard.

She hit the close button on her phone and smacked it face
down on the white damask tablecloth and then scoured the room,
realising her grandparents had slipped away from the party.

Skye regretted not booking a room for the night in the hotel.
Martha and her dad had offered to pay, but she'd rather get home.
She was leaving Cleo, her lovely black and tan rescue dog, long
enough. She'd arranged for a neighbour to slip in and sit with her a
while, open the back door for her to go into the garden to do the
things a dog needs to do. And then again later, to feed her and let
her out again.

Her neighbour had been happy enough to do it, but it wasn't the
same. Cleo didn't really know the elderly woman that well. Skye
hadn't really had a choice. She wouldn't put Cleo in kennels. That
would be all too much for her. Cleo had been through enough in
her short lifetime and suffered from separation anxiety amongst
other things.

Skye glanced at the time again and then back up to the dance
floor, where a moment ago Jade had been dancing with a group of
older ladies. Astonished to see her younger sister now in the hold of
Martha's son, Luke, as they circled the dance floor, Skye watched
with narrowed eyes.

What the hell had happened there? One moment they'd been

about to scratch each other's eyes out, now they were all smoochy, smoochy. Funny what weddings, alcohol and whole load of dancing could do. Not to mention that the three of them were the youngest ones there by a generation.

She huffed out a laugh as she watched.

How odd. They were a surprisingly good match. Who'd have thought?

Neither one of them was in a relationship, not far off the same age, so why not?

Skye sat upright in her chair, unable to slump because of the tight bodice of her dress. She focused on the good-looking pair on the dance floor, fluid, their bodies moving in perfect synchronicity.

Funny how nobody had ever thought to pair them up before now. Possibly because Luke had been in a relationship and Jade had been at university for the past eighteen months. When she was home, she was a royal pain in the arse. Her objection to her dad's choice of wife had been vocal and rude.

And Luke, unsurprisingly, had virtually ignored her. Because he was a prick. He'd ignored them both.

Now, suddenly, they'd relaxed. A sudden release of every pent-up emotion. An easing of self-restraint.

And boy, had her sister let go.

Skye's lips twitched up. She'd love to be happy, to be carefree. The drink had been free-flowing but she'd not had that much. She'd topped up her water glass more than her wine glass. Not enough to forget.

Forget that voice on the end of the phone that chilled the blood in her veins.

She gave a delicate shudder and raised her glass to her lips once more to take a sip of Prosecco that had warmed, going slightly flat because she'd barely touched it in the last hour and a half while she watched the dance floor. Not even tempted to get up and join in. She felt as flat as the Prosecco.

'Are you all right?'

Skye jumped so hard, her drink spilt down the front of her gown to trickle down her bosom and send a shiver over her hot skin.

'Sorry, Skye. I didn't mean to scare you. You just looked so forlorn.' Jacob settled a warm hand on her bare shoulder and gave a concerned rub before withdrawing.

'I'm fine. I was in a world of my own, that's all.' She leaned into him and rested her head on his shoulder as he took a sip of what looked like whisky in his tumbler. His gaze on the newlywed couple on the dance floor.

'They make a lovely couple.'

'They do.' Her hushed voice came out wistful.

'You've not danced all evening.' He jiggled his shoulder, so her head gave a lazy bump against it. 'You should be up there with the rest of the youngsters.' He indicated Jade and Luke.

Skye snorted and grinned up at him. A nice man, she was always comfortable in his presence. The loss of his wife a few years earlier had brought him into her dad's life, just at a time when her dad needed his help too. His business partner of the past almost seven years, the pair had built the company into a well-respected, successful organisation.

After her mum had died so suddenly of a brain haemorrhage, her dad's bespoke plastic extrusion company had gone into a spiralling decline, and if it hadn't been for Jacob, he possibly could have lost it all.

Not only had her mum and dad been married, but they'd been business partners too. More savvy than him, her mum had carried out the administration, accounts and development side of things. Her dad's skillset lay in the engineering, the manufacturing, the employing of a skilled and unique workforce who remained dedicated to the company.

A company that had almost gone to the wall after fifteen years of trading profitably. They'd had to 'let go' some of its loyal staff in order to keep its head above water.

Until Jacob came along.

By then, it was about to be declared bankrupt with too many debts to pay and too little income coming in.

Jacob had bought into it, turned the business around and while he could have bought it outright, he'd recognised her dad's magic and instead had offered an equal partnership.

When Summer had taken off, leaving the family ripped apart once more, Jacob had been there to shoulder the weight of the company. Skye hadn't known him back then. He'd not been a friend of the family. He'd been a vague business partner none of the girls had known.

Over time, he'd become important in their lives.

Her dad was eternally grateful.

With no children of his own, once Jacob was introduced to them, he treated both Skye and Jade like they were his own family.

Once his wife had died of anorexia and it had come to light what a struggle she'd had and how private Jacob had kept it, they'd united. Pulled together.

It was almost like having two fathers. Not quite. A father and a very special uncle. His reserved presence always kept a lid on Jade's explosive nature.

Skye straightened and turned to look at him. 'Do you think it's too early for me to sneak off?'

Jacob leaned back and hitched up his shirt sleeve to have a look at his watch.

The twist of his lips said it all. 'Perhaps a little.' He shrugged. 'Up to you, though.'

She couldn't help the slouch of her shoulders as the prospect of staying for another couple of hours seemed to rip away all faith.

Skye reached for the bottle of Prosecco in the middle of the table and barely squeezed a drop out into her empty glass. She sank back on her chair and then eyed her sister's almost full flute. Sod it, her sister didn't need any more to drink and if she did, she'd have no idea Skye had swiped hers. Skye wouldn't normally drink out of someone else's glass, but this was her sister. What harm could it do?

'Aren't you enjoying yourself?'

She shook her head. 'It's not that. I...'

Blank confusion wrinkled his features. 'What is it? What's wrong?'

She shook her head as she stared out over the dance floor.

He wouldn't understand. Couldn't. He'd not been around when her mum died. He'd not known them when Summer disappeared. He'd barely known them as a family back then. How could he possibly know what they went through? The torture of being told to stay in university, because despite everything, she needed to think of her future. Her dad needed to keep everything together and the only way he could do that was believe he was doing the best for at least one of his children.

Jade had been only twelve.

Her dad had managed to get Jade counselling but all that appeared to do was bring out rot that lay deep inside, dragging it to the surface so it bubbled and festered on display, rather than tortured her in private. She'd been expelled from two schools before she reached the age of fourteen.

In desperation, her dad had put her in a private girls' school.

Skye never could figure out whether it was to save his little girl, or to save his own sanity.

Jade's behaviour didn't improve, she simply had access to

wealthier boyfriends from the boys' school and more expensive drugs.

Drugs, from her behaviour, she appeared to have taken tonight. Skye couldn't be certain that her younger sister's relaxed demeanour came from more than the consumption of alcohol and very little food. Nobody ever eats very much at a wedding. They're all too busy chatting and drinking. A hundred and fifty quid a head and most of it went unappreciated.

She twirled the stem of her glass in her fingers until Jacob placed his hand on hers to stop her. 'Is it the phone call?'

She nodded as her throat tightened. She'd barely been given a chance to acknowledge what had happened earlier, but it lurked like a spectre in the doorway to her mind.

'It really shook me up.' Her fingers trembled as a physical response to her thoughts.

Jacob leaned his head in to hear her above the pounding music. 'Do you want to talk about it?'

Skye nodded and glanced around the room. 'Maybe somewhere quieter. Do you mind? I don't want to drag you away.'

Jacob smiled, came to his feet and put a hand out to steady her as she slipped from her own chair, Jade's glass still in hand. 'I don't think you're depriving me of anything. My duties here are done. Martha and your dad are hardly going to notice if we slip away for a short time.' He nodded at the pair in each other's arms. 'I think they'll be occupied for a while.'

Skye followed him from the noisy dance floor through a wide, corporate corridor into the small bar. The music still played but was considerably quieter. More like a thrum that vibrated through her feet, keeping her heartbeat fast.

Skye hitched herself up onto a stool Jacob offered, taking care with her dress as he took her drink from her and placed it on the bar before he helped her up, a hand under one elbow. With a soft grunt, he perched on the stool next to her, his broad frame looking a little top heavy as though it might tip over.

Jacob inclined his head at her half-filled glass. 'Would you like a fresh one?' He lifted one finger to the young barman.

Quick to shake her head, Skye smiled at the barman. 'No, thank you.'

'You want something different?'

Skye shook her head again. 'I don't mix my drinks and I think I've had enough anyway.' She smiled at the man on the other side of the bar. 'Perhaps just a glass of water, please.'

'Ice and lemon?'

'Just ice.' Lemon for some reason always had the taint of onions whenever she had a slice from a bar. Maybe the chef sliced them alongside the dish of the day, first thing in the morning.

He slid the glass over to her and raised his eyebrows at Jacob.

Jacob leaned on the bar. 'Bushmills for me, please.'

He gave the young man a nod of acknowledgement as he took the whisky he'd poured and cradled it in his hand with an ease that spoke of how comfortable he was.

The barman wiped the counter down with a cloth and moved further down the bar to serve someone else.

Skye turned to Jacob, who patiently waited for her to pick up where she wanted to without questioning her.

'Over the years, we've had to deal with such crap. So many people have contacted us to tell us they've spotted Summer, that she's been seen walking down a street, in a restaurant, in Portugal, Spain, bloody Bahamas.' Skye shook her head. 'But it's not her. It's never her. It's probably bloody me, only I've never had the luxury of going to the Bahamas.'

He chuckled, not unkindly but in appreciation of her self-deprecating tone. He dipped his head to take a sip of whisky. 'Your dad never speaks about it. Not any more.'

'Why would he? Why would any of us? Summer took off seven years ago now. As if we weren't already fucked up with Mum dying, she decided to make her own demonstration of how much more devastated she was than us.'

Skye drank the rest of her Prosecco and put the glass down on the bar with a definitive click. She wasn't sure she believed what she was saying, but airing her thoughts in front of her own family was too hard these days.

The barman strolled back and lifted an unopened bottle of chilled Prosecco from the ice-bucket, raising his eyebrows at Skye rather than interrupt their conversation.

She changed her mind from a moment before and gave him a nod, pushing her glass towards him.

Discreetly, he swiped it from the bar and replaced it with a fresh one.

There was a subtle popping noise as he expertly uncorked the bottle, then filled it with sparkling wine. He placed it in front of her before melting once again into the background.

Lively bubbles bounced in the glass as Skye raised it to her mouth. She took a sip, her eyes narrowing with appreciation. This wasn't the same as the one supplied for the wedding. It was crisper. Drier.

'Mmm.' She took another, deeper drink and then placed it back on the bar, watching as condensation dripped down the outside of the glass to dribble onto the paper coaster.

Without words, Jacob waited for her to talk it through.

'You know, when she first disappeared, I was convinced someone had taken her. Absolutely convinced.'

Jacob's brow wrinkled. 'Why? What would make you think that?'

'Because there were certain things.' She shrugged, her inner guilt crying to be set free. 'She was ragingly angry about me going to university. She was the good twin. The one who stayed at home.' The sheer sorrow of it could drown her if she let it.

Skye leaned her elbow on the bar and cupped her chin in her hand. 'Every time we spoke after I left for uni, we fell out.'

She met Jacob's sympathetic gaze and realised she'd never really spoken with him like this. Without her dad, where she tempered her words and kept her feelings tightly strapped down so she didn't cause upset. 'It wasn't fair to leave Dad and Jade, Summer said. I was the precocious one, the self-centred, thoughtless, smug bitch who got to go away while she opted to stay at home and sulk, pretending like she was the martyr. She was a martyr. She enjoyed playing that role. Believe me. She made the most of it.'

A feeling of disloyalty rolled around and anger filled her stomach in an unexpected rush as the memories flooded back and tears pricked at her eyes. God, she wasn't going to cry. Surely. Crying jags were no longer a thing with her. She was all cried out. Or at least she thought she was.

'We fell out every time we spoke from the moment I accepted my place at university, and she declined hers. We'd both got a place at the same university, different courses.'

Her voice thickened with emotion, and she took another sip of her drink, and then placed it back down. 'She thought I should stay at home, and I thought she was missing her opportunity. We were like a pushmi-pullyu. Both of us convinced we were right.'

She cast Jacob a look from under her brows. 'We were both so young and idealistic, and raging against the unfairness of the world. The unfairness of losing Mum too soon.' She huffed and circled one hand around in the air. 'That was before I realised *nothing* in this world is fair. Not just for us, but for everyone.'

Skye trailed her fingernail across the dripping condensation before picking up her glass to take another mouthful. She'd not even bothered to drink her water.

'What happened?'

'I went away. She stayed at home.' She shrugged, touching her fingers to lips that tingled. 'Dad said it was fine. That I should go. We both should go.' The defensiveness she felt back then rose in her again.

'Then what made her take off, if that's what she'd chosen?'

The confusion on Jacob's face made her reach out and touch him on the shoulder. A quick smoothing of her fingers across his shirt sleeve as though to comfort him. Jacob, who never even knew her sister, looked as confused as she felt.

'That's just it. We have no idea. I really don't believe she just walked out one day and never came back.' She groaned. 'The police checked everything out. They came to our home to search, to check. I came back for a week, but Dad insisted I carry on. I think he believed at least one of us should have a normal life. But nothing is normal once your twin disappears. *Nothing*.'

She leaned in to stress the word before she took a long, deep breath. 'I came back every weekend after that. Jumped on the train on a Friday afternoon and returned on Monday morning. Week after week we searched. We sent out appeals. Contacted her friends.'

'What did the police say?'

'What could they say? They'd covered all bases as far as they were concerned.' Skye leaned her elbow on the bar and cupped her chin in her hand, her eyes feeling heavy. 'Did you know roughly 2.8 million children run away from home each year? Most of them just... puff...' She flared her fingers out as though letting a wild bird fly free. '...disappear.'

His eyes widened and she leaned forward in a conspiratorial manner and pointed her finger at him. 'Yeah. I did my own home-work on the subject. Most of those are between the ages of ten and eighteen.' She nodded. 'You can just imagine when the police hear

of an eighteen-year-old buggering off with a boyfriend because
she's been arguing with every member of her family, they're no
going to take it as seriously as an underage child, unless there'
evidence of foul play.'

'And was there? Evidence?'

She flopped back against the seat, instantly regretting it as her
bodice dug into her ribs. She hitched it up to try to make it more
comfortable.

'No. Nothing.' She sighed. 'For a time, they even questioned my
dad really closely, as if they suspected him of some heinous crime.
Then they concluded she'd taken off. Disappeared. Personally, I
never believed it.'

'Why not?'

Could she tell him about that special connection? A connection
only twins have, more precisely identical twins. If she said she was
psychic, he'd look at her as though she was psychotic. She'd had
that over the years from people who had no idea what it was to be
so close, to share a womb. To share the same egg. Skye and Summer
were monozygotic, which translates into one egg. Split in two.
Which was precisely how she felt from the moment Summer had
gone. That she'd been torn from her other half.

Skye had been transported to a dark place where fear grabbed a
hold of her, turning dreams into nightmares. Nightmares that had
besieged her in the beginning, but of late they had become more an
aura of floating listlessness. As though the other half of her hovered
in that space between life and death. In a liminal state.

Skye eyed Jacob before she decided to keep that information to
herself. There was other stuff she could tell him.

'She withdrew a wad of cash – something in the region of £250,
which was all she had in her current account, and disappeared.'

'So why do you think there *was* foul play?'

Skye blew out a breath. 'If you're going to make a dash for the hills, why only take £250 when you have almost twelve grand in your savings account?'

Jacob's mouth dropped open. 'Twelve grand? An eighteen-year-old? Where the hell did she get that kind of money?'

Skye shook her head. 'It was part of the life assurance paid out when Mum died. Dad wanted to make sure we were all cared for equally, so he deposited the same amount in each of our bank accounts. It was supposed to be our university fund. Only Summer never got to spend hers.'

Skye realised that she might have said something out of place when Jacob blinked at her, his eyes slightly glazed.

Maybe he thought her dad should have invested that money into the company to save it. It hadn't been his money to invest. It had been in their mum's will. Not exact amounts, but a percentage that she'd wanted them to have.

It was irrelevant now.

She covered her mouth with her hand and let out a yawn, blinking her eyes at the same time. This time when she pointed, her finger gave a floppy waggle.

'You know, the irony of it was that for the first time in ages, I could stop thinking about my mum when I went away. I put aside the guilt.'

'Guilt? You shouldn't feel any guilt. Your mum's death wasn't your fault.'

Guilt seemed to accompany her every day.

'No.' She shook her head. 'But I live with the thought that if I'd just listened when she said her head hurt so badly that morning, or come home from college earlier that day instead of going off with my friends, I would have been with her. I would have called 999 for an ambulance. I could have saved her.' And in saving her, she would still have her twin by her side.

Jacob shook his head. 'No, Skye. You have to let that guilt slide now. It wasn't your fault, or your responsibility. From what your dad told me—' he gave a small nod '—and yes, we discussed it, long ago, when we first met, he said there was absolutely nothing that could have been done. In the days leading up to Christine's death she'd appeared stressed.'

Skye blinked at the sound of her mum's full name. Her dad always called her Chrissy.

Her lids became heavy and she let it pass.

'She had a massive brain haemorrhage caused by high blood pressure. The finding was, she probably died before she hit the floor.'

He swallowed some of his whisky, his lips momentarily pressing together, she suspected from the fire in his mouth. His eyes turned sorrowful. 'There was no possible way you could have helped her. It was her time to die. At least be appeased she knew nothing about it. Literally. Nothing.'

She disagreed with him. 'She would have been in agony.'

Jacob shook his head. 'A flash of pain. An instant. Nothing more.'

Alcohol swirled in her mind and Skye relaxed as much as she could in that dress against the high-backed stool. 'I guess.' She shrugged and swallowed, finding it difficult with a tongue that had started to thicken. 'No matter how time passes, and how many people tell me, I will always live with that guilt.' She gave him a weak smile. 'And here I am being maudlin at what should be such a happy day.'

'It's bound to trigger memories.'

'No, that bloody phone called triggered everything.'

'What exactly did the caller say? It was all a bit mixed up and rushed as we tried to get out for the wedding.' Jacob leaned forward and placed a comforting hand on hers to stop nails she hadn't realised she was tapping against the bar. He gave them a light squeeze and let go.

She picked up her glass and against her better judgement she took a last swallow, sending her head swirling even more. 'It wasn't like the other messages. For a start, she knew our home telephone number. We barely ever use it, Dad just likes to keep it because of my grandparents.'

She let her mind drift to her grandparents, who had already retired for the evening to one of the hotel bedrooms, making her wish she had taken that decision to stay. 'And because he's sentimental. Just in case Summer ever changes her mind and tries to contact him. Other than that, we all use our mobile phones these days. But that woman knew it.'

'Who was she? Did she give a name?'

'She didn't say. There was an accent, but her English was impeccable.'

'What exactly did she tell you?'

'That's just it, she wasn't trying to convince me that she'd seen Summer out and about...'

'So, what did she want?'

'She said to tell me...' Skye breathed in, trying to think of the exact words the girl had used. 'She said Summer wanted us to know she never ran away.'

His eyes widened with surprise. 'If she didn't run away, then what happened to her?'

Skye met Jacob's gaze as the trickle of horror that had always lived in her mind gushed forward. A knowledge. A deep belief. A certainty that what she'd always believed was true.

'I think... I've always thought... someone took her.'

13

It wasn't as difficult as the first time. LJ had learnt plenty since then. Since Summer. She'd taught him so much. Little did she know how much she'd helped him.

He'd used the same technique to meet the next girl online. No one had called him out on the profile he'd continued to use, although he'd been relatively quiet. He was surprised how cynical people had become within a short couple of years about the idea of online stalking. Education about the internet had spread quickly.

In fact, he'd noticed a couple of catfishing attempts from enthusiastic suitors himself. He'd dropped them. Pretty quick.

Not because they were the bright ones, but because they were the ones with connections, with happy lives, with reasons to live.

He wanted the sad, the lonely, the bitching-about-their-world girls. The ones who were needy, greedy, who loved a shoulder to cry on, figuratively speaking. The takers, the ones who sucked the joy from the world with their pitiful neediness.

They were the easy ones. He could reel them in like a landed fish. A catfish.

He'd done it a few times now. Dipped his fishing line into the water to see who would bite. Just at the critical stage, he'd backed off. Left them flailing in their tears and dramas and simply walked away. Ghosted them.

Maybe they were the lucky ones. He was only practising on them.

Practice makes perfect and he was ready to try again.

Ready because Summer sickened him. Her body was still poison to him. Why could the little bitch not have died? Why had she been granted the gift of life?

He wasn't about to murder her. That would make him bad, evil. He wasn't a murderer. But if fate had just tossed in that little helpful hand, bringing with it a swift death, it would have been useful.

She'd lost her appeal. Something died inside her along with that foetus. He couldn't class it as a baby. Although it had been formed more than he'd anticipated for his estimation of how far along she'd been. He thought he could have just flushed it down the toilet, but having given it some thought, he wrapped it in the bloodied knickers she'd kicked off and buried it at the back of the courtyard, where there was a wide gap between the stone slabs and the wall. He'd dug it in pretty deep. After all, he didn't need her to know it was there.

He wrinkled his nose. It was all very distasteful.

He wouldn't make that mistake again.

What surprised him was that she'd not become pregnant earlier. He'd been watching out for it at the beginning, but after some time, he'd relaxed, putting it down to the fact that she wasn't fertile. It couldn't be him.

He'd thought it a blessing she wasn't. Evidently, she was. Perhaps it had more to do with her being so unsettled at first. She'd lost weight, fought him continually and then she'd settled.

Maybe that was it. Because she'd accepted her place.

Because of that, everything had changed.

Right now, he didn't feel like touching her. She repulsed him. But what was he supposed to do with her? She might have outgrown her usefulness in one way, but that wasn't the sole reason she was there. Indeed, it was only one small part of the reason he kept her.

Still, she had other uses. It turned out she made a pretty good cleaner.

More so now that she'd come to heel and he knew her terror of him kept her bound to the house. Who would have known she could be trained like a dog?

He tapped his fingers on the steering wheel as he squinted through the windscreen. He'd hoped it was going to rain. That reduced visibility. He was happy with that. He expected it.

The girls didn't. They seemed to think they were safe, even if they couldn't see far through the dashing rain. He thrived on living in the mist.

It wasn't so easy to find places any more that were remote enough not to have cameras poking into everyone's business.

He stilled as the young woman materialised from a narrow passageway in between a row of old houses that were in such poor condition he didn't seriously believe any of them would have such a thing as a security camera or a Ring doorbell.

He'd cruised the street several times before picking it. Only once every few days he'd driven along there. He'd had time. It wasn't far from where he'd originally picked up Summer. Down the back streets which sprawled out from the centre of Wellington. A ten-to-fifteen-minute walk to Morrisons. Not far. Close enough that they felt safe. Far enough so he did.

He smiled as she glanced both ways. Hesitated as though she was sniffing the air. A little flighty this one, more cautious. Unlike Summer, who'd radiated anger. Anger at her family. Anger at being stood up. So much fury it had blinded her to her own safety.

Almost. Then he'd left her just too long. Long enough for her to become aware.

He wouldn't make that mistake again. He'd almost lost Summer because he thought it amusing to watch and wait. No waiting this time. Not much in any case, just long enough for everything to slide into place.

The deserted bus stop on the opposite side of the road seemed to loiter in the shadows.

He'd researched it. Checked out the timetable of a bus that no longer travelled that route. It had been diverted since the council had proved nobody had used it for almost three years. Not one single person, according to the survey they'd apparently carried out in order to prove no one used it. Funny how figures could lie.

Only the dim young woman who was just about to cross over to it had no idea. Wellington wasn't quite her territory. It was his, though. This was where he originated, in the end house, two rows away. If he was seen, no one took any notice. He was just one of the many locals. Only he no longer lived there, but in a flat closer to the Telford Town Centre. When he wasn't at the other place in the hills.

She crossed the road, glanced around at the broken bus shelter with graffiti splashed all over it.

He'd told her he'd be on the 18.48 from Telford Town Centre. It should get there around 19.22.

He glanced at the time. 19.15.

She was keen.

He'd leave it. Let her hang for a while. Not long enough for her to start tapping on her phone, looking for a timetable. That wouldn't do. He relied on the fact that she trusted him to tell her the correct arrival time. Because they'd developed a trusting relationship.

He snorted out a laugh. One-way trust, in any case.

He leaned back in the comfortable leather seat and smiled. He didn't have to do this. That was what gave him the upper hand. At any time, he could change his mind, fire the car engine and drive away, leaving another broken heart in his wake.

He'd broken a few. It had given him a kick.

Did he want to break this one's heart? Or her spirit?

He chewed his lip while he contemplated.

He'd not taken anyone since Summer. She'd been his first and he'd intended her to be his only one. After all, he'd had good reason. Then.

Circumstances changed.

This time, he wanted her. Sweet, sad little girl. No one to love her. No one to care. Living alone with a mummy who was too strong, too possessive, too overwhelmingly demanding.

OCD.

She demanded her daughter make her bed, tidy her bedroom, fold her clothes, wipe the water drips off the inside of the shower cubicle. She had to wash, dry and put away the dishes because Mummy dear worked so hard all day long and just wanted to kick back with a glass or two of gin and tonic when she came home.

Oh, boo hoo!

Mummy brought dinner home for her, didn't she? A ready-cooked chicken and a pack of salad. A Chinese takeaway. A microwave chicken tikka masala, or ready-cooked baked potatoes with a tin of baked beans thrown over the top. A sprinkle of cheese on that.

LJ couldn't understand the ungratefulness.

How pitiful. Selfish little bitch. She was fed, wasn't she? At the age of eighteen, she was damned lucky to have a roof over her head, her own bedroom, the latest damned Samsung phone. Spoilt beyond belief.

Most kids her age would have had to get a job, earn their own keep, find their own damned lodgings. Instead she got to float around, waiting for Mummy to give her handouts before she went swanning around the continent until she started at Durham University in September. A course Mummy was paying for in full. No student debt. Private accommodation.

Money wasn't everything, she would whine, as she craved the company and attention of someone. Anyone. Because Mummy dear wasn't available.

All these mind-numbing details had been shared with him over the past few weeks. Months. It felt like years. She was so boring.

Mummy wasn't short of money. Mummy was short on time for her daughter.

A man-hater. That's what Mummy was.

A terrible experience with a horrible man and it had turned her off all men forevermore. Which also included anyone her daughter might have her eye on. He had no idea what her mum intended once she left for uni. Maybe she should be allowed to fly. Currently, she wasn't allowed to date. She wasn't allowed to bring a boy home. She wasn't supposed to chat on social media to boys. Boys were evil. They were scum. They would take your heart and break it in two. Or they would rape you and leave you for dead.

How right Mummy was.

LJ opened the car door and climbed out, pulling the hood of his fleece out from under the waterproof he'd layered on and tugged it over his head. He slouched. A teenage slouch which he'd managed to perfect, although his man's body cried out to stand upright.

He kept his head lowered and scuffed his way along to the bus stop, knowing she'd not even noticed him get out of the vehicle, let alone approach, so engrossed was she with her phone.

She was messaging him. His phone was on silent, but he felt the gentle buzz from the pocket in his tracksuit bottoms every time she sent a message. He smiled. The bus wasn't just going to be late like he'd messaged her. Stupid girl. It was never going to come.

'Hey.'

She looked up, startled by his voice. She really had no street smarts, did she?

Little innocent.

Instead of replying, she just lifted her chin in acknowledgement and stepped away into the covered bus shelter and hunched her shoulders, turning her back on him.

Bad move, baby.

LJ took the prepared cloth from his waterproof jacket pocket. The phone buzzed again. He smiled. A slow, calculating smile.

'Excuse me.'

She lifted her head but didn't turn.

'Are you waiting for LJ?'

At that, she spun around, surprise widening her eyes.

He stepped forward and as she opened her mouth, drawing in breath to scream, he slapped the cloth over her face and held on tight.

Her phone clattered to the floor, the screen smashing into tiny shards.

He could do nothing about that as she slumped over his arm, her body going to liquid.

Christ! She'd lied about her weight. She was no size eight. Twelve, fourteen, possibly. At the very least. He grunted as she fell against him. She must have tampered with the photographs on her Facebook page.

Did no one have morals these days?

He would have grinned at the irony, but he was too busy struggling to get a hold of her fleshed-out body.

He hefted her over his shoulder, his knees almost buckling beneath him as he made for his car. He dipped one hand into his pocket, almost dropping her as he staggered and then slammed into he side of his car. He touched his finger to the remote and the boot slowly rose.

Summer had taught him that lesson too. He'd not drugged her out relied on her being knocked out by a fist or two for the journey. She'd woken, dazed and confused, just as he'd pulled over at a twenty-four-hour petrol station, luckily for him. He'd leaned into the back seat, punched her lights out again, closed the door without the sleepy attendant even noticing. The camera had been trained on the number plate of the car, not the back door. Nobody had spotted a thing.

This time, he put his precious cargo in the boot. Not so precious. He dumped her heavy weight, which thumped against the boot floor, making the car rock. If she woke, which was unlikely considering the amount of chloroform he'd soaked into that piece of gauze, before he locked her in the boot, she couldn't cause him any trouble.

He clunked the boot lid down and moved away towards the bus shelter.

A smattering of glass circled the broken phone.

As he bent to pick it up, a deep voice came from the other side of the road, through the alley where not long ago she had exited before crossing over.

'You all right there, mate?'

LJ hesitated, head lowered as he scooped the phone up into one hand. His heart raced so when he straightened, blood rushed from his brain to his feet and he swayed, putting out a hand to steady himself. There was another lesson he'd learnt. He'd worn leather gloves this time so when he gripped the upright pole on the bus shelter there was no way he would leave fingerprints.

'Just dropped my phone, mate.' He used the same tone, the same diction as the other man.

'Nasty.'

The guy dipped his hands into his bomber jacket and sauntered across the road towards him.

LJ's breath shortened.

'Retrievable?'

LJ shook his head and instead of showing the other guy the phone with its pink floral case, he pointed at the shattered glass on the ground while he dropped the phone into his pocket. 'Nah, mate. I was due a new one anyway. It's a work phone. One of the old ones.'

The other guy rounded his shoulders against the unseasonable cutting gust of icy wind. 'You do know this bus stop is no longer in use, yeah? If you're waiting for a bus, you're shit out of luck.'

LJ forced his face into a mask of surprise. 'No! My mum told me to pick her up from here. I was just trying to check the timetable.' He pointed to the ragged piece of plastic hanging from the bus stop window and then at his pocket with the broken phone. 'I can't even contact her.'

'You want to use my phone, mate?' The guy held his phone out.

LJ hesitated. 'Nah, mate. She had a new phone, I don't know the number off the top of my head.' He flicked his thumb as though tapping a screen. 'Speed dial, mate. I can't remember the last time I dialled anything.'

The guy nodded his understanding. 'Who does these days? Where's she coming from?'

LJ glanced down the street at his car and gritted his teeth. Couldn't the guy just fuck off and mind his own business?

'Telford Town Centre.'

'Ah, no. That bus has been diverted to the main terminal. You know where that is?'

'Yeah.' No. And he didn't fucking care either. He'd never actually caught a bus for years, except maybe when he was a school kid. 'Thanks for your help. I better get going.'

'No need to rush. It probably won't be there for another twenty minutes.'

Silent, LJ stared at the guy.

The guy's face split into a grin. 'You must think I'm some kind of freak.'

It had occurred to him.

'I've just retired. I was a bus driver.'

As it fell into place, LJ found himself smiling back at the older man, relief kicking in. 'I was beginning to have my doubts.'

The man chuckled. 'Nice to meet you, son. Go pick your mum up. You must be a good man.'

LJ found himself barely able to formulate a reply. 'Thank you. She thinks so.'

The guy turned his back and started to walk away down the road. 'Good luck getting a new phone. Take care.'

'You too, mate.' LJ watched the man fade into the distance.

Stupid fucker.

He turned and made his way back to his car, fired the engine and drove away with a body in the boot.

Rattled by the man, LJ drove in the opposite direction to which he intended for a couple of miles along roads leading through the old part of town and then out to the winding rabbit warren of new builds, and beyond where it opened up to rolling fields and views of The Wrekin before he stopped.

He slipped the broken phone over a hedgerow into a field, just in case Mummy had a 'find a friend' app.

No matter how quick thinking he was, he'd made the mistake of letting someone see him at the bus shelter. He'd not make that mistake again. So, he needed to make sure that if the phone was tracked, it led somewhere far away from where suspicion could arise and start pointing fingers.

He wiped the thin coating of sweat from his brow and hoped

he'd covered his tracks sufficiently. The change of his modus operandi was good. There had never been any true belief that Summer had done anything but take off on her own. No one had ever reported seeing her near Morrisons. This time, they might look for an abductor, but in a totally different place. At the base of The Wrekin where there were no cameras, nothing to flag his car passing through.

14

SUNDAY, 16 JUNE 2019

I try desperately not to squeeze my eyes shut too tight, or he will know. Know that I'm awake. Not that it makes any difference. He'd slap me awake if he was in the mood to beat me, slap me, rape me.

He's not been in the mood since I lost the baby. Seventeen weeks has passed. I count them off as I scrape another notch on the wall.

I relax and drift off again.

My body may have healed, but my mind will always cling on to the memory of that tiny life form I'd held in my hand. I'd rocked back and forth as tears tracked down my cheeks. Until he'd come and taken my baby away. Disposed of it.

I've not had a period since, which is a blessing too.

The scrape of a tray across the concrete floor jerks me awake.

Normally, I'm aware when he's in the building. When he isn't. There was a strange emptiness when he left. Even if he only pushed my food through the door and went back upstairs, I sensed his presence. At least I knew I wasn't completely alone, even if it was LJ.

I barely hear a sound, but the occasional faint cough, or a radio playing, muted and distant. I figured out that he doesn't live here. Not permanently. There must be somewhere else he goes.

When I first arrived, I'd called out. Cried, screamed. For help. For salvation.

No one came.

I'd not understood the varying degrees of silence until now. Now I know.

I realise subconsciously I could always tell if he was there, even if I never saw him. A slight shift in air, a muffled cough, the soft scrape of a chair.

Otherwise, there was silence.

The building is no longer silent. I'm no longer alone.

Someone else is here with me. Other than LJ. It's not him. The sound does not come from above.

Instinct tells me he's brought someone else here. Into this place. He has another captive.

* * *

I sit up and wait for a long moment before I slither off the bed, heading towards the tray on the floor, my movements fluid and silent as I pace on naked feet.

I crouch, lifting the plate to just under my chin. Not trusting LJ, I sniff. Not that sniffing means anything. I wouldn't have a clue if he sneaked a poison into my food. Just as I'd not had a clue he'd put something in a mere cup of tea to make me miscarry.

I pick up the spoon and scoop food up, touching the tip of my tongue against it. There's no warmth to it. Barely tepid. I'd become used to that with my one meal a day. Enough to keep me alive, but not enough to sustain me.

My stomach gives a protesting growl at the delay in eating. I scoop more up, piling the spoon high before shovelling it into my mouth. I let out a quiet groan of appreciation. It may not look good, but it has taste, flavour. He's changed the food. Which means he is eating here too. Which means he is staying.

I assume he works. He has a job. No doubt. He's not often here during the day. When he is, I figure it may be a weekend.

Sometimes he slips enough food through to last me several days. He stacks bottles of water in the corner. That's the clue.

The first time, I had believed he was being generous, giving me extra supplies. The hard lesson came when I'd consumed the lot over the course of the first two days, only to find he didn't return for another three. That was one of the times I'd almost died.

He'd called me stupid then. He often calls me stupid. Funny how that becomes easier to believe each time you hear it.

Stupid. I am stupid. He doesn't use my given name often. I've almost forgotten that. Just, 'Hey, Stupid.' Only occasionally will my name slip out. Then, it seems to surprise both of us.

I hesitate, tilting my head to one side to listen for movement. When I resume chewing, it's slower, more controlled as I stare at the door. A tremor in my hand this time as I raise the spoon to my mouth.

Is he coming for me?

Has he decided I'm well enough for him to resume what he'd been doing before?

The vague click of a door being closed. Not far from my own room. I angle my head to one side to pick up any noises.

I never realised there was another door down here.

Another room.

I thought mine was the only one. I was the only one.

He never allows me anywhere other than straight up the curving steps and into the house. I'm well enough indoctrinated to not even look past my own doorway. The caved passage beyond is always dark and uninviting. Always empty.

I lick the last remnants of my meal from my plate and lower it to the tray.

Something is different. Wrong.

I pick up the bottle of water he'd delivered and drink it down, almost all of it in one go. So thirsty all the time. Living on the edge of dehydration every day would do that. One 500 ml bottle of water a day. Not much. Unless he isn't returning for a while. Then he leaves extra. Maybe to fool me into thinking he'll be gone longer. Always keeping me on the back foot.

Once in a while he gives me tea. I never trust the tea. Not now. Not ever. I normally pour it into the bucket in the corner where I wee when I'm locked in down here. He won't notice. The smell of urine overpowers any fragrant scent of the tea. It's not as strong as the smell of my own sanitary towels when I have to wrap them tight and place them in the small bin beside the bucket. If he leaves me too long, the combined stench is overwhelming.

I reach out to pick up the small cloth that covers another item on the tray. Occasionally, as a treat, he puts an apple under there. Sometimes an orange. I used to rip the cloth off with excited antici-pation in the beginning. Until I learnt better. Until I understood. These days, I'm never interested enough to look until after my dinner. Just in case it's a tennis ball, or a cleaning sponge. He's done that several times.

Mind games. I hate his mind games.

He thinks it's funny.

I don't find anything LJ does funny.

I gasp as I stare at a large slab of cake. Enormous. Enough to last a couple of days, if I needed it to. I glance at my empty dish. Maybe he's leaving for a few days again. Perhaps I should have made my food stretch out.

The cake proves too tempting, though, to a hungry stomach.

I push my finger into it and let it sink into the fresh, soft, dark sponge. Not coffee cake. There's a thick layer of cream running through the middle and before I even think any further, my mouth starts to salivate. Carrot cake. I'm sure of it.

I pick it up and break off roughly a third. Placing it carefully on the plate, I fastidiously wrap the remaining two thirds in the cloth and slip it under my thin pillow.

I'll never make the mistake of leaving something on the tray again. The first time I did was also the last, as LJ had whipped it away. The loud grumble of how ungrateful I was, how wasteful, had rung my ears for days as the door remained closed and he almost starved me to death.

Mind games. Eat it all. Don't eat it all. I win. You lose.

Never again did I leave so much as a scrap. Even if I could barely stomach the liver and onions. My absolute pet hate. I learnt to love it.

When you have nothing, anything is good.

I sit cross-legged on the thin mattress and nibble at the moist cake, eyes closed as I absorb the sheer pleasure of a sugar fix.

Does this mean he's in a good mood?

Will I be allowed another trip upstairs? Allowed to sit in the daylight for a short time while he reads the newspaper?

I finish off the piece of cake and scramble up from the bed. I can't remember the last time I was allowed upstairs. Yes, maybe I do. It was the day I realised I was pregnant. Weeks ago.

My heart contracts and I pull my mind from that dark pathway leading to nowhere. I've been down it. There's nothing there worse than there is here.

I hesitate, listening before I slide the bed away from the wall, lifting one side of it to muffle the scraping noise.

I climb back onto the bed, kneeling so I can bow down and touch the wall where I've scratched in notches to mark the days off. Hundreds of them. Some I started to nick patterns into to define other events. When I'm allowed a shower, when I'm allowed upstairs. When I get to go outside. Once. Only once did LJ allow me outside. I've been permitted to hover on the doorstep, but the only time I was allowed into the courtyard was to hang some washing out.

Still, it gives me optimism. Faith that one day I will be allowed out into the fresh air to let the sunshine kiss my skin. Skin that is parched and thirsty for daylight. Not that I can see it. Not my face in any case. There are no mirrors.

I take the small screw from where I'd unscrewed it from the bedframe. I scrape away at the soft sandstone wall. Short fast scratches.

And then I stop.

A soft scratch comes back in reply.

I breathe in. Hold it.

I raise the screw to head height and tap it gently against the wall.

An answering tap comes back.

Something akin to excitement flutters in my chest as I rest back on my heels. I'm right. There is someone else down here with me. And it isn't LJ.

My heart contracts. Fear mingles with excitement.

I'm not alone.

15

MONDAY, 17 JUNE 2019

I wait in the silence.

Hours pass.

My only way of judging if a whole day has gone by is the arrival of the food tray. Once daily. I take the tray, eat, make a notch in the wall.

I pick a few bits from the remainder of the cake I'd carefully wrapped up the previous day and sit, my back against the chilly wall. Then I wrap it up again, my stomach churning as I wait.

Wait until the faint sounds from the room next door stop. Noises all too familiar. I made them myself in the early days. Until I realised there was no purpose. No one would ever hear my cries for help down here.

Only now there is someone. Someone else he's brought down after all this time.

I skim my fingers over the rough marks on the wall. Check three times, just to be sure. With absolute concentration, I count on my fingers, from the date I disappeared to now. Today.

After all, there is nothing else to occupy my time. What better way to keep my mind working?

Two years, eight months, ten days. Which made it Monday, 17 June 2019. I think.

Painstakingly, I focus. Count through every day, for each year. I have no idea if there was a leap year, or not. It wasn't that important. Although I struggle to remember the mnemonic they drummed into us at school. It seemed so long ago. If Skye was here, she'd know. Thirty days have September, April, lalala and lalala. Hmm. All the rest have thirty-one, except bloody February which has twenty-seven, or possibly twenty-eight. Or was it twenty-nine? How the hell was I supposed to know? I'm not the numbers twin.

My heart contracts. I try to block those thoughts but once in a while they sneak up on me unexpectedly and it's almost as though Skye is there with me.

But she's not.

There's no one to ask. If I mention it to LJ, he'll laugh in his crisp, unkind way. Then he would want to know why.

Anyway, I have to be somewhere in the right region. I figure I'm maybe two or three days out in my calculations at most. Only once had LJ left a discarded newspaper in the bin upstairs, when he first let me up there, but I figure he realised his mistake and I've not seen a newspaper since. Skye would have been proud of me when I backtracked and added an extra thirteen days to bring it in line with my incarceration dates.

That was just before I lost my baby and I know I never marked up my days then. I added a few, trying to guess how long I stayed in my fugue state. It was hard to guess.

In the silence, I unwrap the cake again and push the last piece into my mouth. Wrapping it up hasn't stopped it from going stale overnight, but it still tastes so good.

I blink as I gaze across the small cellar at the opposite wall. Monday, 17 June 2019. I'm absolutely certain of it. Not just because of my markings but because of a deep sense of awareness. I can't stop thinking about Skye. My twin.

The date slowly registers in my mind. Ironic that he'd brought me cake the day before. Today, I believe, is my twenty-first birthday. Twenty-one. Or maybe there wasn't a leap year and I'd miscounted, and he knew. Knew it was my birthday.

Tears I've not shed for a while now prick the back of my eyes. 'Happy birthday, Summer,' I whisper to myself, not really wanting to remember. 'Happy birthday, Skye.'

My chest aches at the distant echo of my mum's voice. 'Summer Skye.'

Twenty-one and I've never lived a life.

I close my eyes and lean my head back against the wall. Twenty-one.

I thought I'd had it so bad after Mum died. I'd give anything just to be back in that position. Bitching about my twin sister. Moaning because Dad was useless at cooking, so that chore had fallen on me. What I'd give to be able to cook again. To make the beds, vacuum the carpet.

What I'd give to be back in the arms of the family I hadn't realised I adored until it was too late. I'd never moan again, if only I was back home.

I press my hand against my heart and feel the slow rhythmic beat of it, knowing that it's full of regrets. I can't believe how petty and futile my arguments with Skye were. How unimportant in the scheme of things. How ungracious and ungrateful I was with my dad, who'd been hurting too. We'd all been hurting. And the hurt meant nothing. Not now. Once it was in perspective.

I circle my arms around my own body and imagine my dad giving me one of his beautiful, strong bear hugs.

The threat of tears turns to a wash that blurs my vision. It's not often I cry these days. I swipe them away with a furious hand.

Dammit, I'm allowed to cry once in a while. After all, today is my birthday. I think.

'Summer Skye.'

It's Skye's birthday too!

My twin. The other half of my soul.

I reach out my hand and cup her cheek as though she's there in the room. As though I can feel her. It's real to me, even though I know it can't be. The warmth of her soft cheek soaks through to the palm of my hand and when her image fades, I curl my hand into a fist to keep the heat from escaping.

Will she think of me today, as I think of her? Or has her life moved on?

I don't doubt they miss me, searched for me, did everything in their power to find me.

Didn't they?

Did they know I'd been taken, or as LJ likes to remind me every so often, they probably think I ran away from home. I was old enough. I'd turned eighteen. Eighteen.

Time has moved on.

Two years, eight months, ten days to be precise. By now they must have given up. Got on with their own lives. While I sit in the same room, with the same rock walls and the same bed all that time, with a trek upstairs for a shower and to clean his house.

How long does a person grieve? It couldn't be sustained for that long. Even I stopped grieving. The grief eventually had fallen away to be replaced by a dull numbness. Fear had also. I no longer care if I live or die.

What counts now are the rewards I get for good behaviour.

According to LJ, he needed to break me in order to put me back together again. A better person.

It was total bullshit. I may be broken, but I'm not done yet. I'm not beaten.

I try to convince myself.

I will never be defeated because no matter how hard he tries, there is no way he can break what's inside of me.

That part of me is encased in ice.

A soft scraping sound stops me mid-thought.

My new neighbour wants to communicate.

I cover my ears with my hands and close my eyes.

I don't think I'm ready for this yet.

* * *

'Skye.'

Skye froze, her forkful of cake halfway to her mouth.

She blinked as she looked around at the others in the room. Jade, their dad, her grandparents. All there to celebrate her twenty-first birthday in the style she wanted. Quiet, cosy, intimate.

There was nothing appealing about going out with her uni friends or throwing a big party. She couldn't face it. Not without the other half of her.

She swallowed as her gaze came full circle to fall on the carrot cake balancing on her fork. Her new favourite since her grandma had bought one from the local farmer's market a few weeks earlier.

That's what she'd requested for after her birthday dinner.

'Skye.'

No one else responded. No one else heard. They continued their quiet conversation as they ate their slices of cake without any acknowledgement that she'd frozen in time.

A numbness crawled up from her chest and flowered out across her face.

She slowly released the breath she held.

Summer.

The unspoken word formed in her head.

Her twin.

With a suddenness that took her by surprise, her mouth watered furiously, and she had no control over the hand that raised to feed her the cake.

She chewed slowly, her eyes closing at the pure indulgence of it. 'Happy birthday, Skye.'

'Happy birthday, Summer.'

She opened her eyes.

Her family's pain-filled eyes stared at her.

There were only so many times she could insist Summer was alive.

16

SATURDAY, 20 MAY 2023, 10.30 P.M.

Nine hours after the wedding

Skye raised her hand to her head.

'Are you okay?' Jacob leaned forward on his stool, his face wreathed with concern.

'I feel a little dizzy. Maybe I shouldn't have had that last glass...'

Jacob hitched himself from his stool and took her by the arm to help her down. 'I think maybe we'll get you home, now.' He turned to the barman, his voice sounding a million miles away. 'Could you call a taxi for me, mate?'

'Sure.' The barman smiled.

Skye's vision blurred and then blackened at the edges. 'Oh, God. I feel awful.'

'I'll take you back to your dad's house.'

'No, it's fine. I'm going home tonight. I left Cleo there. My neighbour was going to walk and feed her. But I need to get back to my own place.' Her body slouched into his and he wrapped an arm around her. 'I've gotta let Dad know. He'll be mad me leaving so early.' Her lips turned to rubber as words slurred out of her.

Jade was supposed to be staying with her as well, wasn't she? Or had she decided to sleep at Dad's house while the bride and groom stayed at the hotel? The memory seemed all too vague, just out of her reach. Was she supposed to do something? Get Jade?

'Is she okay?' The barman's concerned voice came from a great distance.

'Yeah. No worries, mate. She's a little worse for wear. I'll see her home safe.'

'I didn't think she'd drunk that much. She seemed sober as a judge when she first sat down,' the distant voice replied. 'It was dead quick, that. Seemed to hit her like a sledgehammer. Perhaps the fresher air in here got to her.'

The strong arm around her kept her propped up as her head slumped onto Jacob's shoulder and he talked over the top of her. 'Yeah. She must have had more than we thought at dinner.'

'No...' She wanted to protest, to say she'd matched water glass for glass with her Prosecco, but her lips had turned numb, with a dull tingle to them.

'What the fuck, Skye?'

Skye did a slow turn of her head against Jacob's shoulder, idly noticing the smudge of foundation and blusher on his dark jacket as her sister strode through the corridor into the bar towards her. Christ, he was going to be in trouble with the suit hire company. With a clumsy slap of her hand she tried to swipe the smear off but the effort was all too much.

Everything had gone into slow motion as her vision narrowed down to almost a pinprick.

'What's going on?' Jade's voice turned waspish with concern.

'She's had a little too much to drink.' Jacob's voice vibrated through the ear she had pressed against him.

'What? Skye? You're kidding.'

'I've called a taxi. I'll make sure she gets home, if you let your lad know.'

'Fucking A, I'm coming with you. I've had enough of this shit. And of Luke. I thought he was being nice. Turns out he's a fucking arsehole. Thinks he can ignore me for the past eighteen months and then expects a legover just because his mum is marrying my dad. Cheeky bastard.'

Skye felt the puff of Jacob's sigh over the top of her head. She'd normally give Jade a soft reminder to stop swearing, but she lacked the energy or interest to even vocalise. The thought circled her head, 'Potty mouth, potty mouth,' but nothing came out.

'Skye.' The whispered name had her blinking her eyes open, but the voice belonged to no one there.

She stretched out a hand to the image in front of her but it popped like a soap bubble and was gone.

The barman looked up to nod at the open doorway behind them. 'The taxi's here.'

She wanted to say that was too quick. She needed the loo. She needed to throw up. She needed to sleep.

She leaned more heavily on Jacob and was grateful for his solid body holding her up.

'You're a nice man, you know that, don't you, Jacob? Kind.' She leered up into his face and gave him a sloppy smile while she patted his chest a little harder than necessary.

'Great.' Jade rifled through her clutch bag and took out a five-pound note. Waving it at the barman, she said, 'Could you go and let the bride and groom know we've gone home?'

'I don't want to go. I want to say g'night.' The words slurred out and Skye wasn't even sure her sister understood as Jade stared at her, hands on hips.

'Skye, if I thought for a moment that you were capable of making the right decision, I would drop your arse right now. I can't believe you'd risk ruining Dad's wedding after all we've been through to get here. You're not going to say goodnight to anyone you're wrecked. You're coming home with me right now.'

'You're not the boss of me,' Skye sputtered out with a loose laugh.

'Oh, how wrong you are!'

Skye felt Jade's gaze sweep over her before she turned back to the barman. 'And do me a favour, don't mention this. We want them to enjoy the rest of their wedding evening. Even if we won't.' She handed the money over and then held onto it, so it became a tug of war as the barman gripped it. 'Just say to the groom, "Your daughters have left for the evening, they didn't want to disturb you. They send their love." Some shit like that, anyway.'

'You might just mention that the taxi turned up before we could say goodnight.' Jacob shifted Skye's weight around so he had a better hold on her as she slid further down, her cheek squishing against his chest. 'Don't mention me, I'll message them later.'

Skye wanted to protest but every ounce of energy seeped from her. She didn't want to spoil his evening. He could stay.

'Jacob, you don't need to leave. Please. Stay.' Jade's voice had turned gentle as she touched a hand to his elbow.

Skye's knees gave way, and she would have sunk to the floor if Jacob hadn't got a firm grip on her.

'I'll come. Skye's not in a fit state, and she might be a little too much for you to handle. I couldn't live with myself if anything bad happened. I'll see you both home safely. To be honest, it's been a long enough day as it is, and my best man duties are long over. No one is going to notice my absence if I sneak out with you.'

Skye's eyes closed, and Jade's quiet acquiescence was the last sound she heard.

* * *

The closeness in the taxi pressed down on her, heavy and oppressive as Skye lay slumped over her younger sister's lap. Jade's fingers combed through her hair, so Skye drifted off to sleep. Her eyes barely closed for a moment, before they pulled up in front of her house.

Arms linked with Summer's, their heads tilted to the sky, they spun around in a never-ending dance, the bright light of the sun blazing down on them.

'Skye! Skye, dammit!' Jade's harsh voice dragged her back from her dream. 'Wake up, damn you!'

The world exploded, tilting on its axis as she struggled to sit up.

Spinning, spinning, spinning.

Heat blazed over her skin. She scrabbed for the door handle, desperate to get out, to suck in some fresh air.

'Hold on, Skye,' Jacob murmured from the front passenger seat as he spoke to the driver. 'I'll just see them to their door, if you can hang on here for a minute, then you can drop me off home, too.'

'I'm going to be sick.' Her words came out a garbled mess.

'She's going to be sick,' Jade repeated, her voice loud and panicked enough to have Skye cringing.

Jacob leapt from the cab, his voice filled with alarm. 'Hold on. Hold on.'

Skye smacked the heel of her hand against the window. 'I'm going to be...'

The door she leaned on flew open and Skye fell from the cab, the hot acid burn spewing from her mouth as Prosecco and the small amount of food she'd consumed evacuated from her stomach.

'Oh, Jesus.' The deep voice came from somewhere above her bowed head.

'Oh, my God, Skye. What have you done?'

With unfocused eyes, Skye stared down at what had once been

black, shiny shoes that were now covered with steaming bile and alcohol with the obligatory carrot peppering it.

'Oh, Jacob...' The words barely mumbled out of her before another spasm clenched her stomach and more alcohol projectile vomited from her lips. Sick spattered up his impeccably pressed trouser legs before he could step back quick enough, or far enough.

'Shit. Oh, fuckity fuck.' Her sister hauled her up and manhandled her away from the cab as Jacob spoke with the taxi driver in irate undertones.

'Whasshhappening...?' Confusion swirled around, making her brain ache.

'Taxi driver won't let Jacob back in. Says he's not having his cab stink of puke.'

'Oh, God. Tell him to fuck off, then.'

'Yeah. 'Cos I think that would manage to persuade him to allow Jacob back in the taxi.'

Jade rattled the housekey from Skye's small satin clutch bag and pushed it into the lock.

Without support, Skye stumbled forward, her hand shoving at the open door. Her foot caught in the hem of her dress, and she pitched forward, staggered a couple of steps and then slammed onto her knees in the hallway.

The distinct echo of a ripping seam shuddered through her.

Her stomach clenched again, but there was nothing left inside as she braced on all fours and dry retched while a concerned Cleo stood above her and shoved a cold, wet nose into her neck.

17

TUESDAY, 18 JUNE 2019

A moan escapes my lips and I curl into a tighter ball.

'Summer.' The voice whispers in my ear so the light puff of breath on my skin is almost real. Tangible. 'Summer.'

'Skye.'

I blink open my eyes and stare at the wall in front of me. I thought I'd stopped having dreams. My world is too blank for my mind to make anything up.

'Summer.'

I draw in a light breath. It's not a dream. It's not my twin's voice. I place my hand on the wall from where I've heard the noises. My voice when it comes out is low and hesitant, scratchy from so little use. 'Who is that?'

'Charlotte. My name is Charlotte.'

The bedframe creaks as I shoot up and roll to my knees. 'How do you...?'

'He's not here. LJ has gone. We must be quick.'

Confusion still spins in my sleep-drowsy mind. 'How do you know my name?'

I narrow my eyes as I scan the wall. As if I can see through it to the other side, where the girl named Charlotte probably sits on a bed the same as mine.

I wonder if my mind is playing games on me.

There is no way I can hear anyone so easily. Is it my imagination? Am I going insane? I'd heard noises from that wall for the past few days, but they'd been muffled. Indistinct.

After the first couple of times, I'd chosen not to listen and turned music on to drown out any cries for help.

There's no music now.

I move closer, my head tilting to catch the strongest sound.

I'm hesitant. Scared. 'Hello.'

I try again. 'Hello. How do you know who I am?' My voice comes out sharper this time. Demanding. It's not my damned imagination, I don't have one of those left. I know there's someone in the room next door, but how can I hear them so clearly?

There is a pause, I detect a slight snivel. 'The bastard called me by your name by mistake, when he was...' She sighed, sniffed. 'Bastard.'

Bastard indeed. But you know nothing yet.

I press both hands against the wall and rest my forehead there too.

'How can I hear you?'

'I've dug a hole in the wall. Where I could hear you scratching. It's made of something gritty. Maybe sandstone. I've managed to work a little bit of brick or stone free from this side and I think another piece popped through your side just now.'

I remain quiet, wondering if this could possibly be some kind of insane trickery. Another way to punish me, but the voice comes again.

'I hear you scraping. What are you scraping at?'

I drop my hands into my lap. 'The days.' I sigh. 'I scratch in the days.'

There was a pause. 'How many?'

I don't reply. I'm really not sure I should.

'How many days since he brought you here?' she insists, her voice tipping over into near hysteria. An emotion I recognise that I lived with for the first couple of years.

I hesitate. The fear in the woman's voice is palpable even through the thick wall. Is it fair to let her know what a nightmare she's in for? Would I have wanted to know when I first arrived?

No.

There was no chance I'd have wanted to live if I'd known I'd be here as long as I have. Each day at a time. That's how she has to look at it. How I look at it. It isn't as bad now as it was in the beginning. Now he no longer comes for me.

Even sometimes when I count the days back, I can't believe it.

The day LJ gave me a CD player and four CDs, I'd celebrated. A little reward for good behaviour.

The CD I never realised would come in useful to cover up the crying of my neighbour.

Charlotte doesn't need to know yet what good behaviour means.

'Too many.' I eventually answer her as I slip off the bed and pull the frame away from the wall. Soft grey powder is piled into a small hill under a ragged round hole no thicker than my thumb. There's a long, narrow piece of sandstone that has come loose, the edge of it peeping from the hole. I edge it out.

I've not heard her digging through the wall. Then again, I've deliberately tuned out every sound coming from the vicinity of next door. Turned my music up. For my own sanity.

I scramble down to bring my face close to the hole. 'How did you manage to find this?'

'I figured if you were scratching into the wall each day, it must be softish in parts.'

'Not very soft. I have a small nail, though.' I'm a little proud of that. I slip it back into the hole in the bedframe each time I use it. I'm not telling her that. LJ may just be listening.

'I have a knife.'

'A knife?' My heart stutters, races. I feel a little jolt of... what? Jealousy? Admiration? Optimism? Anticipation? 'How did you get a knife? He won't allow me any cutlery. I have to eat with my fingers or he lets me have a spoon.'

'He doesn't allow me any either, but when I arrived, he thought I was still out of it. He used some kind of drug to knock me out. I managed to slip the knife up my sleeve while I was in the kitchen. He left me to sleep the first time he brought me here.' The catch in her throat evokes every kind of horror I have no need to imagine as I've already suffered it. 'I hid it in the tubing on the bedframe.'

I stare at my own bedframe. That would work. Just as I put the nail back every time, LJ has never thought to look. He's tipped my mattress off onto the floor frequently to check underneath, but he's never examined the bedframe itself.

'Is it a sharp knife?' The thought of stabbing it through his neck comes unbidden to my mind.

I'd kill him. Without a second thought if I got the chance. He's deprived me of my life. Why wouldn't I rob him of his?

The big question is, will I be able to leave this place?

On my hands and knees, I feel along the ridges of the wall face, my fingers trembling as they poke into the narrow gap and then come away dusty. 'If he finds out...' I don't want to say it out loud. He's punished me in the past. Now I never do anything to invite punishment. Is that why he's brought in another woman? Another young girl by the sound of her voice. Is she as young as I was when I was first brought here? Stolen. Incarcerated.

'Brush the dust away. Unless he gets on his hands and knees and inspects the wall, he'll never know.'

'What if he finds out...?'

'Then you link your hands and whack him over the back of the neck when he kneels down.'

Terror tremors through me. She has no idea what she is talking about. Perhaps she's seen too many action movies. But no one gets hurt on the big screen. There is no real, physical pain.

Her words are brave, but I know so much better.

Once I'd been brave. I'd tried to escape. Time after time. Different ways.

They never worked. I never escaped. And then the punishment was so much more. So much worse. Each time. Until the last time when he left me for dead. Yet somehow, I survived.

It never occurs even to attempt an escape any more. Why would I? So much time has passed. There is nothing out there for me any longer. Nowhere to go, no one to turn to.

In his cruelty, LJ loves to remind me as often as he can that my family will have moved on. They will have forgotten me by now. Formed lives that no longer rely on my presence.

I'm not the same person I used to be. I'm no longer human. Just a creature. A stupid creature.

That's what he calls me. Creature. In the beginning he called me 'Stupid', but he's found a new name. Creature. It seems even more demeaning.

My mind wanders as I turn my hands over and stare at them. Wrinkled partly through dehydration and partly through scratching at the wall each day, with nothing but the small nail that is slowly wearing away. I wonder what will happen when it finally snaps. Or when there simply is nothing left of it. When it is worn to a little nub.

I wish I'd been bright enough to have thought of stealing a knife.

I'd have used it on his neck as he lowered himself to me. Jabbed it in deep until the blood pulsed out in thick, lazy gluts and his eyes glazed over until he could no longer see me as I slithered from under him and out the door, leaving it locked behind me so no one would ever find him in the dark.

'Summer?' I lift my head. Remember. There is someone there, talking to me. Her name is Charlotte.

I'm not sure how I feel about having this new person in my life. Whether I want her company or not. It's difficult to know. There's a tremoring excitement and yet a blanketing fear.

'Summer, so, we'll talk each day while he's away. Yeah?' Charlotte's voice cracks a little with fear. 'We'll keep each other sane, won't we? Please.'

I shudder and force myself not to fall for this false promise she's offering me. An expectation that I've long since given up on.

Hope I left behind.

18

TUESDAY, 30 JULY 2019

'Summer.'

'Charlotte.' I taste her name on my lips. It's a sweet name. A good name. I don't get to call anyone by their name. Except LJ. Names are all like gossamer to me.

My voice feels rusty and I'm starting to feel tired. I've no idea how to interact any more, but Charlotte wants to talk. Again.

I already know her life story. It was just her and her mum. A mum who meant the world to her. A life she'd loved and been torn away from. Poor Charlotte.

I listen and my heart breaks for her, but now I'm tired.

Each repetition of her story somehow numbs me.

There's nothing I can do to stop her self-recrimination. How stupid she was to be catfished, to be lured in by LJ who was not the LJ she'd believed him to be.

It's my story too.

Stupid, stupid, stupid.

Each time she tells me how stupid she is, she reiterates my own foolishness.

I was naïve. Thoughtless. Self-centred.

It changes nothing.

We're both here. Wherever here is.

'Look!'

She drags me back from my musings.

I don't know where she means, but I automatically glance down at the small hole she's dug out every day for the past two weeks. I hope she's not making it too big. It's not yet, but it's big enough to push something narrow through the gap.

I scramble down onto my hands and knees. My tiredness forgotten.

'Look what I found.' A small piece of what looks like black tubing pops out of the hole. Just the tip of it, so I can pull it with my fingertips.

'Have you got it?'

I stare at the long, black stick in my hand. A trickle of something like pleasure runs through me.

'Where did you find it?'

'It was further along the wall. I was looking for a way out.'

She is always tapping, scraping, scratching when LJ isn't around. Like she's going to find a hidden doorway into a magical universe.

I say nothing. I'd already spent the whole of my first eighteen months doing exactly the same thing. It isn't my place to criticise or disillusion her.

'I thought you could use it instead of scraping with the nail. It's a charcoal stick, I think.'

I sit back on my heels, nursing the precious find in the palm of my hand. 'Don't you want it?'

Silence stretches out.

'We're going to get out of here, Summer.'

She's forever trying to fill me full of hope. Sometimes it kick-starts inside of me, but still mostly I feel flat. Defeated. She couldn't possibly understand why.

I swallow as I stare at the notches on the wall, creeping their way upward from where I started at the bottom, beneath the level of my bedframe so LJ never notices.

Charlotte doesn't keep a tally of her days. Charlotte has more ambition and determination than I do. One day soon she's going to get out of here. She says she's going to take me with her. She reiterates several times a day. Over and over again. Until some days, I put a CD on and turn the music up loud. I know it brings her some comfort, too, but more than that, it shuts her up for a while when I'm too overwhelmed to listen to her false hope any more.

If I don't want the music blasting, I sneak upstairs and away. I've not told her I'm allowed out. Not yet. I think it might destroy her.

'Summer?'

I don't answer for a long time, but Charlotte is used to that now. She knows I sometimes need silence. I've been used to silence for so long. It used to press down in oppressive waves. Now I value it. Treasure it. It's often my escape.

I pluck the nail from my bedframe and scratch in another notch. Another day. I wonder when LJ will return. I'm hungry. My stomach is starting to growl. I know Charlotte doesn't want him to come back because when he does, it will be her he comes for.

I sigh. Not me. Thank God, not me. A wave of guilt washes over me. Is it so unfair that I don't want to be the centre of his attention?

'Charcoal can be wiped away,' I mutter.

I finish scraping and slip the nail back into the metal tubing of the bedframe.

'I don't want my life to be wiped away.' The notches are a permanent illustration of my existence.

I stare at the piece of charcoal in my palm and wrap my fingers around it. It's precious. She has no idea how precious it is.

'Can I keep it?' My voice is barely a whisper, but I know Char lotte is waiting to hear it.

'Yes. It's a gift.'

I feel the unnatural stretch as my mouth curves up into a smal smile. The first smile for years.

'Thank you.'

I've not given art a thought for so long, not since I decided tc defer my place at university. My anger in the beginning had been sc strong, I'd daubed oil paints across canvases in a fit of fury.

Since I was taken prisoner, the thought of drawing has never entered my head.

I study the bumpy surface of the wall and reach out and start a sketch, the charcoal an unfamiliar medium, having only used it a few times during art lessons, but it's not long before the technique comes back, and I fall silent, concentrating on the evolving picture.

19

FRIDAY, 4 OCTOBER 2019

There are tears in my eyes as I outline another drawing on the wall.

This isn't going to end well, and Charlotte wants me to tell her what to do.

'Summer! Did you hear me?'

'I heard.'

'I don't know what to do. Should I tell him?'

My chest expands until it feels as though it's about to implode. What can I say? If I say yes, I know what will happen. If she does nothing, the same will happen. She's doomed either way.

She's filled my heart with the belief that one day she will escape, but nothing has happened so far.

I sigh out the long breath I've been holding.

'It's probably better if you tell him now. He's going to find out anyway.'

'Not if I can escape.'

It's been almost seven months since she arrived.

Doubt had crept in a few months earlier at her ability to escape. There is no escape. Not from here. Not from LJ.

'When was your last period?'

Silence hung.

'Charlotte? When was your last period?' I put a bit more force in my question.

I hear the shaky breath which rushes out. 'I don't know.'

I study my notches on the wall. Intermittently, there's a notch intersected at the top with another notch. My last period was three weeks ago. I know I'll continue to have them as long as LJ leaves me alone.

I never want to get pregnant again. I was surprised I hadn't earlier. Like Charlotte, but perhaps he hadn't starved her the way he had me. The vicious spitefulness doesn't appear as prevalent with her as it was with me in the early days. Her food is delivered regularly. Mine too, these days. Often twice a day if he's here.

I stare down at my emaciated body with a critical eye, surprised I even fell pregnant. My periods don't come at regular intervals. Again, I consider that's because I'm malnourished. Before I arrived here, my periods were regular as clockwork. I swore it had something to do with having a twin. We kept each other regular, our bodies in rhythm with each other.

Charlotte refuses to keep track of the days. I know how long she's been with us. I have it marked on my wall.

I've been good lately.

I've made progress.

LJ's given me far more freedom. Freedom with a metaphorical noose around my neck, but freedom, nonetheless. He's made it perfectly clear I'm not allowed to step foot out of the door.

Even when he's not here, I'd never chance it. Just in case. He knows everything. Has eyes everywhere. That's what he tells me.

If he says not a foot, then I'll not even risk a big toe, because if I do, he'll break that big toe. Or he'll starve me for a week. Or put something in my food so I retch until my stomach feels as though it's going to come up through my throat and the stench of faeces fills the cell when he forbids me from emptying the toilet bucket. A cell that would be locked. With only one small, barred window, high up in the wall, that I can't see out of, even when I drag the iron-framed bed across the small room and stand on it.

It's obvious there are no streetlights. When it's night, it's pitch black. Nothing. I can't even see the hand in front of my face. When I first arrived, I hadn't even realised there was a window. It's small and set right back in the wall. For the first few weeks I'd not ventured from the actual bedframe for more than to do essentials such as eat, or pee. Even when I'd started to investigate, it had been dull outside. Only in the summer do I benefit from that window.

Feeble light scrolls across the pale grey walls in a slow record of the passing of the day. I follow it, sitting or standing in the rays, face upturned, mind a blank canvas just waiting for something interesting enough to paint across it. To activate my brain.

It fires a little when I am allowed upstairs, out of the cell, just for a while.

Charlotte is never allowed out. Not yet.

I never acknowledge I know of her presence to LJ or that I realise I'm not the only one in residence. The consequences of admitting it chills my very being. I'm good at keeping my mouth shut these days.

I would like to help Charlotte, I really would. Our whispered conversations are all about optimism and escape. I'm not so invested in the idea of getting free, but I wouldn't spoil Charlotte's dream. That is hers to keep.

It may be completely vile of me, but having Charlotte here hasn't just given me someone to listen to, someone who has invigorated my brain and offered a spark of optimism. What it also means is I've found myself with a little more liberty while LJ divides his attention between us.

Not really divided.

He's totally taken up with her and I've lost all appeal to him. I keep myself useful. I don't want to be here, but nor do I want to die. Today. Today I want to live with the hope Charlotte has injected into me that one day I will see my family again.

I close my mind to my previous life as I concentrate on the mindless task of cleaning LJ's three-bedroom cottage.

That's one of my rewards.

20

FRIDAY, 3 JANUARY 2020

Funny what you begin to appreciate in life when you have nothing.

Every little edge and corner I scrub, and for that I can listen to music and have the back door wide open. A back door I still won't consider stepping outside of into the high-walled courtyard beyond.

If I'm lucky, LJ will leave me something on the kitchen drainer. A treat. A reward.

A reward is certainly better than a punishment.

I collect a couple of items, take them with me downstairs to my lair. I'm not sure if he means for me to, but he never protests, never beats me, never mentions them after they appeared not very long after Charlotte arrived. Maybe a couple of months after.

Perhaps because he is too infatuated with her to notice. Perhaps because he no longer sees me.

Time doesn't really mean much, but I calculate it to be after Christmas when I add up the days. It's not something I get tired of, counting. After all, other than cleaning, there's so little to do with my time.

I never even told Charlotte Christmas had come and gone. It would destroy her.

I discover the tiny snow globe on the mantelpiece when I'm dusting. Barely the size of a small satsuma. Not that I've seen a satsuma for some time. LJ brought me some once. It must have been a couple of years ago.

I sit for ages. I tip it upside down and watch the tiny flecks of gold and white drift down to rest on the miniature white stag or float around his hooves. One flake catches on the tip of his antler. He's a beautiful stag. It gives me something to sketch on the wall. Another idea that extends into a whole winter woodland scene. I can imagine other animals. A rabbit, a fox, an owl and I include them too. It's a happy scene. My happy place.

I only wish Charlotte could see it. Come into my room, like Jade used to sneak into the room Skye and I shared, just to see what we were doing. Skye would be creating an entire artwork with numbers far beyond my cerebral capability. Figures I could barely get my head around. Whereas I would splash colour onto paper, or canvas, lost in my own world, and garner Skye's jealousy that she could barely draw an outline of a building without having to use a ruler.

There was never a true resentment of each other's talents as we'd grown with the knowledge that we were opposites. We even crossed our arms the opposite way. Like a reflection in a mirror as opposed to the very same person. You'd have to know us very well to notice.

Memories of those happy times pour in and instead of shutting them down like I used to, when I was alone, I open my mind and let them flood through.

Charlotte and I exchange memories. Charlotte more than me because she can't stop talking. Perhaps I would have been the same way if there'd been another person in the room next door when I arrived.

It offers a sliver of optimism.

Not long after the snow globe, a small red Buddha appears on the windowsill in the kitchen. I wonder if it is a Christmas present LJ hadn't wanted, or something he'd received at New Year, because we are in the new year by the time that appeared.

The red Buddha stirs memories. At school we'd taken religion, snippets of faiths other than our family's and we'd linked some of them to our art. I'd designed a beautiful goddess with a flowing dress and flowers in her hair. Such a romantic depiction.

If I remember correctly, the red Buddha was called Amitabha. I muse about it. That it should be brought here at this time when Charlotte has come to give me hope. Buddhists believe red represents fire and it has something to do with life force and perseverance.

Perhaps that's what Charlotte and my little red Buddha have combined to bring me.

I take that down the stone steps too.

I don't have a red chalk, so my Buddha is outlined in charcoal and white chalk. For now.

I have nowhere to keep anything. No ledges to balance them on, so they sit on the small wooden vanity tray that had lain empty up in LJ's bedroom. The room he uses on the odd occasion he stays overnight. It's not often.

I sneak it down too but wonder what punishment will come.

Nothing.

I've not been punished, so I assume they were a reward. Charlotte makes him happy.

It doesn't make her happy, but it gives me more freedom than I've ever had.

But it doesn't give me faith. His power over me is as strong as ever. If not more so. Because I'm frightened of going back to how we were. I never want to go back to that again.

So, I keep my mind closed to possibilities and dreams I used to have of being free. Free from his cruelties, free from this life that had never been meant for me.

I hum mindlessly to music that plays on a continuous, repetitive loop. Eighteen songs. If I'm good and clean properly, he might allow me another two. He seems to have been happy lately, with his new acquisition. More generous than in the past.

I check the drainer and see it's empty. A flicker of disappointment twangs at my heart until I spot it. My present. I pick up the stick of coloured chalk he's left on the windowsill next to the cellar door. Green this time. I already have white, yellow and blue. The first one had been more accident than design when Charlotte had gifted me that small piece of charcoal she'd discovered wedged into a crevice in the wall. It could have been years old.

I'd done some charcoal work at school in my art lessons. A still life. One of the students had posed for us. Despite the suggestion they might remove their clothes, which had almost caused a riot of excitement, the headmaster had put a very definite stop to that.

I'd used it again when I traced a horse in the field at the bottom of our road. The beauty of that medium to define muscle, bone and sinew.

The thrill of having something I could lose myself in pushed aside some of the fear I have of LJ. Not all. Never all because he is never predictable. Never trustworthy.

When LJ originally saw the tiny picture on the pale grey surface of the cell wall I'd etched with the small stick of charcoal, he seemed to like it.

The following morning, there'd been a piece of chalk and another stick of charcoal. I'd wilted with gratitude. An outlet to my thoughts, my dreams, my fears and nightmares. With free rein, I'd started at first with random little designs, the view I had of the courtyard, the winding steps descending into the darkness of my dungeon. The hell hole at the bottom as a scrawling mass of blackness.

I hesitate at the top of the stone steps into the cellar now. Do I dare go down? To investigate?

Would he know if I sneaked past my own cell to the one further along the corridor?

I uncurl clenched fingers from around the stick of chalk. If he catches me, he'll take away my privileges and I may never get them back again.

Charlotte has taught me to be brave again, though.

I take the first two steps with slow hesitance. Is Charlotte worth my freedom? Miniscule as it is, it's mine and I've earned it.

I find myself at the bottom of the stairs and I hold back.

Is Charlotte okay?

I've not heard her since last night. Since the screams and then the gut-wrenching sobs. Sobs I no longer let out. Hers were more of a keening as she rocked after his visit. Like I used to, but now my mind switches off from everything he does.

I'd whispered through the hole in the wall this morning, but there'd been no response.

I creep along the corridor to the end where it turns to the right and the door is there in front of me. I picture the layout in my head. Her cell is side by side with mine, but the entrance is a few feet back, so it's not easily visible until I walk along the hall.

My feet are hesitant.

I raise my hand, about to tap on the door, but pause and place my palm cautiously on it instead.

Unlocked, the heavy oak door creaks open an inch as I lend my weight to it.

I draw in a deep breath until my lungs are on fire, flames about to burst out of my mouth and nose like a dragon. It's one of my imaginings I etched on the wall. In black and white before I had access to more colours.

I give a gentle push to open it wider.

'Fuck!' LJ's voice almost screams the word and my heart slams into my throat.

I've been caught!

I freeze, unsure whether to turn and run or step further into the room to expose my presence.

'What the fuck did you do that for?'

About to answer, I realise he's not talking to me. He's talking to Charlotte.

I edge back from the door, breath stilled in my chest. I can't see anything. I can only imagine as his gravelly voice continues.

'Fuck. Now what am I supposed to do?'

I scuttle down the hallway and dash into my own room, silently pushing the door closed behind me.

I crawl onto my new mattress. One that isn't quite as thin and doesn't smell of anything much. He'd not wished me a happy Christmas, but this is what he'd brought with him.

I curl into the foetal position and squeeze my eyes tight, only now acknowledging that the piece of chalk in my hand has almost crumbled to dust. The four broken pieces rub together as I clench and unclench my hands, desperate not to make a sound.

Instinctively, I know I won't hear from Charlotte again.

Charlotte has escaped. In her own way.

21

Ten hours after the wedding

Skye flung back her head, her throat working like crazy to suck air into lungs that were drowning under the onslaught of water streaming over her head in a rushing torrent. She gasped in through a wide-open mouth.

'Shut your mouth.'

She knitted her lips together.

'Put your head down.'

Her head dropped like it was disconnected from her neck and she opened her mouth again to draw in air.

'Close your eyes.'

Her eyelids were already screwed shut against the vicious soap-suds that leaked in behind them and burned her eyeballs out in any case.

A pathetic whimper vibrated in her throat until Jade pushed a bundle of soft white flannels into Skye's hand so she could press them against her face to protect herself.

'Well, this is a first.'

Skye wilted onto the base of the shower cubicle, propping herself up with her shoulder against the wall as Jade continued to sluice her off. She held onto the flannels with one hand while she crossed an arm across her body in false modesty.

'Cold...' Skye's teeth chattered as her entire body convulsed in huge, dramatic shivers.

Heat ramped up and steam rose from her freezing skin.

'Normally, it's the other way around.' Jade's voice was inappropriately cheery, given the situation. 'I guess I owe you this for all the times you've done it for me in the same situation.'

But it wasn't the same situation.

Skye tried to tell her sister, but the words slipping from her mouth had no substance and slewed all over like melted mercury, unable to hold their form.

She'd held Jade's luscious hair back from her face many a time when her younger sister had thrown up into the toilet bowl after a night of overindulgence, but she'd never had to actually jet wash her down.

Keeping the flannels across her eyes, she gave a feeble slap at her sister to get her to shut off the water. 'Nuff.'

She had no idea if the word came out correctly, but the water stopped suddenly, even though the sound of it still filled her head.

'You know I said you'd lost weight?' Jade grunted as she manhandled Skye out of the narrow shower, making her drop her flannels. 'Well, I lied. You're a fat bitch.'

Laughter spluttered from Skye's loose lips as they both sank onto the bathroom mat. Jade slung a soft, warm towel around her sister and rubbed until Skye thought she might flay the skin from her body.

'Loveyoutoo.' The words rolled into one unintelligible lump.

As Jade tugged an oversized T-shirt over her head, Skye hummed in the back of her throat.

There was something she had to say. Something she really needed to tell Jade.

She closed her eyes as Jade scrubbed a hand towel over her hair, until it probably resembled a ball of tumbleweed, but she had no strength in her to protest. The shower had literally wrung her dry.

She had no memory of getting up the stairs, apart from a vague picture of her hanging onto Cleo's neck with her sister's arm wrapped around her waist as she bumped her up the stairs.

There was no memory of Jacob leaving. Nothing. Except... there'd been another presence. A dark shadow of someone she used to know.

Sadness slumped down on her like a leaden weight and tears filled her eyes with unexpected ferocity.

'Oh, don't cry. I didn't mean it, I was only joking. You're not fat.' Jade scrubbed desperately at Skye's cheeks and offered up a watery smile of her own. 'Still a bitch, but not fat.'

A wave of laughter hit her again as her emotions rock-and-rolled.

With her arm slung loosely over Jade's shoulder, they staggered along until they reached her bedroom. Cleo's icy nose inched under her T-shirt to touch her backside and Skye's eyes widened momentarily, watching everything spin and then slammed shut.

She'd tell Jade in the morning. That important thing she needed to speak with her about.

Her soft duvet was pulled up and tucked under her chin.

Skye felt the weight of Cleo as she climbed on the bed to stretch out full length against her.

She reached her hand out and rested it on the silky fur at the same time as her sister stroked the tangle of hair back from Skye's face.

'You're safe, Skye. I've got you. Nothing can harm you. No one is going to get you.'

Jade's deepest fear was also Skye's secret one.. One she could never admit to, or it would become a reality, that one day Jade or Dad would leave and never come back.

'Shh. You're safe,' Jade crooned.

Skye sighed as she curled onto her side and fell into the waiting dark.

22

MONDAY, 6 FEBRUARY 2023

I squeeze my eyes tight and hope that she'll shut up. Pray she'll go away.

She's persistent, this new girl. This Lilijana.

She's constantly tapping, banging, screaming, clawing. I don't know exactly what it is she uses on the walls, the door, the floor, but I imagine she has thrown the bed around, tipped it over so she can use the tubular frame to ram against things.

'Hey, you.' Her accent is light, understandable. She has excellent English, as though she learnt it from Google.

'I know you are there.'

I didn't want to engage with her. It's nothing to do with me. I want nothing to do with anyone since Charlotte. I thought I didn't have any emotions left, but it broke my heart when Charlotte took her own life. I thought I'd become as important to her as she was to me. I no longer felt like a ghost hiding in the shadows.

It seemed the loss of her baby tore her soul, like it did mine. Only I was already broken when it happened to me. She was still fighting with all of her strength. It appeared she turned the fight on herself. Who would have known?

There was someone else at one time. If I consult my wall, I'll be able to see when, but I can't be bothered these days. We never spoke. Never engaged. I'm not even sure she knew of my existence because I had melted into the shadows once more.

I don't think she stayed long.

It's been some time since LJ brought anyone back.

I thought he'd given up. He'd stayed less frequently in the last six months or so. I was beginning to believe one day he simply wouldn't return.

What would I do?

How long would I wait before placing a foot out of the front door and risk trekking my way through the vast swathes of woodland to find civilisation?

'Hey!'

She smacks something hard on the wall and I leap off my bed as though she's going to break through.

'I know you are there! I have seen you.'

My body jerks upright. I'm like a gazelle, just about to take flight after scenting a lion.

She hasn't seen me. Has she?

'When?'

There's a stunned silence. Then, 'I knew it. I knew there was someone.'

So, she'd lied to lure me. Reel me in. Well, I was tired of being lured in and I wasn't going to play games.

'Fuck off.'

Another silence. Then, 'I would fuck off, if only I could. I need to get out of here. Can you help?'

'No.' My answer is quiet. Subdued. He may not be here now, but he will be back. Who knows when?

The anger drops away from her tone. 'Are you a prisoner too?'

I'm not sure how to answer that. Am I? If I wanted to leave,

:ould I? These days, there's nothing stopping me but myself. Isn't
here?

'Yes,' I whisper, as I slide my bed away from the wall and lower
myself to the floor where the hole is. The hole I've not utilised for
:he past... I flicker my gaze over my scratch marks and take a quick
guess rather than counting from the beginning... over three years
since Charlotte left me. 'Yes, I'm a prisoner, too. There's a hole at the
bottom of the wall. There may be something in front of it, if you
move it, you can hear better.'

I hear the scraping of something, and then her voice, still
muffled, but definitely clearer comes through. 'What's your name?'

I pause. Do I really want this pain all over again? I take in a deep
breath. 'Summer.'

'Summer. I am Lilijana.'

'That's a nice name.'

The silence is awkward. Did I say the wrong thing? I don't speak
these days. My voice is a scratchy rasp from barely being used. It's
so hard. I don't want conversation with anyone. I listen to my music
and clean. That is all.

I don't even want to imagine getting to know this woman over
the next few weeks, or months, or even years and then waking up
one morning to find she is gone and I'm alone again.

I've become quite accustomed to my own company. I don't want
to open my heart up to someone else again. I'm not sure I could
bear the pain another time.

I never had to clean up after Charlotte. After all, I wasn't
supposed to know of her existence, but I wonder if LJ would get me
to do it in the future. After all, he trusts me to do so much more.

'It means innocence and purity.' The bitter laugh transcends the
wall as she brings me back to the present.

'What does?'

'My name.'

'Oh. Mine means summer.' I fail to add it was only one half. Summer Skye. That's what it should be. But the whole has become fractured and I can barely remember what my other half looks like. She's an occasional shadow in dark dreams.

'I've got to get out of here. My family need me.'

What of my family? I'm sure they no longer need or want me. That time has passed. I keep quiet. It's not something I can help with.

'Will you help me?' Her voice is a quiet plea.

'No.' I don't even hesitate. How can I help? There's nothing I can do.

'Why not?' The anger in her voice leaves me unmoved. After all, I'm dead inside.

'He'll kill you.' It was simple.

'I'd rather die than be a prisoner of a monster.'

I hear the tears choking her. Tears I've cried many a time. But no more.

'I'm sorry.' But there is no real sympathy in my heart. I am... flat. Apathetic.

I hear nothing more.

I look around at the floor and walls covered with my sketches, my drawings. Things that bring me comfort and I want to comfort her too. If only I can.

I tug the bottom sheet free of my mattress. It's thin and starting to fray at the edges and I can only think it would be nice if LJ brought me a new one soon. I haven't had new bedding since Charlotte...

On my hands and knees on the cold floor, I crouch, a stick of charcoal in my hand. It's not easy on the sheeting, I have to pin it between my knees to stop it sliding away, but surprisingly it brings me some joy as the charcoal shows up brighter on the white background, the image somehow more powerful.

Somehow, I will get this to Lilijana.

I glance up at the long length of broom handle I'd left propped against the wall.

A smile curves my lips.

I need to do something to help Lilijana. Something to keep her sane.

Even if my sanity has long since left me.

23

FRIDAY, 19 MAY 2023, 6.30 P.M.

My relationship with Lilijana is nothing like it was with Charlotte. Charlotte had been both a fighter and young and delicate at the same time. I'd befriended her, protected her, kept secrets from her so she didn't suffer. In the end, the suffering was so much more.

It took me so long to realise that despite her strength, that one thing broke her mind and losing her baby had been more than she could bear.

In protecting her, my wounds remain raw.

It's never occurred to me that taking my own life is the way out. It isn't in my mindset and now I have to question: does that make me the stronger person for staying, or Charlotte for going?

'How long have you been here?' Lilijana's question stabs through the silence with no warning, no introduction. Not that I need niceties, but perhaps she could say my name like Charlotte used to.

'Summer,' she would whisper and I knew she wanted to talk.

Lilijana very rarely uses my name. She will abruptly start a conversation and finish it the same way.

I never start a conversation. She doesn't want me to.

I tried in the beginning, but there was never an answer. I don't think she considers herself to be rude, just direct.

I leave it to her now. That's the way she prefers it.

We've settled into our strange relationship. I'd like to think my heart hasn't engaged, but I look forward to her short, sharp conversations. Sometimes once a day, occasionally more.

Lilijana has been here just over three months.

I consult my wall and trace my fingers over what appears to be fence posts clinging to a clifftop. This is Lilijana's timeline, which runs separate from mine. I want to keep it apart so when she falls from the cliff, I will not have to disengage it from mine.

Three months, eight days.

That wasn't the question she'd asked me, though. The question was, 'How long have *you* been here?'

'Six years, seven months, seven days.'

If it had been Charlotte, I would have sugar coated it. I'd never have divulged the actual truth. But she is not Charlotte, and her feelings are not my responsibility.

She doesn't need to say anything. The stunned silence simply drifts through the wall between us.

What must she think of me? Does she think I am weak, pathetic? I don't particularly care. Or, more precisely, I cannot bear it. To hear the terrible distress.

I hear them, louder than I used to now the hole remains uncovered. Unlike my ears. I press my hands tight to them so I don't have to listen.

Lilijana is a warrior.

I have to admire that.

She never gives in. Never concedes a single battle.

'I'm pregnant.'

My blood runs cold.

I raise my head where I've had it tucked into my knees while I wait in the silence. 'Oh, God.'

'What will he do?'

I tell her.

How can I not?

Look what happened to Charlotte when I kept my silence in my misguided belief that I was protecting her.

'I don't want his baby inside me. Let him take it!'

'It might kill you.'

'Good.'

I come to my feet from where I've sat on the stone floor sketching my latest muse. My knees and ankles ache with the cold and I hobble across my cell, my stiff hips slowing me down. I've spent too much time downstairs lately, just for the sake of an occasional conversation with Lilijana.

I need the sun on my face now.

I reach the top of the stairs.

He's not here. He's not been for a couple of days. He didn't leave much food, so either he will be back in the morning, or he has left us for good.

The courtyard has soaked in the afternoon sun, and I hover on the doorstep, still not entirely comfortable stepping out there, although I've been braver lately. LJ has said nothing. Even when I have taken one step when he is here, just to test.

Subconsciously, I'm practising for when the day comes that I step outside the front door, because I know once I do, it will be forever.

I turn my face to the sky. Summer Skye. Beautiful, clear blue.

I've not thought of my twin for some time. My mind has been quiet with so little to think about, but Lilijana has fired thoughts that I don't seem to be able to suppress.

My eyes are closed. Skye's voice sounds in my head. 'Faster, Summer. Run faster.'

I look behind me as my legs stretch out, my bare feet racing across the beach. The string tied to the kite tugs at my fingers, and I let go. I stumble to a halt and watch as the kite drifts off. Up, up into the cloudless blue sky.

'Summer!'

My eyes fly open as every bone in my body jerks, as though each individual one has just been poked. My elbow whacks into the wall and I scrabble to my feet, not even realising I'd been crouched on the stones outside, my hand clutches the chalk I'd been sketching with.

LJ's face is a mask of dark fury.

What have I done? This is something I've not witnessed for so long.

A muscle pulses in his jaw.

'LJ. I didn't know you were here.'

'Evidently.' The sneer twists his mouth. 'Don't you have something better to do than while away your time sleeping in the sun?'

I wasn't asleep. I was daydreaming.

I don't answer because there is never a right answer when he's in this kind of mood.

He turns his back and walks into the kitchen.

I scrabble to follow him, anxious to see what he wants me to do. Sick terror roils in my stomach. I will do anything it takes to please him. To obey him. I'm aware his hold on me is unreasonable, but I can't shake it off. Even with the doors wide open, I am his prisoner.

Ignoring me, he turns his back and fills the kettle slamming the switch on with unnecessary force.

'I have something to do for a couple of days. I won't be here. You'll have to see to yourself.'

Surprised he's telling me something he's never bothered with before, I hover in the doorway. There's something different about him. He seems... rattled.

To my surprise, it makes my nerves jitter as anxiety sets in. don't like change. It unsettles me. Like when he brings new girl here. It's nothing but trouble.

I hover, chew the side of my thumb for a moment until he flicks the switch off the kettle before it has fully boiled.

'What's wrong?'

He turns and pins me with that shark-eyed stare as though he's contemplating telling me more. His lips tighten and he turns away to fill a mug with boiling water.

The sickly smell of herbal tea turns my stomach and I know.

I know what he knows.

24

'Summer!'

I jump because I'm not used to Lilijana snapping out my name. Certainly not in the middle of the night.

The sleep I'd been in had been deep and dreamless. Now I blink open groggy eyes, but I can tell it's the middle of the night as there is nothing but pure blackness inside my cell. A reflection of my soul.

It must be cloudy as not even the light from the moon has filtered through in soft cobwebs across the walls from the tiny window.

What will I say to this woman? Another woman who LJ has administered his vile concoction to. His special tea.

He's gone and left me alone to endure her agony with her, knowing that if she dies too, I will be alone again. I don't even want to contemplate how long a body could lie down here before the stench of it reaches my own nose.

She's not started that heartrending keening yet, nor even a soft groan. But then I don't expect that of Lilijana.

'Summer!'

I don't want to answer, but I have to. 'What?'

'You need to let me out. I need to get out of here.'

I blink because that wasn't what I was expecting to hear from her.

'Are you ill?' She doesn't sound ill. She sounds strong. Powerful. Typical Lilijana.

'No. After he left I threw the herbal tea in the bucket I piss in. There was something wrong with it. Nasty stuff.'

'He didn't stay and make sure you drank it?' I knew there'd been something different about him. He would never have made that mistake in the past.

'He seemed to be in a rush. Distracted.'

She'd picked up on it too. I wonder what has happened in LJ's secret world.

'You need to let me out.'

I regret telling her he no longer locks my door. But she'd asked how come I wasn't there sometimes and I'd committed to never telling lies to protect the girls in the room next door. Not any more. Not since my mistaken belief that I was protecting Charlotte.

With a voice full of urgency that turns to pleading, Lilijana smacks something on the wall to make me jump again. 'You can come with me. We will escape together.'

I curl into a ball on my mattress and shake my head as though she can see me. I don't want to go. What would I go to? It's been too long. It's too late. LJ reminds me of that from time to time.

A desperate sniffle catches in my throat and I can't answer. I won't answer.

'Summer!'

She's bullying me. Like LJ bullies me, and I'm not taking any of that crap from her. She can just fuck off.

I cover my ears and wish the wall was thicker and consider plugging the hole with something.

I can still hear her.

'Summer. Let me out. I need to go home. Find my family. I don't want to be here for the next six years. Nor do you.'

I don't want to answer her.

'Summer. I think you have something called Stockholm syndrome.'

I already know it. She doesn't need to poke at me. I know.

'I studied psychology. I know a little about it. I also know you've formed a bond with LJ.'

'I haven't.' The denial spills from my lips. Lilijana isn't as young or as naïve as both me and Charlotte, and possibly the other nameless girl.

'It's not your fault,' she cajoles. Her voice has turned softer now. 'You need to do this. If not for you, then for me.'

I raise my head.

'I can't.'

'You *can*.' Excitement tinges her words.

That's what happens when I answer, when I give someone expectation. False hope. That's why I try not to speak. It doesn't always work. It's hard to remain silent all the time. Although I am getting better at it.

'I think he might have left the key in the lock. I tried to see. Normally there's a shaft of light from the hallway.'

'It's dark.'

'I looked before. When you were sleeping. Before it got dark.'

I would still be sleeping if she hadn't woken me.

'There was something in the lock, blocking the light. He's left the key in.' She is insistent.

'He won't have.'

'Will you have a look for me? Summer?'

I swing my legs around and place my feet on the floor. It may be darker than a sky deserted of the stars and moon, but I can find my way around this place. I've been doing it for years. Everywhere except Charlotte's room. Now Lilijana's. I don't go there. Bad things happen there.

'Summer? Please.'

I slip my feet into my scraggy old plimsoles and pad to the open cell door.

Pausing, I take in a deep breath before I feel my way along the wall to the door at the end. The door I've not been near since Charlotte left me.

A thin light filters through from the room beyond and a small jab of something akin to jealousy digs deep. How come I am not good enough to warrant a light? All these years, and he's never given me a light.

Nor have I taken one. Maybe I could have. But I never did. Is that weak of me? I've taken other things, but in my heart I know he wouldn't want me to have a light. I'm the stupid creature who lives in the dark.

I rest my hand on the thick wooden door and draw in a breath.

'Summer?' There's surprise in Lilijana's voice.

Did she believe I wouldn't come? That I had gone back to sleep as I often do when I don't want to listen any more.

I didn't know myself that I would until I stood here outside this prison of hers.

With shaking fingers, I trace the horizontal lines on the heavy oak door down until I locate the lock and grapple with the heavy brass key that LJ has left in it. Maybe a mistake on his part, but he's never locked my door for years. Perhaps it was deliberate. A test. Like he tested me in the beginning. Like he tests me still.

I don't know if it is, but I don't care.

The key grates as I turn it, and at the same time I twist the old brass metal ring that slides a bolt back.

Before I can push the heavy door open, Lilijana yanks it wide and rushes through.

I'm swallowed up by an embrace that threatens to suffocate me.

My fragile body almost breaks under the power of hers. Thick muscles flex as she holds me close. I want to struggle free, but I force myself to keep still, my muscles stiff with insult and fear.

I don't want to be touched.

Lilijana pulls back. She's not quite as tall as me, but there's flesh on her bones, while I only have skin left on mine.

Before she can disguise it, I catch the flicker of horror in those dark, deep-set eyes of hers.

She composes herself, loosening her hold as though she realises she could break me in two with one more squeeze. She gentles her hands on my shoulders and stares into my face.

'Thank you.' Her accent is thick with emotion.

I give one short nod.

Her gaze flickers along the hallway I suspect she's never seen, if LJ had drugged her before he brought her down.

There's concern in her eyes now, but determination also.

'Summer. We must go.'

I shake my head. The fear in me is even stronger.

I can't imagine leaving this place. I don't care what she calls it. I can't imagine entering a world I don't know. The dread of leaving is far stronger than the terror of staying.

How can I make Lilijana understand?

She snatches at my wrist as I try to back away. I need to get to my room. To curl up on my bed and block out what is going on.

My heart pounds until every inch of my skin pulses with the rhythm of it. I can't catch my breath as heat rushes up my neck to engulf my face.

Lilijana is having none of it. She hasn't even noticed that I'm hyperventilating, sinking to the floor like a two-year-old having a meltdown. Maybe my struggle is imagined or it's only internal.

She wraps one strong arm around my shoulders and holds me up as she steers me towards the stairs. The long length of her high ponytail slaps at me and then rests between us.

Panic sparks the fever of desperation in me, and my breath comes in fast little hitches as she pushes me onwards, past the door to my room. I lurch back, taking her by surprise as I claw at the doorjamb to my room.

'Summer. It's okay. I have you. You're safe with me.'

But I won't ever be safe. 'Leave me alone. I don't want to go.'

She gets a better grip on me and lifts me off my feet, half carrying me until we reach the curving stone steps. She pushes me up ahead of her and into the hallway. My strength cannot match hers.

'Summer,' she rasps, her own breath coming heavy now. 'We can't waste any time, we have to go.' She stops and turns to face me and I notice she's still holding onto me as if frightened that I might flee down the stairs and lock myself in my room. I would if I could but there is no lock on the inside. Only the outside.

'Tell me.' She gives me a light shake, but my thin bones almost rattle in her hands and she lets go with a suddenness that takes us both by surprise. She starts again, this time with more control. 'Summer, which way? How do I get out of here?'

If I told her there was nothing beyond the door but wilderness, would she believe me and return to her room? Her cell. Her prison. I look into her eyes and point along the hall to the front door.

I know it will be unlocked. LJ doesn't see any point in locking it. Nobody comes near and I'm never likely to step through it. I'm far too indoctrinated for that. Or so he believes.

I never have yet. I'm not going to now.

Lilijana reaches for the handle, swinging the door wide as I step back. Back from freedom. Back from the terror of the unknown.

My heart has swollen so much in my chest I can no longer breathe. Not even the fast erratic breaths of a moment ago. It's simply lodged in my throat.

'Summer. Come on. We must be quick before he decides to come back.'

But he's not coming back. Not today. He said he would be away for a few days.

I glance towards the door into the kitchen and beyond, where the safety of the enclosed courtyard beckons to me.

I shake my head and slip back another step. She can't make me go. Not if I don't want to.

It isn't that I don't want to. I simply can't.

If I set foot outside that door, flames will consume me, and I'll be a pile of ash on the ground.

I look over Lilijana's head as her desperate face turns tortured. She really wants to save me. But I can't be saved.

Clouds outside part, allowing moonshine to drift through, and I get a brief glimpse of the driveway that disappears down a narrow track. A track to the unknown.

I take another step away.

'Come on. We'll go. Together.' I can hear the impatience slipping through her voice now. The desperation to leave now, before he returns.

Lilijana reaches for my hand, but I snatch it back and scoot into the kitchen, closely followed by her. My heart threatens to burst from my chest. 'I can't! I can't!'

She reels back from the desperate anxiety streaking through my voice, her own dread flashing through eyes glazed with fear. 'I've got to go. I have family. They don't have any way of looking for me. I shouldn't be here.'

And the penny drops. It's how LJ managed to take her. Because no one would look for her. Possibly her family don't even know yet she's missing, because she shouldn't be here. Not in this house, but in England. As an illegal immigrant, her family can never find her. Her only way out is to escape.

Panic drops from me like a cloak. 'You go.'

She nods. A sharp inclination of her head as we reach an unspoken pact. 'I'll send someone.'

I know she can't. She's already confessed that she's an illegal immigrant. Who would she run to? Who would she tell? She can hardly go to the police. She'd be deported before she could blink.

I satisfy myself with the thought that at least she will have escaped and not been subjected to LJ's remedy to get rid of the poor foetus in her womb.

My eyes drop to her belly.

'I won't bring his evil spawn into this world.'

I'd not seen it the same way. I'd considered the baby wholly mine, not LJ's, but with a flash of insight, I understand. Who am I to judge?

'I will think of you when I am with my family again. I'm going home. I never wanted to live here in the first place. I thought I had a job. A life. I do not. But I will.'

I nod again, but the words choke in my throat as I hover in the kitchen doorway, torn between screaming for her to take me with her into the dark unknown, or staying in my cell downstairs. Safe from the outside world.

She turns towards the front door, her hand on the jamb before she steps down onto the gravel drive.

Tears fill my eyes and take me by surprise. Who would have known I'd form a bond with this stranger?

She hesitates and turns back. 'Can I give a message to your family?'

I blink and a tear rolls down my cheek. My family. What would they think after all this time? What would it do to them? Their lives have moved on without me.

'Summer.' I turn my head as I hear Skye's voice.

Would she want me back?

'Summer!'

My neck spasms and my head gives a wobble as my attention jumps back to Lilijana. Lilijana who spoke my name. Not Skye.

She strides back to me, raises her hand and smudges the tear away with the pad of her thumb. 'Do you have a number I can call?' It's as though she doesn't even know what she has done. Perhaps if she acknowledges the tears, she won't be able to make a run for it.

Perhaps she feels the same about me.

'Summer.' She's never used my name as much as she has today. 'A telephone number?'

How does she expect me to remember a telephone number from all those years ago?

And suddenly it pops into my head. It was the number we had drilled into us in case of an emergency when we were little. In case we needed Mum or Dad. It was our home number. Not that it made any difference. It probably no longer exists. Not after this length of time.

'I have nothing to write on. Nothing to write with.'

Lilijana steps closer and offers up the inside of her arm. 'So I don't lose it.'

'There aren't any pens here.'

A flicker of confusion creases her brow. 'What else is there?'

I glance in the kitchen. On the windowsill is a stick of white chalk and a piece of charcoal from my earlier foray into the courtyard.

I reach for the charcoal, but I can't imagine it's going to make a mark.

Lilijana follows me into the light.

I break the charcoal in two and start to scrub the number in my head onto her arm with the softer, crumblier end. I press hard on her delicate skin, scrubbing a little to define the numbers and use the second half to finish off.

Dropping the charcoal on the kitchen bench, I step back, rubbing my fingers to get rid of the marks on my hands. I can only pray it doesn't rub off her arm as easily as it rubbed off my skin.

I blink. Is that what I want?

I can't leave, but do I want to be found?

Carefully, Lilijana stretches the long sleeve of her T-shirt down to her wrist to cover the number and then she looks up at me.

'Thank you for saving me, sweet Summer.'

I remain silent as she presses a soft kiss to my cheek.

'Are you sure?' she asks one more time, and steps back as I nod.

'Wait!' I say.

Hope floods her eyes, but I step over to the small fridge and pull out a bottle of water and one of the packs of sandwiches LJ left behind. He might beat me when he gets back, but it no longer matters.

I hold them out to Lilijana and disappointment is fleeting. She was never going to get far with me tagging along and she has to know that. I have no strength. If I was to guess, I could just about make it to the curve in the drive.

I'm doing her a favour, really. She'll be much faster without me.

Lilijana takes them from my hands, her eyes holding mine for one poignant moment longer before she takes off at a sprint down the drive, the swing of her long ponytail the last thing I see.

I close the door. Both the one in front of me and the one in my mind.

Devoid of emotion, stripped of everything, I make my way downstairs and curl up on my mattress.

I close my eyes and fall into a deep sleep.

25

SUNDAY, 21 MAY 2023, 3 A.M.

He'd heard the expression 'red mist' but never imagined it could be real. Only it was. LJ could barely see past the thin veil that coloured his vision.

On reflection he supposed it was something to do with his blood pressure skyrocketing as he waited for the opportunity to search for that stupid girl.

Why couldn't they all be more like Summer? Compliant. Quiet.

So quiet, she'd almost bored him to death.

He barely bothered with her these days.

She was more a maid, keeping his house clean, his clothes washed, dried and ironed. He took the chance years ago of allowing her out into the small courtyard just to get some sun on her pallid, sickly skin before she died on him. He'd watched her stand there, looking up at the sky, never even thinking to scale the wall she diligently chalked pictures across.

She was so indoctrinated, she wouldn't dream of running.

Unlike bloody Lilijana.

He screwed his eyes closed and groaned as he gripped his hair in his fists.

He should have known better. She'd fought him from the word 'go'. Never complied fully, no matter what he did to her, how many times he beat her, broke her fingers, starved her. That feral light in her eyes still never faded.

Summer's had. There was nothing in those beautiful sky-blue eyes any longer.

She'd been so like her mum. He'd simply had to have her. Maybe that's why he'd kept her, couldn't dispose of her like the other girls. Two of them he'd buried in the courtyard he allowed Summer to look out over.

It amused him that she sought out this haven. A graveyard, in effect. The bodies were buried in shallow graves at the far corner, where a wide border had been left, presumably for planting herbs or flowers. The earth was soft. Not as soft as he'd wished. Which was why the graves were shallow. Not so shallow scavengers could get at them. He'd managed to pile some fallen stones from the wall on top, to hopefully keep any rats away.

Three it was going to have to be. Though whether the third made it to the courtyard he wasn't sure. He just needed to find her before she caused any more harm.

Stupid girl.

The anger wasn't just directed at her, but himself too. He was the one who'd left the key in her cell door. A mistake he'd never made before, but in his favour, he had been truly distracted by other matters.

As soon as he'd arrived back home, his real home, he'd realised his error, considered whether to dash back. It was hardly a dash. The round trip would have cost him almost three hours. Three hours he couldn't afford. And that was all dependent on traffic.

He'd closed his eyes, envisaged the key and then dismissed the thought. He'd had more faith.

Skinny little Summer wasn't about to disobey him. There was no backbone in her.

His jaw clenched, making a clicking sound in his ear.

If that was the case, how had Lilijana managed to open the door with the key on the outside? It was the only way. He couldn't imagine any other scenario. Was Summer even aware of the existence of Lilijana? He didn't think so. She was barely aware of his presence these days.

He huffed out as he gave it some thought.

It wasn't easy, but the locks were so old. Ancient. All she had to do, if he thought about it, was use something to push the key out the other side and slip her hand through the gap between the floor and the door, retrieve the key and open the door from the inside.

Really easy. Shame he'd not considered that before. None of the other girls had ever escaped. Summer had never managed to. Maybe hers was the more secure room. He allowed her fewer possessions in there, although he'd noticed in the last year or so, she'd sneaked a few down. It was of no matter to him. She could hardly do any damage with a small snow globe and a miniature Buddha. She didn't even have the gall to try.

After Charlotte, he'd tried to make the second room more inviting. Poor, dear Charlotte. She'd perished. Weak and wan, when he'd flushed the baby from her womb, she'd simply given in, given up, refused to eat and drink and lay on her bed, her face to the rock wall.

The slow drip, drip, drip of blood hadn't been from the abortion he gave her, but from the deep gashes, elbow to wrist, she'd inflicted on herself.

At first the shock had numbed him. He'd not expected that from her.

Where she'd got the knife he had no idea. Except the last time he recalled seeing the short, sharp paring knife was when he'd sliced the bonds from her wrists the night he'd brought her there. He'd assumed he'd stashed it back on top of the cupboard in the kitchen out of reach. Out of sight.

Evidently not.

Still, it could hardly be considered his fault. She'd made the choice to use it on herself.

There was nothing he could do to help that kind of stupid.

Lilijana was a whole different matter. Too tough, too feisty. Too determined. His biggest regret was snatching her.

She *could* have opened the door herself.

He narrowed his eyes. Except there wasn't anything in the cave long and narrow to poke through that keyhole. Was there?

He scrolled through his memory, checking out what had almost been a barren room. A room he'd only added soft furnishings to.

He'd hefted the blood-soaked mattress out after Charlotte had died and flung it down the side of the cliff, watching while the vegetation swallowed it up. He wanted nothing to do with it. The smell of blood and death. No one would ever find it down there. There wasn't a likelihood of hikers up there as there were no footpaths and no livestock on this side of the pass.

Once rid of the evidence, he'd furnished the room with a new mattress, and cheerful flowery bedding from a charity shop, together with a lightweight battery-powered lamp, nothing they could use as a weapon.

Perhaps that had been his mistake. When Charlotte took her own life, he'd thought it might pay to make the room more homely.

Summer's room was fine. Just fine! She never protested. Never asked for more.

Lilijana had never stopped whining.

When he got her back, he was going to thrash the truth from her about how she escaped, because deep down he knew she'd not achieved that alone.

He crossed his arms over his chest, leaned against the thick-waisted oak tree and waited, waited. Interminably waited. But he was so sure she would come back to the squat he'd picked her up from in the first place, only three months before. If for nothing else but to retrieve her belongings she'd stashed there. He was fairly sure she knew nothing about how long he'd stalked her, but once she'd served him in that corner shop he sometimes called in at, her card was marked.

She was so like Summer in demeanour, if not looks. Or Summer's demeanour had been before she'd virtually given up. Or so he'd thought. Turned out he'd been so wrong about that. On both counts.

He'd had to have Lilijana.

It wasn't his usual modus operandi. Maybe that was his mistake. A mistake he'd not make again. He'd not got to know her, to assess her character, her strengths, her weaknesses. Not befriended her through social media, nor gained her trust, so it had all come as a total shock when he'd made his move.

The conversations they'd had were brief and he'd thought that was enough. New to the UK, she'd moved here leaving her family behind to join her boyfriend and work for the company he owned.

Only the boyfriend was married, and the company was never his. It was a load of bollocks, this whole on-line dating and friend-ship. Did people never learn?

She was living hand to mouth in a squat with other illegal immigrants until she could find genuine work with a real work permit. In the meantime, she worked for cash in the corner shop, too ashamed of the circumstances to let her family know. A family who might well have clubbed together the air fare to get her back home.

Pride had stopped her.

Poor pitiful girl.

Only she hadn't been pitiful. More pit bull.

He'd not known that when he'd lured her with the promise of decent work, a roof over her head and food in her belly.

It seemed her idea and his weren't the same.

He raised his head and breathed in like a wolf sniffing his prey.

The soft scent of her reached him before his eyes focused on her form, hesitant in the shadows.

With a grim smile, he gave her a moment to slip inside the empty squat. He'd left her belongings there when he'd checked earlier. He'd needed to know if she'd left her passport behind because she'd not had it when he'd taken her. Now he knew for sure she had. It was tucked inside the inner pocket in a threadbare jacket. That and a small amount of cash she'd rolled up in a pair of holey socks, a thin bedding roll and a few clothes. Now, he'd let her load them up, so she was slowed down by the weight of them.

He pushed away from the tree trunk and crept, unseen, down the side of the dilapidated bungalow with half the roof missing, causing the other squatters to move out since the last time he was there.

He paused, his back against the wall. While he waited, he tugged on blue nitrile gloves he'd obtained from work.

The place was a hazard. When he'd checked inside earlier, he'd barely been able to stay for more than a couple of minutes, the stench of raw sewage and abandoned weed filled the small kitchen. The living room, where the hole gaped wide at the night sky, sat in a shallow flood from rainwater that had poured through.

He'd been reluctant to go any further, but he knew where she kept her belongings. Surprised they were still there, under the fall-out, he backed out and waited. And waited. Strange none of the others had taken them when they'd fled. Perhaps the roof had collapsed on top of them and in their rush to get out no one noticed. It must have been soon after Lilijana had disappeared.

Even the homeless had a code. They never normally took one of their own's possessions. Not straight away, at least. He'd have expected one of them at least to return, but evidently they'd not discovered her stash under the broken roof tiles and thick layers of dust.

Still, he waited, but at least now he knew she'd returned.

It briefly crossed his mind to consider where she'd got the burner phone she must have used, but then many of the homeless knew each other by sight if not name and they bummed all sorts from each other. Shared their last.

A quiet shuffle and low grunt warned him that she was there. He stood, stock still, breath held as her booted foot appeared and she slithered out over the low windowsill, cautious enough to avoid the jagged glass poking out from the frame.

With her back to him, she paused, hitched the heavy backpack onto one shoulder and stepped forward.

He leapt at her, snatched the backpack so she fell backwards into him, her slender body no competition for his strength.

He snaked one arm around her waist and slapped the other hand with the chloroform-laced cloth over her mouth. She reared back, her skull snapping close to his face, but he'd learnt that one early on and ducked his head so the impact slanted off his ear. She ripped at his hand, long nails gouging through the thin nitrile gloves he'd pulled on, ripping through to peel the skin from the back of his hand.

Yowling, he snatched his hand away and dropped the small cloth on the ground.

Fury pounded through his veins, setting them alight. As she made a move to break free, he snatched at her hair and yanked so she fell back against his chest. This time he smacked his hand over her mouth and squeezed her nose hard with his thumb and forefinger.

Manoeuvring to get a better hold, his hand released its grip on her.

In the almost silent battle, but for the sound of his own breath, she wriggled from his grasp, slipping her shoulder out of the back pack strap, she whipped around to face him. She rammed the back pack at him and, as he staggered back, his arms pinwheeled to gain balance. She snatched the backpack away again, threw the strap across her body, spun around and took off at a sprint like a gazelle being chased by a lion.

Like the gazelle, she stood little chance as he bore down on her in a heavy rugby tackle to the ground. The loud crack of a branch snapping filled the night air, and he froze, his body sprawled on top of her inert one.

Blood pounded through his ears, making him deaf to all but that rapid flow of gushing liquid.

Winded, he paused a moment before he pushed himself free and kneeled beside her.

'Lilijana?' The whisper rasped from his dry throat. 'Lilijana?'

He reached around and pressed two fingers to the side of her throat and felt nothing. No pulse. He flipped her body over and those pretty hazel eyes stared sightlessly up at him. He choked on his own horror. He'd killed her. Broken her neck. He'd not meant to. Not this time. He'd done it again.

He came to his feet, a slow, cautious move before he took a step back, and then another. He paused.

How could this happen? He'd barely touched her. The weight of his own body slamming down on her legs hadn't done it. He looked at the backpack. The shoulder strap slashed across her throat.

With a step forward, he stood straighter. Blew out a breath.

It wasn't his fault. It was the backpack. If she hadn't slung it around her neck, she'd still be alive. He studied the strange angle of her head. Her neck had been snapped.

He came closer, until his toes almost touched her side, his gaze skimming over the backpack. Where was the phone? Should he look? He wore gloves he'd grabbed from work in a panic as he'd not thought about his leather ones in the finer weather, but she'd ripped the thin nitrile ones, and small beads of blood oozed from the back of his hand. He didn't want to risk any kind of DNA being picked up.

He'd already handled her. Grappled with her. His blood could be all over her clothes. Once more wouldn't make a difference.

He reached out and coaxed the backpack from her motionless body, letting her arm flop back onto the ground.

His eyes narrowed.

With the backpack in his hands, LJ leaned closer and scanned Lilijana's inner arm. The one with smudged black charcoal numbers inscribed the length of it from elbow to wrist.

'Shit!'

'Lilijana?'

LJ's head reared up and fear shot through his veins as he leapt to his feet.

'Lilijana? Where you gone, girl?' The unfamiliar voice echoed in the darkness and LJ hugged the backpack to him as he stepped into the shadows, heart racing in fear of discovery.

Lilijana wasn't supposed to know anyone. Not well. Not well enough for them to come looking for her.

Was this the boyfriend she'd spoken of previously? Had she run to him in desperation?

LJ melted into the tree line and waited as a tall black man rounded the corner of the bungalow, his bald head shiny in the moonlight. Whoever the hell he was, LJ wasn't about to stick around and take him on. As his dad used to say, the guy was built like a brick shithouse.

The moment the guy moved forward, distracted by the

discovery of Lilijana's body, was the moment LJ turned and sprinted through the small copse of trees as silently as possible, the backpack clutched to his chest.

Wheezing by the time he emerged on the other side, he stopped to take in great gulps of air. Sweat trickled down his spine and dampened the thinning hair at his temples.

He patted his trouser pocket, relieved to feel the rattle of keys as he approached his car. He glanced both ways, then reached for the door handle, hoping like hell he wasn't followed.

'Excuse me, mate.'

LJ whirled around at the deep timbre of the voice, fear taking a firm hold on his throat as he faced the man who approached him with a long stride.

26

'I can't believe you lot. When the hell will you respect other people's property?'

LJ squinted at the man in front of him. Built like a boxer with a backpack slung over one shoulder, he wasn't someone LJ wanted to take on. He wasn't the black guy. This one had small eyes and a big chin. Same height as LJ but square. Solid. The type who wouldn't think twice about landing a punch by the look of him.

LJ didn't need that. His face already throbbed like a bitch from where Lilijana had reared her head back. He thought initially he'd avoided the blow, but now his adrenaline had taken a dive, the aches and pains were starting to make themselves apparent.

This guy hadn't followed him from the squat. Chased him. No, he was someone else.

'What the fuck are you talking about?'

The guy flinched. Took a step back. Maybe with his size he wasn't used to people challenging his aggression. But LJ had had enough. He wasn't prepared to give way.

'You've parked over my drive.'

LJ ran a quick check over his vehicle. The back end jutted across the drive of a large, imposing house. Blank windows reflected a twinkle of light from the streetlamp.

LJ spread his arms and shrugged. 'I've not been long. You can hardly whine about it, mate. I mean who needs access to their drives at this time of the fucking morning?'

'Shift-workers, you thick shit. Me! I've just got off a twelve-hour shift and I want to get into my drive.' He pointed way down the street to some anonymous car that LJ supposed he was meant to recognise. 'I've had to park all the way at the end of my own fucking road and walk.'

LJ couldn't give a damn. Did he think he was hard done by just because someone had made it difficult to get into his drive? 'You do know you could get a double decker bus through that gap, don't you, mate?'

Shock registered on the guy's face as LJ stepped around him, clicking the key fob, so the locks disengaged on his own car.

'I don't want to damage my car.' The guy's voice turned from aggressive to more conciliatory, but LJ wasn't in the mood. That veil of red mist still hovered on the periphery of his vision.

He didn't have the time or patience for this shit.

He swung the car door open. 'Not my problem, mate.'

He edged into the driver's seat and leaned over to pull the door shut behind him.

He never saw the fist that ploughed into his face, but his head snapped back, smacking against the edge of the headrest, and his breath whooshed from his body. The door slammed shut against his hand, so his fingers gave a protesting crunch and LJ sat momentarily stunned, watching through his driver's mirror as the man strode down the street in the direction of his car. Obviously with the intention of moving it onto his drive once LJ moved.

Fury grabbed LJ by the throat, and he reached for the door handle. He edged the door open and turned just as a tall black guy with a shiny bald head stepped from behind a van on the opposite side of the road, evidently in hot pursuit of Lilijana's attacker.

His voice boomed along the street and the other guy ground to a halt, almost opposite. The only other guy in the street, because who else would you find out there, other than a fucking shift-worker who'd just finished a twelve-hour shift?

As the bald guy loped across the road, LJ edged his door closed, hit the start button on his pale grey Lexus RX and the hybrid engine engaged the silent mode.

Headlights off, LJ inched his car from the kerb and crawled up the street away from the two men, just as the bald one threw the first punch, evidently mistaking the other man for whoever he'd been pursuing through the copse.

Sirens whined in the distance and blue lit up the sky as LJ turned right out of the road and headed in the opposite direction.

A thin smile curled up at the edges of his swollen mouth at the irony.

27

Something has me shooting upright. The light duvet slips down to my waist as I wait for my eyes to become accustomed to the dark, all the time listening for the slightest noise.

I tilt my head, straining to hear any muffled sound.

Has LJ returned? Was that what disturbed me?

I wait, holding my breath in the silence. And it was more silent than ever, dense and heavy, if there could be such a thing.

I mourn Lilijana's absence, but I know it's for the best. She couldn't stay. Not once she knew what was to become of her when he found out she'd not taken the tea he'd brought her. Even if he believed she'd taken it and it hadn't worked. There would be a far harsher outcome.

It was also for the best that I never left. I can't imagine a life without LJ, a life outside, of freedom.

It's no longer freedom to me, but the horror of the unknown.

I shudder at the thought of stepping outside the front door. When Lilijana stood on the doorstep begging me to go with her, all I could do was stare down the long dirt track that led into the endless forest which surrounds the place.

My chest had tightened so much, I could barely breathe, barely move from where I hung onto the door frame.

Now, I wish I'd gone.

It's too late. Far too late.

I swing my legs off the bed and pause before pushing to my feet as a wave of nausea floods through me. Is it just the thought of being alone again? Because I am completely alone. Definitely no other sound but that of my own heartbeat.

I remember now what woke me.

The key.

I'd left the key on the outside of Lilijana's cell door when I released her.

Which meant LJ would know for sure that I was the one who let Lilijana free. I was to blame, and I couldn't even imagine the horror of repercussions once he found out. And he would find out, the moment he checked the door.

As I stand there, my head reels with dizziness until I get my bearings. I wonder if LJ put drugs in any of the food I've eaten. He's not done that for years, but I remember that feeling of being off-kilter. I can't imagine why he would, unless he'd meant it for Lilijana.

I raise my hand to my forehead, but there's no temperature, just a sluggish feel which I push determinedly to one side.

I sneak to my own cell door and prise it open with the tips of my fingers. He rarely locks it these days. He trusts me.

Instinct tells me he isn't home as I sneak along the dark hallway, which corners at the end before revealing a second door. A door it had taken me several years to be brave enough to approach.

I reach out, take the large key with the ornate brass bow at the end and slip it from the lock.

My mouth is completely dry. I've never disobeyed LJ in years. Not years. I'm docile these days, my feelings almost dead. Almost.

There's an unfamiliar flutter of something akin to excitement in my stomach. In helping Lilijana escape, I've defied LJ.

It feels good.

I push the door wide and step inside Lilijana's cell and draw in a shocked breath as I allow myself another little slip of feeling. What is that? Jealousy? Anger?

I'm not quite sure.

I cruise my gaze over the entire room.

It's so completely different from mine. I'd not noticed when I released her, not looked in as she stumbled out and she dragged me up the stairs to the front door. I've certainly never dared enter before.

The bed at the far side of the small cave-like room is far nicer than mine. A stab of jealousy swims through me. The covers are relatively new, not faded and dusty like mine, but certainly clean as they're the ones I washed just two days ago. I've always assumed LJ gets me to do his washing and takes it away to wherever he lives his secret life away from me. I see now it isn't his. That jars with me. Stings a little.

I've been used and I don't like it. Not one bit.

This time I recognise it. The emotion. A small flame of annoyance ignites.

How dare he treat me less favourably than the others? Am I the only stupid creature?

I didn't expect to find I'd been playing maid to his other resident. One, like the others, who wouldn't have lasted long. Only Lilijana escaped. Charlotte took her own life.

I'm not so sure about the other one. Only one, I think.

Initially, I barely even knew they existed. Apart from the odd sound, scraping, or distant sobbing.

After Charlotte I had never wanted to come along to this room again. It had been too painful and the self-recriminations had stopped me. Like I could have helped her. Stopped her.

I may have wandered the house and courtyard, but I'd gone into hiding in the true sense. Hiding my emotions.

I turn in a slow circle. The room is a mini paradise. In comparison to mine, that is. Perhaps if I lived a normal life, this wouldn't be that great. I envy them the window on the same side as mine. Lower down and so much bigger. Heavy vertical steel bars are there to prevent escape.

My head gives a little jerk and my shoulders spasm. How come I don't have such a big window? One that I can see through.

My whole body tremors as though I have cramp as I make my way towards a window that looks out onto a vista I've not seen before. Instead of the bright verdant valley dropping away beneath the house I see from the lounge windows, this view is of rolling hills, gently sloping into the dappled blue and grey distance, where cultivated fields flow in silver moonlight.

'Summer.' I hear my name and wrap my fingers around two bars, pressing my face between. Beams of moonlight reflect off the bright citric yellow of a field of rape and I hear the voice again. 'Summer.'

A smile curves my lips.

I'm not sure how long I stand there, but when a cloud scuds over the moon and the brilliance of the field dims, I step back, realising it was only my imagination.

I rub my fingers against the smooth indentation lines across my icy cheeks and I know it must have been a considerable time.

I turn my back and look once again at the room. So much nicer than mine.

A vague memory of my shared bedroom from years ago inches its way into my mind, but I blink it away. It's no good having lovely memories, all they do is torture me.

Time has meandered by and while normally it would mean nothing, I know as I walk to the door that I risk being found for every moment longer that I stay.

I push the key deep into the lock on the inside of the room and walk out, leaving the door wide open. Walk away.

Beneath all the deadness I feel, there's a bubble of fury building, just about to burst.

28

SUNDAY, 21 MAY 2023, 10.25 A.M.

The day after the wedding

Heat exploded from her as Skye struggled to get free. The oppressive weight pinned her down as she clawed her way from the depths of her dream.

Summer's tinkling laughter followed her up. 'Skye. I'm here. Come and find me. I'm here.'

Terror punched through her as she wrestled to throw off the weight of the body pressing her into the soft mattress as the events of the previous night flooded in.

'Lie still, would you, for goodness' sake.'

At the sound of Jade's sharp voice, Skye stopped struggling and lay panting. 'I'm too hot.'

'I'm not surprised. Look at Cleo.'

Skye squinted out of narrowed eyes. The dog lay the full length of her side, pinning her beneath the duvet so no air could get in. Skye wriggled to get her arm free just as Cleo raised her head and then belly-squirmed closer. Her wet black nose poked at Skye's ear as she let out a contented groan.

Less than content herself, Skye gazed at her younger sister, who stood above her, a frown creasing her brow.

'I feel dreadful.' Skye writhed until she broke free of the cover and then propped herself up against the headboard as Jade handed her a glass of bubbling, fizzing white liquid.

'What...?'

'Andrews Liver Salts.'

'Yum.'

'It'll make you feel better.'

'Nothing will make me feel better. Ever. I feel dreadful that I spoilt Dad's wedding.'

'You didn't. They never even knew we left. I messaged Dad a bit later to say sorry we'd left without saying goodbye. He said he hadn't realised. I gave that bloody barman a fiver and he never even did what I asked.'

'A fiver was hardly the height of generosity, now, was it?' Despite herself, Skye let out a rough chuckle and then fell silent as she swallowed down the concoction.

'Ah, dear. I've never felt so dreadful.' She handed the glass to her sister and then shuffled Cleo over so Jade could edge onto the bed next to her. Jade lowered herself against the headboard and leaned her shoulder against Skye's.

'It's Jacob I feel sorry for.'

As the memory rushed in, Skye closed her eyes and groaned. 'Oh, no. How is he?'

'I don't know, I've not heard from him since he left.'

'He left? I thought he was going to sleep on the sofa.'

'No. I think it was all too much for him.'

Jade's lips twisted.

'What?'

'Well, after you embarrassingly tried to take his trousers off him...'

'I only wanted to put them in the washing machine.' The vague memory made her squirm with mortification.

'You were grappling with him. It was embarrassing. The man looked horrified.'

Skye put her hand over her mouth, shaking her head. 'No, I was just...'

'Well, whatever you were "just", you frightened poor Jacob away. Just as you decided to black out, he took off down the road at quite a nifty trot. Said he was happy to walk it.'

'How far?'

Jade shrugged. 'To be honest, I don't know where he lives. He's Dad's partner, not exactly my bosom buddy.'

Another soft groan slid from Skye's lips. 'Oh, no. I just assaulted Dad's partner. The poor man.'

'You didn't exactly assault him. More like terrified him to death.'

Skye closed her eyes. 'It could have been worse.'

There was a silence and Skye cringed as she opened one eye to stare at Jade. 'Was it worse?'

'Could have been worse if he hadn't been here when you passed out.'

'Oh, no. Please tell me he didn't carry me up to bed.'

'No chance. I had to do all that myself. I stripped you and put you in the shower first, scrubbed the puke out of your hair. I don't think you can wear that dress again. It's ruined, I think you put your foot through the bottom seam, and the waist split wide open. The bodice parted company with the skirt. I saw your granny knickers. Very nice. Good job you were wearing them. Jacob thought so too, which is probably why he decided he'd leave me to it.'

'What a nightmare. I thought you said I'd blacked out.' She could only be grateful she had. Humiliated, she flopped her head into her open hands.

'You had. Between trying to rip the trousers off Jacob—' Jade let out an indelicate snort of laughter '—and getting you upstairs. I managed to rouse you enough to get you in the shower. I'm not sure you were entirely dry when you stumbled into bed, but I put a towel on your pillow so your hair would dry and not soak through, hopefully.'

Skye slid her hand under her head and felt the rougher material of a hand towel she'd not noticed. Her hair was going to look like she'd been pulled through a hedge backwards. 'So, what could be worse than Jacob seeing my knickers and witnessing my truly embarrassing demise?'

'Before all of this,' Jade waved her hand around, 'Jordon pitched up.'

Skye gasped, her hand going to her chest. She narrowed her eyes and tried to grasp onto a memory, any memory of him being there and came up against a blank canvass.

'Yeah.' Her sister gave a slow nod. 'He was pretty much the worse for wear himself.'

'Ah, shit.'

'Puke, actually.'

'Did he see me?' In all her humiliating glory, ripped dress, pukey hair, make-up more than likely smeared down her face.

'Oh, yeah. And then he took a pop at Jacob, who was just stepping out of the door, because he claimed Jacob must have attacked you. Said he'd never seen you in that kind of state in all the time he's known you. Christ, he really kicked off.'

Skye frowned, a horrible suspicion starting to form. 'How do I not remember this? I mean, really it's a total blank.' She shook her head. 'I can't even... there's not an inkling of memory.' A small spasm took hold of her body and she clenched against the desire to puke all over again.

'You were flaked out on the bottom step, leaning against the wall. You had your eyes open. Basically, the lights were on but there was nobody home.'

'Was Jacob all right? Did he get hurt?' This was even worse than she could have imagined. The poor guy roped into her domestic.

'Jacob smacked Jordon in the nose and told him to fuck off.'

'What?'

'I know. Who'd have thunk it? Dressed to the nines and licenced to kill.' Jade snorted out an evil laugh. 'Honestly, I have nothing but admiration for the man. Jacob stepped forward, smack...' She tapped the heel of her hand. 'Straight under Jordon's nose. Blood fucking everywhere. It was like *John Wick*.' She gurgled out a laugh. 'Wish he'd been around to sort Luke out earlier in the evening.'

Skye didn't feel the same way as her stomach lurched to remind her of the previous night's abuse. 'Oh, no. Blood as well to clean up.'

'No. Not unless you want to wash the doorstep down. There are only a few spots. Jacob handed him his white hanky, spun him around and pushed him down the path. Then off he trotted himself. He yelled over his shoulder that he'd check on us today.'

'Why?'

'Because Dad and Martha were off on their honeymoon first thing this morning, and no one wanted to spoil their trip.'

Skye nodded in agreement. 'Poor Jacob. Poor Jordon.'

'Nothing poor about Jacob. The guy's a hero.'

'Except the puke up his trousers and over his shoes.'

'Yeah, that. But Jordon got everything he deserved.'

'Maybe. But he was right about one thing, I don't normally get wasted like that. I know how much to drink. I had quite a bit throughout the day, but I never had that much. I never felt the effects of it until... until just before you arrived in the bar.'

'What are you saying?'

Skye rolled towards her sister so she could look her straight in the eye. 'I'm saying I think someone spiked my drink last night.'

29

It's cold down here but I'm not sure I want to go back upstairs.

LJ has returned. I know he has. I can feel it in the stir of the air. The odd weight of cruel anger.

Do I want to face him? Risk his wrath at finding me here.

Where else should he find me?

On silent feet, I steal upstairs and hover at the kitchen door.

Back to me, LJ stares out of the kitchen window into the small courtyard. There's a black bin liner on the drainer and it looks pretty full. His hands press hard onto the kitchen surface, either side of the sink. His knuckles are white.

Can he still be angry about Lilijana escaping? His anger can go on for days, I should know.

He can't be angry with me. He doesn't know I had anything to do with it.

'What the fuck do you want?'

The gravel in his voice has me hesitating at the door. I'm not sure whether to step inside the kitchen or scuttle off back to my room.

'Stop hovering,' he snarls, and before I manage to move, he whips around to face me.

I gasp.

One side of his face is fat and swollen, with a bloodshot eye and a split lip. I've never seen LJ this way. Even after Charlotte caught him with her fists. That was a small swelling, a purple bruise on his cheekbone. Nothing compared to this.

There's a part of me that wants to rush to him. Touch his face. Check his injuries. That's my inner tortured, beaten self. The part of me that's been educated to respond that way. To sympathise with him.

The other part of me is filled with glee. Someone got him. Damaged him. Hurt him. For a change. Maybe there is hope. Now he knows what it's like to be on the receiving end.

Who could it have been?

'She's dead.'

The flat statement has me reeling. I crumple against the door frame, knowing all the time that I'm not supposed to know who 'she' is. Not supposed to know of her existence.

'Who?' I try to remain deadpan, keeping my gaze just below his so he doesn't look into my eyes and see the truth. I stare at his chin, the purpled outline of a bruise developing.

'Lilijana.'

I reel at the name. My stomach churns, but I stop myself from crying out.

'The woman in the room next to yours.'

Without conscious thought, my gaze flicks up to meet his and locks on.

'Don't deny you knew her. Stupid.'

Knew. Not know. So, it's true. She's dead. The only way he could know that is if he killed her. I know it's selfish of me, and I do mourn her death, but something more ominous occupies my mind.

It means my message won't have got through. No one will eve[r] know I'm here.

The flicker of anticipation I'd held in my heart extinguishes.

I couldn't go with her then, but I know more now. If I'd know[n] then what I have subsequently discovered, would I have gone with her? I think I might have.

I say nothing because what is there to say? It's not the first time I'm sure it won't be the last. Perhaps I'll be next. Who knows? There's a part of me almost wishes I was next. That it would be over.

There was another hidden part, shy and reticent with a tiny spark of hope.

Lilijana gave me that.

And then he snuffed it out again.

All that effort, the risk we'd both taken and for what? She is now dead, and I haven't moved any further forward.

I thought she was going to be my saviour. To let them know where I was when I never had the courage to save myself. She'd not wanted to go to the police. She wasn't officially in the country. She lived in a squat, but she was going to get her things and go back home. A home she'd thought was bad. Until she came to the UK and discovered how much worse it could be. The grass is always greener... or so I'd thought, in any case. Many of us must think that. Until we're beaten by the wrongness of it all.

'How do you know?' There's a part of me that wants to know where we went wrong. How he knows I was involved.

He snorts and dabs the back of his hand against his split lip to smudge off a pearl of blood that formed when he grimaced. I can only pray she was the one who gave him a good thrashing before she died. That she didn't make it easy. She wasn't the type. She still had the fire in her belly at the time she escaped. Unlike me. My fire is extinguished.

Or is it?

I drop my gaze again so he can't see it. That light. That desire.

If she did it, I can too. Only she ended up dead. Will I as well?

'The telephone number you etched on the inside of her arm.'

My blood goes cold.

'Only you could have done that. Lilijana didn't have access to your charcoal. Your reward.'

'Maybe she…'

'No.' He holds up one finger and the threat stops me in my tracks.

He knows. Without doubt. 'She was left-handed. You wrote it on the inside of her left arm. She would have written it on the right arm, with her left hand.'

He runs his tongue over his teeth, and I wonder how hard he was hit. Are his teeth loose? The devil inside of me wants to see him spit one out.

The idea does nothing more than give me a little jolt of pleasure, but my main concern is Lilijana. I'm not allowed to ask questions, so I wait. And I wait.

LJ draws in a deep breath and then reaches for the black bin liner. He throws it at me, and I catch it, letting out a loud 'whoof' as the soft package is heavier than I thought.

'Get those washed. They need to be drip dried.'

He frowns as he looks out the window, up at the heavy clouds in the sky. I think he may change his mind, but instead he walks past me into the living room. Dismisses me from his mind.

I'm left all alone with nothing more than a bag of dirty clothes and my thoughts.

What did he do to Lilijana? How did he murder her?

Will there be blood stains on the clothes? Did he stab her? Strangle her?

I don't want to look too closely, so I slip the darks into the washing machine separate from the lights. Just as Mum taught me.

My breath catches in my throat.

I've not thought of my mum for such a long time. Why now?

Maybe that lick of optimism hasn't been altogether smothered.

I place a washing tab inside the drum and shut the drawer after adding a small amount of conditioner, trying to rid myself of every thought that swirls around my normally dull, empty head. I touch the buttons to programme it, set the spin to zero. I press the button to turn the old washing machine on.

I chew at my bottom lip as the washing machine clicks on and water rushes in. In the same way it seems to have rushed into my head as I stare out the window.

My reflection gazes back. The old me. The beautiful me with lush hair and bright eyes, a soft mouth curved into a gentle smile.

I blink and the image fades until I stare at a washed-out version and know that wasn't me looking back. It was my twin. Skye.

For the first time in years, I actually want to go home.

Tears fill my eyes to blur my vision and I let memories seep in. Memories I've squelched underfoot for all too long.

30

SUNDAY, 21 MAY 2023, 11.20 A.M.

The day after the wedding

Pain sliced through her head as Skye accepted two paracetamol and another glass of water from Jade.

'You can't be serious. Who would do such a thing?'

Skye swallowed down the pills with several gulps of water. She handed the glass back to her sister and flopped one hand onto Cleo's shoulder while she raised the other to her forehead.

Pain throbbed through her head and the nausea still hovered in a tight ball in her stomach. 'I didn't overdo it, Jade. There was nothing wrong with me, and then there was.'

'Maybe the fresh air...'

'It was before that.'

'Are you saying Jacob spiked your drink?' Disbelief creased Jade's face.

'Oh, God, no.' Skye rubbed her forehead as the effects of the liver salts and paracetamol started to take combined effect. 'Jacob never touched my drink. The barman served it directly to me.'

'So, the barman roofied you?'

Skye blew out a breath. 'I've no idea. How long does it take for these drugs to kick in? Because I actually felt like I'd been hit by a roller coaster in full flight. It was instant.' She glanced sideways at her sister. 'I mean, Jade, you know what uni is like. I spent the first few weeks off my head drunk.' She left it unsaid that the moment Summer had disappeared, she'd sobered up and barely touched alcohol since. The occasional couple of glasses of wine were her limit. It was about control, and she needed to be in control. 'We knew what we were doing was all a bit reckless, but I never left my glass unattended. I never gave anyone the opportunity to spike my drink at uni dos.'

'That's different. You need to protect yourself under those circumstances, we've all been taught that, but we knew everyone last night. Even if some only vaguely. Surely no one at a wedding function would spike a guest's drink?'

'Why not?' Skye scrubbed her fingers through Cleo's thick neck fur. 'There's far more opportunity. I left my drink unattended so many times. I nipped to the loo. I was up on the dance floor.' Albeit briefly, but she left that out.

'So, you're saying it could be anyone from the wedding party? Or the waiting staff?'

'Yeah.'

'But why?'

A shudder ran through Skye as though her veins were running cold, and her nerve endings tingled with a thousand ants dashing over her skin. A spasm clenched her stomach and Skye curled her knees upwards. 'Why does anyone spike a drink?'

'Because they're sickos and they have something they want to achieve.'

'Precisely that.'

'Rape.'

She held her sister's gaze. 'Only I was safe because you and acob looked after me and made sure I got home. If you hadn't, I don't know what would have happened.' She pressed her fingertips into her eyes. 'Oh, I feel so ill.'

'We should inform the police.'

'What can they do about it?' Skye couldn't even look at her sister as her head swirled and her eyes felt like red-hot pokers were being drilled into the sockets.

'Surely they can give you a blood test. Find out if you were drugged?'

'Isn't it too late?'

'I don't know. Dad would know.'

Skye dropped her hands from her face and, despite the pain, pinned her younger sister with an iron stare. 'We're not telling Dad.'

'Perhaps we should.' Jade's voice shook with concern.

'No. Nothing happened. I'm perfectly safe. It was probably just a random idiot, an opportunist, trying to make me look like a fool, and it didn't work.'

'Or a real creep who was about to rape you.'

Skye shuddered and Cleo belly-crawled up the bed until her face was on the pillow next to Skye's. 'It's okay, girl. You would have looked after me.'

'Not if it was your ex, she wouldn't.'

'Jordon?' Skye squinted at her sister. 'Jordon wouldn't do that.'

'From what I saw last night, he was quite ready to assault you.'

Shock trickled through her. 'No, but...' His messages had been quite vicious, threatening.

'But what? How did he know what time you'd be back? Did he follow us? Had he been in the venue?'

'I didn't see him there, but then...' He'd said he was going to turn up at the venue. She needed to read her messages once she could see straight. Check exactly what he had said. She rubbed the frown wrinkles from her forehead. Surely he wouldn't have. There

was a vague recollection that he'd threatened to come around to th
house.

'Exactly!' Jade pointed at her, almost touching her nose, as i
she'd read her mind. 'What if he was so desperate to get you back
he arranged to roofie you, bring you back here and then this morn
ing, hey presto, he's back in your bed with you. All nice and
snuggly.'

'Only it didn't work, because you and Jacob looked after me.'

'Yeah. What if we hadn't been to hand, though? What if the
thieving barman is a friend of his? What if you'd got a taxi home on
your own?'

Skye huffed out and Cleo wriggled onto her back, giving Skye
free access to a tummy scratch like she was the one who deserved
comfort.

'It doesn't bear thinking about.'

'I think you should think about it. If we're not going to let Dad
know, then the next best thing is to call the police.'

'The police? Don't be dramatic, Jade. What can they do?'

'They could stop it happening again. If no one reported these
things, then nothing would ever get done.'

'I don't want to.'

'Don't be churlish.'

'Churlish?' Skye snorted out a laugh. 'Where did you pick that
word up from?'

Jade clamped her mouth closed.

'Jade!' Skye shot her a look filled with suspicion. 'Where did you
hear that word?' It wasn't one Skye recalled in their family vocabu-
lary. There was a hint of the old-fashioned to it that didn't jibe with
Jade's normal speech patterns. Old-fashioned. An edge of supercil-
iousness.

Her sister's ears started to glow a dark red. 'One of my lecturers
uses it. It's quite descriptive.'

'Pompous.'

'No. I don't think so.'

'Do you have a crush on him?'

'No. Yes. Oh, I don't know.' Jade wriggled off the bed and came to her feet, clearly annoyed. 'You're just changing the subject. I'll go and get a pot and you can pee in it.'

'What? What the hell for?'

'So we can take it to the police.'

Skye paused halfway through lifting the cover for her to scoot out without disturbing Cleo. 'Why would we do that? Nothing happened.'

'Someone spiked your drink.'

'But no harm came to me.'

Jade sighed and flumped back down onto the edge of the bed, almost bouncing her older sister off. She raised her hand and cupped Skye's cheek. 'We need to know if your drink was spiked. If it was, was it meant for you, or was it purely some idiot, like Luke, who thought it might be hilarious to see someone off their head?'

Skye drew in a long breath, her fingers going to lips that still felt strangely numb. She blinked as the memory rushed in. Her hand reaching across the table...

'I drank your Prosecco.'

Shock registered on her sister's face. 'What?'

Skye forced her mind to wind back to the previous evening when her memory hadn't been covered by a black cloud. 'There was no more Prosecco left in the bottle, so I leaned over and nabbed your drink. It was almost full. I knew you wouldn't mind. You were off having fun.'

She didn't mean it to sound accusatory, but that's how it came out. Jade had been having fun with Luke, and Skye had been all alone at the table. The injustice of it only now hit her while her defences were down. Jade had been the one to make all the fuss about their dad remarrying and yet she was the one who'd cele-brated hard while Skye had worked to make the event a success.

She stared down the length of her body. Look at her now. Barely able to move unless she wanted to throw up again. But perhaps the roofie hadn't been meant for her, but her sister.

Fear stabbed through her. She couldn't bear the thought of Jade being hurt. They might have fallen out over the wedding, but they weren't normally ones to squabble with each other. If anything, since Summer had disappeared, the pair of them had been close. Closer than before. Skye could be a little overprotective of her younger sister, but that wasn't unusual. Especially under the circumstances.

'So, Luke did it?'

Skye looked sideways at her sister. 'You really think it was Luke? I can't imagine he'd do that. That he'd take the chance. Or that he would be so... juvenile.'

'I wouldn't put it past him, slimy little git. He propositioned me and we'd only been dancing for two minutes. Thought it might be a bit of fun if we got it on in the ladies' loos. You know, bridesmaid and groomsman. That good old cliché.'

'You're kidding!'

'No. I reckon he's a right pervert. You don't even want to know what he suggested.'

'Maybe it was him. Maybe I wasn't the intended target.'

Jade's eyes widened. 'Maybe the roofie was meant for me.'

'What did you do when he propositioned you?'

'Told him to fuck the fuck off.'

31

SUNDAY, 21 MAY 2023, 2.45 P.M.

The day after the wedding

Skye strode out, her long legs covering the ground, and let out a sigh. Getting out of the house with Cleo had been the best decision she'd made. The only decision she could make. A dull fog had settled over her brain. It didn't matter how much coffee she consumed, it simply wasn't lifting. In fact, the caffeine very possibly made her feel worse. Nauseous. Heady.

A big, fat bacon sandwich had helped. The bacon so crisp every drop of fat had been rendered from it. Jade swore by it. The thick doorsteps of white bread stuck to the walls of her stomach. She'd not been able to face tomato sauce, though, no matter how much Jade insisted.

The food now wallowed in her stomach, but the salt in the bacon seemed to be having an effect.

The aimless walk along footpaths through fields filled with soft velvet green shoots which would become oats, or barley – she never could tell which – had done her more good than sitting on her backside in her pyjamas with Jade casting her concerned looks every few minutes.

She'd left her sister behind to pack for university. Not that she had much, just the small rucksack she'd dropped off the previous day, tucking it in the bin shed because Skye had already left for their dad's house and Jade didn't have a key to Skye's small pad.

'I'm not in any danger, I wish I'd not mentioned it to you,' she'd reassured Jade.

The police, when she'd spoken with them on the phone, had been most reassuring. It was probably a random act. She wasn't necessarily their target. Sometimes they don't care who they drug. They'd run through the incident with her over the phone and praised her for being sensible. For getting help immediately and being taken home by responsible people.

They suggested she might want to have a urine test carried out at her local GP surgery to verify, but it was unlikely the drug would still be in her system.

What was the point?

They'd taken her seriously, even logged it as an incident, but why pursue something that had never actually transpired into anything horrific? She was safe. Her sister was safe. There was absolutely no way the perpetrator could be traced. After all, the police could hardly be expected to fingerprint all the glasses used in the room the night before. For a start, they would probably already have been dishwashed.

Skye approached a crossroads in the footpath and perched her backside on a stack of old stone walling that had been propped against an ancient oak tree. A flutter in her stomach matched the fast pace of her heartbeat. Faster than normal. Could a drug do that to you?

Had she really been drugged?

It was supposed to have been a wonderful day, the wedding. A resh start. A new beginning. For their dad, at least.

It had started that way.

Just Skye, her dad and a glass of Prosecco each. And then it all spiralled out of control.

Jade had stormed out a couple of nights previously, refusing to answer the messages Skye had left. It wasn't the first time she'd thrown a strop, but it was the most important. The only saving grace was she'd returned without anyone other than Skye and their dad knowing she'd had a hissy fit.

Just as Skye had believed nothing else could possibly go wrong, she'd taken that call. It was the snowball effect. Everything seemed to be building... building.

No one else appeared to have been affected as seriously by the phone call or in the same way Skye had. The woman who'd sounded so earnest. They'd not heard her. Not caught the break in her voice as she told Skye.

Skye hadn't wanted to make a fuss. Not after the initial shock of the call.

It had been almost seven years since Summer took off into a cold, drizzly night. Everyone else was convinced she'd run. She'd gone because the stress of dealing with home life was no longer something she could cope with.

Guilt still lay heavy over Skye's heart. If she'd been there for her twin, for her younger sister... But she'd needed her own space after their mum had died.

Despite being twins, Skye was the eldest. Only by a few minutes. But those few minutes had shaped their characters. The stronger willed of the two, she'd stuck to her decision and gone.

She'd no longer been able to bear the distress on her dad's face, day after day, as though he was fading away. The opportunity to go had worked for her. Unlike Summer, who'd opted to stay at home and apparently drowned in the responsibility of it all.

The coolness between the two of them had opened into a chasm of loneliness where they barely spoke with each other. When they did, there was a distance, an aloofness.

Skye's chest ached with the memory of it. All so meaningless. Falling out for the first time in their lives. None of it worth the heartache. Regret she tried hard to bury these days surged up until she blinked away unexpected tears as she tipped her head back against the rough bark of the tree.

Skye initially blamed herself for Summer's disappearance. Had her twin been so depressed, she'd packed a bag and simply disappeared?

Deep down, Skye had never believed that was what had happened. The bag Summer had taken had hardly been a holdall, just her normal handbag. Admittedly probably filled with all the crap she always had in there. Everything but the kitchen sink.

But there were items she'd not taken Skye had known for a certainty she would if she'd intended to not return.

There was no way her twin would have taken off without her black and white, soft as down Jellycat. The one Skye kept close herself afterwards, taking him with her when she moved out of university, had him propped up on her dressing table out of Cleo's reach.

She'd not been able to bring herself to move back in with her dad into their family home. Not once their family was no longer whole. The emptiness had wiped away everything homely about the place.

She was glad he was going to sell it. She couldn't wait for it to go. For them to make another step away from the events that tainted all their lives.

Skye leaned back and closed her eyes, absorbing the gentle heat of the sun across her eyelids.

'Summer.' She whispered her twin's name.

'Skye.' The reply came, as it always did, as it always would as long as Skye kept her twin alive in her heart.

A vision of Summer danced behind Skye's closed eyelids. Back to her, Summer's hair swished as she swayed, never turning to face her twin. Skye never saw Summer's face unless she looked in a mirror at herself. It seemed her imagination didn't need to supply that information.

Summer raised her hand and in it she held... she held...

Skye's eyes snapped open as frustration got the better of her and the image faded like mist over a fast-flowing river.

What was she holding?

Skye leaned forward, resting her elbows on her knees as she squinted at Cleo snuffling in the hedgerow, picking up the scent of whatever scuttled there.

What was Summer holding? She tried to evoke the image again, but it had gone.

Skye had never noticed anything in her twin's hand before. Not in her dreams...

She sat upright. Came to her feet.

Yes, she had. Summer often had a paintbrush in her hand, red paint dripping.

This wasn't a paintbrush, though.

Skye paced along a narrow footpath edging a wide field and, automatically, Cleo fell into step two paces ahead, sticking to the footpath, long tail swishing from side to side.

Skye dredged up the memory of the previous day's phone call despite the woolliness of her mind.

Who was that young woman? Why had she made the phone call? Why now?

In the beginning, when Summer's disappearance had hit the news, they'd had so many sightings, so many people contacting them, predominantly out of the goodness of their hearts, concerned, wanting to help, so sure that they'd seen her. None of them ever had. Not friends, not neighbours. When there were sightings, they were of Skye. Not Summer.

Summer had effectively disappeared into thin air.

Then there were the crank calls, the cruel people who thought it was a laugh to fill their family with false hope and send them down blind alleys. Each of them had closed their Facebook accounts after literally hundreds of messages. Kind messages, messages of sympathy, but nothing that led to anything of any meaning.

Unlike those previous messages and calls, Skye believed there was an element of truth in this one. Not just a cruel prank. Who would do that? What would they gain after this length of time?

Whatever the truth behind it, Summer may be trying to contact them. In her heart, Skye knew it. Believed it. This wasn't some loon who wanted to disrupt the lives they'd only just started to get on track. The sincerity in the voice had rocked Skye.

No one else had heard it, but she had.

And she believed it.

Also those whispered words Skye hadn't quite caught. The ones she concentrated on now, unsure whether she'd heard right, which was why she'd not spoken them out loud to the others.

She came to a standstill and peered over the hedgerow into the neighbouring field of sunshine-yellow rapeseed that rolled over gentle undulations as far as the eye could see.

'Summer...'

She closed her eyes and pictured her twin, this time the paintbrush was yellow. She concentrated. It wasn't a paintbrush.

It was a stick of yellow chalk.

Skye drew in a breath and knew for a certainty what the woman on the phone had said.

'She chalked something for you.'

32

One day after the wedding

'Skye!'

She shot upright on her dad's wide sofa where she'd fallen into an exhausted sleep. A startled grunt came from Cleo as she scrabbled to keep purchase on the sofa that Skye had accidentally knocked her from.

Skye drew her legs up to her chest and buried her fingers in the dog's thick fur on her neck.

'Sorry, girl.'

She leaned against the back of the sofa. Wrapping her arms around her knees, she rested her chin on them.

'Summer.'

Cleo raised her head at Skye's whispered word to give her a drop-dead stare and then flopped it onto the thick navy velvet throw Skye had pulled over her legs before she'd drifted off to sleep.

Skye ignored the dog and instead buried her face in her hands.

She'd heard her sister's voice. That's what had woken her.

Summer's voice, not just in her head, but as though Summer was there in the room with her. Close enough to whisper with a puff of urgency in her ear. Close enough for it to be real.

She'd stopped hearing her sister's voice a couple of years ago. It had faded, the substance of it lost across time. Where at one point it had ribboned through her consciousness, entangled in her identical twin DNA, it had faded, a faint whisper in the corner of her mind.

She couldn't rid herself of the continuous revolution of thoughts poking at her until she thought she might go insane.

Each time she remembered, she looked deeper, trying to find something she'd missed before.

While everyone else in the family had been crippled at Summer's loss, Skye had been destroyed. Identical twins, their DNA almost the same. Only their genome differed somewhere deep inside. Perhaps that was where her dad and younger sister found their comfort. In being able to see Summer every time they looked at Skye. Perhaps it diluted the hurt, the pain of her leaving.

Not that anyone would ever convince Skye that Summer had left of her own free will. She'd not believed it before, but now she was convinced.

When Skye had made the decision to leave for Lincoln University, she'd been devastated to realise Summer wasn't going to join her, choosing instead to remain behind with their dad and younger sister. She'd seen it as a betrayal. Dad hadn't wanted them to go initially. He thought they should have a gap year, a year in which they could grieve over the death of their mum. Skye hadn't agreed.

Skye's talent lay in numbers. They were like a picture in her mind. The ease with which she could shuffle them had baffled her mum. Her dad had the same kind of brain. Mathematics.

Summer's talents lay in art. Their mum had called them two

ides of the same coin. Identical in every way. Except their character.

Both of them had been accepted at the same university to study different courses. They would be together. Forever.

Summer had refused. All superior and self-sacrificing, like some bloody magnanimous saint. And she expected Skye to do the same. To put her life on hold so they could sit by their dad's chair and ululate until the pain of their mum's death faded or smothered them all in a dark blanket of despair they'd never be able to fight their way from under.

For the first time in their lives, the twins had been separated and Skye had been furious, barely able to speak to Summer. The odd exchange of messages had been curtailed each time by a lack of conversation other than blame.

That's why Skye was convinced.

Convinced her sister, the good twin, would never have left them, never have left her little sister and their dad. Skye had never really accepted Summer was lost to them.

With no contact whatsoever, there was a high possibility that she was dead after all this time. So everyone tried to convince Skye. If there was no closure though, how could she believe it? Proof of death was what she needed to convince her. Until she had that proof, she'd never accept it.

There was a part of Skye's heart that knew her sister was still alive. Still breathing. Just as Skye was still breathing, even though she found it difficult on occasion. The times she couldn't get her twin out of her mind. Like their twenty-first birthday when she should have been celebrating a landmark, but instead spent a quiet day with her dad and Jade curled up on the sofa watching some stupid chick flick and then having dinner with her grandparents instead of partying.

She'd wanted nothing else, not when all she could hear was

Summer's voice in her head. 'Happy birthday, Skye. Happ
birthday.'

Skye raised her head and reached a hand out to run it ove
Cleo's soft fur as she stared at the framed painting on the wal
opposite. The one her dad had kept.

The one Summer had created for their mum. Blues, greens anc
whites mingling in a seascape of wild, foaming waves crashing intc
one another and exploding into the cloudless blue sky. Oils hac
been her favourite medium, but given anything, Summer woulc
have created a masterpiece. Recognisable instantly to Skye.

'She chalked something for you.' The phrase edged its way back
into her mind.

What a strange way of phrasing it. But the woman had an
accent; perhaps if her first language wasn't English, she'd not quite
said the right thing. Chalked?

Bothered by her intruding thoughts, Skye edged from under the
throw and padded across the floor until she stood in front of the
painting. Her toes curled into the dark, patterned carpet, but her
eyes never left the image, as though she could conjure up her own
twin.

'Summer.'

She heard a soft sound behind her as her quiet whisper
disturbed Cleo, who grumbled at the disturbance and came to
stand silent at her side, as though Skye had beckoned her, not her
twin.

Cleo touched her muzzle into the palm of Skye's hand in a quiet
reassurance that she was there for her. The dog stood tall at her
side. A Huntaway, a breed originating in New Zealand specifically
for herding sheep up in the mountains. Black and tan with features
close to that of a German Shepherd, but with silken, floppy ears
and a soft mouth.

This dog was no sheep-herd. Gentle and intuitive, she knew instinctively when Skye needed comfort. And she needed it now.

Skye rested her hand on the dog's head while she continued to stare at Summer's artwork.

'Where are you, Summer? Where did you go?'

What had the girl who phoned meant?

She said, 'She wanted you to know she never left you. Not of her own free will.'

'You never ran away, Summer. You never did,' Skye murmured as her eyes concentrated on the painting.

'He's crazy. He'll kill her. Like he did the others. One day, he'll kill her, too.'

Who? Who was crazy?

Skye drew in a long breath as her chest tightened in a painful reminder for her to breathe.

'She chalked something for you.'

Why chalk?

Could she believe the woman's words?

If so...

Who had taken her sister?

Where was Summer now?

33

SUNDAY, 21 MAY 2023, 6.05 P.M.

One day after the wedding

The harsh peal of the doorbell had Skye almost jumping out of her skin. Her heart raced as Cleo spun around from where she'd leaned against Skye's leg and charged for the door, her deep staccato bark alerting Skye to intruders.

Skye didn't need Cleo's bark when her dad had a doorbell, but it was a comfort to know she took her role seriously.

'Crate.'

Cleo slunk into the crate Skye's dad kept for her frequent visits, but her guttural growls reassured Skye that if she needed her, Cleo was there ready and raring to go. And Skye wasn't about to lock Cleo in her crate. After all, she had no idea who was at the front door.

An uncomfortable feeling still hung heavy on her after last night's experience, and she appreciated every reassurance she could get.

If it was Jade, forgetting her key again, there'd be a different sound to Cleo's bark. A greeting, not a warning.

Skye swung the front door wide, her heart lodging in her throat at the sight.

Two uniformed police officers stepped forward onto the doorstep.

'Hello.' A quick flash of doubt crossed the officer's face and then cleared before it settled. 'I'm PC Debs Gulliver. This is PC Olivia Hughes. We were hoping to catch Mr Matthews. Are you...?' That hesitation again. Doubt. She dropped her gaze to her notebook. 'Are you Mrs Matthews?'

Comprehension dawned. They were expecting someone older. Good job they hadn't asked if her mum was at home. Skye wasn't sure she could bear the pain of it right now, not with her emotions deeply wrapped in the memory of her twin.

She huffed out a breath. Although that was no longer incorrect as she now officially had a new step-mum. Mrs Matthews was no longer exclusively her mum. She pushed the pain aside.

Still disorientated from her complete absorption with the painting, Skye raised a hand to her forehead.

'I'm *Miss* Matthews. Skye. I don't live here, it's my dad's house. I'm his daughter.' She indicated behind her with her thumb. 'I'm just here to tidy things up after my dad's wedding and organise taking the hired suits back to the shop tomorrow. I thought I'd do it now. Get it over with rather than dropping in tomorrow morning because I have to have it back by a certain time. Midday I think. It's easier to do it this way.' She fluttered her hand trying to get herself back on track, but they'd unnerved her. 'There is a Mrs Matthews, a new Mrs Matthews, but she's not here either because she's on honeymoon with my dad.' She stuttered to a halt at the misinformation and the verbal diarrhoea that seemed to pour from her. Dear God, was everyone affected by a police uniform in the same way, or was it just her? Did she tell a lie? Could they arrest her for telling a lie?

Not exactly a lie, she *was* there for that purpose. The fact she'd fallen asleep virtually the moment she walked in the door and only just roused could be attributed to the date rape drug in her system. If that's what it was. Or an excess of alcohol. Or the fresh air when she'd walked Cleo. Doubt swirled around, with dizziness still pushing at her.

Was that what they were here for? Surely not. How would they know she was here? She'd given her own home address, hadn't she? Maybe out of habit, she'd accidently given her dad's in the confusion.

Hadn't they asked for her dad initially? Oh, God. Her brain. What the hell was she spluttering on about?

Her cheeks flooded with embarrassment. 'I'm sorry. You wanted my dad? Not me?'

The two women officers exchanged glances, and nothing more than a blink communicated their agreement.

'Could we step inside for a minute?' PC Gulliver requested.

Skye stepped back, but the other officer hesitated. 'Is your dog okay? With uniform, I mean? It sounds very big.'

Skye raised an eyebrow. With uniform in particular? Did dogs recognise uniforms? Certainly, Cleo wasn't fond of posties. Any postie. But was that because they effectively knocked on the door every day and ran away? It was a tease to any dog.

She guessed many police officers encountered dogs with behavioural issues.

'Cleo is fine.' There wasn't a flicker of concern. Cleo was well trained and socialised. She just had a really loud bark. Perhaps just keep the fact that she was very big to herself for the moment; the officer was about to find that out for herself. By which time, she would already realise what a sweetie Cleo was.

Relief moved over PC Hughes's features as she scraped her feet on the doormat. 'Last house I visited, their chihuahua took a piece of my ankle. Bled like bug— bled a lot.'

'Oh, no, Cleo wouldn't do that. She's a gentle giant.' Too late. She'd already let her mouth run away with her again.

'Yeah, it's always the little ones. Feisty little beggars. Never give a warning, just go straight for the jugular. Or in this case, my ankle because unless I bent over, it couldn't reach my neck. Having said that, I had to grab it by the scruff of its neck as its owner was frightened to death of it.' She stepped over the doorstep into the hall. 'Ankle still swells up now and again. Worst thing was I had to have a tetanus jab too. I hate having injections.'

Skye moved back. 'Well, at least you won't need another one of those any time soon. Come through. Can I get you something to drink. Coffee? Tea? Water?'

'Water, please.'

'Water, please.' PC Hughes echoed her colleague.

Skye led them through a long hallway to the back of the house where wide kitchen windows overlooked an immaculate garden. One her dad took pride in the upkeep of. He'd insisted on mowing it the day before the wedding just so it didn't go wild while he was away, even though he'd organised for a gardener to come in every week. Standards. He wanted them to know just how manicured he liked his lawn. It was like employing a cleaner and running around the house to make sure it was immaculate before they arrived.

The wide, airy room they'd entered was a house extension that had been completed just days before Skye's mum had died. Another reason Skye would prefer her dad to sell up and move on. It was a heavy reminder of her mum's own personal investment into the house, her love of it, and very possibly the reason why her high blood pressure had been contributory to her death.

'Please sit down. I'll just be a minute.' She smiled at them, stiff and forced, as she turned her back. Her palms sweating. 'Take a seat.'

Skye ran the cold water tap and filled three glasses. She suspected she might be in need of one of them as her throat turned to sawdust. Tempted to run her wrists under the icy water, just to cool down the hot sweat that threatened to overwhelm her, she quickly held them under before she wiped them dry with the hand towel.

Creaks and groans came from the ridiculously cluttered uniforms, with everything but the kitchen sink attached as the officers seated themselves at the breakfast bar. PC Hughes's feet dangled as she settled herself on the high stool and looked as though she'd tip off the edge given the slightest bump.

Skye placed one glass in front of each officer.

She cradled her own in her hand as she leaned back against the wooden-topped bench. She'd taken advantage of the few minutes to chastise herself for being so verbose. She really needed to shut up. Just shut up.

She tilted her head. 'Is there something I can help you with?' She pressed her lips together. Say no more. Wait.

PC Gulliver's jacket creaked as she reached inside a pocket and took out a small notebook and pen at the same time as PC Hughes produced a smart tablet. No wonder they couldn't move, they were so weighted down with all their equipment.

'We were hoping to speak to your dad, but obviously, as you say, he's on his honeymoon. Much as we would prefer not to disturb him, could you give me his contact details?'

A sick feeling churned her stomach. 'Is something wrong? I've only just left my sister a couple of hours ago to walk Cleo. Is Jade okay? What's happened?' Panic rose to clutch at her throat. This was it. This is what happened both times before. Nice officers. Sympathetic faces. Bad news.

She would have swayed if the counter hadn't been propping her up, and she couldn't be sure that was attributable to her spiked drink the night before. More the memory of each time she'd encountered a police officer.

They were already in the house by the time she arrived home the day her mum died. Her dad, face cupped in his hands, sat on the sofa. Defeated.

That one event had destroyed all of them. A catalyst to everything else that had followed. The domino effect.

Who knew certain families were subject to that? If you believed in luck or fate, then you could sure as hell believe that some lives were doomed.

'You have a sister? Jade, yes? To our knowledge, she's fine. This has nothing do with her, we don't believe. Unless...' PC Hughes turned her head and the creaking increased as though it was her head screwing off her neck. 'Does she live here?'

Skye eased out a breath, aware of Cleo sidling from the lounge into the kitchen like she'd sensed her distress. She placed a hand on the top of Cleo's head and as she tried to speak, a dry hiccup erupted from her mouth. 'No. She doesn't. She's away at university. Or she would be if it wasn't for the wedding. She's probably off later this evening. Or first thing in the morning. She's sort of floating between here and my place. That's where she is now, I think. I haven't seen her since earlier this afternoon. She's sorting out a few last-minute things before returning to uni.' Cleo gave her arm a nudge with her nose as though warning her to shut up. Skye stroked her head as a reward. 'This is Cleo.'

PC Gulliver settled back on the seat and smiled at the dog. They were giving Skye a little time to settle. Like Cleo, they could probably sense her panic, smell her sweat. Did they think she was guilty of something? She felt guilty, the mere presence of them stole any sense of certainty from her. Anything could have happened. Anything could happen.

'We have no information on your sister,' PC Gulliver reassured her. 'But we are making enquiries about an incident last night.'

'Incident?' She'd had an incident the night before. Were they referring to that? Had Jordon reported Jacob for hitting him?

'Mmm.' PC Gulliver gave a weak smile. 'To be more precise, in the early hours of this morning.'

'Oh.' They'd all been fast asleep in bed by that time. Although she'd not heard from Jacob since. Perhaps he was sulking since she threw up on his shoes. His trousers. She almost cringed when she recalled what Jade had told her about trying to strip them off him. Instead, she centred her attention on the here and now.

'What kind of incident? If you want to know where my dad was, I'm sure the hotel can verify that he was there all night. They were setting off for Southampton this morning. Probably already boarded.' She looked at her watch. It was almost 6.25 p.m. 'You may not get hold of him for a few days. They've taken off on a thirty-five-day cruise of the Caribbean for their honeymoon.'

Both officers raised their brows. Maybe it sounded ostentatious, but they deserved it. Her dad deserved it. He hadn't taken a holiday since... well, he deserved it.

Skye took a sip of her water and then placed it on the bench beside her. She linked her fingers together and stared back at the police officers. 'Is there something I can help you with, save disturbing him?'

'Yes. Well, we can ask. If not, we'll have to make ship-to-shore contact.'

'I assume you're not going to make him come back. That wouldn't be fair.'

'We'll try not to.' PC Hughes gave her a tight smile and Skye noticed she'd not made a commitment. 'But some things are more important.'

'Than his honeymoon?'

'Possibly.' The officer tapped on the smart tablet she'd placed on the table. 'There was an incident last night, and on investigation, we discovered what we believe to be your dad's landline telephone number about the victim's person.'

'Victim? Oh, my God. Was someone injured?' She thought of Jade telling her about Jordon being punched in the face.

'I'm sorry, we can't discuss the full circumstances at the present time. Would you mind taking a look and confirm this is your number?'

Skye stared at the photograph, black and white, cropped to show a telephone number etched into what appeared to be… 'Jesus.' She leaned forward and peered closely at the image. 'Is that skin? Can I see veins?' Nausea rose like a sea from her stomach and Skye swayed on her feet.

PC Gulliver stood and offered the chair to Skye. 'You might want to sit down, you don't look too good. Are you feeling all right?'

Skye nodded, swallowing the saliva that had pooled in her mouth as PC Gulliver pushed the glass of cold water into her hand.

'No, I feel a little nauseous. A little unsteady. I… umm, I think my drink was spiked last night.'

PC Hughes went still. 'Sorry?'

'I reported it earlier today. And they said to take a urine sample to my GP, but of course they're not open until tomorrow.'

'Did anything happen?'

Anything really bad, Skye assumed, other than being roofied.

'I'm fine. Really. My sister and my dad's best man saw me safely home.' She cast them a glance from under her thick fringe. 'I don't think I drank too much. I'm not…' She shrugged. 'I'm not irresponsible. Whatever it was, it took me off my feet and I have a bit of a black hole where my memory should be.'

'You were safe, all the time?'

'Yes.' Skye nodded. 'Even when my jerk of an ex came around.'

'Your jerk of an ex? Who would that be, then?'

She hadn't meant to mention him. Didn't want to get him into trouble. He might be an idiot, but he wasn't a dangerous idiot and whatever Jade had said, he wouldn't have arranged to have her drink spiked. Would he?

She was flummoxed. She wished she had someone with her. Her sister. Jacob. She'd not seen him since he'd taken off and could only assume he would return his own suit to the shop – providing he cleaned the sick off the trousers. There was bound to be an excess for that.

Skye carefully placed her glass on the table and pressed her hand to her mouth while PC Gulliver pulled up another chair and sat beside her, Cleo in between. She leaned forward. 'If you want to report your ex, you can. Is he harassing you?'

Was he?

Certainly, but not in the way they meant. He was more of a nuisance than a threat. Or was he? It sounded as though he was pretty aggressive the night before. If Jacob hadn't been there, was Jade right? Would he have taken advantage of the situation to, in his eyes, repair their broken relationship?

Skye wasn't quite sure how to word her answer. She didn't want to get Jacob into trouble for whacking Jordon on the nose. That would just complicate matters so much more.

Maybe now was a good time to exercise some discretion and keep her mouth shut. Her fingers shook as she linked them together. There was so much whirling around in her head she didn't even know what to think.

'No, it's fine. I can handle him. He showed up at the wrong time, hat's all. Jacob, he's my dad's best man and business partner. He made sure Jordon went on his way.' Was that subtle enough? 'Nothing bad happened to me.' That was the truth, at least.

'And you say you have reported it?'

'Yes. I reported my drink being spiked.' Not the fracas between Jordon and Jacob.

'And you're happy to leave it at that?' PC Hughes squinted at her.

'Yes. I think I may have been a victim of some kind of random drugging. I'm not even sure I was the intended target.'

'Is this the kind of thing your ex may have done?'

'He wasn't at the wedding. He turned up here when we arrived home.'

'He was waiting for you? At what time? Is he a bit of a stalker?'

Skye squirmed. 'Possibly. But I don't think he'll be back.' Not with his bloody nose... 'I don't feel I need to make an issue of it.' And get Jacob charged for assault. 'I'm satisfied that nothing untoward happened.' Apart from there was a black hole where her memory should be, and she only knew this because her sister had told her. Apart from...

'Apart from you being drugged.'

'Well, yes... but not by him.' She felt obliged to stress that. Jordon may have been a pain in the arse, but he wasn't the one responsible for her roofie. She hoped.

PC Hughes sighed. 'Look, Skye, I know you were safe last night, but if you have any cause for concern about your ex-boyfriend, or anyone else for that matter, I want you to contact us.' She waved her small notebook and then placed it on the table and started to write. 'I'm going to log this on your original complaint and then if you have anything, and I do mean anything that causes you concern, you contact us straight away and it will be on the file. Do you understand?'

'Yes.' Skye nodded and a little knot of fear unravelled in her stomach. 'Thank you.'

The two officers remained quiet while PC Hughes scribbled in her notebook.

Silence was too heavy for her to deal with right now, she needed sound and movement. Reassurance. 'Why don't you enter it straight into the smart tablet?' She asked just for the sake of something to say.

PC Hughes didn't even raise her head. 'Because they're shit, and you can never get a signal and then you get back to the station and find that whatever you thought you'd entered hasn't loaded up and you have to start from scratch with a memory that's been filled to capacity through the day. That's my memory as opposed to the smart tablet's memory.' She sighed. 'I prefer the good old-fashioned way.'

Skye found herself studying the woman. A broad face, dark, heavily hooded eyes with a calmness that came from years of experience. Salt and pepper glittered in hair scraped back from a face devoid of any kind of make-up. Skin smooth. Perfect other than a few crow's feet at the edges of her eyes.

The woman smiled, and those lines deepened. 'I'll enter it up once I get back to the station.'

Skye reached for the tablet as the officer finished and edged it closer. Her heart pounded. Was that her dad's telephone number? 'What did they use to write it?' It didn't look like it had been tattooed on. The edges were blurred and smudgy.

'Charcoal, we believe.'

Something inside of Skye stilled. Her mind, a moment ago dull and slushy, fired up like an electrical circuit springing to life. Oh, dear God... charcoal, as opposed to chalk. Or had the woman on the phone been mistaken?

'Who is it? The person whose arm this has been written on? Is it my sister? Is that Summer?'

'Summer is your sister? I thought you said your sister was called Jade?'

'My twin. Summer. I have a twin.' Her stomach clenched. 'She disappeared seven years ago. We've not heard from her since. The police said she probably ran away. She was eighteen at the time. We'd had a lot of upsets at home. Our mum had died a few months earlier.'

I deserted her. The thought elbowed its way into her mind.

'I decided to go to university, and she chose not to. It was a difficult time.' She blew out a breath, a sense of detachment taking hold. This was it. The day she'd waited seven years for. They were going to tell her Summer was dead.

'Is it her?'

The officer gave her head a slow shake. 'If Summer is your twin, then definitely not.'

Boneless, Skye wilted into the chair. 'What makes you so sure?'

PC Hughes looked up, her gaze direct. 'I really shouldn't tell you this much, but the victim is not your twin. Not your sister, even. She's of a different ethnicity. We don't have the details yet, but possibly Eastern European.' The woman ran an eye over Skye. 'Not your skin tone.'

Skye stared at the image again. It wasn't evident from the black and white photo. Her skin could be any shade from pale through various shades. Not black. That was the only thing she could be sure of.

PC Gulliver reached over and placed her hand on Skye's. 'I'm so sorry about Summer.'

'It was a long time ago.' Clogged with tears, her voice came out a husky whisper.

She felt the slight squeeze of her fingers and looked into the woman's wise eyes. 'I hope you find closure one day.'

Skye stuttered in a breath full of emotion.

It wasn't her twin. It wasn't Summer. Skye swallowed down the tears. She needed to think straight.

If it wasn't Summer, who else would have their telephone number almost tattooed onto their inner arm?

A sudden connection hit her like a freight train driving through the thick clouds, slowing her thought process.

Was it the woman who phoned yesterday? Before the wedding. An accent. Eastern European.

She ducked her head, slipped her fingers from under the police officer's hand and tucked a stray lock of hair that had flopped forward behind her ear to give her a moment.

'It could be our number, but then...' She shrugged. Stopped herself.

She couldn't have explained her reluctance to mention to the police officers the phone call from the day before, except she wanted time to think about it.

She needed to engage her brain properly.

Was that dishonest of her? Could she be arrested for withholding information? Heat rose up her neck at the thought of lying to the police. She'd never so much as had a speeding ticket. She was a law-abiding citizen. Normally.

For some reason, though, Skye needed to think about it first.

She could always go back to them. Call them with more information, tell them she'd just remembered... After all, the events that followed had overshadowed that call.

She had a very valid excuse that her brain had been fried by some kind of drug.

She tapped the screen with her fingernail. 'That could be a five or an eight.' She paused, her gaze scanning the number. 'Possibly even a three.'

'Possibly. We are checking several options out. Not just this number.'

'So, it's not my dad's phone number for sure?'

'No.'

But it was.

Something inside Skye stirred. The writing wasn't tidy, the number looked as though it had been hastily dashed down, lines scrubbed back and forth as though whatever had been used, charcoal, wasn't quite taking. But there was something familiar. An oddity. The number seven had a small horizontal slash across a slightly curved vertical stem, like a rounded belly. Unusual. Old-fashioned. Something Summer used to do. Just as she used to put a small heart above an 'i'. A practice she used to get into trouble for at school. An idiosyncrasy she was known for. The artistic side of her craving freedom to express itself.

What would Dad do? What would he say?

He'd be honest. Open. Spill his guts.

Skye opened her mouth to do just that. 'No. I'm afraid I don't think it is our number.' She gently slid the smart tablet away from her. 'No.' She shook her head. 'I'm so sorry I can't help. I know nothing about it.'

The heat of her lie shot into her face until it pulsed and she wondered if they could tell.

Both PCs came to their feet at the same time, their chairs scraping against the tiled floor.

PC Hughes pulled the smart tablet towards her and then paused. 'Just one more thing before we go. You wouldn't happen to recognise this, would you?' She swiped her finger across the screen and the picture changed.

Skye's chest clenched as she stared at the charcoal image etched into what appeared to be a wrinkled piece of cloth.

She narrowed her eyes and studied it, a curl of recognition halting her.

It couldn't be...?

She almost reached out to straighten the piece of cloth and stopped herself in time. It was a photograph. She couldn't make it any clearer.

She didn't need to.

Disbelief fogged her brain.

Not only did she recognise the style, but she was damned sure she recognised the location.

She pressed her lips together to stop from saying anything.

She needed time to sort out this mess in her head because everything pointed to the impossible.

34

SUNDAY, 21 MAY 2023, 7.35 P.M.

One day after the wedding

Skye took her dad's laptop from the top drawer of the desk in his home office. The fluttering of unease had ratcheted up to thundering terror.

Christ, she needed to check. Surely her drugged brain wasn't giving her hallucinations.

Desperately wishing she was wrong, Skye powered up the laptop, plugging it into the mains as she noticed the 'battery low' light on. Her dad had been using it until the last minute the night before his wedding. He'd obviously not had the opportunity to charge it, or not given it a thought. Why would he need to? He was leaving for a month.

There'd been other things on his mind at the time.

Literally a few hours ago, she would have smiled at that thought, but now she could barely muster more than a brief flicker of acknowledgement.

Surely she was wrong. She had to be wrong. Acid churned in her stomach and she held her breath as Skye typed her mum's date of birth into the password box, selecting that option instead of the fingerprint recognition which correlated to Dad's fingerprint.

Incorrect password. Try again.

She puffed out a breath, running her fingers through her hair as she thought.

Her mum's date of birth. Dad always used that as a back-up in case finger or face recognition failed to work. Why the hell would he have changed it?

She covered her face with her hands and let out a groan. Perhaps she'd typed it in wrong. She knew she hadn't, but all the same she placed her fingers on the numeric keypad and re-entered the numbers.

Incorrect password. Try again.

What? When had he changed it? He never changed that password, despite being advised to. His laptop was only ever kept at home. He never needed to take it to work. He used a desktop there. Good, old-fashioned and reliable.

He'd never changed his password in seven years. Why would he now?

Skye sat back, her hand automatically going to Cleo's head. She looked down at her dog, soft eyes filled with concern.

'What did Dad do, Cleo? Why would he change his password from the one he's used for the past...'

She drew in a long breath, her lungs inflating as the memory of her own words rushed in.

'Dad, it's time. You deserve happiness. You need to move on. Mum loved you very much, but you need to let go. Find your own happiness.'

That breath slid out again. 'Martha. What's Martha's birthday?' She rested her head back against the leather chair and closed her eyes. She hadn't got a clue. He'd only been seeing her for about a year. Martha's birthday didn't register with her. Hadn't they gone away to the Lake District for a couple of days earlier in the year?

She opened her eyes, straightened and reached for her phone. She scrolled through all the WhatsApp contacts she'd used for the wedding and hesitated with her finger hovering over Luke's name. What would he think? After his behaviour the previous night towards Jade, did she really want anything to do with him?

A sigh slipped from her lips.

It was irrelevant. Whatever her personal opinion of the man. Other than last night's fiasco, she'd had very little to do with him. He'd been nothing but a vague, sullen shadow as far as she remembered. The apple of his mum's eye, of course. Her only son. She talked about him often, but he seldom turned up to a family dinner. He'd barely had anything to do with planning the wedding other than turn up for the suit fitting, which Skye hadn't attended.

Her dad said he was a nice lad. Her dad said everyone was a nice lad. Or a nice lass. It could hardly be considered an endorsement of Luke's character.

It was all irrelevant.

She needed information from him. Now.

She tapped on her phone and sent him a message.

What is your mum's date of birth?

35

'Summer! Summer! Come on!'

Skye races along the beach, head back, hair flowing as she charges towards the waves lapping the shore, laughter drifting out behind her.

I cast a quick glance at Mum, who smiles as she tips her head back and lets the sun kiss her golden skin. She closes her eyes behind dark sunglasses and lies back on the sun lounger. I know she's happy. Relaxed.

Still, there's a soft melancholy about her.

This is likely to be our last holiday together. Soon Summer and I will be adults. Independent.

Dad's up at the ice-cream parlour with Jade, they're on their third helping today at the all-inclusive resort in Sicily. Much as I love the gelato here, I really don't need to put weight on just as we head off to uni.

We've applied for places which can accommodate both mathematics and art degrees equally. We've argued a little, but in the end, we settled on the best choices we could make. Because we want to stay together, no matter how far apart our subjects are. That's not as important as being together.

All we have to do now is wait for our A level results.

In the meantime, we're here to have fun. Even though the wristbands are for children as we're not eighteen yet. So, we're not allowed to drink alcohol. Technically.

It's surprising how many adults here, strangers, will accommodate us, let us have a drink they've acquired for us with their adult wristbands.

Mum would hit the roof, if only she knew. It's definitely not something she would approve of. But Skye and I are sensible. We're not going to get trollied. Not while our parents are around. We're far too responsible for that. But it would be good to get a little practice in before we go off to university and start our new lives. Wild lives. Free lives.

We can do whatever we like without ties. Without restrictions. Without the bonds of our parents.

I run for the sea, kicking up my heels, my arms wide as I charge into the surf and fall into my twin's arms.

We circle around and I freeze.

The skyline turns into pieces of a jigsaw and starts to crumble, eating away at the picture. The ice-cream parlour melts, the colours running down to the beach to swallow it up and the scene rushes at us, rolling like tumbleweed towards us as I hug my twin. Not wanting to let her go, but the riptide batters us, pulling us apart until we clutch at each other, unwilling to let go.

I open my mouth to scream, and it fills with sand.

We grasp each other's arms tight as the wind howls, lashing us with its powerful fury. My eyes squint against the debris flying all around. I cling on, tears streaming down my face as we lose our grip on each other, our fingers making one last attempt before we're ripped apart.

The wind drops. Nothing is left. Pitch black surrounds me.

In the silence I sob, 'Skye.'

But my arms are empty.

* * *

'Summer!'

My eyes flash open and I fully expect to see Skye standing over me, her swimsuit dripping with water, but there are only my own tears streaking down my face.

The bed creaks as I push myself up from it, still sobbing. The dream so real I can still feel it.

I pace my cell. I know I have the freedom of the house these days, but this is my sanctuary. My hiding place. Weird, or not, I feel safe here.

Today, though, I am restless. Thoughts of Summer are stronger than they've been for so long.

Is that because I've held out some kind of hope that even though I can't go to her, she could come to me? Would I want her to?

It's not an easy decision when your mind has been tethered down by chains of cruelty that keep your thought processes locked away. No decision is mine. No thoughts my own.

Except LJ has allowed me more space and I'm going to use it.

I jump to my feet, slipping them into a shabby pair of black plimsoles before I dash up the stone steps, breathless by the time I reach the top and a streak of panic filling my chest.

He's not punished me yet, but that means nothing. He'll bide his time. Wait. It used to be so he could drive me to distraction with the fear of punishment. These days not so much. I know it will come. The punishment is often not as cruel as the waiting.

It's just a matter of time.

I check all the rooms. He's here, I know he is.

From the lack of creaking floorboards, he's not upstairs. Not unless he's asleep but I don't think so.

I creep to the top of the cellar steps. Wait. Listen.

He's down there! He must have been in the other room as I dashed up.

Now, he's in my room.

The punishment has begun.

36

SUNDAY, 21 MAY 2023, 7.50 P.M.

He circled the room. Picture by picture. Bit by bit. As though his eyes had just opened for the first time.

How had he allowed this?

In the beginning it had been with cynical amusement. The beauty of Summer's work consumed by the horror of what had become her life. Her punishment. Not just hers, but theirs, too. Because it was them, both of them, who were responsible.

At first it had entertained him. Her vision. Her interpretation.

Now, he saw it for what it was. A grim reality.

He raised both hands and gripped on tight to his hair. Christ. How had it got to this?

What if someone saw this?

Pictorial evidence of a life lived in captivity. In slavery.

He'd never meant for it to go on so long. He'd wanted to make a point. A hard, cruel point. But a valid one, nonetheless.

Had it ever been his intention to progress to this? He'd never meant to take any more young women. It had become a fever. A disease. He'd been consumed.

But now...

He lowered himself onto the edge of Summer's bed, his fingers still clawing at his head. In seeking to punish a monster, he'd become the monster.

A desperate sob jammed in his throat until it edged its way out as a pitiful squeak.

What had he done?

The pleasure he would normally take in punishing Summer evaporated. In its place was a sick realisation that he teetered on the precipice of being caught.

His stupidity had put him at risk. He should never have pursued Lilijana. Then again, he'd had no choice.

It had shaken him, though. He'd come so close to getting caught. To getting found out.

He pushed to his feet, barely able now to sit still. His nerve endings were spitting with sparks of electricity.

Last night could have been the end of everything. If the bald guy had caught him, he would have beaten him to a pulp. Instead, LJ had managed to slip away through some twist of fate. It was ironic that the guy who'd smacked him in the face had probably been the one to take the beating from the man who'd been pursuing LJ.

Would it be all over the news tomorrow? Would Lilijana's death be in the local newspaper? Would there be a connection between the two men fighting and her body?

He thought of trawling the internet. The data coverage there was rubbish. He needed to go home and check. Scan the newspapers, check online.

What would become of him if a link was made? If the homeowner mentioned him, or had taken his registration number. Or if someone along that street had a Ring doorbell. There were cameras everywhere now.

LJ took the stairs two at a time, as though the ghosts of all those women and their unborn children pursued him, their clawing hands reaching for him from the cells below to punish him. Not for his deeds, but his stupidity in putting himself at risk.

What had he done?

Not so much appalled by the actions he'd taken, but the possibility of being caught, his heart raced.

As he reached the top, he drew his phone from his back pocket. Even in the direst of circumstances, he'd never make the mistake of leaving it where Summer could get hold of it. No matter how well trained he believed her to be, he would never risk her disobeying him.

But she had disobeyed him. It was her who had turned the key and opened the door. Not Lilijana.

Summer had freed Lilijana and yet chosen to remain imprisoned herself.

Why?

Why would she do that?

Stockholm syndrome. He knew about it. All about it. He'd studied it out of curiosity when he noticed Summer's responses to his commands, wishes.

He gave a grim smile as he reached the top of the stairs and glanced out of the wide-open door into the walled courtyard. The sound of the washing machine slushed as he took a moment to survey things. She must have put another load in thinking he'd not notice. Her bedding perhaps. He didn't care. The clothes he'd brought earlier in the day were washed, dried, ironed and put in the black bin-bag he'd brought with him. Good, obedient little girl that she was.

Only she wasn't good. She wasn't obedient.

For fuck's sake. He stared out into the fading light. Her drawings had leached out onto the terrace, which until recently had been a sea of weeds. She seemed to have weeded the whole lot to make room for her art.

How had he let this get so out of hand? How had he allowed her to spread this dangerous propaganda as far as he could see?

How?

The answer was clear. She'd become so invisible to him, he'd completely forgotten she existed. She cleaned his house, his clothes, his dishes. He allowed her to prepare food sometimes, although she wasn't a good cook. Neither was he. But the microwave warmed a good ready meal.

This, though, this was too much.

What if someone came here? His cousins, second cousins. Like they had before. Not for a long time. Not since just after his great-aunt's death. Greedy bastards, the lot of them. All wanted a piece of the pie. They'd removed every item of value they could get their hands on until the solicitors had stopped them. Too late for most of it though. Her precious jewellery, her valuable ornaments. If anything was left, they'd have been back for more.

What if they thought to check up on their inheritance that had been tied up in probate for the past several years while all his great-aunt's great-nephews and great-nieces argued their right to the property? A property they believed deserted and derelict. Yet they still continued to fight over it.

The land was worth far more than the property itself.

They teetered on the edge of a legal agreement at long last. He'd been the one to stand back and let them argue, all the while making use of the place. A place none of the lazy arse cousins had even thought to check on after the initial visit from the solicitors for valuation purposes. None of them wanted the property, they all wanted the money.

None of them ever visited their great-aunt when her health was failing. They took her money for Christmas and birthdays, but it was only LJ who came to stay. Who checked on her. Who looked desperately for the will she'd written in his favour, or so she'd told him. Only there was no will. Nothing. He'd searched the entire premises. Taken her old furniture apart piece by piece.

She'd never married, never had children. A hermit in her latter years.

No living nieces or nephews either. Just great-nephews and great-nieces he didn't even know, nor wanted to. Money-grabbing relations who deserved none of it. Only he was worthy. Or so he thought.

Now, it needed to be divided between all of them. Every one of them who believed they deserved their share. Their slice of the cake. Sixteen of them altogether, although probate had realised that some of them weren't quite as strongly related as others. Down the line, the relationship had been diluted. Half-siblings having children of their own. A step-brother who thought he had every right. The solicitors had weeded the unworthy out and now there were nine left. Nine pure bloodline who were entitled to a share of what was left after the solicitors took the biggest slice. The lion's share.

Matters had moved rapidly in the last few weeks.

The time was coming when the property would be valued again.

Which was why he'd moved his own furniture out again and replaced it with the old girl's. Or as close to the old girl's as he could find since he'd wrecked hers, tearing it apart. Chintzy little armchairs that smelled of mothballs and a threadbare rug.

He'd used his own, classy stuff for a short while to impress, to give the impression of wealth and success. It had worked.

He'd also used it to give him a savage sense of superiority.

A superiority he no longer felt as he stared at every piece of evidence on display.

They'd take one look at this, and the shit would fly.

He glanced at his phone. No reception. Never any bloody reception.

That was part of the appeal, though. Wasn't it?

He was completely incommunicado. Which was what he liked. Normally.

Now, though, he needed to get out of here, put things in order.

He circled around. Contemplated.

He needed to contact work and let them know he needed time off, arrange for his workload to be re-distributed without arousing suspicion. He snorted.

Arouse suspicion.

He was pretty sure there would be suspicion, but not for the reason they thought. Questions would be asked in any case. His timing wasn't exactly brilliant.

Who would have thought when he started up with the business that he'd actually grow to depend on it? Need the income and get used to all those home comforts.

Work was going to miss him. But he was hardly in a position to go in with his face in the state it was. He couldn't be seen. He couldn't afford for questions to be asked, fingers to be pointed. Gossip to roll around.

What was he supposed to do?

He stared as the scrawny woman scratched yet another chalk and charcoal scene on the uneven, cracked brickwork, her eyes narrowed in concentration against the failing light.

The desire to kick her, just for the hell of it, almost proved too much.

The best thing was to dispose of her too. Have done with it all. Forever. He could do that. It wasn't like he was unintelligent. He knew exactly the problem he had. It was an illness, but not one he couldn't manage. He was a high-functioning addict. He needed to control it now. Put his life back on an even keel.

Dispose of every scrap of evidence so it looked like he'd neve~ been there. None of them had ever been there.

LJ stared at the disused flower bed running the length of the fa~ end wall. Could he dispose of everything? It wasn't feasible on hi~ own, was it?

Perhaps...

'Summer!' he barked, as he gave in to the desire and delivered ~ swift kick to her narrow backside.

Summer snapped upright hard enough to break her spine a~ she turned to face him, a distant look in her eye and a thin stick o~ charcoal in her hand. The bloody piece of charcoal she'd no doub~ rubbed across Lilijana's arm.

Fury stole in to rob him of his sanity for one split second as he stepped forward.

From the light in her eye, Summer knew her time had come. There was no fear, just a relieved acceptance. She didn't flinch, she never even tried to hide from it.

Except that wasn't going to be the way of things. Not yet. Her time would come, but before that she had her uses.

'I've got to go out.'

Nothing flickered in her expression. Somewhere inside, a small part of him shuddered. He'd done this to her. Made her inhuman. Unresponsive.

He was interested to see just how unresponsive she would be to his instructions.

'I'm going away for a while, but I'll be back in the morning.' He kept it vague. 'While I'm away, I want you to scrub everything clean. Do you understand?'

She gave a single bow of her head, but he could tell the message hadn't sunk in.

'There's a new scrubbing brush under the sink. A bucket in the kitchen cupboard.' He knew because he'd bought them recently.

Just after he'd cleaned up the mess from the previous girl. The one who came before Lilijana.

Shell.

That was her name. She'd lasted two days. The injuries she'd sustained when he reversed over her with his car when she'd managed to pop the boot open from the inside had caused internal bleeding.

He hadn't known until he got her back here and she vomited blood.

She'd bled out on the floor. He'd disposed of her body the same way as Charlotte and the two foetuses. He refused to acknowledge them as babies. They were not.

He'd dug each of them a shallow grave. Deep enough to cover them. There was no chance larger predators such as foxes could get into the high-walled enclosure, but he'd buried them deep enough so other, smaller animals wouldn't dig them up.

As the sun lowered in the sky, shadows touched on those graves, the golden glow from the sunset lighting up the red brick-coloured soil to remind him.

Summer had made a good job of scrubbing the floor clean previously. Bleach had left her hands raw. This time he'd brought rubber gloves.

It hadn't been pleasant to watch the skin peeling from her fingers when she chopped vegetables for their dinner. No, he didn't fancy that again. Not that it would matter as much this time.

He'd disposed of the scrubbing brush in the bag of rubbish he always took away with him. No bin lorries visited here. Nothing. The solicitors had kept paying the electric bill and the water bill to keep the place in good order for when probate was settled. It would be settled soon. In the meantime, no one lived there, to their knowledge, so the place didn't have to be serviced. How they'd never noticed the bills were more than just running costs, he had no idea, other than they probably didn't care. They were getting their cost per hour, and no one had instructed them to have power to the premises cut off.

LJ had deliberately said nothing. He'd not seen the point.

Soon, he'd be gone. The stains might not.

'Scrub everything, Summer,' he reiterated. 'Walls, ceiling, floor. Take it all off.'

He watched as comprehension dawned. A slow, steady enlightenment. Instead of the blank canvas he'd grown used to seeing, a pitiful mournfulness crumpled her face. Soundless, she stood facing him, her shoulders drooping, her head jerking, as he delivered the worst blow yet.

'Get rid of your drawings. The lot. Inside and out. I want no evidence you ever existed.'

Tears tracked down her face.

He turned and walked back into the house. He needed to put things in order so that he could walk away from everything without raising any suspicion.

He circled around, taking note of everything. He needed to leave it all behind.

With a last grim glance at Summer's pathetic body spasming with twitches and tics in the courtyard, LJ picked up the black plastic bags full of clothes and his car keys and left.

37

One day after the wedding

Skye stared at the message from her little sister.

Why do you want Luke's mum's date of birth?

What the hell? How did Jade know? Skye fired back a rapid response.

Where are you?

The word *typing* appeared at the top left of the screen as Skye waited for Jade's reply.

I'm with Luke.

Skye glanced at the time on her phone.

What?? Why?

Because he sent me a message while you were out with Cleo to
ask if I would like go for something to eat.

Her fingers couldn't type fast enough.

Eat? Eat where?

A grinding fear clenched her heart. Why would Jade agree to
see Luke after everything that had happened the night before?
What the hell was she thinking?

Skye couldn't turn her back for a moment without Jade being a
complete twonk.

She waited.

The two white ticks turned blue.

She waited a little longer.

The word *typing* didn't appear again.

What the hell was going on? Was Jade safe?

WhatsApp made the phone burr at the incoming call, causing
Skye's frayed nerves to snap as she swiped the screen with her
painted fingernail.

The video wavered to reveal a watery image filling the screen
and then cleared as Jade brought her face close to the camera and
growled into it.

'I haven't got time to bloody well keep sending messages. I've
just ordered, so you have precisely two minutes.'

'Where are you?' Skye squinted at the screen, trying to pick out
something familiar in the background.

'I'm in the loos.'

'The loos where?' She knew how evasive her sister could be.

'For God's sake.' Her sister rolled her eyes, and the screen froze
to leave that ugly image staring back at Skye for a full second before

t unfroze. Normally she would have laughed and taken a screen shot to send back to Jade, but right now she saw nothing funny about the situation.

'Where the hell are you?'

'Chill out, would you, and keep your voice down.'

'You have a volume control.'

'Well, you don't.' Jade snorted. 'Everything is fine. Luke sent me a message not long after you'd taken Cleo out and said he really wanted to apologise. He felt really shit about the way he'd treated me. I think Dad might have said something to him about his behaviour. Anyway, he said he was wasted last night, and he doesn't normally act like a complete arsehole.'

'There's no evidence of that,' Skye muttered.

'I heard that!'

'You were meant to.'

'Anyway, he suggested we meet up at the Park Street Kitchen so he could apologise in person.'

She could have said how good the place was, but her annoyance with her sister wouldn't let her.

'And you fell for it?' Sometimes, Skye couldn't believe her own sister's naïveté.

'I'm not stupid,' Jade shot back.

'Except you're there with him now, and you never even thought it would be a good idea to let your big sister know your whereabouts.'

'I didn't need to.'

'Exactly why?'

'Because Dad knows.'

Stunned into silence, Skye stared at the image of her sister, now fuzzy once more. 'Dad knows.' She licked her lips. 'When did you speak with Dad?'

'Before he boarded. I sent him a message telling him to have great time and not to worry about anything here, we can deal with anything in his absence.'

'What the hell would you say that for?'

For the first time, Jade hesitated. She lowered her voice and came closer to the camera, hissing out at Skye from the screen. 'Because you said not to tell Dad that anything had happened last night, and I wanted to make sure he hadn't got wind of it. Apparently, he was concerned. Concerned that Luke had upset me, and that's why *you* took *me* home early.'

'Ah!'

'Yes, "ah". I should say so. I let him believe it, too. So, he told Martha, Martha ripped Luke off a strip, and Luke wanted to apologise. I know he was a complete shit last night, but that was the booze talking and I felt a bit guilty for him getting it in the neck, so I agreed to meet him. Just meet him. So he could apologise. And he's been really nice. And actually, he's very funny. So, I'm going back in to finish my meal with him, and then I'll be hopping on the train back to uni, if that's all right with you. I have a lecture first thing in the morning.'

'Send me a message when you get there.'

'Really?'

'You normally let Dad know you're safe. Why not me?'

'I can, if you insist.'

'I insist.' Why did her little sister choose now to be awkward? Ah! She'd always been awkward.

'Because you don't trust Luke not to spike my drink?'

Skye didn't reply, she simply met her sister's gaze over the connection.

'Okay,' Jade conceded. 'I'll let you know as soon as I get back.'

Muscles Skye hadn't realised had bunched up released and she blew out a breath. 'And don't let him near your unattended drink.'

Jade's eyes popped wide. 'Oh, shit!' She slapped her hand over her lips.

Just as Skye's heart boomed in her chest, Jade burst out laughing. 'No. It's not him. Definitely couldn't be. He'd also be really bloody stupid to try something now when both our dad and his mum know who I'm with.'

'And me.' The pulse still thundered in her ears. 'I know where you are and tell him I'll hunt him down if he does anything to harm you.'

Jade laughed again. 'I'm not telling him that. He'll think you're a hard-arse, and you're not.'

Skye swallowed. She wasn't. Was she?

The smile dropped from Jade's face, and she became serious. 'Are you okay with me going back to uni, or would you feel happier if I stayed a while longer? I can miss a couple of days of lectures.'

Skye knew what she wanted to say, but that wasn't fair on Jade. If she dropped behind on her lectures it was always going to be an uphill struggle to catch up. It was one of the reasons their dad had insisted Skye continue going to university when Summer went missing. It was the thing to do. Keep going. Put on a brave face. Soldier on.

Or was it?

If she told Jade about the visit from the two police officers, then she definitely wouldn't go back to uni. Some things were best kept quiet.

'I'll be fine. You get yourself back to uni. Will I see you at the weekend?'

'Yeah. I'll come back. You never know, I might have a date with Luke.'

Skye groaned. A recipe for disaster if ever she imagined one.

'Okay. Take care. Love you.'

'Love you too. And don't speak to any strangers...'

Skye tapped the exit button just as a message popped up from Luke.

Mum's date of birth is 29.03.1974

38

SUNDAY, 21 MAY 2023, 8.45 P.M.

One day after the wedding

Skye tapped Martha's date of birth into her dad's laptop and waited for the information to spool through on the Wi-Fi that had decided to have a go-slow moment.

It had to be the right password. She'd tried both hers and Jade's while she was on the phone to her sister, waiting for Luke to reply. Neither of them had worked and her dad really didn't have much of an imagination for passwords.

A quiet sadness pressed down on her as she thought of Martha's date of birth wiping out her mum's. It was time for her dad to move on. She'd been the one to encourage him. But it still crushed her to know that the memory of her mum slowly faded, year by year, with nothing to keep it alive. Unlike thoughts of Summer, which now carried more significance than ever.

The screen sprang to life and Skye sat for a long moment staring at the programs.

Where to start?

The false fingernails she'd had affixed especially for the

wedding tapped ferociously at the keyboard as she entered her enquiry into the search engine.

She leaned forward as Cleo touched her cold, wet nose to Skye's ear.

Automatically she reached out to stroke the dog's neck, her eyes never leaving the screen.

Her logical mind knew exactly what to do, where to look. She'd just needed to put it into gear.

Companies House search.

There was no point enlisting Jade's help. She wasn't going to believe Skye's gigantic leap in conjecture. And that's all it was at this moment. A fragile link that could be pure coincidence.

In her heart, she knew it wasn't. She didn't believe in coincidence.

The scene on the drawing PC Hughes had shown her was ingrained in her mind's eye. She knew it. She'd seen it herself. Commented on what an incredible view it was when she'd stood looking out over it. Spectacular. Breathtaking. Not something you would ever forget in a hurry.

But was it the same view? Or was she just projecting the image she'd looked at for all of thirty seconds onto a memory of something vaguely familiar from years ago? Is that why she hadn't told the police while they were there? In case they thought she was stupid? In case she *was* stupid. A paranoid fool?

She'd been on the backfoot in any case. She'd hardly expected police officers on her dad's doorstep. Her mind had leapt from one scenario to another like a Duracell bunny on speed.

Skye pulled up the information she needed. She opened her dad's drawer and retrieved a notebook. She scribbled down the address she retrieved from the information on Companies House. Information that was so easy to obtain these days since it was a legal requirement for companies to keep it. Amongst other things, director's full name, date of birth, service address and home address.

She removed the top three pages, so the impression of her writing didn't show through. She'd seen that on a detective programme or something where the imprint showed through and incriminated one of the characters. How many pages did it take to ensure there was no imprint left? She ripped off another page, folded the paper and pushed it into her back jeans pocket, closed down the laptop, slid it back into the drawer she'd found it in and came to her feet.

Hesitating at the doorway to the hall, she glanced up the stairs. Just one more thing. Something else to support her theory. Give it another blade of truth.

Cleo sprinted up the stairs ahead of her, full of anticipation, although Skye wasn't sure what for. Maybe Skye's own eagerness had communicated itself to her dog.

Fooling Cleo, Skye changed direction at the top of the stairs and walked to the opposite end of the landing from her old bedroom.

She stood outside the door to the little box room where Martha had stored some of their things from when they were younger. Partly the reason Jade had kicked off. She felt Martha was boxing them up and putting them out of their dad's life.

She wasn't. The poor woman just needed to create room enough for her to be in his life, and he couldn't live in the past any longer.

Skye edged the door open.

She blew out a breath, wilting against the doorjamb as the scene swamped her senses.

All her childhood memories were here. Boxed up. Ready to ship out.

This was the reason Jade had been so unreasonable. Or it appeared she had. This was her childhood too. This had been her room. Summer and Skye had shared the larger one at the other end of the hallway, but Jade's was now a storage room.

No wonder Jade had hit the roof. With all the other tension surrounding the wedding, she must have been devastated to have found this. Poor Jade.

Skye pushed away from the doorframe and put her hands on her hips.

Where to start?

There were even more boxes than the last time she'd looked inside the room. She tried not to go in there. To snoop.

A niggle of depression touched her as she stared at the neat stacks. All labelled. What would Martha and her dad do with them when they moved house? Would they take them with them. Perhaps they were going to make them all have their own stuff in their own houses. Which made sense. Except Skye barely had enough room for herself and one big dog. There was simply no storage. And Jade was still in shared accommodation.

Perhaps they would hire a garage or storage unit and the boxes would sit there, rotting.

Skye moved a couple of boxes and decided each of the stacks belonged to one of them. There was more than one stack each. In fact, there were several. And to get to the ones at the back, Skye had to move all the ones at the front.

Puffing out, she lugged them one at a time to create a pathway, and squeezed in between them, making a promise to herself that she would definitely lose weight as soon as this was all over, especially after Jade had called her a fat cow, or something to that effect, in her hazy recollection of her younger sister trying to heave her naked body around.

Cleo made a low whining noise in her throat and Skye cast her a quick glance over her shoulder. 'Quiet, or you can go back downstairs.' It's not as though Skye hadn't fed her. She'd done that as soon as the police had left.

With a soft groan, the dog lay full length in the doorway, legs stretched out front and back, showing off her impressive length.

Skye negotiated her way to the far end of the piles of containers and looked at the labels.

Summer – Soft Toys

Her heart squeezed. 'Summer,' she said under her breath. She picked at the edge of the Sellotape sealing the top down and stripped it back. She didn't have time for this, but for some reason she couldn't resist looking.

She stared into the box for a long while until she reached out and pulled Eeyore from underneath a couple of other cuddly toys. Instead of smelling musty and old, Summer's scent drifted up for Skye to catch it. She closed her eyes and hugged the toy close.

After so long, she tried hard not to think of her twin's disappearance, but she was always there. Always present.

That's how Skye knew Summer was alive. She had to be. Skye would have felt her death. She'd felt her desperation. Not for a while. Until recently.

Skye reached over to place Eeyore on the windowsill to watch her and then moved the top box and balanced it on the stack next to her.

Summer – School Photographs, Reports

Skye moved that one too. Her heart simply couldn't cope with looking right now. It was too much for her deal with. Memories were already whipping through her without evoking more unnecessarily.

Summer – Artwork

This. This was the one.

Skye rested her hands on the box and took in a long, slow breath.

She removed the lid and put it to one side while she foraged through a stack of papers of varying size and thickness. She knew what she was looking for. Knew it had to be there.

Her fingers touched on the spiral binding of a sketch pad, and she coaxed it from under the other papers. This was what she'd been looking for, she was sure. Skye's memory of Summer's possessions was eerily vivid. She'd spent the first eighteen months pawing over everything. Each little item, every single drawing. Just to find a clue. To discover something the police had overlooked. She never had. But every item of Summer's was ingrained on her memory.

Without anywhere to comfortably sit, Skye backed out of the passageway of boxes she'd created. With her back to the wall next to the doorway, she slid down to sit cross-legged next to Cleo, who barely acknowledged her except for the flick of one soft ear and a gentle grumble.

Skye stared at the book. Spiral binding. Hard cover. Navy blue. Nothing fancy or artistic. The creations contained inside were the art.

She took a moment to prepare herself while her fingers stroked the outside.

This was slowly going to kill her, she was sure. She closed her eyes to block out the sadness that almost overwhelmed her before opening them again when she was ready.

She held one edge of the cover and flipped it over the top binding.

The rush of memories would have swept her off her feet if she'd been standing. Her chest squeezed tight until she was breathing like she'd run a marathon.

The first time Summer had ever used the medium of charcoal in her artwork. A bowl of fruit. The strokes had been bold and dark, with delicate smudged areas of shading. Darkness and light.

That was what had been so familiar to Skye. Not just the medium, but the style. There was something distinctive about her twin's artwork. She was sure she would recognise it anywhere. There was a certain power that pulled her into the picture. No matter what the subject matter.

She flicked over to a second page.

This still life was of flowers, dead, wilted in a black vase with an ornately curving handle. But the vase wasn't a solid black. There were varying strokes and shades, giving it depth and shape, depicting death in all its horror.

Skye remembered Summer sketching it. She'd begged their mum to let the flowers die. Her mum had been desperate to throw them out, but Summer had won her over. Red roses, whose full blooms still held beauty in their decay, bowed their heads over the edge. Undefeated in death, they still vied for attention.

Skye traced her fingers lightly over the dead roses then down to outline the vase and a smile curved her lips as the memory popped into her mind, vivid and alive.

'Mum, can I break the vase?' Summer grinned up at their mum from where she sat at the dining table, the sketch finished, the vase with its dead flowers in front of her.

Horror had streaked their mum's face. 'Certainly not.'

Skye blinked.

She turned the page. The broken vase lay littered across the table, dead rose petals scattered around.

Love. That's what it's about.

A hammer hung loose in her mum's hand, a wide smile

stretched across her face to make her cheeks crinkle, her eyes sparkle at the sheer destructiveness in the name of art.

Skye blinked away her tears, but not before one dropped onto a blackened petal, smearing the charcoal in a circular blur.

She wiped the heel of her hand across her cheeks, sensing the quiet shuffle of Cleo getting closer to her to offer her comfort. Skye reached out to stroke the dog's head before she turned the page.

The next picture was a scene of a meadow with a cliff in the distance and a sliver of sea on the horizon. Skye could almost feel the long grasses blowing in the wind, smell the fresh salt-laden air.

This was it. This was Summer's style.

Skye stared at it, a frown dipping her brows as she concentrated.

She was damned sure now she saw this. Absolutely positive.

The same style as the picture she'd been shown earlier in the day. If only she'd been able to take a quick snapshot of it with her phone, but both the officers' attention had been firmly fixed on her.

She could barely remember seeing them out the front door. Once they'd gone, she'd sat in stunned silence for well over an hour before the cogs in her mind started to turn and Cleo had nudged her nose under her elbow to remind her it was time for her dinner.

Now she knew without a doubt.

Should she ring them?

Her sister was alive. She was somewhere not too far away. If she was still there.

Skye pushed up from the floor. The ache in her knees told her exactly how long she'd sat cross-legged as blood rushed back to her numb feet.

She raised her head and glanced out of the window as rain streaked down the panes and the only thing visible was her own reflection, with the bare bulb glaring down to light up the room. Another little bugbear that had put Jade's nose out of joint when Dad had removed the curtains and lampshade with the intention of e-decorating and had instead turned the room into a storage facility.

It didn't matter to her. At least she had everything she needed now. All she had to do was find the address she had written down on the page in her back pocket.

It was late. Too late. By the time she got there…

Skye glanced out of the window again, the last ribbons of daylight streaked across the sky in dusky hues of purple and ochre in a final dramatic burst before it was snuffed out.

She stared at the window. A soft blurring of her own reflection stared back at her. She reached her hand out. It wasn't her, but her twin… 'Summer.'

39

SUNDAY, 21 MAY 2023, 8.45 P.M.

I can't do it. I can't.

I'm all alone now. The air would be still except for the shimmer of anger radiating from me. A shimmer I've not felt for years. It's shouldered its way through the numbness.

My chin rests on my knees as I gaze around my cell. The door stands wide. Open to the outside. I think I could walk out of here. Right now. What's to stop me?

Me.

I stop me. Every time. I've had opportunities. Countless. There's something deep in my psyche that won't allow me to leave. My logical brain tells me that I'm programmed. Indoctrinated. That knowledge doesn't make it any easier for me to make the move. To run.

Don't judge me.

Put yourself in my ragged shoes.

There's a part of me so bonded with LJ. I'm not sure it's love. Obsession, certainly. Unhealthy, for sure.

He's changed lately. Moved on and I'm not so sure I'm as in thrall to him as I was. I'm still toying with how I feel.

Whatever triggered LJ's aberrant fear today, I'm not ready to destroy my life's work. I've suffered so much at his hands and I'm pretty sure that when he returns, he'll kill me. So why help him clean up? Erase me from his life? He'll have to do that all on his own.

I roll onto my hands and knees and check my markings on the wall. I still scratch them in every day. My first nail wore down, but I managed to coax another one from the bedframe, leaving it a little unstable and creaky. That one's almost at the end of its life now, too, but I took two more from the other room.

I've not added the days up recently, but I do now. Counting backwards.

I stop at just over the four-year mark. The day I took that first tiny piece of charcoal. My memory of it is vague. Had Charlotte pushed it through the hole in the wall with her knife? Poked it until I could feel it with my fingertips? I wish she'd poked the knife through. Would I have used it then?

My mind wanders as the memory floats like a sheet on a listless wind.

'Summer. Look what I found. You can use it instead of scraping the wall.'

Only I knew charcoal was temporary and the scratches were my story. Proof of my existence. So I continued marking each day with my nail and used the charcoal for its true purpose. Sketching instead. A new story.

I circle around, looking at them. My art saved me, but my scratches into the wall keep me halfway sane.

I trace my fingertips over the marks. Counting. Counting. Each score in the wall a day of my life. And I know exactly how long it's been since I started sketching.

Four years since I started documenting my life story.

I turn and once again sit on my backside as I study the room.

No.

I won't scrub it clean.

This is *my* artwork. *My* life.

I know he thinks he can make me, but something inside me has hardened and I'm resolute. The broken part of me makes a tentative attempt at healing.

Dusk has fallen and I crawl onto my bed, lying on my side with my face to the wall. There's nothing to fear here. I've learnt that over these past seven years.

Ghosts don't exist and only the living can hurt you. Only LJ hurts me.

I close my eyes to blank out the vision of all my hard work. If nothing else, I'm proud of that. Proud that I've left my imprint, if not on the world, then on these walls and across the curve of the low ceiling until it elevates in an arch over the window where I can no longer reach.

One day perhaps it will be discovered. Like the drawings discovered in caves from prehistoric man or the hieroglyphics from the Egyptian pyramids.

I'm no hunter-gatherer, but I'm an artist and my work is as important to me as those cave drawings from centuries ago. Will it be centuries before mine are found?

Who knows?

It could be days.

Some people would damn me for the life I've led. Judge me for what they see as my weakness.

That's what the other girls thought too. They're dead. I'm alive. What does that say?

I'm a survivor and my story is here for anyone to read.

I draw my cover over me as a chill touches my rapidly cooling skin and the ghosts I deny exist come to haunt me.

Charlotte. The unnamed girl. Lilijana.

Poor Lilijana.

What is the point of escaping? She had purpose and a life to go to. Mine no longer exists. They would not want me now. LJ made sure of that. He's drummed it into me. I'm stupid. I'm a mess.

I'm a creature.

I squeeze my eyes tightly closed. There's nowhere for me to go, so I will stay here.

Tonight, I will sleep. I will not clean my artwork off the walls and floors and ceilings and the passageway and stairwell. I will not put it right for him.

He's not coming back tonight.

He's coming back tomorrow.

And when he does, it will be my time to die.

40

MONDAY, 22 MAY 2023, 9.25 A.M.

Two days after the wedding

Skye opened the boot. 'In you get.'

Cleo leapt in, all enthusiasm and wagging tail, mistakenly believing she was going for a walk. Well, she'd already had an early-morning walk and now Skye had other, more pressing matters to deal with.

She slid into the driver's seat and tapped the postcode into her satnav. She made herself comfortable before she set the car in gear and reversed out of her driveway.

Pulling up to the kerb in front of the bridalwear hire shop, Skye scooped her dad's suit from the back seat and trotted inside the shop.

'Hi, I'm just returning the groom's suit for the Matthews' wedding.'

A mature lady with an abundance of steel-grey curls peered over the top of her glasses at Skye and smiled. She moved a garment she was sewing to one side, carefully placing the attached needle and thread on top. She got to her feet and moved from behind a table to step up to the counter. 'Did it go well?' The hint of an Irish accent tinged her words.

'It did. Thank you.'

It hadn't. Not really. Of course, her dad and Martha believed it had, but that phone call had sucked the joy from the whole day. All the way through to the moment Skye's drink had been spiked. From then onwards, her memory had holes.

Today she felt much better having drunk water continuously the previous day to flush her system through. Her mind had cleared. She was focused despite a night of tossing and turning waiting for the day to break.

She forced a smile as she laid the suit on the counter for the lady to check.

The woman looked up, her cheeks crinkling as she smiled wider. 'There are three suits to be returned from the wedding party, I believe.'

'Yes.' She thought of Luke and Jacob and considered it wasn't her place to mention that the legs of one pair of trousers had been doused in puke. Her fault, but not her responsibility. Maybe she would offer to pay the excess once Jacob returned it, but she wasn't going to mention it to this woman. 'They'll be returning their own suits. They're aware of that. This one is my dad's.'

'Ah, very well. They're supposed to have them here by midday, so you might want to remind them.' She lifted her gaze pointedly to the small clock on the wall. It was 9.30 a.m.

Skye stretched a smile. 'I'm sure they'll be here.' She nodded as she kept the smile in place, her face aching from it. 'I'll remind them.'

It wasn't her responsibility to make sure they returned their suits. Was it? She could only assume her dad hadn't paid a deposit on all of them. For the life of her, she could not remember being told to collect all the suits.

She edged out of the door. 'Thank you.'

She slipped into her car and sent a quick message to both Luk and Jacob. Their responsibility now. She'd done her bit.

As she drove away, Skye glanced in her rearview mirror.

Was that Jacob's car just pulling up into the space she'd vacated

Her gaze bounced back off the mirror and she stared straight a the road ahead.

Chest tight, Skye drove through the outskirts of Telford breaking out into vast countryside, and headed for the destination she'd already plumbed into her satnav.

One hour, twenty minutes. There was no point staying stressed for the entire journey. She turned on the radio, but the screechy overexcited voice of the presenter slid under her skin like red-ho needles, making her nerve endings twitch.

Skye touched her thumb to the on/off switch and allowed the quiet shush of the car speeding down the country lanes to soothe her while her mind went wild.

What was she doing?

She was on a mission, right or wrong, and nothing was going to stop her.

She turned off the main A road onto narrow lanes that wound their way higher into the hills, until the valley below was obscured by puffs of white clouds.

It wasn't her imagination that the air was becoming thinner, she was sure.

Her car topped a rise, and she drew to a standstill. Barely wide enough for the car to squeeze through was a small lane off to the left that would take her even higher.

She hesitated. Was she completely mad? What was she thinking of, coming all the way here? Alone.

What if she turned up and she was wrong?

What if she was right?

The signal on her phone barely registered one bar of data coverage.

She could either take the left turn or carry straight on and try to find somewhere to turn around and go back.

Skye blew out a breath, depressed the accelerator and carried on straight ahead.

She'd already committed herself the moment she entered the postcode in the satnav. A postcode that currently showed she'd reached her destination. There was nothing there. Nothing to see apart from lush greenery. No inkling of a dwelling of any kind.

Over the rise and the road started to fall away again before she spotted a small passing place that she tucked her car well into so that it wouldn't be caught by any passing cars. The open view down the hillside was breathtaking.

Skye stared at the satnav. In taking the road she did, it looked like she'd passed her destination, although the voice of the satnav hadn't yet screamed at her to tell her to turn around. Not that she could turn around. A three-point turn on this hillside would end up with her down in the valley in a ball of flames, she imagined, even with the extra width of the passing place.

Skye pressed the buttons for the electric windows to lower each of them several inches so the air remained cool enough in the car while she investigated the house. She'd come back for Cleo the moment she knew where she was. That was the easiest way, otherwise she'd be walking her along a dangerous lane with very little leeway to pull over if a car came. She pictured herself throwing her dog into the hedgerow. No. That wasn't going to happen.

'Stay there, Cleo. I won't be long.'

Cleo's sad whine still didn't persuade her to change her mind.

She'd trot back along the lane. See if she could spot a house anywhere.

She stepped out of the car and made her way back to the

narrow lane. She followed along the steep incline, puffing as she pushed herself onwards, a thin layer of sweat coated her face and drizzled down the length of her spine.

Just as she started to believe she'd entered the wrong postcode into her satnav and was about to turn around and make her way back to the car, the small lane dinked to the left again, opening out to a wide drive, overgrown with weeds almost waist high. A dilapidated house perched on the hillside, the right side of it appeared to be partially buried into the rockface, the front sprawling and wide.

This was it.

The trickle of unease she'd had turned into a flood.

She'd been here before. Years ago. Five, maybe six years.

Her recollection of it was vague. She'd been disinterested at the time. Initially.

This was it. The place she really dreaded to think had the same view as the sketch now in the police officers' possession.

She could still be wrong.

She knew in her heart she wasn't.

She walked a few steps to the house. The bottom wooden doorstep was rotten and collapsed, but she stepped over it and prayed the next step up didn't do the same under her weight.

The doorbell worked and the sound pealed out in the empty atmosphere.

Was she wrong? The place looked completely abandoned.

Was it just a cruel coincidence?

She turned her back to the door and studied the place. She could see the roof of her car from where she stood. But nothing else.

The sweep of the gravel and weed driveway was wide and empty.

If anyone was home, they'd somehow managed to get there without using a car.

41

MONDAY, 22 MAY 2023, 9.45 A.M.

Two days after the wedding

Cold sweat beaded his top lip.

He swiped it off with the back of his wrist before he glanced over his shoulder. He pulled his car away from the kerb and out into traffic that seemed to have become heavy in the past few minutes.

He didn't like being lectured and that's what the jumped-up old hag behind the counter had done. He wasn't used to being spoken to like that. He commanded respect. She gave him none.

Luckily for her, he'd tamped down on his fury, paid the excess for handing back a clean but slightly shrunken pair of trousers and left without any harm being done. Harm was exactly what he'd wanted to do, what he held tightly onto. Before the end of the day, someone was definitely going to get harmed.

He touched the phone button on his steering wheel and when the numbers appeared on the display, he selected the one for work.

'Hey, Carly. How are you?'

Carly's calm, efficient tone brought his heart rate back down a notch as she answered him.

'Look, Carly, I've got a lot on at the moment. I'm going to take some personal days. Let them know I'm not available unless there's an emergency, would you?'

'Yes, of course. Is everything all right?'

He touched his damaged face with his fingertips. Perhaps that hadn't helped the situation with the old woman. She probably thought he'd been in a brawl.

'Everything is fine. I just have a lot of catching up to do and I need some personal space to get it done. No worries, I'll be back in probably next week.' He paused. 'We'll see how it goes.'

Doubt crept into Carly's voice. 'Are you sure you're okay?'

He felt the irritation kick in at her questioning his word. 'I will be. Soon. I'm sure. Thank you for your concern.'

'Oh, no worries. You take care. I look forward to seeing you soon, Mr—'

He pressed the off button as his car sailed along the A road. He didn't need his satnav, he knew the route like the back of his hand. If you followed that, it took you through all the narrow lanes instead of sticking to a minor, but more serviceable B road approaching from the other side of the hill until the very last turn.

He turned the radio on and relaxed as he watched the country-side rush past. A countryside he knew so well. The gentle swell of hills rose steadily as he left behind the flatter fields of Shropshire.

42

Two days after the wedding

I don't think I've ever heard the doorbell here ring before. I'm pretty sure that's what it is.

I curl into a tight ball on my bed and squeeze my eyes closed. Whoever it is will go away. They have to go away. They're not allowed in. LJ wouldn't want anyone here.

He's never said it, but I'm pretty sure I'm not allowed to answer the door. After all, according to him, I don't exist. I am nothing. Just a creature.

The sound peels out again and I lift my head. I'm not entirely sure the front door is locked. When LJ left last night, I can't recall hearing him locking it, and I never went back up there to check.

After all, who would want to try and get into this house? This hell hole.

It's so remote, or so I'd believed until Lilijana took off, disappearing into the night. She obviously found civilisation.

Still, no one would come here. Risk this house of horrors.

Would they?

A shaft of guilt stabs at me as I look around my room, my cell. haven't done as LJ instructed.

For the first time in years, I've disobeyed him. I've not cleaned single inch of my artwork from the walls, or the ceiling, or the floo I couldn't. It's my salvation.

I wonder if he'll kill me for my disobedience.

He's murdered for less. I now know he has. There's not just dark side, but a sickness in him that's grown over these last fe years. From the time he started bringing other young women here When it was just me, I understood. He was obsessed. There's n obsession now, but perhaps he's trying to replicate that origina rush he got when he first brought me here. That excitement. Tha fanaticism that's worn off.

No longer enthusiastic, he's purely sadistic.

Another ping of the doorbell and I start to wonder if this is why LJ wanted me to clean up. Did he know someone was coming?

I let my gaze wander around the room.

Does he think it's a mess? Is he ashamed of it?

I don't think it's shameful. I love it. Everything I know is here.

I swing my legs from the bed and place my feet on the floor.

Have they gone? The bell hasn't sounded again for a few moments. Perhaps I need to check. To investigate. After all, LJ wouldn't want someone wandering around here uninvited.

He'd want me to deal with them. Get rid of them.

I leave my shoes off and sidle up the narrow, winding stairwell until I'm almost at the top. The sliding door into the hallway stands open. I can't see anything unusual, but my heartrate quickens.

Someone's here.

That animal instinct I've developed over the years tells me there's someone in the house with me.

I sniff the air. There's a different smell to it.

A freshness.

I'm not alone.

43

MONDAY, 22 MAY 2023, 11.15 A.M.

Two days after the wedding

Without really understanding why, Skye reached out and gave the old-fashioned doorknob a gentle turn. The door made a light cracking noise as it opened as though the heat had made the dry, flaking paint stick to the doorframe.

She let out a soft gasp.

Should she go in?

She'd never done anything like this in her life. Why would she enter someone else's property?

The answer was clear in her own mind.

Because she had to know.

She let the door swing wide and stepped inside a short hallway. A stairway disappeared upwards to her right and a wooden sliding door in the void under them was ajar, exposing the top step to what appeared to be a flight of stairs going down presumably to a cellar.

Darkness beckoned to her, but she took a deliberate step away, a shudder pricking at her skin.

She knew what she was looking for. The view.

It had been so long ago that she'd visited, the house was unfamiliar. She'd only been once. With her dad. She barely remembered why she'd accompanied him, but she had. Moral support, she supposed. Not long after her mum had died. Just after the new partnership had been forged.

She stepped through the room on her left into an old ramshackle kitchen with cupboards that slewed at slight angles. A small curtain covered the void under the sink, like her grandmother used to have in her kitchen. From what she could remember of the old lady.

A window looked out onto a walled courtyard, but where she would have thought there'd be a window overlooking the front of the house and the driveway, there wasn't.

Skye opened the backdoor and took a quick glance out at a small courtyard. High walls closing in and almost barren. Except for weeds starting to poke their way between paving slabs, wet and shiny from what could have been a cloud burst.

She closed the door and stepped back into the kitchen. None of it seemed familiar. She couldn't recall being in this room.

Skye tracked back through to the hall and followed it until it opened out into the wide expanse of a room she remembered with gut-wrenching horror.

She stood for a moment as the pain in her chest made her recognise how shallow her breathing was.

The sick realisation that what she'd considered a delusion, a fantasy born of optimism in finding her sister, was in fact true. She stumbled back a step and dipped a shaking hand into her handbag to rummage for her phone.

Dear God, she needed to phone the police. She was right. She'd been right all along. Why had she doubted herself? Why hadn't she told the police? For the same reason many didn't tell the police. The fear of looking stupid.

Because after the first two years of sightings and reports, of false hope and misinformation, the police had stopped listening, stopped believing. If people disappeared for that length of time, either they were never coming back, or they were already dead.

This time, though, she was right, and she should have told them.

This empty vessel of a house was the place her sister had been. Whether that was recent, or not, was another matter, but she had been here. The view from the window was the one the police had on the sketch. The sketch of that incredible, unmistakable vista Skye had no doubt now had been created by her sister.

Her fingers wrapped around her phone as she took in her surroundings. Old floral furniture she didn't recognise from before, when there had been sleek black leather sofas. Everything was so old and mismatched, as though it had been picked up at a charity shop.

Skye squinted at her surroundings, horror grabbing at her throat. It looked clean. Everywhere looked clean.

It wasn't deserted. It was someone's residence.

Someone did live here. But who?

Had it been sold in the interim? New people moved in?

It seemed a strange coincidence and not according to her research. The address was still on the official Companies' House register of directors for her dad's business from what she'd read the night before.

Maybe the register hadn't been updated.

She looked at her phone and as it recognised her face and sprang to life, Skye let out a soft groan. No service. No freakin' service.

She closed her eyes and then popped them wide as a voice she recognised spoke from the doorway behind her.

'Summer?'

44

MONDAY, 22 MAY 2023, 11.40 A.M.

Two days after the wedding

Mind full of the tasks he needed to complete, he let the music and inane chatter of the radio wash over him as he plotted. He glanced in the mirror as he took a turn onto a smaller track.

Broom handles poked up from where he'd stashed them in the boot with more cleaning products. Bleach, disinfectant, soda crystals... whatever the hell you used those for. Window cleaner, anything to scrub off evidence of their presence and, just in case, he'd picked up a five-litre container of general cleaning fluid they used at work. He kept it under the sink in his apartment. Just in case. You never knew when that kind of product would come in handy. There was another one in the house, but he suspected Summer would have used most of it by now.

When he'd thought about it, he realised there was no way Summer would be able to clean off everything in one go. For a start, it would take her an age with that small scrubbing brush.

The soft flutter of panic made his chest clench. He had to get out of there as fast as possible.

A grim smile plastered his face. Stupid girl. He could imagine her on hands and knees, scrubbing as tears fell. She'd have stayed up all night, just to please him, but there was no way she would have everything finished by the time he arrived.

She'd be terrified of him. Cowering in the corner like the timid mouse she'd become. Despicable. She made his stomach curdle.

He thought of the other items he had in the boot. The thick black plastic liner. The shovel. He'd needed to buy a new one of those as he'd broken the handle on the one in the basement the last time he'd used it when he'd slammed it so hard into the ground until it vibrated up his arms as it hit solid rock.

He slowed down to edge past a white car parked in one of the passing places. He glanced in as he passed but there was no one there, just tinted windows half down.

Bloody tourists. It never ceased to amaze him how many idiots did that, just to get out and take a look at the view. Maybe take a photograph while another driver crashes into their car and knocks it off the edge of the precipice. Fools. All of them.

They were called passing places for a reason. Not parking spaces. Inconsiderate fools.

He narrowed his eyes. He'd not seen a dog up at the window, so perhaps a young couple had left a baby in the car seat while they jumped into the bushes to have a piss.

Or some old couple who decided to have their morning coffee and a biscuit as they dangled their legs off one of the outcrops of boulders further down the winding lane, never giving one thought to the fact that the boulder may not be secure. Nothing in this area was secure. There were always rockfalls off the edge.

Whichever. It didn't concern him.

LJ took the sharp turn onto the narrow dirt track up to his house. It would be the last time. He wouldn't be back. Once probate was settled, the solicitors would sell the property and he could buy something new with the measly share he inherited, together with the savings he'd made over the last few years.

Something without all the dark memories this one held.

A fresh new start.

Maybe he'd join a dating app. Find a nice young wife. Someone with more about her than his previous one. Weak willed and pathetic, the woman had never had any backbone. If he told her she shouldn't eat something, she didn't.

When she'd faded away, anorexia getting the better of her in the end, she wasn't missed. Her estranged family hadn't even come to her pathetically small funeral. He had informed them, but they'd not spoken to his wife in all the years they'd been married. It was a bitter pill for her to swallow, but she'd been better off without them. He'd made sure she was safe. Happy. As happy as a miserable person could be.

Perhaps his next wife would have more about her.

He needed to start with a clean slate.

It had all become too heavy for his shoulders to bear the weight.

Before he left, though, he needed to make sure there was no evidence of his presence there.

Summer should be well on the way to cleaning up her mess.

The lemon scent would be strong and astringent as he went in. If she'd not diluted it properly it was going to make his eyes sting too.

The car switched to electric and glided silently up to the front of the house. He stared at it for a long moment. It had been a good place. Useful.

Its usefulness had run its course. It was time to get rid of it. Wipe it off his radar as such. With no trace.

He reached over to the passenger side of the car and picked up the plastic carrier bag with the scrubbing brushes and let out a grunt as he lifted the container of cleaning fluid. He opened the boot and slid the long-handled brushes out.

LJ imagined the little mouse of a woman staying up all night, scrubbing those walls and floors until there was nothing left, no evidence of her existence, just to please him. She did a lot to please him these days. It got on his nerves. She'd lost everything. All appeal.

Like the house, she had to go. He had the equipment to see to it. Although it wasn't something he relished. He'd never actually taken a life before. Not intentionally.

Arms full, LJ hesitated, leaving the boot open.

Why would the front door be open? He'd not noticed it immediately. It wasn't wide, but ajar. He'd shut it behind him when he'd left. Not locked it perhaps, but then he rarely locked it. After all, they'd never had a visitor in years up here and Summer would never dream of venturing beyond the back doorstep, never mind the front one. She was too scared. Too programmed.

Still, someone had opened the door.

He didn't like that.

He thought of the car in the passing place.

He pushed it wider with his foot and quietly placed all the gear he'd brought from the car just inside the kitchen and then walked towards the door into the courtyard to see if she was there.

Summer may have cleaned up, but it looked more like the deluge of rain in the early hours had washed the chalk from the paving slabs and the stones. There was a partially smudged small sketch creeping up one side of the wall. He wouldn't have noticed if he didn't know what to look for.

He'd have to speak with her about that.

She needed to erase it.

He needed to erase everything else. His existence in this place.

Once he disposed of poor, pathetic little Summer, who would right now be in the cellar, scrubbing the ceiling.

His mouth twisted with distaste. It wasn't a pleasant job, but it had to be done.

After today, he'd not return.

He stepped back through the kitchen into the hallway and towards the door down to the cellar that was slid open on its runners about a foot, enough for pathetic little Summer to slip through.

He raised his hand to slide it back further when a soft sound from the living room had him pausing.

A quiet gasp? A gentle movement?

LJ turned and made his way there.

With her back to him, long hair shining like he'd not seen it for so long, beautiful and sleek, Summer stood with her back to him, her attention on the view from the expanse of windows.

'Summer?'

She turned around, her face set in a mask of stone-cold fury.

Her lips barely moved. 'I knew it was you. It had to be.'

45

MONDAY, 22 MAY 2023, 11.50 A.M.

Two days after the wedding

'Jacob.' Her lips, stiff with tension, barely moved.

His own battered face reflected her horror. 'Skye.' He breathed the word out, disbelief whispering on the air.

'The car... it's yours.'

She inclined her head, her gaze centred on him. Had Jordon done that to him? Blackened his eye and split his lip?

'Skye,' she confirmed, her eyes narrowing as the import of it truly hit her. He'd not sold the place. It still belonged to him. Only he'd furnished it differently. Why would he do that?

Why would he do any of this?

She needed answers.

'Not my twin. Not Summer.' She licked lips that had gone dry. 'Why would you think I was Summer? You don't even know her.' She paused, cocked her head to one side. 'Do you?'

She squinted at him. This was just too surreal. 'You didn't know our family until after Summer had gone. Disappeared. Absconded.'

Or had he? Had he known her before she was...

Taken.

Skye knew. There was no doubt in her mind why Jacob thought for that split second that she was Summer. Because he saw who he expected to see. Not her. Not Skye, but her twin. There was only one reason he would make that mistake.

She puffed out a breath.

This was why she was here. To find the sister he'd stolen. Kidnapped. Kept.

What she hadn't anticipated until last night was who? Who had taken her twin?

Not in her wildest dreams had she imagined it was someone they knew. Knew and trusted. Trusted and loved. Someone so close, her stomach tightened, the burn of nausea heavy in the pit of it.

They'd taken Jacob into the family fold. As much as he'd saved the family business, they'd saved him too. After the death of his wife.

She tried to swallow but the spit had dried in her mouth.

How had his wife died? She couldn't remember. Was it anorexia? She'd never met her. It was at the beginning, when he first got to know her dad.

'Skye.' He reached out a hand in gentle appeal but there was something in his eyes that sent a shiver along her spine.

With a sharp step back, her heel rammed against the rotted wooden frame of the floor-to-ceiling window. She froze, a whimper catching in the back of her throat. 'Don't come near me. Don't you touch me.' The frame crumbled beneath the heel of her shoe and her foot sank into the soft, decayed wood.

He angled his head to one side. Skye almost heard the cogs in his head calculating how hard he needed to push for the window behind her to burst out of its frame and to tumble down into the rocky valley below. Taking her with it.

She didn't want to move, to get closer to him, but if she didn't

want to be his victim, she needed to slip past him before he had th
opportunity to make up his mind.

'So, it was your car I passed down the lane.' He gave out
rueful snort as he shook his head. 'I should have recognised i
but you'd reversed it right into the hedgerow. I never saw th
registration plate.' He huffed out a laugh. 'Silly me. I was other
wise occupied, and let's face it, white Ford Fiestas are prett
common.'

She flinched at his demeaning tone. How dare he?

That wasn't the worst of his sins, though.

Uneasy in his presence, she needed to get out of there. Phon
the police and leave it to them. She wished she'd already informe
them before taking off on her own. Not for a moment had sh
considered she wouldn't get a signal.

She was predominantly a city girl. Why would she conside
data coverage?

But she was in the middle of nowhere. A possible data
blackspot.

It was just her and Jacob.

A slight movement had her darting her gaze beyond him to the
open doorway.

'LJ.' The soft, almost childish whisper had Skye's heart leaping
into her throat.

A slash of absolute fury passed over Jacob's face as he spun
around to face the door.

The slight, waif-like woman leaned against the doorframe, her
shoulders hunched as though her body was curling in on itself, a
twitch gently consuming her body. Her hair hung in long, tangled
tresses, almost reaching her knees. Eyes that should have been an
exact replica of Skye's were dull and lifeless. Skin, grey and gaunt,
stretched over high cheekbones.

Skye took the opportunity to step away from the window, side-stepping to remove herself from Jacob's reach, but she couldn't stop the name that spilled from her lips in an agonised cry.

'Summer.'

The woman's eyes flickered to her, widened briefly with a flash of something indefinable, perhaps recognition, and then turned dull again. Her skinny frame twitched with a continuous motion of fidgets and spasms.

Skye couldn't be certain whether her sister was a drug addict, or if she had some kind of neurological disorder, but she'd never seen anyone so emaciated.

My wife died of anorexia.

Shock tore at her soul. He was a monster.

'Summer.' This time the name came with more assurance. She ignored Jacob, even though his body had tightened beside her. 'It's me.' She kept her voice soft, as though she was talking to a child. Because the person in front of her was delicate. Fragile.

Horror unfurled in her stomach as Skye watched her twin sister. Eyes downcast, flickered up and away, over Jacob and down again. She had one arm crossed over a tiny waist, the hand gripping the wrist of her other hand as if she was trying to hold herself together.

Her sallow, thin skin was wrinkled like there was no substance underneath to keep it stretched taut.

'Go to your room, Summer.' The low vibration of Jacob's voice held such threat that Skye's insides turned to liquid.

She'd never heard him use that voice. Never once seen that look in his eyes. Except...

'It *was* you, that night.'

She'd seen a flash of something she'd thought at the time was her imagination. She'd mistaken it for annoyance at her throwing up on his shoes, but now she recognised it for what it was.

Fury at being thwarted.

Terror flooded her and she swayed on her feet.

He craned his neck to look sideways at her. 'Me? What was me?' His eyes pierced her as he stabbed the question out to make her flinch. It didn't stop her, though. Her own bubbling fury could match his any day.

'The night of Dad's wedding. You *did* put something in my drink. It had to be you. There was no one else. It wasn't Luke. He came nowhere near me. It was you.' She shook her head, no idea how he'd achieved it, but certain that he had.

He gave her a grim smile. 'It wasn't difficult. It never is. You women never take enough care. You think because someone is nice, they're not going to do something bad.' He wrinkled his nose as he sneered down at her.

She kept her body still. Stiff. 'I thought you were nice. I thought you were my dad's best friend.'

He snorted as he made a half-turn back towards her, leaving Summer hovering in the doorway as though she couldn't bring herself to go but was terrified to defy him.

A lick of anger started to build, a small fire-lighter in the depths of Skye's belly. He'd done this to her sister. *He'd done this.*

She glanced at the ghost of a woman behind him. A husk. That was all that was left of her beautiful twin.

All because of this man. This brute.

'I've never been best friends with Allan.' His nose wrinkled in a sneer of disgust. 'We were colleagues, associates. Never friends.'

Shock rocked her back on her heels as if he'd slapped her. That had never been the way of things. 'He asked you to be his best man.'

'More fool him.'

'He thinks you're his friend.' And with good reason. Jacob had been in their lives for years. Knew intimate details about all of them.

'I'm not. Never have been. Why would I be?' He paused before delivering a well-calculated blow. 'He killed your mum.'

Shock staggered her. A sharp cattle prong to the heart. She shook her head in denial.

'My mum died of an embolism. A haemorrhage in her brain.'

'Caused through the stress of leaving your dad.'

'What? What?' Her mouth fell open as she glared at him. 'Don't be so ridiculous. Mum wasn't leaving Dad. She adored him.'

'She didn't adore him. It was me she loved. Me she wanted.'

'She didn't even know you.' She shook her head with disbelief. He was a madman.

'Of course she did.' He flung out an arm and Skye took a step back. Her gaze skittered to her sister, who slumped against the doorframe, her head bowed, her narrow shoulders still jittering in gentle convulsions, her head bobbing. 'We worked together.'

Confusion rolled over Skye in clouds to fuzz her memory.

'We didn't know you before. Mum never knew you.' Her words faltered, stuttering from a clumsy mouth. Before her mum died, before Summer disappeared, she wanted to say, but the words refused to tumble from her mouth. The man had lost all sanity.

'Of course you didn't, do you think I'm stupid?' White spittle rained down on his bottom lip as he snarled at her.

Summer's head shot up, bloodshot eyes turned wild like a spooked filly about to bolt.

Skye took the unintended warning from her twin and held both hands, palms out to Jacob in a conciliatory manner. 'I'm sorry, I don't understand. Please help me. Explain to me what happened.' If she could buy some time, she could come up with a plan.

He tilted his head to one side as though assessing whether or not she was worth his time. Whether her question was borne of genuine interest.

'Your mum, Christine, was an incredibly bright woman. Beautiful, elegant.' His eyes melted into a faraway look for a moment before his dark gaze snapped back to Skye. 'When I first met her, she was single.'

The shock jolted Skye. What? He knew her before? Before Dad?

'Christine Lawrence. We were at university at the same time, not the same one, but nearby. We met at uni nights.' Skye stilled. This had to be some kind of sickness. Who would cling for so long?

'She was my first love. I worshipped the ground she walked on. Lady Christine, I called her. She used to laugh and claim I'd be better calling her Lady Muck. I never treated her like that, though. She was precious. I loved her.'

His eyes narrowed in contemplation. 'I truly believed she loved me too. We had one night together, and that was it. She met your father and never looked at me again. Not once. I would have pursued her, but my sister died at around about the same time. Tragic circumstances.'

His voice became distant for a moment, filled with regret. 'It wasn't until years later that I met her again. My company was carrying out an audit on a company Christine worked at.' It was as though he no longer wanted to acknowledge that Christine was her mum. Their mum. He was thumbing a wedge between them. 'She'd taken on extra work to help out Allan's failing company. He might have said it was Christine's death that caused its demise, but it was already floundering.'

The tight smile never reached his eyes. 'She was going through a rough patch at home. She felt invisible. As though no one needed her any longer. Allan was preoccupied with saving his business while she juggled two jobs, her own and propping his business up too. You girls were about to go to university and Jade, well, Jade was... as she always has been... a little bitch.'

The burn in Skye's chest threatened to burst into an inferno. How dare he! How dare he insult her little sister? Jade could be difficult, but that was hardly a surprise given their family history.

'he real surprise was that she wasn't a paid-up member of the mental health community. She hadn't been a difficult child when their mum was alive. All her rebellion had come after. Before that, he'd been a sweet, normal girl approaching her teenage years. They'd never had any behavioural problems with her before their mum died. Before Summer was stolen.

He roamed his eyes around the room, frantic and crazed. 'She came here, you know.' He stepped over to the wide panoramic window and stared out at the valley stretching for miles. A thin layer of dust and dirt had built up on the outside of the windows over the years, but couldn't disguise the beauty of it, breathtaking in comparison to the ugliness of his heart.

In the distance, a dirigible skimmed closer to the horizon, the vision so incongruous, it could have been a Zeppelin from some steampunk movie. There was something about the image that grounded Skye for a fleeting second. Made her consider they were not completely alone. But whatever help they needed, they'd have to travel a considerable distance.

Her mind whisked to her twin sister, her heart clenching at the prospect of their demise.

She thought of Cleo locked in the car and could only hope someone would find her if something bad happened. If Jacob lost it completely and murdered them both. Although Summer was evidently scarred for life, she was alive, so maybe he wouldn't kill now, if he'd never killed before.

She gave a shudder. What if he had? Maybe there was no hope.

Her poor dog. If only she'd brought Cleo with her. Not that Cleo could do any damage. She knew Jacob. She was hardly likely to turn on him, to defend Skye. But at least she would have been free to run instead of cooped up in a car that would get steadily hotter during the afternoon.

When Skye had left Cleo, she'd had every intention of returning reasonably quickly.

Skye gave herself a mental shake. She still had every intention of going back. She couldn't think any other way.

With his back to them, Jacob moved closer to the vista and fell silent for a moment as though he pictured that time when their mum had visited. A time Skye had no knowledge or memory of.

Skye took the opportunity to take three cautious steps toward her sister. The tension in her twin was palpable, but she was willing to ignore it. If she had the opportunity to grab her and run, she was taking it. The only concern was how far it was down the dirt track to the narrow lane and her car tucked into the passing place.

At Jacob's slight move, Skye's attention centred back on him. 'She loved this view, did my Lady Christine.'

She'd never been called Christine. Not in their household. Dad had called her Chrissy. Just plain Chrissy. Yes, she'd been beautiful and elegant and gracious, but Jacob's desire for her was unhealthy, bordering on obsession. How had they never seen this side of him?

Skye stared at Jacob's broad shoulders, almost blocking out the view.

Perhaps they'd never wanted to. He'd befriended their dad, not Skye and Jade as much. He'd been their dad's partner. He'd saved the business. But why?

She reached behind her and took hold of Summer's wrist, her fingers wrapping around a bone so fragile, she imagined she could have broken it with just the slightest pressure.

With noticeable determination, Summer yanked her wrist from Skye's hold, taking her by surprise at the unexpected strength as Skye sensed rather than felt her twin move away from the door, into the hallway and out of her reach.

It had never occurred to Skye that her own twin wouldn't want to be touched. Of course she wouldn't. What kind of hell had she lived through that she didn't even trust the touch of her own sister?

A sister she hadn't seen for almost seven years.

In fear of Jacob turning around, Skye fumbled to ask him a question and keep him talking. 'Why was she here? Why would she have come out here? There would be no reason.' She edged around the word 'mum' in case he became edgy again.

He raised his arm and rested the heel of his hand on the window. The soft bloom of heat spread to make a dusky cloud on the glass. He lowered his head to look straight down into the ravine and Skye found herself praying that the window would give way and Jacob would plunge down to be swallowed up by the deep crevice below.

'I phoned the company she was working for, said I'd injured my foot and couldn't drive, but I needed the documentation that day. Nothing gets up here quickly, so I asked if she could hand deliver. It was something we were both working on together, so it was natural they sent her.'

He turned his head. 'Did you know, she never even recognised me? At first. Not until I reminded her. By then it was too late.'

A sick shudder ran through her as the implication of what he was telling her hit home. She could barely force the words from her lips. 'You drugged and raped her. Just like you were going to do to me.'

With the speed of a serpent, he whipped around to glare at Skye. 'My relationship with Christine was consensual!'

She slapped a hand on her heart and staggered back a step.

The gentle touch of her twin's hand between her shoulders took her by surprise. Steadied her, but her breathing still came in juddering gasps. 'You raped my mum.'

She knew. She should have kept her mouth shut, but she knew. She had to have it confirmed. 'Why? Why would you do that to her?

A second time. Because I don't believe for one moment she went willingly in uni, either. I think you did something underhand there too.'

Like fog clearing from the hills, her vision was suddenly clear. He'd date-raped her mum in university. Then he'd done it again, years later. The sickness in him was so dark. So evil.

'You don't understand. You can never understand. From the minute I saw Christine, I loved her. Wanted her.' His voice turned bitter. 'He stole her from me, you know. Like he stole from me before.'

'But you took others. You took my sister.' She swallowed as the pain of it hit her. 'You would have taken me too, if Jade hadn't come along. We thought it might have been the barman. Or Luke, at first.'

'You stupid little girl. Of course it was me.' He sounded as though he was proud of it. 'It's not hard to hide a tablet in the crease of a palm. The little fizz of it disguised by the bubbles of a drink.'

This man hadn't just done this once. He'd practised. Perfected.

He stabbed his thumb into the soft flesh of his hand. 'I helped you onto the stool, and you couldn't even remember when I took the glass from your hand for a split second and placed it on the bar. It was easy. A moment in time. You naïve child. Naïve women who think they are protecting themselves and yet all the time leave themselves wide open, vulnerable, to—'

'Predators.' The word shot out, like a bullet.

He stopped dead in his tracks.

The air filled with tension as they stared at each other across the divide, both of them breathing heavily as though they'd just fought the first round of a boxing match.

'Were you going to bring me here?' She resisted looking over her shoulder at the insipid version of herself. 'Was I a replacement?'

Jacob's eyes shifted over her shoulder and back again to rest on her.

The warmth of her sister's hand withdrew and a chill set in where the pressure vanished.

She understood now that she was on her own, that whatever move she made, decision she took, her twin was too indoctrinated to help. How long had she been given the freedom of the house and yet chosen not to leave? What kind of sadist could have that impact? That reach?

An evil one.

A bastard.

Skye ground her teeth until her jaw ached as loose threads started to pull together. Her mum's anxiety, the high blood pressure. The reluctance to go into work, which she'd hidden from their dad. The memory had slipped away like a wisp of smoke on the wind, but it jammed back in with jarring clarity.

'You didn't have consensual sex with my mother. She would never have been unfaithful to my dad. Not back in university and not this time. You deceived everyone. You drugged her so she had no idea what had happened. The guilt and shame of that was what drove her to distraction until her brain could no longer cope and exploded in a shower of self-recrimination.'

'I never...'

'You did,' she shrieked. Quieter... 'You did,' she said, with more conviction. 'You drugged her, so she had sex with you.'

'She loved me. When she woke up in bed with me later that same afternoon, she understood. She knew we were meant to be.'

Skye shook her head. 'She never did. You drugged her, and then guilted her into feelings she never had because somehow, she believed she was at fault.'

A slash of realisation crossed his face, and that same realisation laid a ghost to rest in Skye's heart. With her own heart pounding abnormally, she knew in an instant. He'd used GBL from her own dad's factory. GBL was used as a paint stripper but when administered orally it converted into GHB in a person's body. It was kept in a secure lock-up, but of course Jacob would have access to it since he worked with her dad, but where had he managed to source it before? When she'd looked him up on Companies House there'd been a list of companies he'd previously worked for in that industry. None quite as specialised in that area, but the opportunity to acquire that chemical would have been there. How many times had he used it?

Disgust unfurled and she spat out, 'She died because her blood pressure shot up so high. High because you'd drugged and then blackmailed her. She didn't love you. She never loved you.' The words tumbled from her lips unfettered. 'My mum, *Chrissy*,' she stressed, to ensure he understood she'd been theirs all along and not his. 'She adored my dad. She adored us. And you took that away. You took away her life.'

She glared at him across the room. 'And then you took away my dad's by befriending him.' She flashed her arm behind her. 'And you took away the one consolation he could ever have. One of his daughters.'

His skin paled in the face of her attack.

'No. It wasn't that way.'

'It fucking was.' She rarely swore, but this time it warranted it, and she stepped forward into his space, no longer afraid. Too furious to even think about being afraid.

'You. You absolute fucking arse. I thought you were intelligent.' She watched the shock flash over his features, almost as though she'd dealt him a physical blow. 'Clever you may be, but you have no emotional intelligence. My mum never loved you. She adored my dad, she adored her children. She didn't want to be with you. We were her world, and you took that away from her, from all of us.' She slashed her hand to incorporate her sister. 'The only way you

ould achieve that was by drugging her. That's not love. That's ille-
al. It's evil.'

He recoiled at her words. The horror on his face making her
vonder for a split second if she was wrong, and then she looked
nto his eyes. Dead.

'I'm done with you.' She swivelled on her heel and took the two
teps she needed to get to her sister. 'We're going. I'm taking
Summer with me.'

Shock crashed through her as his heavy fist slammed down on
her shoulder, almost forcing her to the ground as her knees gave
way, her handbag slipping from her shoulder to fall on the floor, the
contents spilling in crazy abandon. 'You're not taking my girl, my
beautiful Christine.'

Ice froze in her veins. He had no idea, no concept of the real
world. Did he think Summer was his? That she was Christine? In
his twisted mind, did he believe her twin was their mum?

'Jacob.' She looked over her shoulder at him, thought to appeal
to his real self. The sane person beneath the deranged mind. 'I'm
going to take Summer and go.'

His stillness compressed all the air in the room until she could
barely breathe.

'No.' His voice was smooth. Deathly. 'You're not going anywhere.
You're going to stay here. With me.'

Skye froze as he reached for her with both hands.

46

MONDAY, 22 MAY 2023, 12.15 P.M.

Two days after the wedding

Her twin's face was devoid of emotion as Jacob snaked arms around Skye that were surprisingly beefy.

Having only ever seen the man in a suit, or at the very least a neat white shirt and smart trousers, the shock of his strength sent terror streaming through her veins. His gentle hugs had never hinted at the strength in him.

She recalled Jade's sense of wonder when he'd smacked Jordon in the nose. She'd been full of surprised admiration.

Any misdirected admiration was now whipped away in whirl of terror.

Her scream pierced the air and still her sister never moved, never acknowledged Skye's presence, just stared through the window into the distance without a word, or a flicker of awareness.

As though she'd seen or heard it all before. As though her senses had been numbed, her nerve endings burned out so she felt nothing.

With his arms wrapped around her, Jacob hauled Skye up, her

legs thrashing in mid-air, the soft soles of her pumps barely made an impact as she kicked at his shins. Not much shorter than him, Skye's head came to just above his.

Terror froze her mind for one long second and then adrenaline powered it back up again as she recalled the self-defence lessons she'd attended at university. She wasn't as young as she had been then, but her muscle tone and strength were still good.

She stopped struggling and persuaded her muscles to liquify until she hung limp in his grasp, the dead weight of her slumping against his chest. She flopped her head forward onto her chest.

The heat of his breath puffed out over the back of her neck as she realised the exertion had taken its toll on him too. She whimpered as he took a step forward, her body in his arms, but she forced herself to remain inert.

Skye dragged in a deep breath, grasped the arms around her with her hands, dug her nails into his forearms and flung her head back. The sharp crack of his nose breaking gave her a stab of satisfaction. Satisfaction which lasted less than a millisecond.

White spots pricked against the blackness of her vision as her head reeled, but the moment he dropped her on the floor with a pained yowl, she landed on all fours and then was off at a run. Instinct had her wrapping her fingers around Summer's thin wrist and yanking her along behind her.

The drag of her twin's feet slowed her down, but she was determined not to leave her behind.

She headed straight along the short corridor for the front door, dragging Summer's resistant body with her. She staggered, bounced off the wall as she fought against the dizziness that threatened to take her down.

The naked roar of an injured bear bellowed from behind and Skye risked a quick glance over her shoulder, letting terror rip through her as she gasped in raw breath after breath.

Blood gushed from a nose that skewed sideways and Skye realised with a quick jolt of pride she'd broken it.

Narrowed eyes glared at her through tears, but the deadly fury beneath sent a shiver through her.

'Summer, come on.' She stared at her sister's blank face, the heels of her naked feet she was dragging, the wrist that was pulling out of her fingers, slipping slowly from her grasp.

She realised she had no choice.

She let go.

It was her Jacob was after. Her he wanted to kill.

If he hadn't killed Summer by now, he was unlikely to. Wasn't he?

For one brief moment, her mind cleared. She'd escape and come back with the police for Summer later.

She slammed into the closed front door and wrenched at the doorknob. Shock and panic rolled into one as she yanked again and realised it was locked. Her gaze skimmed up at the bolt that had been thrown across at the top.

She reached up and slid the stiff bolt free with a strength born of desperation.

Skye threw another anxious look over her shoulder as Jacob barged past Summer, flinging her against the wall so she slumped against it and slid to the floor while he bore down on Skye.

Skye hauled at the doorknob with both hands, determined it would give way by some miracle and burst open.

This time, when he banded his arms around her, he didn't bother to pick her up, he simply bear-hugged her back to his chest and crushed the breath from her.

With one hand, he covered her mouth and nose, and she realised the frantic wailing noise came from her.

As he cut off her air supply, pinching her nostrils together, stars spangled behind her eyelids and her struggles slowed. Her mouth opened like a fish under his palm, desperate to draw in air. He shifted her weight and the soft, fleshy part of his thumb brushed against her lips.

Skye bit down with all the hysterical strength of a woman who was fighting for her life.

His skin ruptured and blood seeped into her mouth. His yowl almost burst her eardrum as he yanked his hand from teeth that were clamped on. He spun her around and the last thing she saw was his bloodied fist coming straight for her face.

47

Two days after the wedding

My body twitches, little uncontrollable spasms that I can't control.

It's silent now.

Not that the screams had pierced through my senses. It's been so long since I reacted. I realised long ago that no matter what I do, how hard I plead, I can influence nothing. So, I might as well shut down. Don't let anything through. Not sound, not emotion, not feeling.

Lilijana was the latest to have raised my hopes, only to have them crushed once more under LJ's heavy boots. I can't remember the girl in between. There was someone. Not anyone I got to know. Not like Charlotte. Charlotte was my friend for a short while. Only for a matter of a few months. I still remember her, though.

I raise my hand and press it against the cool of the living room window where I retreated to, so I never had to witness LJ dragging this latest one off into the underworld.

The fever inside pushes down, making the air thick and humid, hard to take in as it sits like water in the bottom of my lungs.

My fingers make a little convulsion against the glass as I stare at them, knowing that it's an indication of the desperate desire inside to draw this out. Draw until the pain subsides and the memory of the woman who looks just like me fades.

My gaze slides from my long, slim fingers to the pale reflection of my face in the windowpane. Not just like me. Maybe long ago, that would have been the case, but now I stare back at a watered-down version of the woman I've just seen. I used to be. Sepia to her full colour.

'Summer.' My own name hovers on lips that barely open these days. Only to eat and breathe. Talking is something I no longer find necessary. After all, who is there to listen? And those who have listened have never lived to let my words slide from their own lips to someone else's ears.

I study my watery reflection and let the numbness wash over me. It doesn't matter, I tell myself, as my gaze falls on pale lips. Her lips. My lips.

'Summer,' her voice whispers in my ear.

'Skye,' I reply to my reflection.

'Skye.' My sister. My twin.

The first inkling of emotion flutters in my chest.

I have a twin. My sister. My soul. The flip side of the same coin. My mother used to say that. Identical twins. Perfect mirror image of each other. Opposite in nature.

I crook my head to one side to stare into the reflection of my eyes. Her eyes. Only hers had more colour, more vibrancy, more life. Is that because she had lived while I hovered at the edge of death? A living purgatory.

'Skye.' My lips form the words, my warm breath puffing out over the window to mist my view. 'My twin.'

The thoughts force their way past the thick fog lying low over my mind and pierce my conscience.

LJ was taking Skye down into the basement, through to the room beyond that was carved into the hillside. To the room where he puts all of them to start with. To lock her up until she's so hungry and thirsty she will eat anything, drink anything. Do anything. Even if she knows the food and the water are drugged. She'll take it. She'll have no choice but to take it. And then he'll do what LJ does.

The real torture will begin.

I give an involuntarily shiver and my nerves respond, jumping and jiggling until the Mexican wave works its way through my body and out of my fingertips.

Acid burns in the back of my throat and I take my hand from the window to place it against the hot skin of my neck. 'Skye.' The name, so foreign to me, trembles against the hand cupping my throat.

I can't let him do it. Not again. Not this time.

Not to my twin. My love. My life. A life I no longer live.

My head gives a gentle wobble as I search the room for a weapon. But LJ's not stupid. He doesn't keep weapons here. Nothing any of us could use to escape, or to harm ourselves. Or worse still, harm him. Because he has been harmed in the past.

I know he keeps a knife somewhere, because he's let me use it on the odd occasion, but I don't know if he leaves it or takes it with him.

He's not as slick as you'd think he'd be with the amount of practice he's had.

We've all got the drop on him at some time or another. Mostly, it's ended badly. Only Lilijana escaped.

There have been, to my knowledge, four of us if my guess is right and I was the first. Then Charlotte, then the girl with no name, and lastly Lilijana.

Skye is the fifth.

And the reason she's here is because of me. Because I helped Lilijana escape.

A flutter of something unfamiliar moves in my chest and then dies. It could have been a flicker of joy. I don't know. I probably would no longer recognise it. Possibly a little panic. But even panic doesn't normally happen these days.

I no longer care. Or do I?

Skye is here because of me. Because I asked Lilijana to contact her in a moment of hope. Of idiocy, and now, because of me, my twin is captive and she's going to be subjected to the same torture I've endured.

All these years. I think of the nail I use to mark the wall worn almost to a nub. I don't want to have to find another.

It's my fault.

I touch shaky fingers to my face and the surprise of that hits me more than anything so far. My cheeks are wet. Tears streaming from my eyes. Tears I've not shed for years.

Because it's my fault my twin is here.

'Skye.' This time the name breaks from my lips in a tortured cry.

My movements are still slow and measured, the way I've been taught, but inside there's an urgency.

My head jerks as I scan around.

Skye's black leather handbag lies abandoned on the floor, its mouth open, the disgorged contents scattered where they fell.

I crouch by the side, my knees cricking and grinding, and I study them.

It's silent now.

My dextrous fingers skim over the contents. A packet of tissues, a small pair of earrings in a little see-through bag, a plastic box of breath-freshening mints. My hand hovers over the bunch of keys.

Are they any good? I pick them up, push the longest key between my middle two fingers and contemplate it. My mind is dull, deadened, but I force it onwards. The keys aren't good enough. They would do nothing but put a dent in him.

LJ is far too strong. Much stronger now that I am weak.

I need something...

I sit on my heels and pull the oversized bag closer.

She has a book in it. Not much good. A paperback which would have no effect if I hit him over the top of the head. He'd turn into a wild boar, the pig that he is, and he'd ram me against the wall, so my lungs explode, my ribs crack. I think he's done it before. I possibly have a number of ribs that have been broken by his brutish strength.

I drag my wandering attention back to the task at hand.

A small phial with 'e-liquid' written along the edge of the gold container. I have no concept of what that might be. Is it poison? I give it a small shake and true to form, the liquid makes a quiet slushing noise.

E-liquid. What a strange word.

I can't imagine any ordinary person deliberately carrying poison with them. No one in their right mind would put a toxin in their body on purpose. Would they?

Whatever the case, it's an unknown quantity. I have no idea what it could do. He's hardly going to drink it. Inhaling it would just be stupid.

I drop it to the floor and stick my hand inside the bag for the next item.

A phone.

I blink.

A phone.

The screen is blank. Black.

The last time I had a phone, it had buttons on the side. This didn't appear to have anything.

I stab at the screen, and it comes alive. Face recognition. What the hell is face recognition?

The keypad pops up and asks for a password.

I have no idea, but I tap in our date of birth.

Too easy.

The screen remains blank. Just like my mind. It's been so long. Six years, seven months, seventeen days. Only this morning I counted. During the time I tried to ignore the fact that LJ wanted me to scrub the place clean.

I'd gone into the courtyard and washed away the small amount I'd sketched out there. It was always washed away by the rain in any case. It didn't pain as much to dispose of those drawings. They were dispensable, as I'd discovered every time a storm had come and washed it clean.

They never meant as much as the ones in my tomb. They're too precious. Significant.

Several times it's occurred to me that maybe I should give up scoring the wall every morning, but it's become part of my artwork, my mural. Something LJ doesn't notice as it depicts a fence line winding in crooked stripes into the distance where the sun sets through a blaze of glory. The blaze of glory is only in my mind. What I'd like it to be. With only chalks, there can hardly be a blaze, but a soft going down of the sun beyond the deep valley cut into the hillside. An insipid death of daylight.

My neck gives a painful wrench and drags my concentration back.

The screen goes blank. I bring it up to my face and tap the glass again. This time the phone opens all on its own, and a complex screen pops up.

All I want is the phone.

I tap the icon with a phone on it, and then the keypad. I know my home phone number. That's all. And 999.

No service.

I sink down further. It used to be that you didn't need a signal to dial the whole of 999 but just the two first digits and it would prepare to connect. Perhaps that's no longer the case. Or maybe there is no service up here, full stop. I can't recall LJ ever using a phone.

What would be the use? I don't even know where I am. I have no idea if I can speak coherently to anyone.

The phone slips from my numb fingers onto the floor in front of my knees and I rummage in the almost empty bag.

Hand sanitiser. How odd.

My fingers snag on a slim tube. I draw it out and cradle it in my hand.

Pistachio.

The word pops into my head as I look at the pale green tube.

Pistachio.

A word I've not encountered since my life before I died.

Pistachio.

Pretty.

I frown at the first real acknowledgement of awareness.

Am I coming alive again?

I pull the tube apart and a flat glass nail file drops onto the handbag. Long and pointy.

I curl my fingers around it. I've never seen such an instrument. Last time I saw one of these, it was shorter, metal. Which would have been far more useful than this.

I stare at my ragged fingernails, bitten down to keep them from getting in the way of drawing. I don't need to look at my toenails to know they are long and gnarled with a strange yellowing colour, only cut when LJ remembers to turn up with some nail clippers his face distorted with revulsion. He would still never dream of trusting ne with something I could use as a weapon. Against him. Against ne. Not after Charlotte. Anything could happen.

I sniff as I stare at it. A strange flutter in my tummy.

Is this what I've been looking for? Regardless, there is nothing else.

Coolness touches my skin as I come to my feet and make my way to the top of the cellar stairs.

Almost like a radio has been turned on, my auditory senses kick in with a ferocity that knocks me back a step as I realise what I'm hearing is my twin's low guttural tones, the one she used when she protected me. The eldest twin, from birth she was the stronger willed, the one more likely to stand up for herself. And, more importantly, for me.

It sweeps me straight back to my childhood.

48

'Just ignore them, Summer. They're just stupid little gits.'

'Skye,' I rebuke under my breath, knowing if Mum heard her use that word, she'd be in trouble. Git. Such a lovely, naughty little word. But Mum didn't like us using it. She said it was a contemptible word. We should use twerp instead. Twerp. Like that had any power in the description of the little gits we were talking about.

It was easy enough Skye telling me to ignore them, but she wasn't the one left at school on her own all last week. She was the one who'd had tonsillitis and been off sick, leaving me to fend for myself.

Fend, because she was the troublemaker, and no one knew the difference between the two of us. Skye was the feisty one. The one who never backed down and as we wore uniforms to school, no one could tell us apart. Not even when we wore our hair in different styles.

Only, once the little gang of four boys, our seniors by two years, had found out it was her who was ill, it had been hell. There wasn't a morning they hadn't pushed me over in the dirt, an afternoon when they hadn't spat at me and called me a witch. With that final day on my own, they'd chased me all the way to my front doorstep. Sobs had torn from my throat as I'd rushed inside the house.

Why couldn't I have got tonsillitis at the same time as Skye? If that had been me ill, Skye would have faked it so she could be off too. We might look identical, but I wasn't wired the same way inside. That was our dad's expression. It meant we were different in a special way from each other.

Only Mum could tell us apart and that wasn't always, but once we opened our mouths, she knew. We could fool a whole myriad of people by pretending to be each other. Even Dad and Jade struggled. But Mum knew...

No matter how hard I tried, there was no way I could pull off imitating Skye while she was off sick.

Mum had sent in a note. The teacher had acknowledged it and spoken my name out loud. 'Good that you haven't caught the dreaded lurgy, Summer. At least I won't have difficulty this week telling you apart. Perhaps you can take Skye her homework and help her complete it.'

Skye didn't need help. She was the one with all the intelligence. I was the creative. We both had our strong points, and neither one of us was jealous of the other's.

Except sometimes, I wished I was her. Strong, gobby and no nonsense.

I'd cried in her arms, in hushed sobs so as not to wake baby Jade, telling Skye all about it. All about those mean boys, while Mum gently hummed from the kitchen, oblivious to my heartache.

The weekend provided a welcome break from the bullying. My nerve endings had frayed by the time we returned to school on the Monday, despite having my twin back with me. They'd found my weakness and now they might believe Skye was weak too.

'Oh, bum.' Skye skidded to a halt. 'I've forgotten my reading book. Wait there and don't let the bus go without me.'

I opened my mouth to protest but Skye sprinted back the way she'd come, leaving me at the bus stop as she disappeared beyond the high hedgerow that led down the long narrow passageway to our house.

I sighed as I leaned against the lamp-post next to the bus stop.

Mum had started to let us come to the bus stop without her over the past few weeks since Jade was going through a phase of keeping her up all night and falling into a fitful sleep just as we were ready to go to school. Our house was barely a stone's throw from where the bus pulled in. There were no roads to cross and there were plenty of other children around.

Not that any one of them raised a voice or a fist to defend me against the savages once Skye was at home sick.

The boys were too clever to let on to the bus driver that they were doing anything untoward and at eight, I was still a little timid to speak out against them.

I felt their eyes on me the moment they walked around the corner from their houses further up the street. All four of them.

The ginger one with eyes swollen almost shut as though he never had a good night's sleep. The tall one with beautiful skin and thick black hair in a trendy style that was shaved just above the ears. The one with ruddy plump cheeks that almost swallowed his piggy nose that fat freckles smattered across, and the skinny one with glasses who trailed behind, his knobbly knees poking from beneath his wide-legged grey school shorts, while all the others wore long trousers. Of them all, he was the nastiest. In Skye's opinion it was because his legs were permanently cold.

Plump cheeks stepped forward, his face already pinched into a sneer. 'She's all alone, little witch. Where's witch number two?'

'Right behind you.'

Slightly out of breath, Skye jogged from behind the hedge and, without slowing pace, came straight up to the four boys. She swung her blue canvas bookbag, weighted down with all the books I'd brought home for her to read. It smacked the first boy straight under the chin. His plump cheeks wobbled as he staggered back.

'Whoof...'

He fell straight into the tall one, who flung up his left arm and accidentally punched the ginger-haired boy in the face. All three of them went down in a heap, with the little guy underneath, broken glasses on the ground by his side.

As they scrambled to get up, Skye looped her arm through mine and lifted her chin. 'Don't ever touch my twin again. Or you'll have to answer to me. Just because I'm not with her, doesn't mean I don't know. No matter how long I have to wait, I will get you.'

She turned just as the school bus pulled up at the stop and with a cherubic smile pushed me ahead of her with the small gaggle of stunned, silent children who were boarding.

Not one of them opened their mouths to tell on her.

The bus driver leaned forward so he could see past the queue. 'Come on, boys. Stop messing around or I'll be having words with the headmistress about you.' He scanned them, giving a dark frown. 'If you're having a punch-up, I'll have the lot of you up in front of her. She'll have you in detention for the rest of the term. Understood?'

The boys nodded, brushing themselves off as they scrambled to get to their feet, picking their bookbags off the ground.

Skye held on until I boarded ahead of her and then stepped up the two steps. She leaned back, her hand on the grab rail, her face angled away, but I heard.

'Touch my twin again and I will come after you. I'll get you!'

49

MONDAY, 22 MAY 2023, 12.45 P.M.

Two days after the wedding

Skye's cheek scraped across the cellar floor as Jacob flung her down. Undefeated, she pushed to her knees, only to have a hard boot stomp on her back and force her down again. Down so her gaze skimmed over a floor covered in chalk illustrations.

She froze, panting out through an open mouth as she stared at the horror depicted in a mad frenzy.

The pressure remained on her spine and Skye forced herself not to struggle. She needed to breathe. She needed to gather her strength. She needed to be ready for his next move.

Because she sure as hell wasn't about to get any help from her twin.

In her naïveté and bravado, she'd come to rescue Summer and, in failing that, also failed to reach her twin. Perhaps there was no rescuing her.

Summer was under Jacob's control so far that she wouldn't dare disobey him. Summer had already demonstrated that by pulling back out of Skye's reach. She was more scared of leaving than staying.

Skye took a moment. Raised her head to scan the room, entirely covered in a mural of death and horror. A continuing story of a life lived in sheer terror. Her sister's artwork a depiction of brutality and fear. Incomprehensible in its insanity and yet its sheer enlightenment came to Skye in a balloon of knowledge.

She'd come to save her sister. But her sister was no longer salvageable.

Nor was Summer about to rescue Skye.

Summer had been paralysed by fear. The naked dispassion in her gaze tore at Skye's gut. Her twin never even acknowledged her. Her mind had been tortured and twisted into something alien. The trauma of being incarcerated had damaged her spirit beyond recognition.

'Lie still!' The gravel in Jacob's voice was something Skye had never heard. Never witnessed. Not to this degree.

Her dad had mentioned on occasion how strong a leader Jacob was. Not a bully. Not an out-of-control fiend. Purely a businessman. A professional. The man who had rescued her dad's business.

But to what end?

She ground her teeth and sucked in a breath as the foot in the small of her back lifted only to be replaced by a heavy knee, accompanied by a hand to the side of her face, which ground her soft cheek harder into the rough stone floor.

Skye lay still, her breath coming out in little bubbles of saliva and blood through puckered lips. 'Why?'

His breath puffed across her forehead, and she blinked tears from her eyes, but she couldn't rid herself of the vision of ghoulish creatures depicted across the wall that were being sucked into black flames coming from a fiery mouth of hell.

She squinted at the charcoal drawing of a pair of hands, holding a small child.

Her stomach lurched. Not a child. Not even a baby. A foetus.

The implication rose. The horror her sister had endured. Not only to her person, but to the baby she had carried. Had there only been one?

'Why what? Why this?' The dark chuckle from Jacob emanated an evil she could never have imagined.

'Why us? Why my dad? Why did you make his business successful, and yet all the time... this?'

'Because I hate him.'

'That's not a reason.'

People hated others but did nothing about it. Took no retribution. This had been far more than just that. He'd dedicated his life to the destruction of not just one other, but an entire family.

The sob she released had no effect on him as he grabbed her hair and yanked her head upwards so he could growl into her face.

'You have no fucking idea how much I hate Allan. Every day I live with the thought of destroying him time and again.'

Skye tried to shake her head but there was no wiggle room, he held her hair bunched in his fist so tight that it would be wrenched from her scalp if she tried to escape.

'Tell me,' she whispered, as tears tracked down her face and dripped off the end of her nose to dissolve little spots of chalk and charcoal.

'I hate him because he ruined my life. So, I ruined his. I just stuck around to watch the torture. Even then, he managed to crawl his way out of the hell I'd created for him.'

An involuntary squeak came from her lips as he tightened his grip.

'Your bastard of a father could fall in pig shit and still come out smelling of roses.'

'Why did you help his business to succeed, if you hated him so much?'

'Because I could. It was the best way for me to stick around.' Droplets of saliva spattered across the side of her face as bitter laughter puffed out of him. 'It was within my power to build him up, but I watched him suffer every day for the loss of Christine, and the disappearance of that stupid creature you call your sister. And now I can pull the rug right out from under him for a third time when you're not there to greet him after his extended honeymoon. When I walk away because I have a better offer and his business falls apart again without my support. This time he will be a broken man. I'm determined.'

Skye thought of the thirty-five-night Caribbean cruise they'd embarked on for their honeymoon. They'd have no idea until they returned that she'd gone missing. Jade had returned to university. It wasn't unusual for a number of days to go by without them speaking with each other. A quick message every couple of days. They were both busy and Jade's exams were looming.

Work would have no idea for at least another ten days as she'd taken holiday herself to recuperate from the wedding and all the preparations.

Thirty-five days was going to be a stretch. But really, what were the chances Jade would be able to contact her dad on his honeymoon cruise? They'd wanted privacy. It was their honeymoon, he wasn't going to pay for Wi-Fi when he could pick up occasional messages when they sailed into port.

Worse still was if they discovered something was wrong while they were away and were unable to get home easily. The torture of that scenario played in her head.

Skye let out another sob.

'Why? Why would you want to destroy him?'

How could it be about her mum? That was odd. A quick fling

couldn't make you so invested. So focused on destroying another person. It smacked of a thin coating for the real reason.

A soft sigh of resignation hissed out of him as he settled back on his haunches and relieved her of his overbearing weight.

'Because he destroyed mine when he raped and killed my sister.'

Everything inside Skye stuttered to a halt.

'My dad killed your sister?'

50

MONDAY, 22 MAY 2023, 12.45 P.M.

Two days after the wedding

I'm not entirely sure what it was that pulled me back from the edge of my catatonic state, but everything is too bright, too loud, too full on. Like the dying embers of an ocular migraine where the flashing lights subside, leaving your sight naked and exposed.

By the time I stand at the top of the cellar steps, the nail file clutched in my hand, voices drift up from down there in the dark.

I can see in the dark. I've lived in the dark. Now my eyes zero in on the stone steps curving around to the left. Sucking me into that hellhole. The one I go into willingly and without complaint these days, even though there are bedrooms upstairs. This is my place. Where I belong.

LJ trusts me to return to where I belong. Trained me.

I take the steps one at a time as voices carry up to me. LJ's low, threatening gravel. Skye's tone soft, almost soothing. It won't work. I've tried that tone myself many times. Just when I thought I'd turned him around, he'd rebel, slamming me into the wall, or the door, or the floor.

LJ's back is towards me, his head bowed as he crouches over Skye's body, one knee pressed into her back.

Her face is turned sideways towards me, eyes squeezed shut.

A familiar pose.

My gaze flickers up to the wall, where it curves over to blend with the ceiling. The exact spot I've charcoaled in deep graphite greys almost exactly that scene. A scene I've experienced beyond imagining.

Ahead of the familiar figure on the floor is a window to another world, in pastel hues of aqua and lemon with a splash of rose and lilac.

My world.

The world I'd love to live in. If only things were different.

I skim my gaze across the ceiling and down the next wall. All covered in various shades of black and white. Not hues or tones. Black, white and grey, as I was taught, do not belong to the visual spectrum.

At the startled squeak, my shoulders jerk and my neck does its spasmodic twitch and I'm back in the room. Back where I belong.

Only there's someone in my place. On the floor in front of me. Prone.

She looks like me. Or should I say, she looks like I would look if my life had been normal. Different. If I hadn't been enslaved. But she's not me.

She is Skye.

My sister. My twin. My soul.

I shift my attention to LJ and the scratchy threat in his voice. I've heard this tale before, so many times. A little like a broken record and almost word perfect. This time I don't switch off. I listen to the story and hear the agony in poor LJ's voice.

'She was seventeen when she first met Allan.'

Funny how he rarely uses the term *your dad*. As though

omehow that over-familiarises the situation, bringing his relationhip closer. Connecting them. Us. Not wise. It's better he distances imself from any emotion.

My fingers loosen on the nail file, and I hover in the doorway as f I need his permission to enter. Which I do. I need his authorisaion for every single move I make, there isn't a thing I'm allowed to lo without LJ's express consent. Not even pee. Even when he goes ut for the day, I must remember to ask his permission to pee, because if I don't and he finds evidence in my bucket, I'll have cold urine dumped over my head in the dead of night.

It's a ritual. A procedure. I know the rules now. There is nothing left for him to teach me. Once the lesson is done, then he can relax the rules. I'm now allowed to pee in the toilet. It's a luxury he can take away at any given moment as he likes to remind me frequently. Like he takes away my freedom of the house.

But he's trying to teach my twin.

By the savage expression on her face, she's going to put up a fight. Not that it will do her any good. In fact, more harm than good. I know that from experience.

Her eyes flash open and the blind fury banked up in them has me taking a step back, my attention jerking back to LJ's story.

'I was away at university and Allan catfished her. They didn't call it that back then, but he'd met her, so one of her friends told me when I turned up to check on her.'

Catfished. That was the terminology. That's precisely what LJ had done to me. Catfished.

My lips spread into a cynical smile.

Skye's head gives a small jerk. I think that's why my head bobs all the time. LJ damaged the nerves in my neck and I'm aware my head is permanently on the move.

My attention drifts back to him, although it doesn't have to.

I've heard the story before. I didn't believe him when he first

told me. I don't believe him now. I simply learnt never to speak ou
Never protest.

I keep my silence now, let him talk it out.

You'd think that might calm him down, make him a little mor
tolerant. It won't. When the story ends, the frenzy will begin.

I don't want to be here for the frenzy. I know what it entails.
hover for a moment, consider if I should turn and dash up the ston
steps, through the kitchen and wait for him out in the courtyard
I'm not sure why he brought her to my room. I assume it's to lor
over the punishment he's eked out to me over the years. A boastfu
proclamation of all he has achieved.

'She had no idea he was so much older than her.'

Nor had I. Ironic. Or a deliberate cynical plot to duplicate wha
had happened to his sister.

Skye keeps silent. Maybe that's the best way. I'd asked questions
which caused more anger. Questions like I thought catfishing wa:
relatively new terminology.

I was then subjected to a rant from LJ about catfishing being a
much older term than even I in my wisdom could imagine. That the
word originates from the 1913 book *The Catfish* by Charles Marriott.
Everything since then has hung on the same theory of disequilib-
rium brought about by the obsession of someone masquerading in
a way as to beguile and tempt.

He'd beguiled and tempted me in the form of a seventeen-
year-old boy.

His claim was that my dad had done the same to his sister.

I couldn't, no, I still can't see it myself. Not my dad. Apart from
anything else, was social media even a thing back then? I think not.

Did he mean Dad misled her?

I close my eyes and picture the man I've not seen for over six
years. Eyes drawn with sadness emphasised with dark purple

bruising to depict all the pain he has endured. Deep creases either side of his mouth. Stress lines. My fingers itch to pick up my charcoal and sketch again, but I make myself hold on to the here and now.

Not my dad. I couldn't believe it. Still can't, no matter how many times LJ has insisted.

But LJ does.

The anger in him will build. Higher if he thinks you doubt him. Worse still if you argue against his rampage. Don't question his word.

Some kind of empathy creeps over emotions I thought long dead.

Please don't argue, Skye. Please don't.

My chest starts to ache. It hasn't done that in so long. I have no emotions. I am a stupid creature. I am nothing. I feel nothing.

I draw in a deep breath.

I do now.

LJ leans his face closer to Skye's and sharp pains shoot through my chest. This isn't right. I don't do this any more.

My breathing quickens.

'Do you know what he did to my little sister?'

Skye let out a soft sob, unable to shake her head against LJ's cruel grip.

'He fucking raped her.'

Black rage fills my twin's eyes as her furious glare hits me full on like a thunder cloud. As though she's seeking some kind of rebuttal from me, some kind of denial of the fact that our dad, our precious father, raped a young woman.

He didn't. I bloody well know he didn't.

That's not for me to say, though. I'm not about to interfere. To have LJ turn on me. Like he always turns on me. Although less so these days now that I've become a shadow.

Spit bubbles from Skye's mouth as she clenches her teeth together and lets out a growl of fury from deep inside.

LJ is already in his zone, though. 'She was only eighteen and he was twenty-one. He knew she was innocent.'

How many eighteen-year-olds are innocent these days? Even those days. It's not so long ago. I've often wondered if it was true or if he was simply in denial. Did Dad have sex with LJ's younger sister and get her pregnant? I could live with that. I couldn't live with the thought that he'd actually raped her. My dad. LJ has never convinced me. Because I know my dad. I know how wonderful he is, what a gentle person he was. How he adored my mum. Us. His three daughters.

My dad was not a rapist.

LJ in his insanity believes he is as he continues his rant.

'And when he got her pregnant, he walked away without a backward glance. No care, no humanity. No offer of help.'

LJ cranked Skye's head up until I thought he might snap her neck. I took a slow, cautious step forward, but he was oblivious to my presence.

'She died. In a pool of blood and afterbirth, not to mention the foetus.'

I close my eyes and my inner vision is filled with thick viscous scarlet soaking the palms of my hands and that tiny little baby curled into a C shape. In my mind's eye, the baby is more formed than in actuality. I know that. But my imagination fills in the details. She was my baby, and he took her away from me.

'Why?' A pained gasp floats from Skye's lips.

'Because by the time I knew about it, by the time she confessed, it was too late.' His grip slackens and Skye's head slumps, so her cheek rests on the floor once more. She puffs out small pants in relief, building her strength as I used to build mine, but to no avail. She will not win.

I snap back. What did LJ say?

Confessed? I've not heard him use that term before. Why would she have 'confessed' to him? Her brother.

I stand a little straighter and my head gives a gentle wobble.

'What do you mean too late? What did you do?' The hoarse whisper comes from Skye's mouth, not mine, but the exact question had formed in my head.

'I was just helping. Her pregnancy was too far along the way before I found out. I never realised she was so far gone. She was so... little.' The silence stretched out as I pay more attention.

This isn't his normal spiel. In his tale, he finds his sister, blood pooled around her and the fully formed baby dead beside her cold corpse with a photograph of my dad in her hand.

I narrow my eyes and focus in on him. He's rattled. Really rattled. He didn't expect this. Her. My twin sister, Skye.

There's already a connection. When he took me, I was a stranger.

They know each other. How?

He knows Dad and that sends a vicious spike through me. I've always believed he knew *of* my dad. That was different. This was vengeance for my dad's part in his sister's death. Her elected suicide. Or so I'd been led to believe. Like Charlotte. But he actually *knows* him in the here and now, not the past.

My stomach churns, little gas bubbles popping inside so my pulse rate increases, my breathing becomes shallow.

'What do you mean? What did you do?' she grinds out. Blood oozes from between her lips and drips a pattern on my floor mural.

My mind drifts.

I could use a small slip of sheet from my bed, like I have in the past, and smear that blood into an arc to form part of the picture. I've done it before with my own blood, letting it dry to a rusty brown hue. Now, brown can be a hue.

I seek out the 'painting'. Dried blood. My blood. Baby's blood. Dripped between my fingers in a splash pattern. Splodges.

I tear my gaze away and force myself to concentrate on them.

He hesitates as though she's caught him out.

'It wasn't me. It wasn't my fault. I was *just* trying to *help*.'

The words coming from him are ever so slightly skewed, the meaning altered.

This is different. I've seen him furious. He loses control on a regular basis. But confidence? I've never known him to lose the ability to control a situation. But somehow, she has him squirming, metaphorically speaking.

I think it's her tone. She's the only girl, woman now, I've ever known who isn't batshit scared of him. But then she knows him. Is that what makes the difference? She knows the other LJ. Jacob, she calls him.

Is that what the J stands for?

'Then whose fault was it? What happened, Jacob? Did she try to get rid of the baby? Abort it?'

I look a little closer. His face spasms in pain.

That's it.

She's *not* scared. Not in the frantic, clawing desperation the rest of us have shared. Those sky-blue eyes have a colourless coldness to them. A slide of cunning behind the fear.

Just like the time she beat those boys up. When she hid behind the hedge deliberately. She never told me. She made out she'd forgotten something, but really, she'd bided her time and then smacked them with her books, knowing they'd humiliated and tormented me. Knowing they'd continue to bully me, and the bullying would escalate unless she put a stop to it. My saviour.

She'd been frightened of them, of course she had. But she'd sorted them.

The realisation that she believes she can do it again hits me.

She has no chance of sorting LJ.

He is evil personified.

I can see it in the set of his jaw.

Somehow, though, she's coaxed a little truth from him. A truth I believed I already knew. But it transpires the version I knew was not the whole truth.

His grip slackens, his voice drifts as though in resignation and recognition that he needs to acknowledge the reality of it.

'Your dad got my sister pregnant and then deserted her.' This time, he fails to add the word rape.

'So you've said.' She doesn't move, but I see her muscles relax as she lowers her head to the floor as though conserving her energy. Then what? When she was on her own with you. What happened then?'

I know. In a sudden blinding insight, I know.

'You gave her abortion tablets,' I whisper, as I step closer to his side, understanding the truth of it. My voice comes out a husky gravel, unused to being used.

He untangles his fingers from Skye's hair and covers his mouth with his hand. For the first time since I've known him, there is an inkling of pity stirring inside.

Pity that is quashed in a millisecond as I realise my dad, our dad, had nothing to do with his sister's death. That despite LJ's insistence that Dad raped his sister, LJ was the one who had killed her. It hadn't been suicide. She hadn't taken her life out of desperation and a sense of abandonment.

I blink and the vision of my own tiny baby fills my mind's eye.

The crushing pain of loss fills my heart and takes me away while I scan the curved roof of the cave and look for the scene that will give me solace. Give me hope. The scene I etched on the corner of my bedsheet and ripped off to give to Lilijana. The scene that has brought my twin back to me.

Only this time, the scene doesn't bring me solace, it brings only a sharp pain of injustice, so when I breathe in, my neck feels like I've been stabbed.

I tighten my grip again on the nail file.

It's my fault. I'm the one who brought Skye here by sending that message out with Lilijana and I'm the one who permitted this to happen.

Guilt floats through every other emotion to shoulder them aside.

Guilt.

I haven't felt that in forever and it's almost foreign to me.

Almost.

But the memory of it moves me closer so I sidle up to him. Closer than I ever would voluntarily.

'I thought your sister committed suicide.' The rough edges of my voice scrape away at my throat.

He glances up at me, a dismissive sneer on his lips, but there's a shift in his demeanour, as though he's wrong-footed. Doubt in his eyes I've never noticed before. It flickers, and then it's gone. But I saw it and I pick away at it like a blunt fingernail at a scab.

'You said Jane took her own life. That she died and the baby along with her.'

'What difference does it make?'

Skye glares sideways at him. 'The distinction between suicide and murder. It's a big difference. It makes you the one guilty of your sister's death. Not her. Not our dad. It had nothing whatsoever to do with our dad.'

Movement is so blindingly fast, it bursts from him in a flame of rage.

His fist connects with the back of Skye's head and her face smashes into the stone floor.

This time, her cry of pain lances my heart.

'It wasn't my fucking fault. If it hadn't been for your dad getting her pregnant and deserting her, I wouldn't have needed to take those measures.' Breath wheezes out of him in a gust of fury as he wrenches her head up by her hair and wraps his other hand around her throat.

I know what comes next. He'll apply pressure slowly, firmly, until sparks float behind closed lids and she drifts off to another world until that grip slackens to let in sips of air. Precious air.

If the grip slackens, because this isn't his usual response. He knows her. He didn't know me, never knew the other girls. Now he no longer has the upper hand, figuratively speaking. There's a loss of that inner control.

I know him as LJ, but is Jacob the same person with the same reactions? I think not. This is more passionate, more erratic than his usual calculating style.

His mask has slipped for the first time since I've known him. Six years, seven months, seventeen days.

The mask that's been in place since the day he killed his own sister and her poor, innocent baby. His guilt laying the blame at everyone's door but his own.

My gaze drifts to the images. Charcoal and chalk. My hands. My tiny baby.

He could have killed me, too, and left me down here to rot. I'm fairly sure one of the girls is in the garden. Dug in, not too deep. Charlotte, I suspect.

The memory of those digging sounds as I sat at the top of the winding stone steps float into my mind.

Cuh, ssh, puh.

Cuh, ssh, puh.

Huh, phooo...

I drag my gaze back as my twin tries to draw in a breath.

Tears stream from her eyes. My eyes. It doesn't seem right.

Does he have her by the throat? Or is it me?

He's murdered. Murdered his sister and her baby yet still all these years he's blamed my dad and in effect blamed me. His denial has been my jail sentence. A sentence based on a lie.

A *fucking* lie.

A dark rumble of something deep and unrecognisable starts in the pit of my belly. A clawing, gasping desperation.

Skye's perfect, flawless skin turns a mottled pink, and her beautiful mouth opens, begging for air.

'Let her go.'

The words come out of my mouth with a soft calmness and LJ doesn't even look up.

I am nothing. Just a stupid creature.

Skye's eyes start to bug out of her head and thin threads of red sprinkle through the white. My gaze starts to stray up the wall to find that part of the mural, the part that shows my eyes filled with thin black lines as I die, but I drag myself back.

'LJ.' My voice is hoarse, but forceful, and he casts me an unconcerned glance. Because I'm unimportant. A creature that ceased to exist for him long ago. 'LJ,' I repeat. 'Let my sister go.'

He lets out a derisive huffing snort. One that underpins exactly what he thinks of me. Of her. Of us.

I step closer. 'Let... her... go.'

'Go to your room.' His lips pull back in a snarl.

'*This* is my room.'

Surprise flickers over his face as though he'd forgotten where he was.

I have nowhere else to go. This is my room. My life. The only existence I have known for six years, seven months, seventeen days.

All that is about to come to an end.

I step forward and my hand clenches around the glass nail file as his fist tightens around Skye's neck.

'I said... let Skye *go!*'

I pull my arm back and punch with all my might, not knowing if the instrument has enough strength, or my arm enough power for the sharp end to pierce his skin.

The jolt vibrates all the way up my arm, sending my nerve endings dead for a moment before they return to life with a lightening tingle.

LJ jerks. Surprise widens his eyes.

His hand releases its hold on Skye's hair and grabs for the soft tissue at the side of his throat where my hand still holds the glass nail file.

Warm blood coats my fingers as he drops the hand that clenches Skye's throat and she flops to the ground, hoarse gasps dragging in precious air.

LJ's fingers grasp at mine, but they easily slip from his, coated in blood as they are.

He fumbles, his fingers sliding from the slick glass blood-coated nail file. Time and again, he grabs. He slides. He grasps. He slips.

And I stand and watch with a distant detachment.

Do I care?

I'm not sure. There's a heaviness to my chest but I feel no desire nor urgent need to help him. He's getting what he deserves.

His mouth is wide, eyes staring as he seems to focus on Skye's body curled in front of him.

Blood dribbles from the corner of his mouth as I side-step him and touch Skye's shoulder.

'Skye. Skye. We need to go now.' I use the tone I had with Charlotte. As though she is a child and she needs to be coaxed. Protected.

Skye raises a tear-streaked face to mine, her eyes bloodshot, her mouth swollen and bruised. I imagine that was how I looked so many times after LJ had taken his bad temper out on me.

Poor, innocent me.

I never deserved it. Not any of it.

Nor does Skye.

I pull at the sleeve of her cardigan. 'We need to go.' I take a firmer hold on her elbow and start to pull. She shuffles towards me and hasn't even looked over her shoulder to see where LJ is yet.

I'm ambivalent. She can either see him, or not see him. It makes no difference to me. All I know is that for now we are safe. I have paralysed him with one puncture of what, from memory, is his carotid artery.

His fingers are slick with crimson. A beautiful, rich crimson that coats his entire hand and drizzles down into the sleeve of his white shirt. The shirt I never expected him to wear as he normally wears a T-shirt or a hoodie and jeans or joggers.

I pull Skye away, my free arm now wrapped around her, lending her support as I drag her towards the door. She doesn't need to get blood on her. No more than she already has of her own dripping down her chin onto the V of her T-shirt that is exposed under the cardigan, and my handprint on her arm.

I manage to get her to her feet, but she staggers. As I let go, she slumps against the wall, barely able to keep herself upright.

I hesitate.

I glance behind.

LJ is now on his knees and elbows, his forehead almost touching the ground. I think, from memory of yoga that we used to do with Mum for fun, it's called a downward dog. And he is a dog.

No. That's too good for him. He's a beast.

He raises his head, and his gaze catches mine. A pleading light fills them as he gives a feeble slap at the glass nail file as if to plead with me to take it out. I'm not sure I could, even if wanted to. The glass is too slick, too slippery. Too deeply embedded.

His strength waning, he cranks over onto his side and his thick

...ody hits the floor with a dusty whoof I imagine smudging much of my latest artwork. No matter.

Distracted for a moment, I draw my gaze around the room.

Six years, seven months, seventeen days. Now it's time to leave. Leave behind a whole life depicted during that six years, seven months, seventeen days over the walls, the low arched ceiling and the floor. My artwork has almost reached the door and it seems fitting, just as I've run out of room for my story.

I can continue it elsewhere.

My gaze falls on the pretty little snow globe and the miniature red Buddha.

I step around LJ, swipe them up and tuck one into each pocket of my shabby old hoodie.

LJ lets out a last guttural grunt, his fingers still reaching for that nail file that only has a couple of inches still protruding. Strange how in certain situations strength comes from nowhere.

I need more of that power now to help my twin sister up the stairs and into the living room, where we need to collect her bag and belongings scattered on the floor.

I turn and her eyes connect with mine. There's an expectation that hers will be filled with horror, but instead there's a tough understanding flickering through them. She nods her head once and holds out her arms for me to support her.

I turn and lock the cellar door behind me. I pocket the key.

As we reach the top of the stairs and step through into the hall, I can see the oxygen has started to reach Skye's limbs. Her colour has gone from grey to puce as blood pumps through her deprived system. Her strength is returning.

We pause. Both of us heave in great gasps of air as Skye slumps against the opposite wall.

I scrub my hands against my jogging bottoms to wipe the blood off and reach for the door to the cellar, sliding it into place.

I step back, my gaze skims over the panel that settles with quiet groan. If I didn't already know there was a door there, I woul never guess.

No one will ever guess.

I feel a touch on my shoulder, and I turn to stare into Skye summer-blue eyes. Her eyes. My eyes. The handbag she's retrieve dangles from one limp hand.

I can't smile. I no longer know how.

She does. It's weak and it's forced, but it's a smile as she wrap her arm around me and draws me towards the terror of the outside world.

'Let's go home, Summer.'

She tugs the door open. 'Oh, Cleo!' Skye turns to me. 'She mus have managed to squeeze out the car window.'

A huge hound greets us, her tongue lolling as though she's run a long distance to find us.

And suddenly the bonds break and I step through the door into the sunshine.

Free.

51

THREE YEARS LATER

Art.

Art is my salvation as I pick up my brush and swirl it into the deep purple and then daub the oil paint onto the canvas in thick, generous swathes. The brush strokes swish through, blending with the black of the night sky to lift the colours into pre-dawn.

Art saved me then as it saves me now.

I don't have to talk to express myself.

I have barely spoken since the day my twin sister came for me. Saved me. Although, in many ways, I saved myself too. Kept my sanity, if you can call my current state of mind that, with my artwork.

I blink as Skye comes out of the house. Our house. The one I've known my whole childhood. The one with happy memories like the warmth of a security blanket. The house Skye bought for us both to live in together as Dad moved into a new one with his new wife. Martha.

I like Martha.

Skye makes her way down to my little summer house at the

bottom of the garden, Cleo trotting at her heels as though, some-how, she's attached to her through an invisible lead.

The bond between them is so strong, I let my mind consider whether it's as strong as the bond between twins. It's not jealousy. Far from it. Purely idle curiosity.

I have no feelings, nothing. LJ made sure of that. He scoured them from me. I feel nothing. Empty inside, it doesn't even worry me that the possibility is I will never feel again. Although there is a brief flicker from time to time.

Maybe I will. Maybe I won't. It's as though everything has been wrapped in cotton wool, so all sensations are dulled.

There are vague curiosities.

Cleo has an inner sense, I believe, as she moves from Skye's side to mine and rests her chin on my knee as I perch on the stool. The soft black fur of her head radiates the heat of the sun and I close my eyes. There is something there. A pleasure I feel unfurling inside like the gentle opening of a new leaf. Emerald-green, fresh with life.

Any pleasure I experience comes to me in colours. Like the red of the thumb-sized laughing Buddha I keep with me all the time. The one I took when I left LJ. Its presence had seemed so incongru-ous. I just had to have it. A reminder. A warning. A comfort.

The second item I'd brought with me had been a present to LJ that first Christmas after he'd bought into Dad's company. That Christmas when Dad and Skye had apparently come for Sunday lunch. They'd sat in the lounge of that house and brought him that gift while I'd been downstairs in the hidden cellar. Strange how I'd felt such a connection the first time I held it. Strange also, that Skye had looked over that fantastic vista, not knowing one day that view would save my life.

'Summer.' Skye keeps her voice low. She knows instinctively not to frighten me with a sudden move, or a loud voice. I was incarcerated alone for far too long and my sensory perception is delicate. Sensitive.

She smiles as I open my eyes, but I know there is no expression on my face to mirror hers. Identical twins we may be, but her hair is not filtered through with grey steel like mine, her expression not ravaged by trauma and the touch of evil like mine. I don't like to look in a mirror. Lines of despair cut deep into my cheeks like brackets carved either side of my downturned lips. Resting bitch face, they laughingly call it these days. I would have laughed at that at one time, too.

Not now.

There is no laughter inside of me. Instead, a dark, opaque veil is pulled over my emotions. I know they are there, but I can't quite reach inside to extract them from the depths where they hide, too scared to express themselves.

Skye comes around the easel to stand by my side and stare at the nightmare I've created. That's where my emotions roil around in agony and despair for the whole world to see.

If they care to look.

For some reason, they don't. All they see is a dark beauty. The evil I portray doesn't suck them down. They admire, with no concept of the torture I endured to produce this for their wonder. Or maybe they do. Maybe theirs is a morbid fascination about the girl who disappeared and, on her return, never spoke of her experiences.

Because if you don't speak, no one can pull the truth from you. No matter how nice the police had been. They believe me to be mute. And I can be.

In the early days, I'd had to stay in hospital on a drip with Skye by my side. Jade had come and gone, looking after Cleo and seeing to Skye's needs. Not quite knowing what to do. Dad and Martha flew back from Barbados once the ship had docked and they could grab a flight back.

Several psychiatrists had attempted to get me to speak, but after a while, they'd drifted away, their interest waning.

If you say nothing, you can't engage.

The only people I engage with are my family. And only when I want to. On my terms.

Skye's lips part. 'Incredible.' The word escapes her on a puff of awe. I know she sees. She knows. She is the only one who will ever know. 'Will it be finished in time for your show?'

Instead of answering, I wipe the brush on the paint-spattered cotton cloth I keep across my knees and incline my head as Cleo draws back from the smell temporarily to lean her shoulder against my hip. Her hot breath puffs out across my thigh, and I feel the comfort in her closeness.

I sit back and study what I've created. Almost finished.

A whirlpool of emotions being sucked into a black vortex of death.

It seems that is what the public wants. None of them had been locked in a dark cellar for six years, eight months, four days.

Which actually turned out to be seventeen days longer as I had miscalculated slightly. Possibly been unconscious for longer than I realised. Missed a couple of leap years.

It's of no consequence now.

That's not what the public see.

None of them suffered the dark cruelties I've been subjected to. But they are all willing to hold their hands up and proclaim understanding of this pain, of this deep, searing agony and desperate plight of evil.

Skye is the one people believe to be the artist. She is the face of Summer. While Summer languishes in privacy, scared to be seen. Unwilling to face the world.

I look around the garden, the house. This is my world.

My gaze falls on Skye.

We are twins! Who would know?

Skye sweeps her hair up into a messy bun, letting soft ringlets fall to her shoulders, and paces the art gallery with soul-baring confidence where my paintings have become an overnight success.

The sinister story of my disappearance and mysterious return buoys them up, attracts buyers, is only enhanced by Skye's quick flit into the gallery. She does it for me, as I can't. I can't walk into a room with people. Can't talk to men. Any men. Except...

My dad hovers at the top of the garden in the doorway to the house. Our house. Mine and Skye's. He still looks unsure around me. I think my return devastated him almost as much as my loss. Not because he didn't want me back, but because the me he would have wanted was long gone and he's not quite sure how to be around me.

If I could smile, I possibly would.

Instead, a sweat breaks out in tiny beads across my top lip and along the length of my spine, so my flesh shudders in ripples.

Skye's eyes narrow, a split second before Cleo raises her head and then takes off, up the garden full pelt, her hackles just rising enough to let Dad know he'd taken her by surprise. Her body stiff. Funny that, because Cleo is normally 'guard-dog-aware', which makes me feel comfortable. Protected.

By the time she reaches him, she's all wagging tail and loose limbs again. After all, she's known him since she was a pup. Five years old now. She'd never known me before, but she welcomed me into her family immediately from the moment she stood on that doorstep after forcing the car's back window down until it broke, as though Skye had summoned her. And now she loves me.

Whether that's to do with me being genetically the same as her mum, or if it's because I'm damaged, and she knows I am.

Damaged is too fine a word.

I'm broken.

Some would say I'm lucky. Lucky I'm still breathing. That's jus a matter of opinion.

I watch my dad's approach and can't help stiffening. Fear reside too deep inside for me to make a pretence of anything other tha that.

Skye rests her hand on my shoulder, sensing my discomfor even though I have said nothing, barely moved.

The smile on Dad's face is easy enough but it doesn't quite erad icate the anxiety in his eyes. He's always gentle with me. Slow tc approach.

He has no idea what happened. All he knows is that I'm not th same child who stole out the door that day. No longer his little gir who came back to him, yet still his daughter.

As he reaches us, Skye steps forward and wraps her arm: around him. It's comfortable. Natural. 'Hey, Dad, where's Martha?'

He returns her embrace with a bear hug, one I already fee sucking the life from me. Claustrophobia squeezes at my throat and my fingers dig into Cleo's soft pelt as she comes back to my side, offering me protection. Comfort. She never seems to mind my grip.

Dad pulls back from Skye's arms and smiles at me, and the ache in my chest relaxes. He's not going to try hugging me too. I see the small hesitation in his expression and know that he would love to. Not today, though maybe someday. 'She's nipped to the newsagent. Our newspaper never arrived this morning. She likes a flick through the Sundays.'

Sunday. The day Dad and Martha come every week for morning coffee and a catch-up. That's what they call it. What they really mean is a check-up. On me.

I'm not very demanding on Skye, but there are certain skills I no longer have. Like using a sharp knife. Cooking.

I'm good at cleaning. My whole life was about cleaning while I was with LJ. I can't help myself. If there's a speck of dirt, a smear of grease, it has to be cleaned. Skye jokingly tells me it's a fair exchange. I clean, she cooks.

It's not a fair exchange. She's given up her life for me. Her love life. Romance.

There are no men in her world either. That's her sacrifice. Secretly, I think she's started to see the owner of the art gallery. She talks about him so much, I'm almost convinced that I'd like to meet him.

She's told him about me.

Maybe one day soon I'll be brave enough to say yes; after all, her life is not mine to ruin.

Martha arrives and pauses at the patio doors. Her whole body seems stiff and unnatural as she makes her way towards us. The strain on her face slowly evolves into horror.

She holds the newspaper out and my blood runs to ice.

'Allan, oh, Allan.' She stares at my dad as she offers the newspaper to him. 'You're not going to believe this. Look, Allan.'

Dad reaches out, his face leaches of all colour and the paper flops in his hand.

The black and white photograph of a man, dark eyes empty and soulless, stare out at me and my breath halts in my chest.

If Skye was close enough, I'd probably have squeezed her hand until her fingers broke. As it is, the loud crack of my paint brush rends the air between us.

Skye stares at the photograph, and the multitude of colour photographs below it, and does a slow head turn until her eyes meet mine. Her chin drops and her lips part.

I know my face remains blank. Just as I schooled it to. Six years, eight months, four days of incarceration taught me that much.

Dad lifts his head, eyes filled with tears, and he stares at Martha.

'It's Jacob.' He holds the paper out and turns to Skye. 'Jacob's been dead all this time.'

Black and white, LJ's photograph stares at us from a page of horror.

The body of a man has been discovered in an abandoned cottage at the crest of the Shropshire Hills. In a macabre twist to his disappearance three years earlier when he abandoned his job as an executive director and simply vanished after telling staff he needed to deal with family issues, police confirm that the decomposed body is that of Leonard Jacob Edwards.

In a sinister turn of events, police believe that Edwards had been leading a secret life, using a cottage which it transpires was in the name of his great-aunt, who passed away almost ten years earlier. The property had been the subject of a family feud and legal dispute over entitlement for some considerable time and was thought to have been deserted.

According to a source, Edwards's body was discovered in a cave which was built into the hillside and could be accessed through a small cellar with a hidden door. When previous checks had been made on the property by solicitors and estate agents, no search had been made of the cave and access had not been visible until the new owners started renovations.

A tide of utter devastation washes over me as I stare at the photograph of the man who incarcerated me for a huge chunk of my life.

Stockholm syndrome.

Rationally, I know this is what I have, but that doesn't mean to say I can rid myself of it. Tears burn the back of my eyes, but I can't cry. Because I'm not supposed to know who he is. Who Jacob is. To me he was always LJ.

And LJ is dead.

52

Dad holds the newspaper in both hands and rattles the pages as he falls silent for a moment, his eyes scanning down the remaining text.

His hand drops one side of the paper, and he brings it to his face to cover his mouth with shaking fingers.

I see the concern on Martha and Skye's faces and the dog rushes over to presumably try to play because Dad's on his knees on the ground.

Dad ignores her and instead slowly raises his chin until he can study each one of us. His eyes deep and penetrating. I hope he can't see anything in my soul.

I drop my gaze so it's not a possibility.

'I don't believe this.' His voice is weak, a rusty whisper.

'What?' Martha kneels beside him and touches his shoulder.

He flinches as though he was in a world far beyond ours and shakes his head. He places the newspaper on the grass in front of his knees and a small sob comes from him.

It's been a while since I saw him cry. The last time was when he arrived back from his honeymoon and Skye and I were waiting.

Skye's bruising was almost entirely gone by the time they arrived home almost a week later. They could hardly afford to charter a plane, so grabbed the next available flight home.

Even when you knew what to look for, the last vestiges of LJ's fingerprints were barely discernible on Skye's neck, especially when she took to wearing high necks and scarves for a couple of weeks.

Skye has healed. To an extent. She'll always bear the internal scars.

Of course, there's no cure for me.

My attention shifts back to Dad. Dad, whose skin is ashen, his eyes red-rimmed. He shakes his head.

'They're saying he was a monster. They've found bodies in a courtyard garden.' His mouth drops open and his gaze widens as he stares at Skye. 'This is... dear God. We've been here. The first year after he bought into the partnership.' He looks around at Martha. 'Skye and I visited this house, years ago.'

I could tell him exactly how long ago, but I don't see the need. It would only complicate matters.

Skye must feel same as she remains silent too.

My head does that wobble. The one I almost have control of these days, but it still does it from time to time when I'm under a good deal of stress. Stress. No matter what happens from here on in, I will never again suffer the stress I was under when LJ owned me.

'Oh, my God.'

Martha leans in, curious to know more, but I notice Skye, like me, is wary of asking questions. We don't necessarily want the answers. LJ may have been a psychotic murderer, but his reasoning to his mind was clear. Dad raped his sister. No matter how hard we deny it, the suggestion of it still taints our thoughts.

'I never knew.' Dad shakes his head and I notice a small bald spot has started to spread from his crown.

'Knew what?' Martha has taken to rubbing his back with comforting motions.

'I knew his sister. How could I have known his sister? All those years ago. Thirty years ago.'

Dad scrubs his nose on the back of his hand as he sits back on his heels and drops the newspaper from his other hand. He takes in a deep breath and blows it out slowly. 'When I was at university...'

And here it comes, I think. The confession.

'I was in my final year.' He raises his head and stares at Skye for a moment, his gaze skitters to mine and away, so he doesn't unnerve me. He's learnt to do that. To not suffocate me with his joy of having me home and his desire to take me into his arms and squeeze me so tight, hold me close so I would never run again. Because that's what he believes, what we allow him to believe.

Because what really happened will forever remain our secret. Skye's and mine.

Why damage another member of the family with the terror I have suffered? With the guilt it would bring. It wouldn't just damage but destroy.

His breath hitches before he looks down and continues. 'It wasn't long after I met your mum, we were besotted.' He flicks an apologetic glance at his new wife. His wife of three years, but she will always be new to me. Lovely, gentle Martha.

'The new intake arrived. I was on Student Services. We were asked to help out with some of the kids that were having a hard time settling in. I was a mentor, in those days.' He raises his head, and he looks around at us, pain etches deep into his features, making him look suddenly old. 'You wouldn't believe how much pressure is put on us, as young kids, to look after other young kids with mental health issues and family problems.'

'I was allocated a young woman called Jane.' He shakes his head, a little puff of self-deprecating air escaping his lips. 'Jane

Edwards.' His mouth twists into a one-sided, regretful smile. 'She was so young. So very innocent.' He shakes his head. 'She should never have been there. She'd obviously led a very sheltered upbringing. But her older brother had said it would do her good after the death of both their parents. He was in my year, but at Manchester Met, instead of Manchester. Not far, so he thought he could keep his eye on her without, I suppose, stifling her.

'She went out one night and got completely wasted. By the time we realised she'd been raped, she was already around three months pregnant. Actually, maybe four.' He raises his hands and grips hair that has turned a wispy salt and pepper since I've been gone, instead of the thick chestnut I remember from before. 'She didn't even know she'd had sex.

'It was all very difficult. She was too scared to tell her brother. Too terrified of what he might say, what he might do, because they couldn't afford to keep a baby. He took his role very seriously. Quite a disciplinarian by all accounts.

'She knew she had to get rid of it, but she just kept delaying it. I really tried to help. Really, I did, but it was out of my league, and she wouldn't let me tell anyone else. Swore me to secrecy. Her flatmates hadn't a clue. There were three lads and two other girls. They'd go out and party, while she hid in her room, only coming out once they'd left for the evening.' He shakes his head as he smooths a hand over the newspaper. 'I told one of the lecturers, but they went on long-term sick and it never got followed up. The only other person I told was your mum.'

He falls silent while the soft sound of birds chirruping and the dog panting fills the emptiness. He wipes the sweat from his face, shaking his head. 'We were all so young. So horribly young. That responsibility should never be put on the shoulders of a student. At that age, we think we're wise, we're invincible, but in reality, we know nothing.' He blows out a breath as he rests back on his heels. Quiet for a moment.

'What happened?' Martha leans forward and rests her face against his shoulder. 'Tell us what happened.'

'She took her own life.'

My chest tightens and I refuse to look at Skye. Did she think the same as me? Is she confused?

My head gives an almost imperceptible jerk in response to the spasm in my neck.

Dad never raped Jane.

I'd known that in my heart, but LJ had hammered it home to me. Literally, physically and mentally. With his fists and his voice. Made it part of my life. My dad had raped his sister. He knew. Thought he knew. All this, yet he was wrong. So wrong.

Lives ruined because of mistaken identity.

Dad hadn't raped Jane. He'd tried to help her.

'Rather than tell her brother, she committed suicide. We found her...' He stutters to a halt, his hand covering his mouth once more and his eyes squeeze shut to block out the pain. 'Your mum and I, we found her with her baby by her side in a pool of blood on the kitchen floor.'

He drops his hands to his knees and cups them as though holding something precious. 'So small, and yet perfectly formed.' The sound of him swallowing fills the air.

'They died alone. I've not thought about it in years. Tried to bury it. The inquest ruled that she'd taken abortion tablets too late in her pregnancy and it had killed both mum and daughter.' He raises his head and tears stream down his cheeks. 'I have no idea where she got them from. We didn't have the internet back then. Not like today where anything can be bought. I always thought someone must have obtained them for her.'

Martha lets out a pained sob. 'Oh, how tragic. If only she'd told her brother, I'm sure she would have had all the support she needed.'

Dad raises his hand and touches his fingers to his forehead. 'I don't think so.' He lifts his head and looks first at Martha, and then Skye. He doesn't include me. I'd missed out on a huge chunk of their lives, but it wasn't for that reason.

'It was LJ. Not Jacob.' He stabs the newspaper with his forefinger. 'This is LJ. This demon who they say is responsible for the deaths of several women. They don't know how many. They've found at least two bodies and they're still searching the grounds.'

Martha takes in a shaky breath. 'How come you didn't know who he was when you met him again? Surely you recognised his name?'

He scowls in confusion. 'I don't believe I ever met her brother.' His brow furrows in deep crinkles. 'He was there, I believe, but we never met. I was too bloody terrified. I was young. Guilt for not finding her earlier weighed on me, for not following up with someone in more authority, but I never realised... I had no idea she would do that. There'd been no indication she was mentally unstable. I don't think I looked at anyone in that coroner's courtroom. Not a single person.'

'Did he ever mention it to you? Did *he* know the connection?' Martha cups his cheek, her own face riddled with sympathy.

Dad shakes his head. 'No. Never. Perhaps he didn't know it was me, just as I had no idea it was him. I mean... Edwards is common name, and this was years... twenty... before he came into our lives. Jane never called him Jacob. She always called him LJ. It has to be coincidence.'

Coincidence is something I don't believe in.

Every step, every move, every single contact and encounter from LJ had been contrived, manipulated, controlled. Our entire family had been stalked by him for decades. Lured, seduced, coaxed.

Imprisoned. Incarcerated. Raped.

All this time, Dad had believed him to be a good man. A man who had helped save his business. Dad had been completely hoodwinked. Unaware of all the dark, sinister machinations.

I cast a furtive look from under my fringe at my twin and keep my silence. As she keeps hers.

My poor, sweet, naïve dad.

To tell him anything at this point would be to destroy him.

My fingers itch to pick up my broken paintbrush, but even I know it would be inappropriate, so I wait for the tide of despair to wash over my family while my emotions close down so I can block LJ out of my life.

I turn my head to look at my easel, the back of my canvas facing me. I know what is on the other side.

I lived through that hell.

I survived.

53

TWO DAYS LATER

The phone rings in the empty house and I stand by it, my hand hovering.

Skye is at the art gallery preparing for my next show. She won't be long, and she's left Cleo with me, just as she always does when she leaves me.

Sean is the name of the man at the art gallery. She's going out for a glass of wine with him afterwards. Just for a short while.

I'm happy for her. She needs company, someone more than me.

I'm not sure how I will feel if she brings him home, but I'll cross that bridge when I come to it.

I don't like to go out of the front door. Occasionally, Skye persuades me to go for walks with her and Jade and Cleo. Jade doesn't bring her fiancé, Luke, Martha's son, on those occasions. They're just for 'us girls'.

Luke is quiet around me, but I sense his curiosity. He'd love to ask me what happened.

I'm silent in his presence. Never alone with him. I'd never feel comfortable alone with him.

While we girls walk in shaded woodland, or open fields, or

across abandoned beaches in the autumn, I speak then. Sometimes. If I feel like it. Often, I'm content to listen to their inane chatter of work and life and the upcoming wedding.

Skye said Luke was a bit of a wanker when she first met him, but he's started to grow on her, and Jade and him make a lovely couple.

I think I probably won't go to the wedding. Jade won't mind. She will understand.

I like solitude. Most of the time. Maybe I'll stay at home and dog-sit Cleo.

The peal of the telephone edges into my consciousness.

I don't like to answer the phone. Sometimes, though, Skye rings the telephone we still have in the house. Our old number. I won't have a mobile phone. That would be too much exposure to the outside world. Danger lurks there.

I will pick up but say nothing while she speaks. Gentle comforting words that she will be back. She'll come home soon. She knows this gives me comfort.

I feel safe in this house of my childhood. I like to be alone with just Cleo for company.

Skye is still aware that sometimes I need reassurance.

If I feel unsafe, I will crawl into the wardrobe, persuading Cleo in with me until Skye returns home to find and rescue me. Just as she rescued me before.

I don't do that as often these days.

Now, I stand in the hallway.

The phone is insistent.

I pick it up and hold it against my ear to listen.

'Hello...?'

My blood runs cold. This isn't Skye. My fingers tighten on the receiver as I prepare to hang up.

'Hello...? Is anyone there? Is that you, Summer?'

I swallow at the familiar voice, the slight accent. I'd heard it in those dark days. A comfort. A spark of hope. Not for long, but I'd never forget.

'Hello...? Can you hear me?'

'Lilijana?' I whisper.

'Yes.' Her voice is also quiet. 'Summer. I hoped you had escaped.'

'Yes.'

'He's dead. I read it in the newspaper. Saw it on the news. They said he had been there for some time.'

'Yes.' Did she want to know my secret? It wasn't a story I was willing to tell. There was something I wanted to know.

'Around the time I... escaped,' she says.

I feel a catch in my throat. 'I thought you were dead.'

A bitter laugh floats through the phone. 'Almost. The bastard left me in a coma for eight months. He broke my neck and left me for dead. I'm lucky to be alive. If the break had been higher, I would not be. Lucky for me, he never snapped my spinal cord.' She's silent for a moment. 'I had to re-learn to walk and I'm very slow. But I'm alive.'

My throat tightens on a sob. 'Yes.'

'You, too.'

'Yes.'

'I've not phoned before, but I still have the photograph of the number you scraped into my arm with the charcoal. I hoped when I saw the newspaper that you'd managed to escape him. They said there were bodies, but I just had this feeling... you're alive.'

'Yes.' It's all I can say, all I can give.

'We're safe, now.'

'Yes.'

But we're not. We'll never be safe, because there will always be monsters out there. Evil waiting to be given its chance.

'Take care, Summer. Live a good life.'

'You, too. Bye, Lilijana.'

'Goodbye.'

I place the phone down and walk back into the brilliant sunlight flooding the garden, so it pops with vibrancy, and I make my way back to my easel and paints, faithful Cleo at my side, my hand softly touching the top of her head.

I notice for perhaps the first time radiant colours leaping out at me from glorious flowers I swear have come into bloom since yesterday, the splashes of brightness draw me to my easel, and I lift a fresh canvas onto it.

I pick up a brush and reach for the tube of sunshine yellow Skye bought me months ago. The tube I have never opened. Never touched. Until now.

I squeeze a blob of it onto my palette and smile as Cleo settles herself, her chin resting on one of my feet, her warmth soaking through my plimsole, up my leg and into my chest, where my heart starts to defrost.

Today is the day I start my new life.

ACKNOWLEDGEMENTS

The bones of *The Good Twin* had already started to come together in the form of one of the DS Jenna Morgan series. But the subject matter, in the form it originated, was considered too dark.

For some reason, I felt compelled to re-visit Summer. She kept dragging me back to her story.

As a mum of two daughters, like many parents, my greatest fear was not only that something bad would happen to them, but what if something bad happened but we never found out what? Or why? Each of us knows that we can help our loved ones, if only we are there for them.

What happens if we're not?

As usual I have a list of people I'd like to thank. There are so many these days to whom I am so grateful, for their support in all manner of ways. If I've missed anyone, I apologise.

First, to those who let me borrow their names.

For some time now, I have gathered names of real people who attend my talks, and my book release parties, both on Zoom and in person. I hold competitions for them and pick out a name or two on the understanding that the character I create can be anything from murderer to murdered, dog-walker to police officer.

It's never easy to choose names, so, to these wonderful people who throw themselves at my mercy, I am exceedingly grateful.

Sometimes, it's the quiet ones... thank you, Debs Gulliver. Debs won a bottle of Prosecco at my book release event, which inadvertently (haha!) I had left at home. When I contacted Debs to arrange to deliver the (possibly new...) bottle, Debs mentioned she'd rather be named in a book. So here you are, Debs! At least four times just in the acknowledgements.

My other volunteer is the lovely Martha Brindley, who won during my online Zoom book release party. I hope you enjoyed her part in this.

Christine Lawrence also won the prize of being featured. But did I make her a lady?

I hope I did them justice.

To the fabulous Gina Morgan, who cannot have her name in my books for the simple reason that it would be too close to my DS Jenna Morgan (who is technically named after her anyway, but I didn't realise you could do that kind of thing at the time I wrote the first one). Gina supplied me with an object to mention: a snow globe.

And not forgetting someone (who I have forgotten) who suggested I include a red Buddha (I hope it wasn't a Red Bull).

The Care Bear was suggested by the lovely and supportive Nicola Southall. Little did I know when I wrote it that it was pink with a very angry face.

The word 'dirigible' comes from the lovely Natalie Peake (or possibly her sister Katie Fouracres). I'm sure both of them will welcome a mention.

For the wonderful support of Andi Miller and her Facebook group, Books with Friends. They have always got my back.

Ross Greenwood, for his excellent critiquing and continued support.

To my amazing husband Andy, who sometimes stares at me as though I'm an alien as he asks where on earth did I get that latest idea? For a man who spent thirty-three years in the police force, I'm proud to say, I can still shock him.

To my incredible daughters, Laura and Meghan. I am so proud of you both.

To my sister Margaret, as always, for reading through my manuscripts and loving every story I write.

To my brilliant editor, Caroline Ridding, at Boldwood Books, who just understands...

It was our decision this year to have our utility fitted out and as every wise person knows, you should always allow extra time for this to happen. What we never anticipated was that the work needed to be put back a month. This in itself was no major issue. However, coming to the end of my deadline, with me frantically trying to wind up the story, it was discovered by the electrician that our house had a major fault with the consumer unit. Literally everything ground to a halt as initially six, and then three, electricians spent several days over the following three weeks testing the entire house and putting things safe. This meant that during daylight hours, we had no electricity. Little did I realise how disruptive this would be.

At the most critical time in my manuscript, I could not work.

When I let my editor know, Caroline immediately said, 'Have a six-week extension.' And so I took every minute of it.

I cannot praise British Gas enough for the team they sent to sort us out. They were incredible, hard-working, knowledgeable and, best of all, they had a sense of humour.

And just when we thought it was all over, we discovered a water leak...

ABOUT THE AUTHOR

Diane Saxon previously wrote romantic fiction for the US market but has now turned to writing psychological crime. *Find He Alive* was her first novel in this genre and introduced series character DS Jenna Morgan. She is married to a retired policeman and lives in Shropshire.

Sign up to Diane Saxon's mailing list for news, competitions and updates on future books.

Visit Diane's website: www.dianesaxon.com

Follow Diane on social media:

facebook.com/dianesaxonauthor

x.com/Diane_Saxon

instagram.com/DianeSaxonAuthor

ALSO BY DIANE SAXON

DS Jenna Morgan Series

Find Her Alive

Someone's There

What She Saw

The Ex

Standalone

My Little Brother

My Sister's Secret

The Stepson

The Good Twin

THE

Murder

LIST

**THE MURDER LIST IS A NEWSLETTER
DEDICATED TO SPINE-CHILLING FICTION
AND GRIPPING PAGE-TURNERS!**

**SIGN UP TO MAKE SURE YOU'RE ON OUR
HIT LIST FOR EXCLUSIVE DEALS, AUTHOR
CONTENT, AND COMPETITIONS.**

SIGN UP TO OUR
NEWSLETTER

BIT.LY/THEMURDERLISTNEWS

Boldwood

Boldwood Books is an award-winning fiction publishing company seeking out the best stories from around the world.

Find out more at www.boldwoodbooks.com

Join our reader community for brilliant books, competitions and offers!

Follow us
@BoldwoodBooks
@TheBoldBookClub

Sign up to our weekly deals newsletter

https://bit.ly/BoldwoodBNewsletter

Printed in Great Britain
by Amazon

38909405R00205